Praise for Matt Cost's
Clay Wolfe / Port Essex Mysteries:

"*Mouse Trap* is a vivid story that mystery and thriller genre readers alike will find involving on many different levels."
—Diane Donovan, Senior Reviewer, *Midwest Book Review*

"A fast-paced, sexy, and intriguing read! Exciting twists and turns and added thrilling lures will ensnare readers and keep the pages turning!"
—*InD'tale Magazine* on *Mouse Trap*

"Matt Cost's *Mind Trap* pits former homicide detective turned private investigator Clay Wolfe against a dangerous cult leader in the town of Port Essex, Maine.... a twisted and chilling tale of control and manipulation. The ultimate 'what if' on steroids."
—Bruce Robert Coffin, award-winning author of the Detective Byron Mysteries

"This gripping plot moves with lightning speed until its explosive and thrilling conclusion. Cost's jam-packed plot should appeal to all lovers of private detective fiction. I eagerly look forward to the next book in this series."
—Joseph Souza, acclaimed author of *The Perfect Daughter*, on *Wolfe Trap*

Novels by Matt Cost
aka **Matthew Langdon Cost**

Historical Fiction

I Am Cuba: Fidel Castro and the Cuban Revolution

Love in a Time of Hate

The Goff Langdon Mainely Mysteries

Mainely Power

Mainely Fear

Mainely Money

Mainely Angst

The Clay Wolfe / Port Essex Mysteries

Wolfe Trap

Mind Trap

Mouse Trap

MOUSE TRAP

— A Clay Wolfe / Port Essex Mystery —

MATT COST

Encircle Publications
Farmington, Maine, U.S.A.

Encircle editor: Cynthia Brackett-Vincent
Cover design: Deirdre Wait
Cover images © Getty Images

Published by:

Encircle Publications
PO Box 187
Farmington, ME 04938

info@encirclepub.com
http://encirclepub.com

Acknowledgments

If you are reading this, I thank you, for without readers, writers would be obsolete.

And thank you to the wonderful writing community that has welcomed me with open arms and made me feel at home. This includes so many fantastic people it would take an entire book to note, not just writers, but reviewers as well.

I am grateful to my mother, Penelope McAlevey, and father, Charles Cost, who have always been my first readers and critics.

Much appreciation to the various friends and relatives who have also read my work and given helpful advice.

I'd like to offer a big hand to my wife, Deborah Harper Cost, and children, Brittany, Pearson, Miranda, and Ryan, who have always had my back.

I'd like to tip my hat to my editor, Michael Sanders, who has worked with me on several novels now, and always makes my writing the best that it can be.

Thank you to Encircle Publishing and the amazing duo of Cynthia Bracket-Vincent and Eddie Vincent for giving me this opportunity to be published. Also, kudos to Deirdre Wait for the fantastic cover art.

Dedication

To you, the reader.

Chapter 1

MONDAY, JULY 6TH

"Sometimes bad genes need to be stamped out and good ones need to be fostered," Bridget Engel said. "There's really no difference between mice and human beings when it comes to genes." She wore a gray suit, and her blonde hair was cut short in the style that Hillary Clinton had made popular.

Victoria Haas was careful to not let her fork drop to the plate and her mouth fall open in astonishment—not the expected response of ladies of power in business and society. Women who gaped did not drink the 2015 Chablis 1er Cru Fôrets for lunch in the swank private dining room of the exclusive Port Essex Harborside Hotel in the company of the CEO of Johnson Labs, one of the premier biomedical research companies in the U.S. and Maine's third largest employer.

Victoria had been coming here for as long as she could remember, while Engel had only moved to Port Essex some ten years earlier. Yet, she'd never known about this ornate oasis just off the main dining room. It appeared that this private room was reserved exclusively by Johnson for business functions and engagements.

What did Engel mean by *stamped out*, Victoria wondered? She'd brought up the subject in passing, asking how one could ensure that one's baby was genetically gifted, only to be somewhat taken aback by the abruptness of the answer. She bought some time taking a bit of the Cobb salad. Even though her ship had passed Engel's at many political and official functions in previous years, this was the first time they'd met for a social engagement.

"How does one go about stamping out bad genes?" Victoria asked, taking a small sip of the chardonnay. She was also blonde, but was much more fashionably dressed, with a shirtwaist dress, dirndl skirt, Chanel slingbacks, and a string of pearls around her neck.

Engel was looking through the wall-size window into the main dining room, a window Victoria knew was mirrored on the other side. There were four tables in the room she was surveying, but only one occupied, by three men and a woman. This was the room that Victoria knew well, one that she'd eaten in countless times. It was one of the men at the table who'd caused Victoria to bring up the subject of babies. She'd known him since she was a little girl, even having had a fling with him after her senior year in high school, but she'd barely seen him since, as their lives has led them in two different directions.

"It used to be easier," Engel said, her attention drawn to the other room. "There was a time when the poor, the disabled, the promiscuous—the *inferior* could be sterilized. Instead of having them grow up to be criminals filling our jails, or letting them starve to death because of their own imbecility, the United States used to prevent those who were manifestly unfit from continuing to reproduce."

"Do you know those people?" Victoria nodded her head at the window.

"The two men with their backs to us work for my company," Engel said.

Victoria nodded, taking another sip of the Chardonnay. She knew that Engel's company, based nearby in East Essex, did genetic experiments on mice in an effort to eradicate disease, but she wasn't quite sure where sterilization came in. The waiter approached and poured another scant inch of wine into their glasses.

"It seems that sterilization has long been out of favor," Victoria said. "Perhaps there are other ways to… ensure that deficient genes are not passed on to one's offspring?"

Engel turned from the view of the other room and focused on Victoria. "We've made great advances in the past few years. Soon, disease will be a thing of the past."

"That doesn't take care of the slovenly or the stupid, though, now does it?"

"No. No, it doesn't."

"You said something about fostering good genes?"

"Why are you asking?"

Victoria looked at the man facing her in the other room. He was the answer to something she'd been contemplating for some time now. She wasn't getting any younger and, for the past year, she had felt this emotional void, an emptiness only filled when she imagined bringing an extension of herself into this world, something larger than her work, her money, or anything she'd ever known.

"I've wondered about what it might be like to have a baby," Victoria said.

"Tiresome," Engel said, and the two women laughed.

"But truly," Victoria said. "I have thoughts of becoming a mother."

"I know the Haas family has impeccable genes, and have for generations," Engel said. "What of the father?"

"I haven't chosen a father as of yet."

"Does that mean you're holding tryouts?" The two women looked at each before breaking into giggles.

"In a way, yes," Victoria said. "I certainly don't want my child to be average."

"Or your husband."

"I don't believe I said that I was looking for a spouse." Victoria's tone changed from jest to business in a split second. "Just a baby."

"Men can be a nuisance. How do you propose picking a father?"

"I have somebody in mind. I have had his background looked into—in all the usual ways. But if I wanted to do a DNA check on him, how would I go about it?"

The waiter opened the door, and Engel waved him away

impatiently. "You could simply ask them to submit to a test. A swab from the inside of the cheek or a blood sample would do fine."

"That might be a bit delicate."

"He doesn't know that he's applying to be the father?" Engel asked.

Victoria blushed. "Not exactly. How about a hair?"

Engel shook her head. "You'd have to be sure to pull out the follicle and part of the scalp to be certain, and that would be noticeable."

"How, then?"

"Are you... sexually active with him?"

"Not for nineteen years."

Engel laughed. "I'm sure the poor *dummkopf* doesn't stand a chance against a woman such as you. Tell you what—why don't you seduce the poor fool and bring me a sample of his semen? I can have people at the lab analyze it and let you know whether he's worthy of being the father of your child or not."

* * *

"We must first establish the need for utmost confidentiality as concerns any and all of our business dealings and any such information, trade secrets, intellectual property, or any related knowledge you may be... exposed to as you go about your work for us."

The legalese hung heavy in the air over the table in the fancy function room of the Harborside Hotel where they were eating. The clean-cut fellow with the five-thousand-dollar suit had uttered the words more as a threat than a statement; the other man, his duds no less expensive, nodding in rhythm almost as if listening to music. He must be the lawyer, Clay Wolfe thought, wishing they would get to the point. Not that he was invited into Port Essex's inner sanctum for a fine lunch every day, but still...

"Of course," he replied. "That is a standard clause of my contract."

"I have a, um, slightly more binding non-disclosure agreement that I'd like you to sign."

The man had said that his name was Rex Bolton and that he was chief operating officer of Johnson Laboratories. On second glance, he was not as well manicured as Clay had originally thought. His sandy blond hair was tight on the sides but tousled on top, and lines creased his face suggesting worry rather than age.

"I don't see why that would be a problem," Clay said, nodding. He hadn't recognized most of the dishes on the menu and had ordered a Cobb salad. The waiter came and went so quietly and with such self-effacing efficiency that he was almost invisible. Unlike the quite impressive Frederick Remington statue in the corner next to a large mirror that made the room seem bigger than it was.

There were two tables separating Clay and his business partner, Baylee Baker, from the two men from Johnson Laboratories. This was to provide the minimum six feet of social distancing in this time of Covid-19. Baylee was slender with legs that went on forever, a bit of bronze to her skin, and brown hair that matched her eyes. The words *Real People* were tattooed on the inside of her left forearm. The glass of white wine in front of her was nearly untouched, unlike the surf 'n' turf, scallops and Angus tips, which she'd demolished, much to Clay's amusement. The woman had an appetite.

The lawyer—whose name had yet to be divulged—looked at Baylee. "Absolute confidentiality, Mr. Wolfe, is what we need and expect."

"Miss Baker is my lead investigator and a partner in the firm," Clay said. He took a sip of the expensive scotch that he sure hoped was going on someone else's tab.

"Nonetheless, we must insist," the lawyer said.

Clay leaned back in his chair. His hands pressed lightly onto the elegant tablecloth. He ignored the lawyer and spoke directly to Bolton. "I could tell you that I won't include her in the case," he said. "But I'd be lying. If it's a deal breaker, then I'm sorry." He steepled his fingers under his chin, his cards played, ready to accept the outcome however it went.

"I'm sure that we can have Miss Baker sign the NDA as well," Bolton said.

The lawyer reached down to the chair beside him, taking up two thick-stapled copies from a briefcase and sliding them across the dual tables. "Please sign where indicated." It seems he'd been prepared for this eventuality. They didn't appear to be men who were surprised by much.

"What do you know about Johnson Laboratories, Mr. Wolfe?" Bolton asked when they were done, the paperwork safely stashed back in the lawyer's briefcase with copies for Clay and Baylee slipped into a thick envelope.

"They—you—employ quite a few people in the area," Clay said. "You've got a complex in East Essex." He shrugged. "Testing with mice or something like that."

Bolton smiled, a smirk that didn't reach his eyes. "We're the largest employer north of BIW with over a thousand employees. This includes over two hundred men and women with doctorates or other advanced degrees who investigate the genetic bases of cancer, disease, autoimmunity, and many other disorders. JOHNS is known for biomedical research that bridges translational and clinical contexts. We integrate mouse genetics and human genomics to understand the underlying cause of human health and disease. There have been nineteen Nobel Prizes associated with our work."

"So, you do test with mice," Baylee said.

Clay fought back a chuckle. That was about all he'd gotten out of the mumbo jumbo that Bolton had just spouted out, too.

"Yes, Miss Baker. As a matter of fact, we *are* the world's supplier for over nine thousand strains of genetically defined mice."

"That's where all those rodents come from," Baylee said.

"More importantly, they are mammals," Bolton said. "Very similar to humans in many ways. We have even created a humanized mouse."

"A humanized mouse?" Clay asked.

"Mouse models with human immune cell engraftment represent ground-breaking platforms to evaluate compounds to treat a variety of human illnesses, from cancer and infectious diseases to allergies and inflammation."

"Oh, I see," Clay said. But he did not see at all. He did deem it best to not be an ignoramus when trying to land a case from a man in a five-thousand-dollar suit. "How about you tell us why you're here and what you need from us?"

"We are worried that our research has been compromised," Bolton said.

Clay nodded. "You must have your own security. Why us?"

Bolton looked at the lawyer, who said, "You understand that breaking the NDA could possibly be a treasonous offense, and that you could be prosecuted as a traitor to the United States of America."

"You think the Russians or the Chinese are hacking you? Like they did with the Covid-19 vaccine? Because I'm sort of under the impression we should just be sharing that stuff, you know, if it's going to save human lives." Clay wondered, what could possibly be hacked in regard to mice?

"It's more sensitive and delicate than you could imagine, Mr. Wolfe." Bolton's voice expressed exasperation.

"Perhaps I should get my lawyer to read through the NDA before I go any further," Clay said. His lawyer was his Grandpops, eighty-four years of age, still with a keen mind.

"That might be for the best," Bolton said.

"What can you tell us about the case?" Baylee asked. "Without possibly compromising our freedom?"

"I like your directness, Miss Baker," Bolton said. "Quite simply, somebody has been stealing mice."

He's worried that it's an inside job, Clay thought. But stealing mice? It was quite a leap from that to treason. The mice must be pretty special, possessing something so sensitive, that if he, Clay Wolfe, leaked, he could be arrested as a traitor and thrown into some place like Guantanamo without charges or trial. This was serious shit.

"And you suspect your own security team of being involved?" Clay asked.

"We don't know who to suspect," Bolton said. "But it is concerning."

"I think before we get into the nuts and bolts of this, we'll have our lawyer go over the NDA," Clay said. "It shouldn't take long. Perhaps we can get together tomorrow and move forward?"

"Time is of the essence, Mr. Wolfe," Bolton said.

"Of course, I understand."

The lawyer reached into his case and retrieved the NDA and slid it back across the table.

"One of our security team disappeared over the weekend," Bolton said. "He was on the night shift for the fourth. Showed up to work. Was last seen about 2:00 a.m. Never checked out. Never went home. Just gone."

Chapter 2

"You ate at the fucking private club of the Harborside Hotel?" Crystal Landry, administrative assistant, asked while snapping her gum. "Aren't *you* special?"

"Come on back, and we'll toss it around," Clay said. He and Baylee had just arrived at in the office after their hoity-toity business lunch.

"I know that you're a dandy, but the private club? At the Harborside Hotel?" Crystal repeated.

It was true that Clay was a stylish dresser. That day, he'd picked out a white, starched and pressed shirt, with a light blue waistcoat and tie that matched. At the same time, he purposely skewed his tie slightly and left his hair tousled—a casual, slightly unkempt look which was seen to by his hairdresser every two weeks. He kept a two-day goatee and mustache using an electric razor, and his cheeks and neck were smooth. At just barely six-feet tall and 180 pounds, with sandy hair and blue-green eyes and a winning smile, he was the whole package, or at least the local girls seemed to think so.

The private investigation firm was located on the second floor above an art gallery, with outside wooden stairs. The reception room was Crystal's domain, nondescript in a Sam Spade sort of way. A simple desk with a small waiting area and dim lighting. The sound system was top notch, country music now trickling from the speakers with a twang. Crystal preferred the old-style country. When Baylee had been receptionist, the music selection had been mostly jazz.

The switch from jazz to country was not the only change. When Clay promoted Baylee to lead investigator, prior to her becoming a partner owning a quarter of the firm, he'd hired Crystal on as the new receptionist. It had taken almost a year to come to grips with the fact that her language was too coarse and her manner too brusque to be a receptionist. Clay was faced with firing her or changing her job title. He went with the latter. Now, she was the administrative assistant.

Truth be told, Crystal was a whiz in the research department and had proven invaluable many a time. They'd purchased a software application, LocateNOW, that Crystal knew inside and out. She could find a person, missing money, or past details faster than you could say scat. So what if they lost the occasional customer because Crystal's vocabulary would make a sailor blush and a mobster cringe? Business was still booming, especially after being in all the news media about that 'first son of God' thing the winter before. That'd been quite the case, Clay thought with a grin.

The interior office would've embarrassed Sam Spade with its lavishness, except for the torn and ragged couch on which Clay had grabbed many a nap, and even slept the night through a few times. The true gem of the office was the stunning view out of the picture window overlooking Essex Harbor, the sun and steely water complementing his cherry wood desk and fairly new L.L. Bean chairs. They'd talked about moving to a larger space with two offices so that Clay and Baylee could each have their own, but it was hard to leave this view behind. And it was nice to share a space—though it meant they each occasionally had to take their work out to the reception area, having to bear Crystal's cursing when the other needed privacy.

"Do share," Crystal said. "Who're the new clients?" She plopped into one of the chairs as Clay went behind his desk in front of the window and sat next to Baylee, whose workspace was kitty-corner to his own.

"We signed an NDA, and then thought perhaps we should have Grandpops take a look at it before moving forward," Clay said.

"NDA? You mean like one of those things the president gets everybody he comes in contact with to sign? What's the world coming to when you need a piece of paper so you can cheat on your wife, you know what I mean?" Crystal grimaced. "But I'm guessing they're not having you sign that to get into your pants."

"Something about keeping our mouths shut or being prosecuted as traitors to our country," Baylee said. "Sex might've been better. The lawyer was hot as shit."

"If you like the sort of boy who grew up in a country club, went to private school and the Ivy League, all before joining his father in his law practice," Clay said.

"You say that like it's a bad thing," Baylee said. "That young fellow would be whimpering for me to stop long before I was through with him."

"And now that image is in my head for the rest of my life," Clay said. "Let's get back to our potential case, shall we?"

"Let 'er rip," Crystal said.

Clay drummed his fingers on the desk. "We didn't really get much."

"They were from Johnson Laboratories," Baylee said.

"The place out in East Essex with the mice?" Crystal asked.

"That's them," Clay said. "They are fearful that their research has been compromised. That mice have been stolen."

"You mean they got some mice that are really good at getting through a maze, so somebody came along and jacked them?"

"They seemed to suggest that their work is more important than mice navigating a maze," Clay said. "But honestly? I didn't get much from them. I'm going to run this NDA over to Gene. If nothing else, we should be able to make some serious bank from the guys with the five-thousand-dollar suits."

"As long as we don't end up in Cuba," Baylee said.

"Cuba?" Crystal asked.

"Gitmo. Our prison in another country," Clay said. "What do you got on tap for later this afternoon?" He directed this question at Baylee.

"I'm meeting with Kalinda and her head bodyguard," Baylee said. "Five o'clock out on the Point."

"That's right. Guess we'll both be out there. I'm having dinner with Victoria Haas at her mansion."

"Well, la-di-da," Crystal said. "I'll be home eating left-over fucking mac 'n' cheese and tater-tots."

Clay laughed. "How about you spend the afternoon seeing what you can put together on Johnson Laboratories. What they actually do and whatnot. Best to have at least a clue about our client's business."

"Gotcha, boss," Crystal said, "they probably have some press releases and a corporate summary and bios on their website. I can download that and print it out?" Clay nodded, marveling that she got out a whole sentence without an f-bomb in it, as she walked out of the room, her thin, bird-like legs skimming across the floor.

Clay finished up some paperwork before heading home in the late afternoon to his grandfather's house. Gene "Grandpops" Wolfe, was still sharp in every facet of life, even at eighty-four years of age. He had taken a nasty spill a few years back, helping prompt Clay to retire early from the Boston Police Department, where he'd risen to the rank of homicide detective. At the time, Clay had felt himself sliding down the path of the jaded and cynical. He had come off a bad patch, haunted by shooting and killing a man. So, when Grandpops had fallen, it just seemed easy enough to hang up the badge, move back to Port Essex, and open up a private investigator business.

The house was an old sea captain's place, up the hill and overlooking Port Essex and the harbor, with a wide porch running the length of the front. There was a widow's walk perched on the roof—a small, railed platform with an enclosed cupola from which, legend had it, women would watch, often in vain, for the return of the ships carrying their husbands. Clay lived in a studio apartment above the detached garage.

As a lawyer, Gene had been the most-hired defense attorney in the MidCoast region, an advocate for the wealthy, and had been paid handsomely for his efforts. The last ten years of his career had been spent working *pro bono* for the poor. Clay wondered if this was some sort of penance. The man was now silver-haired with a beard of the same hue, carefully trimmed each and every day, tapering to a point on his angular chin.

"What brings you back home?" Gene asked. He sat in a rocking chair on the porch, a half-filled cup of coffee next to him.

Clay sat down several chairs from him. He'd not been inside his Grandpops' house since the outbreak of Covid-19. They tried to get together several times a week, either here, on the front porch, or around a fireplace in the backyard. When the winter came, that would all change, but the here and now was simple enough for visits outdoors. It was a perfect Maine day, about 72°, sunny, with a light breeze coming off the harbor.

"Got some work for you," Clay said.

"What? You got another client who wants to rake their cheating spouse over the hot coals of divorce and alimony?"

"It does include an NDA," Clay admitted. "What do you know about Johnson Laboratories?"

"They do cancer research using mice, I believe," Gene said. "Plus, the CEO, can't remember her name, made PETA's dirty dozen list of most cruel companies."

"For abusing mice?"

"I would assume." Gene took a sip of his coffee. "My understanding is that they are doing lab experiments on them and are allowed to do so because mice are not classified as sentient animals, even though they are highly sensitive, intelligent, and social creatures."

"Great. Maybe that's why they want me to sign an NDA. Although,

I can't see them prosecuting me as a traitor to the U.S. for leaking news of the poor treatment of mice."

"Traitor? There's no way you could be charged with treason, as far as I can tell. Maybe espionage or domestic terrorism. Maybe they're doing more with those mice than trying to cure cancer."

Clay tossed the packet, now in a folder, onto Gene's lap. "If you can take a look through that sometime today, and let me know if it's just a precaution, or if it's likely to put my face on every television as an enemy of America—that'd be great," he said. "Don't even know what they want me to do yet, so I can still decide to say no if I don't like it. I think they just want me to find out who is stealing their mice."

Clay drove down the hill and took a left on Commercial Way. He thought about avoiding the traffic of this main drag through town but took too much enjoyment in seeing the place he'd grown up in, left, and returned to. He knew the owners of the small businesses lining the street. They'd been in the stands cheering for him as he'd led Port Essex to a state football championship. They'd been teammates, cheerleaders, friends in school, with the occasional outsider who moved to town and managed to fit in.

Port Essex was, at its heart, an old fishing village comprised of stalwart people working tough jobs for many a generation. Over the past thirty years, that way of life had been slowly blending with the opening of artsy shops, restaurants, and businesses catering to a blooming summer population. The world had discovered that for two months of the year—July and August—Port Essex was, quite simply, one of the most glorious places in the world to live.

There were two distinct pieces to the horseshoe-shaped town. The downtown that Clay drove through now, and the Point, on the far side of the harbor, home of the wealthy, often part-time residents, sometimes renters, and a smattering of locals who spent much of the year here. The further out the Point you went, the bigger the houses got. Victoria Haas lived almost all the way out, on the Atlantic Ocean side, next door to her parents.

The Haas family had been in Port Essex since the early 1900s. Cornelius Haas had made his money as a robber baron in New York City industry, and bought a house in Port Essex on the Point, originally only for summer use. In the 1950s, his grandson had become a permanent resident, for seven months of the year anyway, the other five spent in warmer climates. Victoria Haas had used the money, power, and networking of her family to become an influential fashion designer in her own right.

Five years back, she'd bought the house next to her parents as a vacation home. Two years ago, she'd abruptly retired from the fashion world and became a seven-month resident. Clay had known her since grade school, and, while not the closest of friends, they'd maintained contact through the years. The summer after graduation—Clay from Port Essex High and Victoria from Exeter Academy—they had run into each other at a party.

Victoria wasn't pretty in the traditional sense. There was a hook to her nose, and her frame might be called robust, but there was an inner beauty that shone forth that made her attractiveness much more than the sum of its parts. Many years later, half-drunk in a bar, he'd been trying to explain that idea when his equally soused neighbor had leaned over his barstool, laughing. 'They got a name for that in French,' he'd said, '*jolie laide*, a beautiful ugly woman.' Clay had often been drawn to things of distinctive beauty rather than traditional allure.

They'd been drawn to each other that night and later had found themselves rolling around naked together in the backseat of his Chevy Nova. Afterward, they'd sat at the sandpit until the sun came up, just talking. It was then that she'd shared her secret with him, one that made it hard to shrug off their hooking up as the one-night affair it was meant to be. It made him feel bad for her, bonding them in a strange way.

Clay had liked her well enough, but still, there wasn't any chemistry as far as he was concerned, but rather, a guilt in breaking things off after having been allowed into her confidence. He quickly realized that she thought differently and held a torch for him. It was college that had finally sent them their separate ways, and he'd gradually stopped answering her phone calls.

In the years since, they'd run into each several times, especially since he'd retired from the Boston Police Department and moved back to Port Essex. Her business enterprises had her traveling the world, but she always seemed to return to Port Essex. Maybe it was her parents being there, even though Clay guessed she had no real love for them, at least not her father.

Out of the blue, the previous Thursday, Victoria had called Clay at his office and asked him to her house for dinner. He was not sure if this was a business or pleasure call, but he welcomed either one. He was leery of resuming their relationship, if you could even call it that. But it'd been some time since he'd been with a woman, and sex with the young Victoria Haas had been extremely satisfying. A piece of Clay's mind was intrigued by what carnal delights might await him with the more mature and worldly woman who he'd seen around town.

These were his thoughts as he drove out to her mansion on the Point. Part of him hoped that the evening would end in pleasure, even if his other brain felt uneasy about where that would lead. Were it strictly business, that would be okay, too, for to be retained by the Haas family would most certainly be lucrative. And there was the pull of the intimacy of her terrible secret, once shared and never since mentioned, pulling him toward her, for what reason he didn't understand.

Her house was small in comparison to her parents' place next door but was breathtaking in its modern style. It was basically five cubes built on stilts with mostly glass walls, floor to ceiling, and solar panels on the roof. He was disappointed not to see the inside as she met him at his Jeep and brought him out back to the patio and pool overlooking the ocean, the waves crashing on the rocks just feet from where they sat.

Victoria had a round, wide-brimmed hat, dark glasses, with pearl earrings that matched her necklace, and a white dress that reached to her sculpted calves. There were buttons in the front, but the first came at her waist, leaving a vee of exposed skin, her generous breasts barely contained within. The kimono sleeves billowed slightly in the breeze. Her skin was white with just a hint of an amber glow to accent her red lips. Her smile was fetchingly crooked, the nose with its curve begging to be traced by his finger.

"Would you like a scotch?" she asked.

Clay looked at the rolling drink cart and saw a bottle of Macallan with a large '18' on it. He was betting that *smooth* would be an understatement. "Absolutely," he said. He also liked that she'd left it in the bottle and not put it in a decanter. It seemed a mix of wealth and normal—if a $300 bottle of brown liquor could be considered normal. His second exorbitantly expensive brown liquor of the day.

"I pegged you for a scotch drinker," she said.

They sat and sipped and caught up. She told him she went by Victoria and not some shortened version, had turned most of the day-to-day operations of the Haas Brand over to others, had never been married, and was looking to move onto another chapter of her life. This new chapter seemed to suggest that what she'd hoped to be her legacy—the fashion empire she'd created—was not the fulfilling endeavor she'd thought it would be. There was a longing in her for something more, what she could not say.

"And there's really no Mr. Haas?" he asked.

"No."

"Never?"

"Not even close," she said. "I mean there have been men, but they all seemed to be shallow fellows who fell short of being worth my time. Perhaps it's my fault. Who knows?"

"I'm sorry to hear that."

"And you, Clay?" she asked. "You've never been married?"

"No, not even close," he replied, smiling, and they clinked glasses.

A man came out and began setting the patio table.

"Why not," she asked after a pause," if you don't mind me asking?"

"Guess I haven't found the right woman," he said. He didn't mention that he had commitment issues.

"Do you date?"

"Not currently," he said. He didn't mention that he did, often, but that it rarely lasted longer than a few months.

The man returned with a serving tray and placed it on the table and left.

"I thought we'd have the quintessential Maine meal of clam chowder and lobster rolls," she said, standing up. "I hope that works for you?"

"Sounds great," he said, following her over to the table.

The man rolled over another drinks cart and parked it by the table. "Would you like to switch over to beer or white wine?" she asked.

"A beer would be great," Clay said.

Victoria nodded at the cart. There were four beer cans in a pail of ice. "Would you grab one for me as well? I hope IPA is fine with you? It's from Bateau Brewing up in Gardiner."

Clay had never heard of it, but dutifully grabbed two cans and poured them into glasses before sitting down.

The clam chowder was excellent, the lobster roll even better, and they each had another Bateau IPA. Afterwards, they took a stroll down a short path onto the rocks and sat in two Adirondack chairs.

"A little different than the first time we met," Victoria said. "Drinking Pabst Blue Ribbon and going for a ride in your Nova."

"You remember my Nova?" he said, and then mentally kicked himself.

"One of my best memories," she said.

Clay blushed. "We were so young."

"That was the best summer of my life."

"Glory days," Clay said.

"What?"

"Bruce Springsteen's song about glory days."

"Ah, yes," Victoria said. "Something about a football player who could throw the ball, right?"

Clay smiled. "A baseball player who could really throw a speed ball."

Victoria stood up and stepped down to the water's edge and stared out to sea. "That summer, those were certainly my 'glory days.'"

"Correct me if I'm wrong," Clay said, "but haven't you built a multi-million-dollar fashion business and been jet-setting around the world? It seems I read about you or see you on television on a monthly basis in exotic locations, rubbing elbows with celebrities."

"What happens when you realize your dreams of youth, and that those particular glasses are half-empty rather than half-full?" she asked.

Clay stood up, his mind trying to prevent his body from approaching her and his mouth from spilling forth with something likely corny and romantic. He failed. "Well, you have always turned all the boy's heads."

Victoria spun around, sorrow, longing, and lust filling her eyes. "Do you still own your Nova?"

Clay smiled. "No. I have a Jeep now."

"Not much of a backseat to a Jeep," she said.

"Nor in a Nova, if I recall correctly."

"We're not kids anymore. We could just go to my bedroom."

Clay leaned forward and their lips locked, the waves drowning out any misgivings he might have had, or perhaps it was just the blood pulsing through his veins. Whatever the case, next thing he knew he was in Victoria's bed, and he'd once again started something he wouldn't know how to extricate himself from.

He woke in the middle of the night, gathered his things, and slipped away. After Clay left, Victoria rose from the bed and went into the bathroom, carefully removed the condom from the Kleenex it was wrapped in and put it in a plastic baggie.

Chapter 3

Baylee was not the type to fall about around celebrities. Pop music wasn't even her favorite genre, being slightly edged out by both jazz and country. But this was Kalinda. The woman was a cross between Beyoncé and Rihanna, bursting onto the music scene when Baylee was sixteen, Kalinda's age, too.

At the time, Baylee would have switched lives with the singer in a heartbeat. Especially if she had known that her own future would include killing an abusive husband. But now? After putting the pieces of her life back together and working towards her inner truth? Baylee Baker was quite content with her life. Of course, there were things that she wanted, but they were within her grasp. There was nothing about touring the world, a different city every night, that interested her.

The songs spoke to her over the years, though, and she recognized a kindred spirit in Kalinda. Because it had happened to her, she knew the suffering that an alcoholic father could inflict. Baylee understood betrayal by one's mother. Being used by boys. Being abused by men. It was a road that Kalinda sang about, and Baylee had lived, and the lyrics connected them over the years.

When Crystal had put through a call from a woman in L.A. claiming to be Kalinda's administrative assistant, Baylee had thought somebody was pranking her. It wouldn't be beyond Clay to pull such a stunt, and, even after agreeing to be the local liaison for the pop singer's bodyguard team, she still waited for somebody to jump out and yell 'gotcha'. Baylee remained just the least bit suspicious even as she rolled up to the gated drive of the mansion on the Point.

"Baylee Baker to see Kalinda," she said. The words felt false in her mouth and worse once out in the air.

The gate slid open. There was no laughing group of her friends on the other side. Baylee drove forward through some trees. A modest mansion appeared, the driveway curling around a fountain in front. Two black Cadillac Escalades sat silently just past the entrance. Baylee parked beyond them and got out of her Subaru, pulling her mask on. She thought it probably needed a wash.

The front door opened, and Kalinda came out. She wasn't dressed in shiny glitter and heavy makeup, but her signature cornrow braids tumbled to her shoulders and a wide smile adorned her face. Her eyebrows looked to be painted on and gave her the look of a wild cat; her nostrils flaring when she smiled. She had on shorts that reached halfway to her knees, and a T-shirt that said, *Straight Out of Port Essex*. A woman with Capris and a plain black T-shirt followed one step behind, the latest iPhone clutched in one hand.

"You must be Baylee Baker. I'm Kalinda and this is Aisha. Don't worry about the mask, we will social distance today. Afterwards, I'd like it if you had a test every couple of days."

"Hello." Baylee nodded. She pulled her mask off.

"Come, we'll sit by the pool."

It wasn't a large pool, but it did overlook the harbor. Port Essex looked quite picturesque from here, Baylee thought, the perfect coastal Maine town. Fishing boats mixed with lobster boats mixed with sailboats and schooners, filling the enclosed harbor.

As if reading her thoughts, Kalinda said, "What a beautiful town. Have you always lived here?"

"Yes, ma'am," Baylee said. Perhaps she was a little starstruck.

"Call me Kalinda. Don't make me feel old, please."

"I'm sure that it pales in comparison to L.A., Kalinda," Baylee said, trying out the name, rolling it off her tongue, perhaps drawing it out too much, Ka-lin-da.

"If you mean by 'pale' that the air is crisp and clean and not filled with smog, that *is* a fact." Kalinda laughed. "I'm very much looking forward to spending the next month here. Do you sail?"

"No, can't say that I do. I do have a friend with a fishing boat and a small sailboat who would be happy to take you out, if you wanted," Baylee said.

"Is he trustworthy? To not sink us, that is?" Kalinda asked.

"He grew up on a boat and then went off and became a SEAL for a while. I think you'd most likely be safer with him than anybody in the world."

Kalinda looked at Aisha. "We'll have to put that on our list." The woman was already pecking the possibility into her phone.

"I'm sorry about your tour being canceled," Baylee said.

"It's as if Atlas shrugged, don't you think?" Kalinda asked. "And the world came to a screeching halt? Sometimes the pause button is a good thing, though."

Baylee thought it interesting that the pop singer had referenced an Ayn Rand book. "Port Essex is a good place when you have to hit that pause button," Baylee agreed. "What is it, exactly, that you want from me?"

"Aisha can fill you in on the details, but long story short? Every once in a blue moon, some whacked-out dude thinks I've been singing directly to him, and that we should be together, or some other fucked-up fan shit. Aisha takes good care of me, but certain activities will require back-up. I trust you can be flexible?"

"Absolutely. How flexible are we talking?"

"We will let you know within three hours if you are needed. Usually much longer in advance, but no shorter."

"That's not a problem. I'll clear my case load of non-essentials."

"And your home schedule?"

"I'm sure Flash and Ollie will understand if I have to leave all of a sudden."

"Who?"

"My basset hound and my one-eyed cat."

Kalinda laughed. "You'll have to bring them over to visit. Rodriguez, my Chihuahua, would love to have some company."

"Flash would be incredibly happy to visit. Ollie is not so much for the car and thinks strange dogs are pin cushions. Probably best if I left him home."

"Fair enough," Kalinda said. "We'd also like to pick your brain on local knowledge. Anything we should know in regard to places, people, and such, but Aisha can get that from you."

"Like I said, been here all my life, and one thing I've learned is which places and people to avoid," Baylee said with a grin.

"What do you know about Johnson Laboratories?" Kalinda asked.

"Johnson Laboratories?"

"Yes."

"I believe they do scientific testing on mice to try and cure human disease," Baylee said weakly. "But I don't know much more."

"I'd be most interested in knowing what their local reputation is, if you could ask around."

"Sure. It'd help to know why?"

Kalinda shrugged. "I'm doing some work for them. If I'm going to associate my name with theirs, I need to be sure they're not involved in anything unethical or morally dubious. Last thing I need to find out is that they poisoned thousands of kids with some supposed medical breakthrough then covered it up, if you know what I mean."

Be pretty bad for the kids, too, Baylee thought. "Gotcha."

Chapter 4

TUESDAY, JULY 7TH

"On page six, paragraph three, what do you mean by trade secrets?" Gene Wolfe asked.

They'd brought another chair into the office, and he sat on the other side of Clay from Baylee, the three of them facing Rex Bolton, and his lawyer, who was now known as Steve Lewis. Everyone wore a face mask.

Gene had explained that non-disclosure agreements were often kept perfectly vague to pressure participants to reveal even less than that which was actually fair game. They'd gone through the hefty packet, clarifying intention of meaning here and there, but overall, he had no real problem with it, as long as Clay and Baylee understood that they indeed needed to keep their mouths shut on this one.

They'd crossed out several articles when Gene demonstrated that the information could be found with a simple Google search. When Gene finished, Crystal made the changes in the computer and printed out two copies, and Gene and Steve bent their heads together to make sure it was all okay. Clay, Baylee, and Rex made small talk until they returned. Politics was studiously ignored.

Finally, the contract was complete and to both side's approval, and they sat down to hear what the job actually required.

"We're concerned that thieves are targeting our mice," Bolton said.

"You're really hiring us to find lost mice?" Clay asked.

"In essence, yes."

"Not just any mice," Bolton said. "Humanized mice."

"What do you mean by that?" Clay asked. "In layman's terms."

"A humanized mouse is a mouse carrying functioning human genes, cells, tissues, and/or organs. By doing this, we are able to model actual human conditions and see how such mice react to certain diseases and then work towards a cure."

"How do these mice get human genes?" Clay asked.

"Injection followed by engraftment."

"Engraftment?"

"Basically, this is when the body accepts the transplant and starts to make healthy blood cells incorporating the genetic manipulation."

"And this injection occurs when?" Baylee asked.

"When the mouse is in its embryo stage."

"Before birth?" Clay asked.

"Yes."

"Okay, so you have mice being stolen that carry human traits," Clay said. "But my understanding is that you sell these mice all over the world. Why all the hoopla over national security?"

Bolton shifted in his chair. "We sell mice that help advance the extinction of certain human diseases," he said.

"But that's not the purpose of the mice that are being stolen?" Clay asked.

"This's the part that you had to sign the NDA for."

Clay nodded. "I figured as much."

"And that is our cue to exit," Steve said to Gene. The two of them went out to the reception area, shutting the door behind them.

Bolton stood up and walked behind Clay and Baylee to the picture window overlooking Essex Harbor. They swiveled in their chairs to stare at his back.

"About five years ago we got funding to expand into a new area in our business. Instead of merely remedying problems, we've been working toward improving life." Bolton spoke in a low voice so that they had to lean forward to hear him. The sun over the harbor seemed to be shining directly upon him, and Clay half-expected him to raise his arms in the air as if he was the creator of the universe. "Instead of only working to eradicate cancer and the like through an understanding of the underlying causes of human health and disease, we began moving in the direction of enhancing life."

"Genetic engineering," Baylee said.

"Yes. We've developed a new breed of mice. This new strain is called SHAIM." Bolton turned and faced them. " SuperHuman Advanced Intelligence Mice. It is the SHAIM that are being stolen."

"That's a shame," Baylee muttered so only Clay could hear.

Clay smirked. "You sell mice that've been humanized, so that other laboratories and scientists around the world can do experiments to eradicate certain diseases, but this SHAIM thing is different. They've been altered in other ways?"

"We alter the DNA in the genome."

"What is the genome?" Baylee asked.

"An organism's complete set of genetic instructions. The good, the bad, and the ugly, we call it," Bolton said.

"You take out the bad and the ugly and add more good?" Clay asked.

"Exactly."

"How?" Baylee asked.

"A process of microinjection into the embryo."

"You mean the fetus?" Clay asked.

"The early stages of conception are usually referred to as the embryo stage and the latter part is the fetus until birth," Bolton said.

"And what's so dangerous about these stolen mice? What can they be used for? It's not like they're going to be trained up into an army. They're mice."

"The potential exists to transfer this science to humans. That, after all, is the end game of this particular project. We're not in this to improve the lives of mice, now, are we?" Bolton went back around the desk, sat and leaned forward. "This is a top-secret program."

"And why not use your own security team?"

"I'm afraid that they might be compromised. I don't know who is involved. Our CEO, Bridget Engel, asked that I use an outside source. That would be the two of you."

"If you don't mind me asking," Baylee said, "shouldn't you be bringing this to the federal government? The CIA, FBI, secret mercenaries on the payroll? I mean, you're talking about technology that would allow somebody to develop super soldiers and the like. This is serious shit."

Bolton pinched his bottom lip with his fingers. "It was actually just one mouse. And it was *not* stolen. A theft *was* attempted but failed. It was found in a small container with air holes in the bathroom facility of the Black Lab where the experiments take place."

"Ha. The Black Lab?" Baylee said.

"Over the past ten years we've added numerous endowed chairs, or faculty at the top of their specific field, through private donations. In this case, the doctor who is heading up the SHAIM program is named Martin Black. We name the specific labs after the head researcher or the donor. In this case, the donor was anonymous."

"Why the bathroom?" Clay asked.

Bolton shrugged. "Our best guess is that the thief got spooked and dumped it before passing out through our security checkpoint. As you can guess, we are very stringent in regard to coming and going from the Black Lab; in fact, from all the labs."

Rex Bolton had signed the contract officially engaging the services of Wolfe & Baker Enterprises. They overcharged him. Probably because he wore a five-thousand-dollar suit. Maybe because he was backed by wealthy anonymous donors doing secretive things right next door in East Essex. Whatever the case, they were pretty flush with money, that day having been employed by one of the largest businesses in Maine, and by one of the wealthiest entertainers in the world the day before. If all went well, they'd be due a vacation, not that Covid-19 was conducive to much travel these days. It might have to be a staycation.

Crystal knocked and entered the room after processing Bolton's retainer. "Guess we got fucking doctor mouse as a new client, huh?" she said.

"Looks that way. What'd you find on them?" Clay asked.

"Not so much, as of yet. Pretty well-funded place, mind you."

"Where's the money come from?" Baylee asked.

"They make a fucking bundle selling rats."

"Mice," Clay said. "No government money at all?"

Crystal plopped sideways on the couch with her feet up. She wore a zebra-striped dress that almost made it to her knees. Her hair had been recently permed and tight coils covered the top of her head.

"Yeah, sure. They made some $300 million selling rats and mice, but another $100 million split between grants and private donors," she said.

"Private donors? You mean people give them money like they would to a charity?" Baylee asked.

"Sure," Crystal said. "They're one of the foremost organizations in the world battling fucking cancer, go figure. They had private contributions of over $40 million. Between that and grants, they are able to continue expanding their business."

Clay shook his head. "I can't even get my head around numbers that big. Maybe we should've charged them more."

"What'd they hire you for, boss?" Crystal asked.

"Can't tell you that," Clay said. "National security."

"Fuck that," Crystal said.

Clay grinned. "Okay, can you keep a secret?"

"If I have to."

Clay looked around the room and then back at Crystal. "Come on over here. I can't be shouting across the room." He waited until

Crystal pulled the chair closer. He then leaned over the desk so that he was only about six inches from Crystal and whispered, "Somebody tried to steal a mouse."

Chapter 5

Crystal was still cursing at him under her breath when Clay and Baylee left, having asked Bolton for a tour of Johnson Laboratories, and especially the Black Lab, where the errant mouse had been found in the bathroom. He knew that Crystal wouldn't believe that they'd been simply hired to find a mouse, not that he had ever put much stock in NDAs anyway.

The coast of Maine wended in a northeast direction, so what often felt as if you were going north was really traveling east. This was the case with East Essex. It was north and then east out a peninsula that jutted slightly further into the Atlantic than Port Essex. Maine had almost 3,500 miles of coastline—more than California—a fact that Clay was reminded of every time he took a drive along the capes, points, peninsulas, and necks that comprised the area where land met sea. It amazed him to think that he could quicker drive to California than he could navigate the many ins and outs and arounds of the coast of Maine.

The top and doors were off the Jeep. Baylee had on a baseball cap to keep her hair from flying wild. Clay thought that was pretty damn sexy. The road made a big sweeping turn out over a bluff overlooking the ocean, and there was a small pull-off area for people to stop and enjoy the sweeping views of the Atlantic Ocean. Clay slowed down and eased the Jeep off the road. Port Essex could be seen back to the right, or at least the Point could be, and East Essex to the left. Something in him wanted to share this spot with Baylee.

"This is where your parents died?" Baylee said after a long minute.

"Yep. And my grandmother as well."

The cliff in front of them tumbled down some hundred feet to the rocks below. At high tide, these rocks were mostly underwater. Now, they jutted from the ocean bed like the jagged teeth of a sci-fi dragon or some alien creature. There was a wooden fence preventing people from coming too close to the edge and a map with a description of something or other on a stand in the center.

"Gene told me it happened out this way somewhere," Baylee said. "I always guessed this was the spot."

"My dad, Mack, drove the car right off there." Clay pointed to just left of the map mounted on a wooden stand.

"You come out here often?" Baylee asked.

"I haven't been out here except to drive by since Grandpops brought me just after it happened. I was eight years old."

"I'm sorry."

"My dad tested positive for cocaine and alcohol. Not too much to drink. Just too much of the white powder. Guess the stress of family and work was too great for him."

"Sometimes shit just happens," Baylee said.

"They were on their way back from the Botanical Gardens. They went to see the Christmas lights. Had dinner after, and then drove straight off this cliff. No tire marks. No way of knowing what really happened. Did my dad have a heart attack? Fall asleep? Did he drop something on the floor and lean over to get it? There wasn't a single skid mark on the road. Chitty-fucking-bang-bang without the magic."

"We should come back and bring, I don't know, some sort of memorial, lay some flowers?" Baylee offered gently.

"Maybe just a bigger fence," Clay said. "And some reflectors."

"What do you remember about your parents?"

"My mom," Clay said, "she had that sort of big heart and warm smile that made everybody feel special. My dad? His presence commanded every room. When he came through the door, every eye turned to him, and when he spoke, every ear listened."

"Those are good memories," Baylee said.

"Yeah, I suppose."

"My father was drunk and abusive, and he died when I was twelve. My mom stole my boyfriend when I was nineteen."

"Makes you question bringing kids into the world, doesn't it?" Clay asked.

"You mean, are we destined to be the same people as our parents?"

"I've been angry with my dad since he died. Why did he choose cocaine over me?"

"You know it's not that simple," Baylee said. "Sometimes we go down the wrong path. Sometimes we just make bad choices. Even good people do that."

"Still, helluva world to bring kids into, if you ask me."

"We're not the same people as our parents. We're not."

"Is that what your therapist tells you?"

"Don't be a dink. That's what I know. But... you could stand a session or two talking things out with somebody, and you know it."

Clay chuckled, a dry laugh that floated out over the bluff. "How'd a couple of orphans like us wind up together?" he asked.

What he didn't ask was if she thought they'd ever stand a chance of being together. He knew, somehow, that it was not yet their time, especially as he'd just started seeing—if that's what you called it—another woman.

"Is this ethically okay?" Baylee asked as they pulled back onto the road for the last few miles to Johnson Laboratories.

Clay wondered if she was reading his thoughts. "Is what ethically okay?" he asked.

"The fact that we've been hired to find who is trying to steal superhuman mice from JOHNS, and that I've also been asked to do research on them by Kalinda."

"Why do you suppose she asked you to do that?" Clay asked.

"She said she was doing some work for them and wanted to make sure their reputation was squeaky clean, so she didn't suffer any blowback, if they, say, poisoned a bunch of kids with a vaccine they created."

"She must be doing some publicity or promotion for them. Maybe a commercial? Or speaking at a fundraiser? Or even singing?"

"Sounds about right."

Clay shrugged. "I don't see why that would be a problem. No real conflict of interest. We're investigating an attempted theft for the company, and you're gathering some background material. If anything, we can charge both parties for doing one job."

As he gazed out at the land- and seascape, he thought it was the kind of day that epitomized why one lived in Maine. The temperature sat at 78°. There was a light breeze coming from the west. Not a touch of humidity in the air. Nor a cloud. The sky was a hard blue. The road was empty of traffic. There wasn't much going on in East Essex and not much reason for tourists to visit. He was with a beautiful woman whose company he greatly enjoyed. They passed over a small bridge and a store to the left, an inlet of the ocean sparkling behind it.

"Do you think this makes us anti-pest control?" Baylee asked.

"What's that?"

"You know, usually people call the pest control people when they want to get rid of mice. We, on the other hand, have been hired to prevent mice from leaving the building."

Clay laughed. "You get to work as a bodyguard for Kalinda, and I get to protect mice. Seems fitting."

"Wasn't that a movie? Rat Patrol?"

"TV series. Grandpops used to watch reruns when I was a kid."

"They weren't really catching rats, were they?"

"Nope. Germans. WWII. North Africa. The one guy used to say, 'Let's shake it,' when it was time to move, especially if they were in a hurry."

"I think that's one of Kalinda's songs."

"Let's shake it?"

"Yep. 'Let's shake it until we heal the ache, let's shake it until there's no escape.'"

Clay made a note to listen to some of Kalinda's music on Pandora. This certainly sounded like it might be a song he'd enjoy listening to with Baylee. Maybe after dinner back at his place one night. Or not, he thought, reminded that he'd just had sex with an old flame the previous evening. Why did he complicate his life so, he wondered? And then answered his own question. It was because he feared becoming too emotionally invested in a relationship, thus, he sabotaged any real chance at happiness. Meaningless flings and short-term dating were acceptable as long as there was no chance of it turning into more.

"There it is," Baylee said, nodding to the left.

The sign, simply saying JOHNSON LABORATORIES, was not overly big, as if the company wasn't trying to attract attention. Clay had looked them up and realized that they did daily tours of the facility, at least in normal times, but these had been canceled due to Covid-19. It seemed that a larger sign would be more conducive to people finding the place. He turned onto the road and up the hill. East Essex was a peninsula about three miles long, almost an island really. JOHNS was located at the beginning of this finger of land, where it was still fairly thick, probably a couple of miles wide, before tapering down to a point at the end.

As they crested the ridge, the buildings of Johnson Laboratories came into view. A large circular building stood front and center with a much larger sign out front. This was the reception building where they'd been directed to report. Clay and Baylee got out and looked around. From his research, Clay knew that there were twelve buildings on the campus that housed thirty-seven separate labs, the reception area, maintenance, security, and offices. The buildings were arranged in a U-shape, running along the top of the ridge and then down the hill and along the Atlantic Ocean frothing on the rocks below them.

There were two receptionists, a man and a woman, both young and smartly dressed. The woman led them to the elevators and took them to the fifth floor. She knocked on the door that said, *B. Engels, CEO*, and ushered them inside. There were three people inside at a conference table that would fit twelve. They were spaced out and not wearing masks. Rex Bolton stood and gestured for them to sit, and they removed their masks as they did so. When in Rome, Clay thought, do as the Romans do.

"Clay Wolfe, Baylee Baker, this is Bridget Engel, the CEO of JOHNS, and Harley Lange, the head of security," Bolton said, sitting back down. "We get tested twice a week around here for the virus, so I hope you're okay going maskless?"

"That's fine," Clay said, stealing a look at Baylee who nodded.

"Welcome Mr. Wolfe and Ms. Baker," Engel said.

She was about five inches over five feet tall, had blonde hair, and soft blue eyes. Her hair was cut in a pixie style with face-framing bangs, and her smile was warm. She wore a light gray pantsuit and what looked like a very expensive silk scarf. Altogether, quite the agreeable package, if clothed and made up for the corporate world.

Clay and Baylee nodded their greetings.

"My sources tell me that you have a knack for solving mysteries, Mr. Wolfe, as do you, Ms. Baker." Engel didn't beat around the bush with small talk.

"We've had some successes over the past year," Clay said.

"I should say," Engel said. "Heroin and cults all in a year's work? Oh, my."

"It's been a busy year," Clay said.

"Am I to understand that those cultists were upset with pure white blood being diluted with... inferior strains, and thus decided to leave earth behind?" Engel asked.

"In a nutshell, yes," Clay said.

"What a shame," Engel replied. "Although I have to say, I've never understood people who create more complications than solutions."

"There was certainly very little rationale at work in their thinking," Clay said. "They lost me at the whole 'first son of God' thing."

"But you seemed to be up for the challenge."

"And now mice," Baylee said.

Engel chuckled. "Not just any mice, Ms. Baker. I understand that Rex has told you about SHAIM?"

"SuperHuman Advanced Intelligence Mice," Clay said. "I did have some questions. What is meant by SuperHuman?"

"They are stronger and smarter than normal."

"And how do they get that way?"

"You understand that some... mice... are going to be naturally stronger and smarter than others, Mr. Wolfe?"

"Yes, I suppose."

"We pinpoint shared mutations in the DNA of those mice, DNA sequences that make them different. We then replicate this mutation and inject this into the genome of the embryo." Engel tapped her pen on the desk. "In a nutshell, as you say, we are exchanging the weaker DNA out for superior DNA. I am sure that the scientists will be able to better explain it."

"Okay, I guess." Clay was not sure that he really understood, but close enough. They messed with the part of the mouse that determined its physical and mental traits and made them better. "Why is it called SuperHuman? And not SuperMouse? Or Mice?"

Engel smiled. "Good question, Mr. Wolfe."

"And the answer is?"

Engel rolled her tongue over her lips in a clockwise motion. "We inject the embryos with human DNA."

"Not SuperMouse DNA but human DNA?" Baylee asked. Engel nodded yes.

"So, you're taking DNA from superior human physical specimens and injecting it into mice at the embryo stage. And when they're born?" Clay asked.

"What are you asking?"

"Are they actually stronger and smarter than normal mice?" Baylee asked.

"Oh, yes," Engel said. "We've had mice that are twenty times stronger than a normal mouse."

"Holy cow," Clay said. "And are you having similar success with their intelligence?"

"Slightly less, but yes, still very significant advances have been made. Intelligence is a slightly trickier trait to determine and positively alter genetically."

"Why mice?"

"Humans and mice share 97.5 percent of their DNA," Engel said. "Chimps are about one percent higher but there is less... concern over mice as test subjects than chimps."

"And the purpose of this genetic engineering is to eradicate disease?" Clay asked.

"Genome editing, Mr. Wolfe, is much more precise than simple genetic engineering. We are working to remove certain diseases not just from the individual mouse but from their offspring and all of their descendants as well by manipulating their genes."

"But you are also making them stronger and smarter," Baylee said.

Engel nodded. "The Black Lab has gone past the initial work of simply altering pathology and has indeed gone a step further to creating superior organisms. We are working to eliminate maladaptive DNA that infringes upon the purity of the... mouse and weakens its natural superiority."

"Isn't that done with plants and animals already?" Baylee asked. "To beef up the cows, so to speak. I just saw somewhere that they were going to release genetically modified mosquitoes into the Everglades to wipe out a certain strain that carried Zika virus or something like that."

"The work we are doing will be used to improve human lives, not that of animals, plants, or insects," Engel said.

"Is that legal?" Clay asked.

"As of now, the FDA doesn't approve of, nor will it grant money for, genome editing of a human embryo. The Chinese scientist, He Jiankui, who produced genetically edited babies, was recently found guilty of conducting illegal medical practices and sentenced to three years in prison." Engel stood up. "That is why we're doing trials on mice. I've another meeting." Her words were abrupt, her eyes on the expensive watch on her wrist. "Rex and Harley will bring you down to the Black Lab."

They were ushered to the elevator and back outside. Rex pointed to a building down the hill a quarter of a mile on the shoreline. "That is the Black Lab. We can walk, if you don't mind?"

Clay and Baylee replied that was fine with them, and Rex led off. A sidewalk ran along the U-shaped drive that curled down to the Black Lab.

"Is there no path through there?" Clay nodded towards the space between them and their destination. "Looks like there's a dirt road."

Rex looked briefly at the narrow, rutted road Clay was now pointing at. "It doesn't go all the way through," he said.

"What's in there?" There appeared to be a clearing in the center surrounded by recent growth trees.

"An old graveyard," Rex said. "This tract of land was donated by Robert Johnson back in the 1920s as a research facility. An old graveyard sat in the middle of the land, and part of the deal was that it couldn't be touched. That wasn't a problem back then when the entire complex was one building. Now that we have twelve buildings and need parking for 2,000 cars, it has become much more difficult, but we've honored that original deal. Not only do we not encroach upon the cemetery, but we've left a buffer of at least a hundred yards around it."

The Black Lab was a nondescript three-story affair. Right inside the front door were two security guards manning a metal detector and a walk-through x-ray machine that looked straight out of *The Matrix*, Clay thought. Bolton told them that most of the buildings had several different research labs operating within them, but the Black Lab was the only occupant here for security purposes. This was just a tour of the facility. The interviews of employees would start later.

"As you can see, there is no fear of anybody getting away with stealing a SHAIM," Harley said. He was not what Clay typically encountered in a security guard. Harley was slender with meticulously groomed blond hair that almost reached his shoulders.

Clay was half expecting the SHAIM to be pumped up rodents reading Nietzsche. In reality, he could barely distinguish them from the mouse he'd trapped over the winter in his apartment above the garage. A total of fifty-seven people had access to the Black Lab, including two maintenance workers and four security staff. It would be tough to interview all of them, so Clay asked for copies of their employee files to research and hopefully whittle down the number to something more manageable.

"Do you feel that we're stepping on your toes, Harley?" Clay asked as they walked back up the hill.

"No, sir, I don't."

"Good. I thought it might be awkward, us coming in here to investigate the theft."

"There was no theft," Harley said. "A mouse was found in a box in the restroom. They never would've gotten it out of the building past my team."

"Have any thoughts on who it might've been?" Clay asked.

"No, sir, I don't. Speculation is above my pay grade. My job is to prevent any theft taking place, and yours is to find who may've been contemplating said attempted theft."

His tone of voice suggested to Clay that Harley wasn't telling the whole truth, the head of security quite naturally resenting that outsiders had been brought in to investigate what he believed to be his domain. Fair enough, Clay thought.

*

"You ever been out to the point here in East Essex?" Clay asked Baylee as they pulled down the drive.

"Sure," Baylee said.

"Could be the most beautiful spot in all of Maine, which means all of the world. What say you and I grab some sandwiches and drinks from the general store and go sit out there on the rocks and have ourselves a picnic?"

"I say that sounds like a lovely idea, Mr. Wolfe. It sure beats the PB & J I got back at the office."

The general store was the small-town type of place where you could pretty much find anything from food to hardware to toys and fishing tackle. They also had a deli counter and made mighty fine sandwiches. Clay resisted buying beer and opted instead for just a water, as did Baylee. As they drove out towards the point, Clay marveled at how many houses there were on just this tiny spit of land. He idly wondered what percentage was owned by out-of-staters. As they reached the end of the point, the road curled around to the right with parking spots all along the side of road. Only about half of them were occupied.

They found a spot isolated from other people enjoying the view and settled down next to each other. It was a comfortable seat, on a wide flat rock protected from the small breeze by a larger stone and just out of reach of the spray coming off the waves as they hit the rocky shore. Clay had a hot roast beef and cheddar, while Baylee had a pastrami on rye.

"We split the files and look for any glaring signs of debt or propensity for illegal activity, youthful indiscretions and such?" Baylee asked.

"Yep. As good a place to begin as any other, I suppose," Clay said. "Start with the most recent hires."

"I'm betting somebody was bribed. I mean, who wants a mouse with superhuman characteristics?"

"You mean, who doesn't? I imagine a foreign government of some sort would be the most likely candidate. And unless they have activated a mole that has been biding his time for just such an opportunity, having gone to the best schools, and gotten his PhD for just such a chance, it's most likely an inside job. Somebody was bribed."

"Are you suggesting a mole might be trying to steal a mouse?" Baylee asked.

"Ha," Clay said. "I believe I said bribery was more likely."

"Or blackmail," Baylee said. "We should keep an eye open for possibly embarrassing situations. Affairs, predisposition for sex with animals, things like that."

Clay laughed. "I guess that might be blackmail-worthy."

* * *

"So, you're telling me you hooked up with that crazy broad that you were seeing the summer after we graduated?" Westy asked. "The one you didn't want to date but you felt bad for her about something you wouldn't tell me?"

Clay looked at his buddy with a wry grin. Weston Beck had been his best friend since third grade. They'd played, studied, and fought together. They'd shared their first drunk and ensuing puking session. Clay's house had been in town and easier to sneak out of at night and thus had been the more regular choice for weekend sleepovers. Clay had been the quarterback and Westy the running back on the Port Essex state championship football team their senior year. When Clay went off to Boston University to pursue a career as a policeman, Westy had enrolled in the Navy's SEAL program and eventually gone to the Middle East.

Westy had gray eyes, was only six inches over five feet, but his shoulders were wider than most doorways and his chest resembled a barrel. His left arm was fully tatted up—a Viking warrior, then patterns of knots leading up to the bone frog, and finally the trident ink adopted by the SEALs. The images took on a life of their own in the rippling muscles of his arms. His hair was short and tight on top, but a powerful beard sprouted from his face, wild and groomed at the same time.

Clay and Westy were currently sitting along the railing of the Pelican Perch, the outdoor topside deck of the establishment below, looking out across Essex Harbor to the Point. They'd just gotten two beers from the bar, which had nary an empty seat, even if there were only half as many as normal for social distancing purposes. It was five o'clock, after all.

"Yeah, that's the long and short of it," Clay said.

"And you did this why?"

"Stupidity."

"So, just to be clear, are the two of you going steady?"

"How about I throw you over the railing?" Clay said.

Westy merely laughed. It would take three Clays to throw him over the rail, and they'd most likely go with him.

"You remember who she is, don't you?" Clay asked.

"Sure. She had a charming hook to her nose, or something like that."

"She looks better now, believe it or not. Filled out in all the right places."

"'Filled out' could be construed as hefty," Westy said. "Not that that is a bad thing," he added.

"She's real nice. And *not* hefty."

"Now you sound like a woman."

"Don't be sexist."

"OK. A liberal woman, at that."

"See that house over there," Clay pointed across at the Point. "The one with the red trim?"

"What about it?"

"I believe that's the one Kalinda is staying in."

"The singer?" Westy asked.

"For sure. Baylee met with her yesterday about doing some bodyguard work. She's in town for a month."

"No shit? Faith loves her. Maybe you could introduce her?"

Faith was the wife, and mother to Westy's son, Joe.

"See what I can do," Clay said. "Or rather, see what Baylee can do."

"She coming over?"

"Yep. Should be here any minute. You can ask her yourself. Her and Cloutier both, I think."

Westy looked at his phone. "I got a half-hour, and then I got to git."

"How's the fishing been?"

"Good. Real good. That reminds me, meant to tell you. You know Daryl Allen?"

"Squirrelly little guy with greasy hair that only looks at you sideways?"

"Yep. That's the one. I was pretty far out the other day, about fourteen nautical miles, and saw a ship going by. Odd place for a ship, unless it was headed to Eastport. Then I saw a boat headed right for it. It came alongside the ship, which I thought interesting, so I put the binoculars on them. I thought it might be a drug thing or something. Then a Jacob's Ladder tumbled down and a man descended into Daryl's boat and off they went."

"You saw it was Daryl Allen?"

"Didn't get a look, but it was his boat, sure enough. The *Mary Ellen*."

"Huh, how about that? No other cargo or anything else changed hands?"

"Nope. Just the one person. Pretty sure it was a fellow."

"What was the ship? One of Eimskip's?"

"Don't think so. Name was in Russian. Believe it was called *Ivan Sereda*."

"You know Russian?"

"A little bit. Pretty rusty now."

Of course, Clay thought, Westy knew a little Russian. Spending time in Afghanistan will give you the basics. His response was interrupted by the arrival of Baylee and Cloutier. Cloutier was of medium height with a slightly round face and glasses. Her smile was ready to her face, and she was known to emit deep belly laughs.

She was also, Clay thought, one of the smartest people he knew.

"Any chance you good-looking fellows want to buy a couple of hot babes a drink?" Baylee asked, pulling up a stool next to Clay. Cloutier sat on the far side of Westy.

"Sure," Clay said. "Where are they?" He turned and surveyed the bar and was smacked in the arm for his troubles. Luckily, the bartender came over and got the new drink orders.

"Speaking of hot babes," Baylee said with a sly grin. "I haven't asked yet, but how was your dinner date with Victoria Haas?"

"Uh, good."

"What's she want?"

"Just catching up, I guess."

Westy grunted, a sound that could perhaps have been a suppressed chuckle. Luckily, this was lost in the arrival of drinks.

"Enough of that," Clay said. "Tell everybody about Kalinda."

"She was real down to earth," Baylee said. "Nice. As a matter of fact, she wants to go sailing, and I told her that I had a friend with a sailboat that might take her out." She leaned forward to look down the railing at Westy.

"I can do that," Westy said. "I'd have to bring my first mate along, of course."

"Who is that? This guy?" Baylee jabbed her thumb into Clay's chest.

"Nope. Faith. Have to get somebody to watch Joe, but that should be easy enough."

"I'll give her your number."

"Great. Thanks," Westy said. "Hey, I got to git." He put a twenty under his empty Budweiser bottle, pulled his mask over his bushy beard, and left with a wave of his hand.

"Yeah, I should go as well," Cloutier said. She took the last swig of her beer. "Denise is making dinner tonight. Rare thing, so I best not be late."

That left Clay and Baylee. She'd swung by and fed her dog and cat before coming and had nowhere to be. He had even less waiting for him at home. Two drinks later they moved to a high-top and ordered food. Covid had created a need for social distancing, leaving half the tables as normal, and spaced chairs at the bar, but it was still no problem getting a table as the night ensued.

Chapter 6

WEDNESDAY, JULY 8TH

Clive Miller wasn't a patient man. That's what'd gotten him drummed out of Afghanistan four years back.

He had gun-metal gray eyes pinched around a thin nose. A long face set upon a long neck. Clive was just under six-feet tall and slender. Thus, in his thirty-one years of life, many people had taken him for being weak. This was not the case. He was wiry strong. That coupled with a meanness and anger borne of an abusive father, and Clive Miller was not a person to mess with.

The first person to discover this was a fifth-grade bully picking on the small fourth-grade Clive. The principal had pulled little Clive from the bully's inert form, but not before he'd broken the boy's nose and kicked out two of his teeth. He'd discovered that day that you got a vacation from school for doing something he liked—namely, kicking the shit out of somebody.

Luckily, his dad being in the military, they had changed schools and towns and states every three or four years, and he got to start fresh. By the end of each permanent change of station, Clive had pretty much exhausted other boys willing to take him on, no matter the age, and the school was ready to permanently expel him. Sometimes they had hung on knowing that his departure was imminent. Never once had they given warning to the future school of the impending arrival of this young psychopath. They were just happy to have him gone.

Clive wasn't sure about joining the military upon graduating high school. He didn't think that he'd much care for being ordered around. When his old man had gotten new orders, one of the last squadrons to be transferred out of Brunswick Naval Air Station just down the road from Port Essex, Clive had just graduated at nineteen years of age. He'd decided to stay. Got a job doing road construction. It was hard, dirty work, but Clive didn't mind. He might've stayed there forever if his boss hadn't been such a dick.

When Clive's lawyer had suggested to the boss's lawyer, the man still being in the hospital, that Clive would join the army and leave the town and state forever if the charges were dropped, the offer was accepted. The police had been happy to drop the case, and Clive had signed the papers and went off to basic. Afghanistan was fucking hot, but Clive was in heaven. He didn't mind humping around carrying the fifty pounds of battle rattle. He got to shoot people. He found that killing people was even more fun than kicking the shit out of them.

Outside the wire, most of the time, all bets were off, and Clive volunteered for that duty as much as possible. Not in the Green Zone but in the forward operating base, known as the FOB. Clive was able to operate with impunity. The other soldiers were either in agreement with his tactics or scared as shit of him. The thing was, anybody could be Taliban. Who was to say whether the dead person was a T-man or just a local? As long as Clive didn't leave anybody alive to talk, why then, he could do whatever the fuck he wanted.

Clive liked his life in Afghanistan. He could have stayed there forever but for do-gooders. It turns out the XO drew the line when you slit the throat of a nine-year old terrorist haji.

Before he even had time to breathe, he was being court-martialed. Luckily, he was back walking the streets of the U.S. before the fake news got hold of the intel and vilified him, turning him into some kind of monster for doing what he was being paid to do: kill the enemy.

With nowhere else to go, he'd carried his duffel with all of his possessions and took the bus back to Brunswick. Back in 2016 that was, and he was torn between finishing the job on his old road construction boss, or robbing houses, or dealing drugs when Bolts found him. He'd thought they'd bumped into each other accidentally at the time but had since come to realize that nothing was by accident with Bolts.

Now, Clive Miller was a fixer. He took care of problems that arose. Once given a task, his hands weren't tied, and he was well-paid for his troubles. There were two simple rules. Eliminate the problem. Don't draw attention. Most of his time was free as there weren't that many issues that required his particular skill set. Yet, enough so that when he was given a job, it was like a vacation, and the idle time was like going back to work.

He'd thought Bolts was just your normal business executive who didn't like to get their hands dirty and preferred others to do it for them. Then Bolts had sent Clive to New York City to eliminate a problem a few weeks earlier. Seems that some fellow was nosing around where he shouldn't be, in this case, asking questions about a business called Freikorps Iron that Bolts had an association with.

Clive couldn't figure out why it was called Freikorps Iron as it was simply an office in a nondescript building on the Avenue of the Americas in midtown Manhattan. He figured that this was just the back office of the business and went about with his planning. He seldom dwelled on things that didn't concern him. What did concern him was eliminating a Jewish fellow who was sticking his too-big nose in where it didn't belong.

He'd made contact with the man, suggesting that he had incriminating evidence against Freikorps Iron, and made plans to meet him at a café, where he planned to earn the man's confidence and then lure him to an abandoned warehouse on the East River and kill him there. But something tipped the man off that Clive was not on the up and up. Clive never knew what, but halfway through a cup of coffee, he learned the man was pointing a Jericho 941 pistol at him under the table.

Clive was pondering this unforeseen circumstance when Bolts walked into the café—not that he had even known Bolts was in the city—approached the counter, and bought a cup of joe. Bolts walked behind the man with the coffee, produced a gun from out of nowhere, and blew the man's head into a scattering of skull fragments. Bolts then turned the pistol on a woman eating a sticky bun with her young daughter and killed them both, before shooting the teenage clerk and the dishwasher. Without a word, Bolts walked out the door. That had been some shitshow. Clive never did hear how the whole thing had played out. Bolts had just told him to get the hell out of there and go back to Maine.

Bolts had called the day before with a job for him, and try as he might, Clive couldn't keep the fucking smile off his face. It had to be done fast. Clive called the *Port Essex Register* and asked for the woman. She readily agreed to meet with him at Koasek Park, out in the back parking lot, where it wasn't so busy. All he had to do was tell her that he worked at JOHNS. He told her that he would be in a dark truck. Clive let her get there first.

There were seven cars in the lot, people off hiking the short trails within the park. When Clive pulled in next to Mary Jordan, he saw the look of anxiety slide from her face like syrup off a pancake. She was a petite woman with round glasses and a light sweater even though it was quite warm. She had perky breasts poking the material outward. He liked that.

Clive kept the truck running. She got out of her sedan and opened the side door, inquiring whether he was indeed 'Tim'. He nodded that he was. She got in and shut the door. A couple came out of the path from the woods and walked towards a Honda.

"I understand you're writing a story about JOHNS," Clive said.

"Yes," Mary replied. "You said you work there?"

"What's your story about?" he asked.

"Do you know anything about Area 38?" she asked.

"I might," he said. "Who else knows about the story?"

"My editor knows I'm doing something at JOHNS but not the nature of it."

"Husband?"

"No. He'd worry that I'd gotten into something over my head. What can you tell me about Area 38?"

The couple drove off in the Honda. They were now the only two in the lot. Clive held up the stun gun disguised as a cell phone and pretended to be opening something up. "I have pictures," he said.

Mary Jordan leaned over, and he pressed the stun gun into the top of her chest and let the voltage fly. She spasmed and twitched, her eyes bulging, but he held the weapon against her chest until he could smell the flesh burning. Drool seeped from her lips and a thin strand of blood hung like an elastic from her right nostril. Just to be safe, he put duct tape over her mouth, plastic zip ties on her hands, and bent her forward. There was a short chain attached to the underneath of the seat, and this he hooked to the zip ties so that she couldn't sit upright.

He would come back later to disappear the car. First, he'd take Mary Jordan to his home. He'd pull into the garage so that nobody saw her, not with her bent forward. He had plenty of time to find out what she knew about JOHNS, Area 38, and who she might have shared information with. Clive figured that Mary would be scared enough to spill her guts without being tortured. That, he would do for fun.

Bolts had asked that he make her death look like an accident, but it'd been too long since he'd killed somebody slow, and by the time Clive was done with Mary Jordan hours later, there would be no question that her death was some accident.

When he tired of his games, he'd end her life in a novel way. He was toying with the idea of pouring gasoline down her throat and then lighting her on fire from the inside but that would be messy, and he probably didn't have the time. That would be for a weekend at his cabin in the woods. Once dead, he'd cut her up into pieces, double bag them, and take them out to sea in the morning to be thrown overboard for the sharks. He knew a guy who would take her car for parts, no questions asked. Mary Jordan would cease to exist.

Chapter 7

Late in the day on Wednesday, Clay got a text from Victoria Haas asking if he could come out and see her. She said it was important.

He drummed his fingers on the wheel as he steered through downtown Port Essex. He tried to focus his energy on the case. The security guard, Harley, had definitely been a bit bristly, as if his toes were being stepped on, or was it something more? Clay made a note to begin the employee background check with him. What better person to steal a superhuman mouse than the head of security?

Then there was the CEO. Bridget Engel. She had seemed friendly enough, though it certainly wouldn't hurt to know more about her. Clay pulled off the road, into the parking lot of a small lobster shack, and texted Crystal to find out what she could about Engel. He almost pulled out, and then added Rex Bolton's name for Crystal to research and hit send.

Caught in traffic, Clay began reading license plates, and estimated that roughly half were from out of state. Maybe more. Port Essex went from a sleepy town of about 16,000 people year-round to over 24,000 for the months of July and August. Port Essex was possibly the most beautiful place in the world for those two glorious months, and those of means recognized this, choosing to own a house here, mostly out on the Point where Victoria Haas lived, as just one in their collection of homes around the world. A walking bridge traversed the inlet connecting this downtown with the far side for those who didn't want to search for parking.

And then, of course, there were the tourists who rolled into town for a few days to a week and ran amok, trying desperately to fill every second of their vacation with memorable images that they could post to social media to show how exceptional their lives really were. Families that clogged the sidewalks window-shopping while complaining about being bored. Men who came to play golf, get drunk, and wreak havoc. Pretentious couples who thought that everything was so quaint and would stop a crowd to get a selfie at the drop of a hat.

Of course, all of these people were catered to and welcomed. They may not have been the beating heart of Port Essex, but their wallets were certainly the veins that brought the money streaming in. In September, the locals would all give a big sigh of relief, count their money, and budget to survive until the following July. For better or worse, it was their town.

And it *was* his town. Clay had been born here. Had grown up here. Sure, he'd gone away. Had needed to leave. Clay had wanted to be a cop ever since his parents died. So, he'd gone to Boston University, got his B.S. in Criminal Justice, joined Boston PD as a beat cop, attended the police academy, passed his Civil Service Exam, and was a homicide detective by age twenty-nine. He hadn't understood what he was missing until he returned. It was sort of like when he'd wrenched his knee playing football his junior year in high school. He didn't know how bad it was until it was better.

On the face of things, Clay had the ideal life. He lived with his Grandpops in his hometown. His private investigation business was flourishing. He got together several times a week with his best friend, Westy. Every day he worked with Baylee, a woman whose company he greatly enjoyed. There was a core group of others who made his life full. At the same time, he felt like he was floundering. What was it all about?

The man who answered the door was the same gentleman who'd served Clay the lobster rolls and clam chowder last time he was here.

He had a pair of bathing trunks and a towel in his hand and told Clay that Ms. Haas requested that he join her in the pool and then led him to a changing room. The suit fit perfectly.

Victoria was floating in the center of the pool on a rectangular-foam float. She wore a white bikini that made her skin almost appear tan. Her lips were very red and dark glasses covered her eyes. "Come on in," she said.

Clay stepped into the pool. The water was warmed, but not so much that it wasn't refreshing, and he eased his way down the steps before diving under. He could certainly get used to this way of life. "Feels great," he said, coming up next to her float.

Victoria slid off, careful to not go under and ruin her make-up or hair. She dipped herself down as far as her neck. "Thanks for coming over. I was feeling lonely."

"Hard to feel lonely with this view," he said, looking out over the Atlantic where several small islands dotted the water.

"Some people feel lonely in a crowd of people," she said.

"I suppose so."

"Would you care for a drink?" she asked.

"I might swim for just a bit first," he said. "I haven't been in a pool this summer yet."

"By all means. I'm going to dry off."

Clay watched as she walked slowly out of the pool, the wet and white bikini almost translucent. She had definitely filled out in all the right places since high school. And he most certainly needed some time in this refreshing water to cool his jets. He did some lazy laps back and forth for about ten minutes before emerging from the pool.

Victoria sat at a table, having donned a lace-trimmed sheer mesh robe hanging open over her bikini. She was quite fetching. Her incredible sexiness was augmented by the fact that she held a glass of brown liquor in her hand. Next to the table was the rolling bar with a bottle of the Macallan 18-Year-Old Sherry Oak Single Malt

Scotch Whisky shining forth from the top, next to an ice bucket and an empty glass, presumably for Clay.

Opera music drifted from hidden speakers, the beautiful foreign voice ranging in emotion seemed appropriate for the time and place, even if it wasn't Clay's typical cup of tea. The scotch was, though, and he poured himself a double. It was almost as if he could see the Italian words tumbling out across the rocks and into the crashing waves.

"You have a wonderful physique," Victoria said.

Clay was six-feet tall with shoulders that didn't embarrass him when he was in a bathing suit, and perhaps a hint of abs peeking through from his midsection. He tried to work out on a regular basis. The pandemic had cut into his basketball time, but the gym had finally reopened. He'd even ventured out jogging, not that he cared for this form of exercise much.

"And you are a beautiful woman," he said.

"I love your eyes," she said. "I don't believe I've ever seen anybody with that combination of blue and green in my life, other than you, of course."

"What they see is not bad either," he said. Mentally, Clay kicked himself for this corny and lame reply, but she appeared not to notice.

"Ever thought about having kids?" Victoria asked out of the blue.

Clay had a light buzz and was enjoying the evening immensely. He could definitely get used to this way of life, he thought again, looking out over the rolling waves. A schooner was working its way around the point to enter Essex Harbor. If it was not time to be with Baylee, this certainly was not a bad spot to wait.

"I guess when the time is right, I might," he said.

"Would you father a child with me?" she blurted.

Clay's heart skipped a beat, but he believed he'd retained an outwardly stoic expression. He'd hopped into bed with her once, and now she wanted to have kids with him? Whatever it was, this was a new one to him. He chose no reply as the best possible answer.

"I've been yearning for a child and," she looked away, "it's not a feeling that appears to be going away. In fact, the idea has been growing inside of me for a few years now." Her face was impassive behind the dark glasses as she stared straight out to sea. "Yet, there does not seem to be a Mr. Victoria Haas stepping forward to fulfill the role of father."

"You could adopt?" Clay said, albeit weakly.

"I want a child of my own flesh and blood, Clay. A part of me to nurture and raise and continue on who I am after I'm gone."

"Are you suggesting that we get married?" he asked.

Victoria laughed, a pure and hearty chuckle that caught in the breeze. "I don't believe that I'm cut out to be tied to one man for my entire life. That whole 'for better or worse, till death do us part' thing, kind of throws me for a loop."

"What, then, are you asking?"

"You know my history. I want a child to spoil and provide for, to love like I was not," she said.

Clay looked around at the grandeur that was her estate, and then thought of her parents' house next door that was even more regal. But he did know her story, and her teenage years had been far from a fairy tale. "It's a pretty big ask," he said.

"Not really," Victoria said. "I'd say it was pretty simple. We go inside the house, and this time we leave the condom off."

Who was this woman, Clay wondered? He couldn't figure out if her words were merely logical—or entirely crazy. "Entertaining the notion of becoming a father is actually pretty huge."

"I want your sperm, Clay. I want you to help create my child. You don't need be the *father* to the child. You're a good-looking and intelligent man. Good grades, high IQ, and apparently very healthy. I've had you checked out."

What did she mean that she had him 'checked out'? Clay didn't like the thought of people investigating *him*. That was his job. "And my role would be?"

"Deposit your seed in me. Nothing more."

"And if I want more?"

"I told you I had you checked out. You're no better suited for a serious relationship than I am, but I've an undeniable maternal instinct within me. You have no such need."

"What's in it for me? I donate some sperm in a test tube and walk away?"

"How about $20,000? And you can donate the sperm the old-fashioned way, if you so desire. But once I am pregnant, we stop." She stood up, her body flowing upward from the chair, a crooked smile that was entirely sexy and a body that was still indelibly imprinted upon his mind.

"I'm not certain that I'd be okay with having nothing to do with a kid who I fathered."

"Perhaps that's why I like you," Victoria said, sitting back down. "Could you pour me another finger? No ice."

Clay poured two fingers of the brown liquid and topped himself off as well. "Not that I wouldn't greatly enjoy the first step of the equation," he said. His mind told him to stand up and walk—no, *run*—away, but his body and mouth once again had different ideas.

"I'm not interested in getting married," she said.

"Neither am I."

Victoria rose and stepped forward to adjust the umbrella. This caused her to press against his leg with her midsection. "Sorry," she said. "Think I need a bit of shade. How about you?"

"I'm fine for now." The sun felt good, but he knew that he'd burn soon if not careful.

"I might be willing to allow you to be known," Victoria said.

"Known?"

"The child will know that you are the father. The two of you may visit with each other. But I have full, and unequivocal, custody."

Clay sipped from his glass. The scotch was almost gone. How had that happened, he wondered? This was certainly a quandary. He'd spent the previous day with Baylee and knew that he had strong feelings for her, emotions that he'd never known. At the same time, he understood that they weren't ready to be together, that their baggage was just too much. In short, he wanted a relationship with Baylee, and that is why he couldn't have sex with her. Now, here he was with a stunning woman who wanted to have sex with him but refused to have a relationship with him.

"That's certainly worth contemplating," he said.

"What say we go inside and get out of these damp bathing suits?" she asked. She stood and poured him a bit more scotch and plunked two more cubes into his glass as she straddled his leg.

"Sure," he said. His voice might have had a bit of a rasp to it. "Whatever you say."

Victoria brushed her fingers across his cheek and down to the scruff on his jaw. "Come," she said, taking his hand and stepping back so that he could stand.

Clay let himself be led back into the house. "My clothes are in there," he said, nodding at the changing room by the back door.

"You don't need them yet," she said.

The scotch roared in his head. Lust deluged his body. "I'm not certain I'm ready to be a father," he said as they entered her bedroom.

Victoria stepped past him, shutting and locking the door. "Do you find me attractive?"

Clay stood stock-still. "You are beautiful and sexy," he said.

She let the thin, translucent robe fall to the ground. "Have you ever played Russian roulette?"

Clay could barely think. "Russian roulette?"

"Yes. One round in the chamber. Chances are good that nothing will happen."

"What?"

"Let's give it a try. A test run, if you will. One chance in six. There is an eighty-three percent chance that I won't get pregnant." She undid her bikini top and stood inches from him, her breasts firm, her nipples erect.

"Eighty-three percent chance?" he said.

"You talk too much," she said stepping out of her bottoms. She stepped into him, wrapped herself around his body and turned her face up.

Clay leaned down the last few inches and crushed her lips with his own. After a minute, she wiggled his bathing trunks down to his ankles. He picked her up and carried her to the bed.

*   *   *

Westy was quite happy with himself. He was currently chugging back towards the harbor after having caught a ninety-pound bluefin tuna. He'd used a bent butt rod and picked it off the surface as it chased the mackerel bait across the water. The market price being about $17 a pound for bluefin, that single catch should earn him about $1,500. Not bad for a day on the water.

Westy's ancestors had settled in the Port Essex region back in 1718. Fleeing rising rents and religious persecution in northeastern Ireland, these Scottish immigrants found their way to the Massachusetts Bay Colony. Known for being a hardy lot, the Reverend Cotton Mather had encouraged them to come to New England and carve a slice of civilization out of the wild lands. Many of these Scotch-Irish Presbyterian Ulstermen had settled further into the interior and northern parts of the colony, but Westy's ancestors had stopped in Port Essex.

His family had fought in the American Revolution, the War of 1812, missed the Spanish American War as it went so quickly, but returned to serve in WWI, WWII, Korea, and Vietnam. It was no wonder that he'd graduated high school and entered the military, attending SEAL training, and then shipping off to Iraq and Afghanistan for the next eight years.

When they weren't fighting wars, the Beck family had been fishermen in Port Essex for over 300 years now. That was quite a legacy. Westy was the only family member left on the water in Maine, his parents having recently moved to Edisto Beach, South Carolina, and his son, Joe, yet too young to enter the family tradition. There were no uncles, aunts, cousins, or any other Becks left.

A boat was cutting across the water heading east up the coast. Westy put the glasses on it just out of idle curiosity and saw that it was the *Mary Ellen*. Daryl Allen's boat. That was interesting. Of course, the man was most likely just returning from fishing. Except that he was going the wrong way, and it was the wrong time of day to just be going out. It was unlikely the man was on a pleasure trip.

Cashing in on the bluefin tuna would have to wait, Westy decided, turning his own boat, the *Gordana*—named after his grandmother—to the starboard and up the coast.

*   *   *

Clay's phone rang, the old traditional rotary-style ringtone, and he quickly slid out of bed to avoid waking Victoria. After a brief respite from the first, furious coupling, they had decided to chance the Russian roulette and gone for round two, a more enjoyable and pleasurable journey of intimacy and exploration. Afterwards, they'd both drifted into a light slumber, now interrupted by the ringing. Victoria was sitting up in bed as he gathered his phone. He took a moment to appreciate her naked torso before looking at the cell, noticing as he did that it was just after 10:00.

It was Faith Beck. "Hello."

"Clay, is Weston with you?"

"No, why?"

"He hasn't come home. That's not like him."

Chapter 8

Baylee went out to Kalinda's rental mansion on the Point at five o'clock. It seemed that Aisha, the personal bodyguard, had to go up to Bangor to pick up the pop singer's husband who was flying in from Europe. Baylee was needed to escort Kalinda to a sound studio down in Brunswick where she was making a recording for a promotional video.

Kalinda and Aisha came out the front door as Baylee pulled in. Aisha went and got in one of the identical Cadillac Escalades. Kalinda motioned to Baylee and walked to the second SUV. "Mind if I drive?" she asked. "I so rarely get the chance."

"No problem," Baylee said.

"I'd rather drive something less fancy," Kalinda said. "But my publicist says I need to keep up my image, and Aisha says this is safer than most." She pulled the vehicle onto the road and hit the gas.

Baylee smiled. This woman was matter of fact, down to earth, and just sort of a regular person. "Where's your husband coming from?" It seemed that they were now in the same pod and didn't need to wear masks when together.

"Paris."

"Are flights allowed into the U.S. from Paris?" Baylee blurted out before she could stop herself.

Kalinda chuckled. "Yes. It's the other way that's banned. Unless, of course, you are a movie star and a celebrity. Then," Kalinda winked, "exceptions can be made."

"It must be nice," Baylee said.

"Fame does have its perks, but they're certainly offset by the downside."

"Like what?"

Kalinda looked sideways at Baylee. "No offense, but like having to have a bodyguard when you want to go out in public."

It was Baylee's turn to chuckle. "Fair enough."

"I can't imagine what it would be like to be a child who has to grow up with famous parents, you know?" Kalinda said.

"I guess that'd be pretty difficult."

"On top of that, they'd be judged in everything they did. *And on pop news tonight,*" Kalinda did a pretty good newscaster voice, "*it turns out that Kalinda's son Bobby isn't very good at math, scoring a 73 on his latest quiz.* Or worse, he's a klutz who makes a habit of running into things and is a YouTube sensation by age eight for falling down."

Baylee hadn't really considered the many downsides of being a celebrity, but it was obvious that Kalinda had put a great deal of thought into that particular subject. "It certainly isn't something I have to worry about."

"Do you want children?" Kalinda asked.

"Not until I can care for them properly, and there is a man in the picture who can do the same," Baylee said. "The last thing this world needs is another messed up kid."

"Amen to that."

They drove in silence for a few minutes before Baylee asked, "What's the name of the sound studio we're going to?"

"It's called Music on the River. Supposed to have the best sound in all of Maine, if not New England. Been around about ten years in an old mill building."

"If it's the mill building on the river in Brunswick, I know the place, or the building anyway. There's a bunch of businesses in there."

"Are you married, Baylee? Or have a boyfriend? Or both?"

"None of the above."

"Why not?"

"I was married once," Baylee said. "It didn't take."

She neglected to tell Kalinda that she'd killed her husband for raping and abusing her. Chances are, the woman knew that already, as she'd most likely done a background check on her.

"Why don't you have a man in your life now?" Kalinda asked. "If you don't mind me asking."

Baylee was rather enjoying the just-us-girls banter. "I seem to be getting on better without one then I ever did with one."

"Good for you."

"How about your husband? You two get along?"

"Yes. Yes, we do," Kalinda said. "I have to admit, though, that part of that is we aren't constantly together. I go out on tour four months out of the year, or I used to anyway, and John has to go on set for filming. That, coupled with other engagements in life, and we end up spending more time apart than together, but it works for us."

They rode in silence for a bit, reaching Route 1 to turn left onto the road that was extremely busy in the summer. There was no stoplight, and Baylee counted sixteen cars in front of them before they finally got their opportunity to risk their lives cutting across and in front of steady traffic zooming along at sixty-plus miles an hour.

"What are you recording today?" Baylee asked.

"A jingle for a promotional video," Kalinda said. "Not really my thing, but it's for a great cause, so why not?"

"Yeah? What's the cause?"

"The company I asked you about. Johnson Laboratories."

"Johnson Laboratories? Is a good cause?"

Kalinda looked sideways at Baylee. "You don't think so?"

"No, I'm not saying that. A jingle for a company that does testing on mice?"

"Their work is going to change the world."

"How so?"

"Their progress toward eradicating diabetes and cancer, to name two. What's not to like?"

"Fair enough," Baylee said. "What rhymes with mice?"

Kalinda laughed. "I went with dice, but you'll get to hear the whole thing when we get there."

* * *

The *Mary Ellen* went around the Point in Port Essex with Westy chugging along behind at a safe distance. It was a good four miles by car to East Essex but less than a mile by boat. Westy watched through his binoculars as the *Mary Ellen* pulled into Paradise Inlet and moored at a wharf. Two men got off and walked down to a weather-beaten cabin and went inside.

Westy looked at his cold storage where the bluefin tuna was. It'd be fine, even if he didn't get a chance to sell it until the morning. He definitely wanted to get a peek at what Daryl Allen was doing, but he didn't want to have his $1,500 catch go bad. Just a quick look-see, Westy thought, and then home.

He dropped anchor, got his Sig Sauer from the lockbox, and then put his inflatable dinghy over the side and clambered in. The far side of Paradise Point from the wharf was an empty stretch of trees and rocks, and he paddled the small vessel there and tied it to a tree. It was still a few hours until sunset. Westy worked his way through the woods and came up behind the cottage. He wished for darkness and thought about waiting, because he did hope to get the bluefin back before his wharf closed shop for the day.

There was a cluster of houses, from simple cottages to large homes, with several people in view. Luckily, the cottage was on the woods-side of the road, and Westy was able to come up behind it and approach the back window without being visible. At least he thought so. That was not actually the case. He was looking through the window at a man that may have been the Russian he'd seen a few days back when he caught movement out of the side of his eye.

He moved to dodge, but something heavy and cold smashed him a glancing blow to the skull. On his back, stunned, he saw what appeared to be a ball-peen hammer descending upon his forehead. Then, nothing.

First there was pain, and then light, which caused more pain, and then Westy opened his eyes, but just barely. There were two men sitting at a table. Westy's Sig Sauer pistol and his Ka-Bar, the SEAL issued knife, sat on the table between them. It looked to be the kitchen through an arched opening of about six feet. They were talking back and forth but he couldn't hear them past the roaring in his head.

Westy was sitting on a chair in the middle of the living room. There was a couch to his left and a painting of a lobster boat behind it. On his right was a window covered by a blanket, with an armchair kitty-corner to it. His arms were tied behind him and attached to the chair by what felt like some sort of nylon rope.

One of the men was most definitely the Russian he'd seen climbing aboard Daryl Allen's boat. He had a broad face with a thin nose and lips that could've been drawn with a crayon, they were so flat. The other man had a balding forehead, narrow face, an unnaturally long neck that made Westy think of a stork, and gun-metal gray eyes.

Those eyes turned towards Westy, and he quickly closed his own to mere slits. He'd not picked his bearded chin up from his chest or moved in any other way. After a minute he opened them back up. The two men had returned to talking. Westy realized that his legs weren't bound. Carefully, he moved one and then the other to be certain.

He could probably stand and run out the door or through the window before the two men could react. They would most certainly catch him, and either kill him, or return him to his captivity. There was the hope that somebody would see him and report it to the authorities. There was no clock to be seen and no outside light coming in, so it was hard to tell what time it was. It could be the middle of the night for all he knew.

Then, Westy had another idea, one that he liked better. He knew that he had to act before they came to check on him. He steeled himself against the throbbing misery that was his head, counted to three, stood up, and charged the table. The two men looked up in surprise, Stork-neck reacting first, pulling a pistol from a shoulder holster just as Westy reached them. He crashed into the table, flipping it over, sending the two men sprawling backward, before crashing to the floor.

Stork-neck kicked him in the side, a pain that he couldn't even feel over the agony still pulsating through his skull. He wondered if it was fractured. He was kicked several more times and then picked upright, still bound to the chair. It must be a sturdy chair to have not broken. Truth be told, it was only in movies that chairs splintered like they were hollow.

"You just like pain, don't you?" Stork-neck said.

Westy could smell blood in his beard. He said nothing.

"What the fuck you theenk you do?"

The man was most certainly a Russian, Westy thought.

"He just wanted to come in the kitchen and speak with us, is all," Stork-neck said. "So, what do you have to say?"

Westy said nothing. He certainly wasn't going to tell them the truth. That'd be a dead giveaway to the fact that his Ka-Bar, scabbard and all, was now down the back of his pants.

"Why were you following Vlad?" Stork-neck asked.

Westy didn't think the man's name was really Vlad. They wouldn't be sharing that information. Not unless they meant to kill him. And then Westy realized that they most certainly were going to kill him. Whatever they were up to, it was far too serious to risk leaving him alive to talk.

"Wasn't following him," Westy said. The words came out as a croak.

Stork-neck slapped him. "You most certainly were. Vlad picked you up as soon as you changed direction. I watched you creep up behind the house and look in the fucking window. Don't lie to me."

"I was following Daryl."

Stork-neck went to hit him again, paused, and furrowed his brow. "Daryl? What the fuck for?"

"Owes me money."

"What for?"

"He bought my old truck. Half down. Said he'd get me the other half in a month. That was six months ago."

"Fuck me with a mop handle," Stork-neck said. "That is just too fucking bad for you, isn't it?"

Westy stared straight into those gray eyes and imagined himself cutting them out one at a time. "You mean because I won't be getting the second half of my truck payment?"

"Ha. You are one cool fucking cucumber for somebody destined to be at the bottom of the ocean before sunrise."

"I theenk we let him go," the Russian said.

"You theenk wrong," Stork-neck said. "I don't need the police passing around some artistic rendition of my face and asking questions about me. Besides, look at this fucking guy. I can almost feel him ripping my guts out with his eyes. I wish I had more time to play, especially after you called and ruined my earlier sport, but now we got two bodies to dispose of."

"Two?" the Russian asked.

"Yeah, I got me one of those fucking lying newspaper reporters in my truck."

There was a knock at the door. Stork-neck pulled his pistol out, walking toward the door. Westy noted that it was Heckler & Koch VP9.

"Look out," Westy yelled.

The Russian punched him in the face, and it was like July 4th all over again, except this time the fireworks were exploding inside his head.

"Open up. It's me, Daryl."

Stork-neck opened the door and let Daryl Allen in.

"What's he doing here?" Daryl asked.

"Came to collect that money you owe me, Daryl," Westy said. "Then I'll scram out of your hair."

"Sorry, my friend, but die you must," Stork-neck said to Westy as he walked back into the center of the room. "I certainly don't need a pencil sketch of my face circulating, now, do I?"

"He has to die?" Daryl asked.

"He seen my face. If you'd told me you owed him money, then we might have avoided the whole thing," Clive said.

"I don't owe him any fucking money," Daryl said.

"You buy a truck from him?"

"Fuck no, I don't even know him."

"You said his name was Weston Beck."

"Yeah, okay, I know who he is, but I ain't never even talked to the fucking guy, much less bought his truck."

Stork-neck laughed a harsh rattle. He walked over and grabbed Westy by the beard, pulling him upright from where the Russian had knocked him to the floor. "You're good. Real good. I'd like to see how long it'd take to make you scream like a little girl, but I think we need to make your death look accidental. Two missing people from a town this size in one day is bound to raise red flags. No, you need to be found dead, and by accident, and not cut into little pieces."

An hour later Westy found himself tied, with his hands again behind his back, to a winch on his own fishing boat. They were following Daryl in the *Mary Ellen* out to sea. Stork-neck was at the wheel under the standing shelter with his back to Westy. The Russian sat on the tackle box across from him. There was a canvas duffel bag leaking blood next to him. Westy had been led to believe that it contained the cut-up pieces of a woman, perhaps a reporter.

The plan, apparently, was to dump the hunks of human body parts into the ocean for the sharks. Then they were going to scuttle the *Gordana* with Westy aboard and let it sink to the bottom. They deemed it best if his body was not found, but the boat, or pieces of it were, suggesting that he'd sunk and drowned. Daryl had not liked the plan one bit, but Westy could tell that he was terrified of Stork-neck. He wished that Daryl was the one captaining this boat, for he thought he might talk some reason into him.

The Russian sat with his head in his hands, suggesting that he didn't like what was happening any more than Daryl. Stork-neck, on the other hand, was singing joyfully at the boat's wheel. The lyrics were some butchered version of "Fifteen Men on a Dead Man's Chest." The sea was relatively calm and the moon white with only a sliver missing, erasing the stars to dim pinpricks in the night sky.

Westy was able to turn his head to ensure that Stork-neck still had his back to him. The Russian was lost in his own thoughts. Carefully, Westy eased the Ka-Bar from the back of his jeans. He fumbled the blade free from the scabbard, happy to have the sea and the song drown out any noise he might be making. He wasn't able to hold the steel and saw through the ropes but managed to wedge the Ka-Bar between the wall and his butt, and then cut himself free.

Did the Russian have a gun on him, Westy wondered? As if reading his mind, the man picked his head free of his hands and pulled a pistol from his waistband. Westy had hoped to take out Stork-neck and then turn his attention to the Russian. Even if he managed to do that now, there was no way he wouldn't be shot and killed at this close range. If he took out the Russian, which held a low degree of probability now that the man held a weapon in his hand, then Stork-neck would most certainly kill him before he could get to the man.

He hated to turn tail and run. But that is what the situation demanded. Or turn tail and swim would be more correct. As they passed between the tip of East Essex and Hog's Head Island, Westy made his move. He came to a crouch, throwing the Ka-Bar underhand at the same time, the blade sinking into the Russian's arm. One step and then he threw himself over the side as bullets fanned the air over him.

Westy had been able to hold his breath for just over three minutes back in his SEAL days. That time was slightly less now, but necessity would certainly help. Hog Head Island was only about 400 yards away. When he came up for air, he saw lights sweeping the water, and heard yelling, and then he was swimming underwater again.

Chapter 9

Once back in the Jeep, Clay texted Baylee. Can you talk?

Almost back to Port Essex. 10 minutes?

Westy is missing.

The phone almost immediately rang. Clay said hello, put it on speaker, and started the Jeep.

"What's going on?" Baylee asked.

"Don't know. Faith called wondering if I knew where Westy was, is all I know."

"Not like him to be out this late."

"Not without telling his wife, that's for sure," Clay said.

"He's not answering his phone?"

"Straight to voice mail."

"What's the plan?"

"I'm on my way to the Knox Wharf where he moors his boat."

"Pull over," Baylee said. And then repeated herself, this time muffled.

"What?"

"We just passed you. I'll ride over with you."

Sure enough, Clay saw a figure emerge from a Cadillac Escalade and come jogging down the road. There wasn't much traffic at this time on Tuesday night and he was able to back the Jeep up to meet her.

"Where you coming from?" Baylee asked, climbing in slightly out of breath.

"I was, out, uh, visiting Victoria Haas."

"Visiting, huh?" Baylee pulled her seatbelt on. "You don't think he's just down to the Pelican Perch knocking a few back, do you?"

"Not like him," Clay said. "But I guess if his boat is back, that will be the second place we look."

"So, you've been out visiting Victoria?"

"Yeah."

"She make you dinner?"

"No. Just drinks."

Baylee looked at the time on her phone. "That's a lot of drinks. You need me to drive?"

"No. I'm fine."

They rode in silence until arriving at the Knox Wharf. Westy's boat was not at his mooring. It being past ten o'clock at night, there was nobody around to ask if he'd been seen.

"Maybe he broke down," Baylee said. "Most likely he's just out there floating along looking at the moon."

Clay called the Coast Guard. A fellow he knew faintly by the name of Pete answered. Pete knew Westy well. He promised to roust two crews and get both Coast Guard boats stationed in Port Essex out on the water, searching. He asked if Clay wanted to go along. Clay said no, thinking of Murphy and his aluminum motorboat. Three boats on the water were better than two, or so he figured.

The sun was a fiery ball of yellow and orange just above the horizon signaling a new day when Clay's phone rang. They had rousted Murphy from sleep and put out in his aluminum skiff, the vessel barely large enough to hold the three of them and not meant for deep water. Luckily, it was a calm night, and they had let the Coast Guard go out further while they trolled along the coast, so far, to no avail.

"This is Clay," he barked into the phone.

"This is Pete. We got him."

Clay gave a thumbs-up to Baylee and Murphy. "Where is he?"

"We're headed back to the Coast Guard Station now."

"What happened?"

"He hasn't said. Found him on Hog's Head Island. Just about frozen to death. He'd been in the water. Pretty bad wound on his forehead."

"What about his boat?"

"No sign."

"You got an ambulance meeting you?"

"He refuses. The police are meeting us there. He says he wants you to take him to be checked out."

Clay mouthed *Coast Guard Station* to Murphy who was steering the skiff. "I'm on my way. About ten minutes."

"Same for us. See you there."

The phone went dead. As Clay repeated the information and then punched in Westy's home phone to tell his wife, Murphy opened the motor up all the way. It took them eight minutes. They pulled into the dock at the same time as the Coast Guard cutter.

Westy was wrapped in a blanket with an angry red wound the size of a shot glass in his forehead. He might have been a sorry-looking figure if it wasn't for the anger emanating from his being like a kettle on the boil.

"What happened to you?" Clay asked.

"I'll tell you on the way to the urgent care," Westy said.

Clay neglected to tell him it was not yet open, and they'd have to go to the hospital in Brunswick. From the looks of Westy, the better technology and care would also be important. "You cleared to go?"

Westy looked at the two policemen and Pete. The officer named Sean, who Clay knew from the gym shrugged. "After you get done there, come down to the station and tell us what happened."

"Let's go," Westy said.

"Hey, Sean, can you give Baylee a ride out to the Point to pick up her car?" Clay asked. Murphy didn't have a car, and it would save him a boat ride out and around the Point.

"Sure, no problem."

"Go home and feed your dog and get some sleep," Clay said to Baylee. "Call me when you wake up, and I'll catch you up."

Clay could tell that Baylee was set to argue, but not feeding Flash was inviting the basset hound to wreak devastation on her furniture. She nodded and followed Sean to his patrol car as Clay and Westy climbed into the Jeep.

Once on the road to Route 1, Clay turned to Westy. "You wreck your boat?" he asked.

Westy cursed using words Clay had never heard from his friend. "You remember I told you about seeing Daryl Allen picking somebody off a Russian fishing boat?"

"Yeah."

"Yesterday afternoon I saw him cutting around the Point instead of coming into his wharf, which was already kinda weird. He had a guy on board, and I got curious and followed him over to East Essex. I moored my boat and snuck up behind the cottage they went into, and some fucker came up behind me and hit me with a hammer."

He repeated every detail of the ordeal, including the supposed reporter in a duffel bag. Westy was efficient but brief, never giving more than he needed. Whether this was SEAL training or concussion pain, it was hard to tell. He was also angry that his boat was most likely at the bottom of the sea at this point.

After he'd dove overboard, he managed to make it to shore without being spotted. The two boats had first swung toward the mainland of East Essex, thinking he'd gone that way, time that had allowed him to reach Hog's Head Island and crawl ashore.

When they didn't find him, they figured he must be on Hog's Head Island, and they'd come ashore looking for him with flashlights. He would've taken them out then and there, Westy said, if he wasn't seeing triple from the blow to the cranium and weak from blood loss and cold. So, instead, he'd crawled into a crevice between two rocks and laid low until they'd gone on their way a bit before sunrise. He had been waiting for the warmth of that sunrise to take the chill out of his bones when the Coast Guard Cutter had spotted him.

"The Russian's name was Vlad?" Clay asked.

"Maybe. Could've been an alias."

"You didn't get the name of the guy who hit you with the hammer?"

"Nope. But his face, right down to his elongated neck, is etched in my mind."

There was no fracture of the skull but most definitely a concussion, a diagnosis that Westy shrugged off as if it might've been a mosquito bite. The doctor thought he should stay a night for observation before leaving but that wasn't an option.

Halfway back to Port Essex, Clay finally broached the subject. "What are you thinking this was all about?"

Westy shrugged. "Somebody's got a fucking death wish?"

"Yeah, that too, but I mean, why?" Clay gave his friend a minute to answer, and when he didn't respond, continued with his questions. "Was the Russian the same as the one you saw the other day?"

"Can't be sure. Maybe."

"They must have something pretty big to hide."

"You think?"

"Drugs? Human trafficking?" Clay asked. "You ever see that series, *The Americans*? Could be Russian moles or handlers traveling back and forth through Port Essex."

Westy closed his eyes and groaned. "Are you really pulling intel from a television series?"

"Okay, okay, I got another one for you. I told you some about the case out to JOHNS?"

"JOHNS?"

"Johnson Laboratories," Clay said. "This is all highly classified, but I doubt you even talk to your wife about such things, much less anybody else, so I think the secret is safe with you. They are creating something called SHAIM, or SuperHuman Advanced Intelligence Mice. They're genetically engineering mice that are stronger and smarter than other mice."

"What does this have to do with Russians? Plus, the guy who hit me wasn't Russian, he was as American as you or me."

"The technology they're developing can be applied to humans. Hell, they may already be using it. What if the Russians are trying to steal this scientific know-how for their own nefarious purposes?"

"I just got concussed. Let's try to keep words like 'nefarious' out of this."

"Whatever. JOHNS hired me because somebody tried to steal one of these super mice. Maybe it was your guy with a hammer, and Vlad the Russian."

"And fucking Daryl Allen," Westy said.

"Him, we should be able to find."

It was almost noon when Clay's phone buzzed just as they reached the outskirts of Port Essex.

It was a text from Cloutier. Can you talk? Can we get together? I have something I need to run by you.

He waited until they pulled into the parking lot of the police station before texting back. Can it wait? In the middle of something right now.

One of my reporters, Mary Jordan, is missing. Never made it home yesterday.

"Shit," Clay said aloud.

"What is it?" Westy asked.

Clay told him.

"Fuck," Westy said.

"You thinking what I'm thinking?"

"That's who was in the duffel bag."

Chapter 10

FRIDAY, JULY 10TH

The two men were sitting in an Audi A8. The sun was sliding down towards the rim of the deserted gravel pit.

"What the hell is going on?" Harley Lange asked.

Rex Bolton didn't answer.

"I thought my file was sealed. Not for public consumption."

"It is."

Harley rubbed his eyes and shook his head. "Why am I the first person they want to talk to Monday morning?"

Rex sighed. "You're the head of security. It's the obvious place to start."

"You're sure they don't know anything?"

"How could they?"

"Why'd you bring them in to investigate, anyway?"

"It wasn't my choice. Engel wanted it."

"That bitch. What does she have to do with it? It's not like she's ever even here. Jet-setting around the world and going to cocktail parties is her fucking job description."

"She's the CEO, Harley."

"She doesn't often act it. Seems to me she spends most of her time being a board member to that one company with the foreign name."

"Exactly. We pander to her when she takes an interest and then do what we want when she's away. I believe there's a saying, when the cat's away, the mice will play?"

"Why didn't you talk her out of it?"

"Just relax. They don't have any idea about you. They just want to ask some questions about the facility's security. You stick to the script, and everything will be fine."

"It was a bad time in my life," Harley said.

Rex wondered why he was always tasked with hand-holding weak-willed peons who were afraid of their own shadows.

Rex had grown up in Michigan. His father, Edgar Bolton, was a self-made multimillionaire who had started off as a salesman before opening his own die-cast machine manufacturing firm selling to the automobile industry, and eventually branching out into real estate and investments. The Bolton Group was currently worth a hundred million. By the time Rex was seven, they were wealthy. By the age of fifteen, he'd traveled extensively, including much of Europe, Japan, China, and Russia.

He'd attended MIT in Cambridge, Massachusetts, and while not a particularly exemplary student, graduated with a degree in Computer Science and Molecular Biology in five years. The year off between his sophomore and junior years had been the best of his life. He'd hiked the Ural Mountains with a friend who'd found himself taking a mandatory vacation from Yale. Life had been so much simpler back then. He and Rick had backpacked their way along the boundary between Europe and Asia, smoking weed, occasionally eating some whacky mushrooms, and living as one with nature.

After four months, they'd emerged from the wilderness looking for some female company in the city of Perm, Russia. There, for the first time, Rex fell in love. He met Lada on the banks of the Kama River, and when Rick returned to the States, Rex stayed on. For six months, Rex and Lada were inseparable. Lada showed him the city during the week, and they took adventures into the country on weekends. Cocktails, vodka, and wine at small pubs, followed by Lada's home-cooked meals, or small cafés paid for by Rex—this was the norm every night.

The sex was unbelievable. Lada would do anything, try anything, and was insatiable between the sheets... or in the car... or the woods—wherever they happened to be. They explored the city, the countryside, each other, drank and fucked like there was no tomorrow. Rex had never since found a woman like that, perhaps the reason why he was thrice divorced.

His father had shown up on his doorstep in the middle of August 1995 and read him the riot act. If he didn't return to MIT in two weeks, then Bolton Sr. would cut him off. Rex was young and headstrong and ready to defy his old man, but Lada talked him out of it. He packed his bags, promised to return, and went back to college. They kept up long distance for some time, but then things had fizzled. Then, five years ago, Rex got a Facebook friend request, and their correspondence had rekindled.

In the intervening years, Rex had graduated MIT, gotten married, and opened his own biomedical research company. The blissful matrimony lasted three years, and he was on the downhill slide of marriage number two when the recession of 2009 wrecked his business. When he turned to his father for a bail out, the bastard had refused him, and pulled all financial support, telling him it was time to make it on his own.

Rex had made it two years on savings and the goodwill of friends, a group whose numbers dwindled month by month until he had finally been forced to take get a job like any other peasant. Chief Operating Officer at JOHNS. He'd planned to be there for two years, max. This was his ninth year in this godforsaken hellhole in northern New England. It was as bad as Michigan, if not worse.

"I can't lose this job," Harley was whining. "I got payments."

"You're not going to lose your job," Rex said. "Just tell them that you know nothing, and keep your mouth shut about your past."

"This Clay Wolfe is starting to make a name for himself around town."

"He's a fucking putz." Rex turned and looked at Harley. "You just need to relax. You want I should send Stephan over to spend the weekend with you?"

Harley smiled, his shoulders settling, and his pout disappearing. "Is he around? That would be great."

*　*　*

It was initially a somber crowd that gathered at the Pelican Perch the day after Westy was found on Hog's Head Island, with few jokes about the hammer impression in his skull, now swollen to the size of a golf ball. Clay, Baylee, and Crystal had locked up the office at five o'clock and walked the short distance to the bar that seemed to keep vigil over Essex Harbor like the watchtower of a seaside castle keeping a wary eye out for approaching armadas. They had spent the past two days working through the employee profiles of Johnson Laboratories and were set to start interviewing people on Monday.

Westy arrived right after they'd secured a high-top table in the corner overlooking the water, and just in time to include his drink order, Budweiser, with theirs. It was his first time out since giving his statement to the police, which had included a sketch of Stork-neck, the one who hit him with a hammer, and the Russian, possibly named Vlad. Clay noticed a slight bulge under his shirt in the back of his jeans and knew that he was most likely packing. Clay wondered what weapon he'd chosen from his collection, seeing as his Sig Sauer had been lost the other night. Maine had no rules against concealed carry—meaning no special license was needed—and Westy would be ready if they came after him again.

The police had swooped in on the house where Westy had been held, but it was long since empty, cleaned out and wiped down. Not a single print had been lifted. The owner was a ninety-three-year-old man who'd recently moved into a retirement community. His son and daughter came up from down south—one from Georgia and the other from Florida—to help move him, but had then gone back home, not yet sure what they were going to do with the cottage, sell it, or keep it. They claimed that they didn't know anything about their father's place being a hotbed of criminal activity, and there was no reason to doubt them. The police didn't have much, if anything, to go on.

Not that anybody appeared to know what kind of criminal activity it actually was. Of course, Westy had been assaulted and kidnapped and then transported with the intention of his eventual murder. But why? This was partially the reason for this get-together. Yes, to catch up and touch base, but to begin the wheels turning on their own investigation. The police had also come up empty on Daryl Allen. The man had dropped off the face of Port Essex. He lived alone in a trailer. His truck was parked at the wharf where he moored his boat, and said boat was missing. The man had disappeared like Houdini's vanishing elephant some hundred years earlier.

"Faith and Joe get off okay?" Clay asked once they all had drinks. His was a Baxter Stowaway, his favorite beer and one that happened to be on draft at the Pelican.

"Yep," Westy said. "She's kind of pissed off at you."

"Me?" Clay asked.

"Seems every time I get involved with you, she gets sent inland to weather the storm."

"What does this have to do with me?"

"I guess I mentioned that your interest was piqued by Daryl picking some guy off a Russian fishing boat, and that's why I followed him the other day."

"So, *I'm* to blame for you deciding to follow them the other day?"

"Looks that way."

"Am I also to blame that you let some guy who you said resembled a stork sneak up on you and strike you with a hammer?"

"Yeah, probably didn't go too well when you showed up hammered after being gone all night," Baylee said with a smirk.

"Bet you still have a splitting headache from getting hammered," Clay said.

Their laughter was cut short by the glare in Westy's eyes. "Nah, I'll take the blame for that. If it wasn't for the angry bump on my head, Faith would've done me a lot worse when I showed up after being out all night."

"I bet she would've shot your fucking ass," Crystal said. Then her face reddened, and she snuck a side glance at Baylee.

They were interrupted just in time by the waiter who came to get their food order. They decided to start off with some apps, nachos, spinach dip, and fried cheese sticks.

"What I want to know," Westy said, moving the conversation forward, "is what does this have to do with the case you're working on?"

"Why would it have anything to do with our case?" Baylee asked.

"Clay mentioned that you are investigating the potential theft of mice that have some super gene in them? Seems to me this might be of interest to the Russians," Westy said.

"Just because you saw Daryl picking up a guy from a Russian fishing boat doesn't mean anything," Clay said, sneaking a glance at Baylee.

"You were the one who brought it up," Westy said.

"So what? Daryl picked up a guy off a Russian ship." Clay said.

"Well, it *is* a little more than that," Westy said. "I mean, the guy was most definitely Russian. And they were going to kill me just because I followed Daryl, and saw their faces."

"But it wasn't the Russian who hit you," Clay said.

"Nah, the Russian was a bit squeamish about the whole thing, actually. It was the odd-looking fellow that I have a beef with, mostly."

"It does seem possible that the Russians could be involved in the JOHNS business," Clay said. He looked at a dark cloud coming from the west and wondered if it might rain. "The fact is, the attempt was unsuccessful. JOHNS has tightened their security. There is little reason to believe that whoever it is will try again, much less actually walk out the door with a mouse."

"I don't much care if they aim to steal a mouse or not. I just want a lead on who hit me in the head and tried to kill me," Westy said.

Clay shrugged. "For what it's worth, we've gone through the employee files on the theory that, whoever it was on the outside, they had to have help on the inside even to get a mouse out. We've flagged twelve people we want to interview."

"Why those twelve?"

"Six of them are in debt, we suspect two of having affairs, and another one has been reprimanded for being a disruptive coworker." So much for client confidentiality and signing an NDA that threatened imprisonment in Guantanamo Bay, Clay thought.

"I count nine."

The food came out, and Crystal got herself another Margarita.

"One of them has Chinese citizenship, another one makes regular visits to China, and the last one is a Russian."

"No shit," Westy said. "Right here in Port Essex? Working at a top-secret facility?"

"They've gathered the top scientists from around the world," Clay said. "Something about JOHNS being the preeminent mouse-testing facility in the world."

"Are there any other fucking mouse test places in the world?" Crystal asked.

"It seems that the Russian should be number one on your list," Westy said.

"Why's that?" Clay asked.

"We all know that the Russians are the bad guys," Westy said. "Don't you ever watch any movies?"

"How about Natasha Romanoff from *The Avengers*?" Baylee asked. "The Black Widow is Russian and badass and on the side of justice."

"Didn't you warn me about not getting intel from the movies?" Clay asked Westy.

"Okay, okay, how about because there was a Russian guy there the other night when Stork-neck tried to kill me?" Westy replied.

"We thought we'd start with the head of security first, and then maybe the Russian," Clay said.

"I guess the head of security is a good place to start. And yes, then the Russian," Westy said.

"Not only is Harley Lange in charge of security, he's in the midst of a pretty messy divorce and is looking at some rather substantial alimony payments," Baylee said.

"Seems he was having an affair with a security officer at his former job," Clay added.

"Might be enough to turn you into a fucking traitor, I guess," Westy said. "I mean, if you need the money bad enough."

"Well, that, as well," Baylee said. "But what if you were some macho guy, you know, married and skirt chaser and all, then you get caught on camera in the broom closet in the carnal embrace of another man? That might be something you don't want surfacing."

"Yep. I can see how a macho man would do just about anything to stay in the closet," Westy said.

"You mean in secret or with his lover?" Baylee asked with a wicked glint in her eye.

"Whose lover?" Cloutier pulled up a chair with a grim hello and waved for a beer.

"We were going through the list of names to be interviewed," Clay said. "For the JOHNS case."

"Aren't johns what prostitutes call their customers?" Cloutier asked.

"Suppose so," Clay said. "We haven't come across any employees hiding a prostitute in their trunk, but the head of security seems fairly intent on keeping his being gay a secret."

"Hard to be a gay man in Port Essex," Cloutier said.

"Darn fishermen and rednecks," Baylee said. They all looked at Westy.

Westy didn't react at first. His head was down staring at his beer. As if the words had finally settled in, he looked up. "Give me a break. I haven't recovered from being hammered."

"Seriously, though, don't be outing him if you don't have to. I'm not part of the queer community that believes that everybody needs to publicly express their sexuality. If he wants to keep it a secret, that's his business," Cloutier said.

"Fair enough," Clay said. "Does the news lady have any news for us?"

"They found Daryl Allen," Cloutier said.

"I know Daryl a little bit," Crystal said. "He'll spill the beans, sure enough. Can't keep his mouth shut."

"Doubt it," Cloutier said.

"Why's that?"

"He's dead," Cloutier said.

They all looked at Westy who raised his hands. "Not me. And leave me alone. I'm not up to your weak wit and underhanded attacks."

"Yeah, well, you better pull yourself together," Cloutier said. "You can expect a visit from the police. He was found in your boat, which is partially submerged out on the Pumpkin Ledges. Coast Guard helicopter spotted it."

"If they weren't looking, he wouldn't have been found," Westy said. "Nobody goes in there, not if they know what they're doing. That's the Bermuda Triangle of MidCoast Maine."

"Cause of death?" Baylee asked.

"No word from the ME yet."

"Somebody's tying up loose ends," Clay said.

"Another lead dead in the water," Baylee said.

Cloutier grimaced. "You got anything else to follow up on?"

"Like Clay was saying, we're going to start interviewing the JOHNS employees who we red-flagged for one reason or another," Baylee said. "The first one on the list is Harley Lange, head of security."

"Yeah?" Cloutier asked. "Does being gay make him public enemy number one?

Chapter 11

MONDAY, JULY 13TH

"Thank you for making time for us, Mr. Lange."

Clay and Baylee had decided to both be present for this first 9:00 a.m. interview on Monday morning. They'd then split up the rest of the first batch for more efficiency.

"Not a problem, Mr. Wolfe. Good to see you again, Miss Baker." Harley Lange smiled and nodded, and Clay noted once again his blonde locks swept back from his face and hanging down past his ears. Not the usual close-cropped haircut favored by security personnel, usually ex-military or ex-cops. His eyes were a dazzling blue, and his features fine-boned.

"We just wanted to go over some of the security protocols that you have in place, and pick your brain in regard to the attempted theft at the Black Lab," Clay said.

They were on top of the hill in the main administrative building doing the interview in a conference room that could've seated twenty easily. Bridget Engel was away on business, but Rex Bolton had met them and made sure they had what they needed.

"I understand," Harley said. He had on a gray suit with a white shirt and green tie. The suit jacket and pants were of the slim-fit variety, showing off his chiseled and lean body.

"Can you reiterate for us the procedures in place to ensure that none of the research of the Black Lab... escapes?" Clay asked.

"As you saw the other day, every employee passes through a backscatter X-ray just like they have in airports," Harley said. "This provides an image that will show anything, including a mouse, even if hidden underneath their clothing. Everybody has a key card to pass through any door in the facility, and every swipe is recorded."

"Anywhere hidden on their body, right, but not in their stomach or their rectum?" Baylee asked drily.

Harley paused as if in thought, his eyes for the briefest moment distant, before replying. "No, Miss Baker. I suppose somebody could swallow the mouse or stick it up their ass and get away with it."

"And you have scanners for personal effects as well?"

"Yes. Purses and small bags are allowed. Taking work to and from the lab is discouraged—actually banned."

"So, the computers are on a closed system?"

"Yes. As a matter of fact, the Department of Homeland Security set up our program, including Einstein, which is an early warning system that improves the situational awareness of intrusion, real-time identification of malicious cyber activity, and its prevention over time."

"To be honest, that is above my low-tech skills," Clay said. "But it'd be sufficient to say that the highest level of protection possible has been implemented and that no red flags have been raised?" Clay asked.

"You could say that," Harley said.

They spent another half hour having Harley take them step-by-step through the process of arriving and leaving the building. It was quite elaborate, and Clay understood why the would-be thief had chickened out and dumped the mouse in the restroom. There was little chance of slipping the rodent out undetected.

"Do you have any suspicions, Mr. Lange?" Baylee asked.

"Of who might have been responsible for the failed attempt?" Harley asked.

"Yes."

"No. None at all. I don't know the scientists very well, no more than a hello or a nod in the corporate dining room."

"You did the security clearance on everybody?" Clay asked.

"I've only been here for three years."

"Where did you work before?"

"Charles River Laboratories in Connecticut."

"Why did you leave?" Baylee asked.

"I knew Rex from passing. When the job of head of security here opened up, he encouraged me to apply."

Clay leaned back and eyed Harley for about twenty seconds, the silence loud in the large room. "How many candidates were there?"

"I'm not sure, but they whittled it down to five, and I was selected."

"Because you knew Rex Bolton?" Baylee asked.

"Because I was the most qualified," Harley said. A glint in his blue eyes suggested he wasn't very happy with the direction the conversation was headed.

"And you had a glowing recommendation from Charles River?" Clay asked.

"They gave me very favorable marks."

"Why do you suppose that was?" Baylee asked.

Harley swung his eyes towards her. They'd moved pass the glint stage and were now blazing. "Because I'm good at my job."

"They didn't just want to get rid of you?" Clay asked. "Be done with you. Wash their hands and move on?"

"What the fuck are you suggesting?"

"I had an interesting conversation with a person at Charles River who said that you left under a cloud," Baylee said. "That the administration there would've fired you, but they were worried that you would sue them. To avoid that, they agreed to give you a positive recommendation."

"They're lying," Harley said.

"I understand that you've recently been through a fairly messy divorce?" Clay asked.

"Stay the fuck out of my personal life, Mr. Wolfe."

"Would it be fair to say that you owe a great deal of money to your ex-wife? As well as alimony? I mean, she works as well, you have no kids. Why was the settlement so lopsided?" Baylee asked.

"Because she's a bitch, is why," Harley said, his words seemingly spit out of a wood chipper.

"It had nothing to do with the reason for you leaving Charles River?" Clay asked.

"I told you that I parted from Charles River on excellent terms."

"Were you carrying on an affair on the premises of the laboratory?" Baylee asked.

"No, I was not."

"I spoke with your ex-wife on Friday," Baylee said.

"She's a lying bitch."

"She said that you were caught on camera bopping one of your security team."

Harley glared at her.

"Do you keep up with Michael Thompson, Harley?" Clay asked.

"I'm going to kill that bitch."

"Is she lying?"

Harley went from defiant to deflated in mere seconds. "No."

"You admit to having breached security protocol and carrying on an illicit affair with a man who worked underneath you? Michael Thompson?" Clay asked.

"Yes."

"Are you being blackmailed to keep this a secret?" Baylee asked.

"Secret? That sack-of-shit ex-wife of mine tells everybody she can. Even some stranger who calls her on the phone, apparently," Harley said.

"Are you concerned that you might lose your job here at JOHNS if the administration were to find out what you'd done at Charles River?" Clay asked.

"Rex knows. He knew when he hired me. All of my old friends

and coworkers know, thanks to my ex-wife. No, I don't think that it would be effective for somebody to blackmail me with this. At the same time, it's my personal fucking life, and I choose to not share it publicly. That's why I moved to nowhere Maine, to escape all the snide glances and snickers."

* * *

Victoria Haas was back in the very private room of the Harborside Hotel having another Cobb salad and drinking expensive chardonnay. Bridget Engel had called to say that she'd gotten the final test results back for Clay Wolfe's sperm sample. Victoria thought it amusing they were having a lunch date to discuss a man's sperm, but supposed certain professionals did this sort of thing on a regular basis.

"You've made a good choice." Engel dropped a folder on the table between them. "His results are some of the purest I've seen. No hints of illness, hereditary or otherwise. Good solid German bloodline."

Victoria blushed slightly. "I don't think it matters, but thanks."

"What do you mean?"

"He won't return my calls or messages."

"You mean to tell me the skunk had sex with you and is now ghosting you?"

"It seemed to be going well. He even came back for a second time. Now? Nothing for the past five days."

Engel took a sip of wine. "This man? Clay Wolfe. He has been employed by my company to investigate an attempted theft. Perhaps he is just busy?"

"You hired Clay?" Victoria's mouth gaped slightly, a mistake she quickly corrected. "To investigate something at Johnson Laboratories?"

"That was what was happening last week while we lunched," Engel said. "Right out there." She nodded at the window to the larger dining room.

Victoria looked into the room, remembering watching Clay and Baylee Baker have lunch with the two men from Johnson Laboratories. She wondered if that bitch, Baylee, was the reason that Clay was ghosting her. She was a beautiful woman, Victoria had to admit, thin like she'd never been herself, in a healthy way, her features so perfect they might've been chiseled by fucking Michelangelo. Or maybe Engel was right, and there was a simple explanation for Clay's silence.

"I wouldn't give up too easily," Engel said. "As I mentioned, his test results are off the charts. His ancestry can be traced back to Charlemagne. His blood is as pure as the driven snow. I wouldn't pass up the opportunity of having a child with him, if at all possible."

"The second time he came back we didn't use protection," Victoria said, feeling naughty talking about it, but enjoying the rush at the same time. "I think that might be what scared him off."

"If you do succeed in getting pregnant, by him, or by another, have you given thought to the best way to ensure the health and mental well-being of the baby?"

"You mean like vitamins and things like that?"

Engel set a card on the folder between them. "There are certain things that can be done, if one has the money. Disease, deformities, and mental defects are the plight of the poor. Not of the wealthy. If you find yourself pregnant, call this number."

* * *

After a full day of interviews, Clay returned to the office, pausing at the door just shy of 5:00 in the afternoon. He took a moment to enjoy the new inscription on the glass door. *Wolfe & Baker, Private Investigators.*

"Hey there, boss, I was just about ready to leave," Crystal said. "How'd the interviews go?"

"Long and tedious," Clay said.

"Baylee coming back as well?"

"No, she went home to feed Flash and Ollie." Clay dropped his briefcase on the floor by the door to his office. "What's happening here?"

"Let's see," Crystal said, thumbing through the papers on her desk. "Victoria Haas wants you to call her. Is that the rich babe out on the Point?"

"Yep."

"Doesn't she have your cell phone number?"

Clay had studiously ignored the many calls to his cell phone as well as text messages. "Anything work related?"

"You know that Russian ship you wanted me to look into? The *Ivan Sereda*? It looks like NORAD is keeping tabs on it. Questions have been raised and a spokesman told ABC News about a year back that they had 'eyes' on this fishing boat and suspect that it might actually be a spy vessel."

"So, it's a government-owned ship?"

"I think everything is fucking government-owned over in Russia, isn't it? That's why they're called commies, because they own everything in common?"

"I'm not sure about that. Not since Gorbachev, I think." Clay smiled. "Does it have a ship log, or something like that, saying where it's going and where it came from and when and all that?"

"Nah. If it comes into port in the U.S., there'd be a record, but as long as it stays out in international waters? No fucking clue. That is unless you're NORAD, and you're up in the air in one of those fucking invisible planes like Wonder Woman pilots."

Sometimes, Clay wondered if Crystal was back on the heroin. She had proven brilliant in her ability to research and find information, but in other ways, she was like a foul-mouthed twelve-year-old. Wearing either mask, she was enthusiastic and friendly, much like a Labrador retriever.

"Any more hits on employees at JOHNS?" Clay asked.

"I got a couple more. Nothing too serious. One went on a two-week trip to Russia about thirty years ago. One of the maintenance men who has clearance to the Black Lab, Buddy Clough, appears to have a bit of a porn addiction, and this might involve underage girls. Not proven, not charged, and not convicted, but he was interrogated regarding that. Or so says Nan down at the police station."

"Okay, I'll add them to the interview schedule," Clay said.

"I don't know if Rex Bolton counts as an employee or not, but he spent some time in Russia back when he was in college. Took a year off and went hiking with a buddy and when the friend came home, our boy Rex stayed on."

"Interesting," Clay said. "Where in Russia?"

"Place called Perm. Near the Ural Mountains."

"Any idea what he was doing there?"

"Not yet."

"Keep digging. Anything on Bridget Engel?"

"Not so much. Woman has a pretty busy schedule. Not only is she the CEO here, but she sits on the board of a whole bunch of institutions and companies. What do you do when you're on the board of some company?" Crystal was looking at her computer screen. "ProHealth, Freikorps Iron, London Labs—"

"Might be worth checking all of them out," Clay said.

"All of them?"

"Can't hurt. How many boards is she on?"

Crystal counted with her fingers. "Seven."

"Give you something to do while me and Baylee are over to JOHNS this week."

"Guess somebody has to run the business," Crystal said.

"Thanks for holding down the fort."

"Sure thing, boss. You want I should lock up?"

"No, I'll leave my office door open in case anybody comes in wanting to pay us oodles of money for some cake job."

Crystal laughed. "Like being hired to find who tried to steal a fucking mouse?" She was still laughing as she walked through the door.

Clay was catching up on office business when his phone buzzed with a text form Cloutier. Where you at?

Office.

Be over in 5.

K.

He figured she was coming over to see if he'd found out anything on her missing journalist, Mary Jordan. Clay had nothing for her. It was just past 6:00. He was having dinner with Grandpops tonight at 7:00, although it shouldn't take long to say he had nothing.

The outside door opened and closed, and Marie Cloutier came into his office and settled into one of the chairs across from his desk.

"What do you know about Chad Gagnon?" she asked.

Clay furrowed his brow. The name had a familiar ring. "He was the security guard at JOHNS that went missing?"

"That's the one."

"Not much." Clay had not previously included Gagnon on his list of people he didn't know much about.

"You're investigating a theft at JOHNS, aren't you?"

"Attempted theft, yes."

Cloutier waved her hand impatiently. "Whatever. They hired you to investigate an *attempted* theft right around the same time one of their security guards came up missing, and you haven't even looked into it?"

"No." Clay drummed his fingers on the desk. "I gotta admit it slipped right off my radar."

"It sounds like there could be a connection."

"Yes, yes it does." Clay stood up and turned to look out the window at the harbor and over to the Point. "What makes you ask me about Gagnon?" he asked.

"There's been a notebook sitting in our break room for the past week. Nobody seemed to be claiming it, and then it struck me that it might be Mary's. The police took everything else, even her computer."

"But not the notebook because it was in the break room."

"There was no name on it, and only two pages had writing. The first page had the name Chad Gagnon, followed by the words 'Area 38' with a question mark."

Clay turned back to face Cloutier. "Area 38?"

She tossed a notebook on the desk. "Yep."

He sat back down and flipped to the first page. CHAD GAGNON. AREA 38. In big block letters.

"You said Mary was doing a story on JOHNS?"

"Yep."

"What was the angle?"

"She wouldn't say, but she was pretty amped up about it. We were supposed to sit down the day after she came up missing."

Clay flipped to the second page. JANE DOE. PLAYING GOD.

"For a reporter, she sure don't write a whole lot, now, does she?" he said.

"She was keeping this one real close to the vest." Cloutier leaned back, pushing her glasses firmly back onto her face. "Either one mean anything to you?"

Clay shook his head. "Not at the moment. Area 38? You got me."

"How about 'Jane Doe, playing God'?"

"I take it Jane Doe is an alias."

"An anonymous source would be my guess," Cloutier said.

"Some people think that the genome editing that JOHNS is researching and experimenting with oversteps the boundaries of what humans should be messing with."

"Playing God."

Clay nodded. "I'd sure like to figure out who this Jane Doe is."

"I wonder if the police found anything," Cloutier said. "She must've had something on her computer."

"I can put out some feelers, but ever since Chief Knight retired, communication with PD has slowed to a standstill. The new guy is by the book and has threatened to suspend anybody leaking any information. Word is, he isn't so hot on PIs, or the press, for that matter."

"Perhaps I'll bring Commander Hansen a nice bottle of whiskey," Cloutier said. "That usually helps loosen his tongue."

"You might as well give him the notebook to sweeten the deal," Clay said.

"You going to look into the disappearance of Gagnon?"

"Yep. For sure. No such thing as a coincidence, right?"

"Gagnon, Mary, the attempt on Westy, and then Daryl. Whatever is going on, it's some serious shit."

"Almost like somebody *is* playing God," Clay said.

Cloutier stood up. "You need to come by for dinner some night. Denise would love to see you. She's barely been out since the whole Covid-19 thing."

Clay stood up as well. "Having dinner with Gene tonight, but after that I'm pretty much free any night."

"No women in Clay Wolfe's life these days?"

"Not so to speak," he said, thinking about Victoria Haas. Was she a woman in his life?

"Well, you have a plus one on your wedding invitation, so you should get busy looking." Cloutier was getting married in the beginning of October.

"Always thought it best to be single for weddings," Clay said. "Inhibitions tend to go down. Who do you have in the bridal party?"

Cloutier laughed. "Most of them are gay," she said. "But there is one Baylee Baker."

Clay's face reddened. He'd walked right into that one.

Chapter 12

FRIDAY, JULY 17TH

"Do you have progress to report?" Rex Bolton asked.

It was Friday afternoon and Clay and Baylee had just finished up the last of their interviews. The three of them were sitting in Bolton's office at JOHNS.

"Not so much," Clay said. "A few ideas to chase down." He shrugged.

"What's next?"

"Harley Lange. Interesting story. He was having sex during work hours at Charles River with a male co-worker, and they knew about it, yet still gave him a sterling recommendation, and then you hired him. Did you know this?" Clay asked.

Bolton cleared his throat. "I was led to believe it only happened the once."

"Yet, you still hired him?"

"He was the most qualified candidate for the job." Bolton held his hands palms up. "He made a mistake based on weakness. He promised me that it would never happen again, not here, and it hasn't."

"His wife divorced him for that affair—that's not a red flag for future trouble?"

"I'm not sure that that was the reason for their divorce, but I can only imagine that finding out your husband is gay would be a serious blow to any marriage," Bolton said. "To be quite frank, we've had a hard time attracting top quality security to East Essex. We're not in the middle of civilization, exactly."

"You seem to attract the best scientists from around the entire world," Baylee said.

"That is different. If you're a scientist, the prestige of working for JOHNS is worth moving here for them. Not much prestige in being part of the security team."

"Did you share with Bridget Engel what you knew of Harley's dismissal from Charles River?" Clay asked.

"Are you interviewing me now? I thought this was just an update on your progress."

"Just trying to be thorough in our investigation, Rex," Clay said.

"Your turn," Bolton said, side-stepping the question. "What've you found out?"

"Not much," Clay said. "We'll have to continue with the interviews. So far, we're drawing a big fat zero."

"Do you understand the importance of what you're investigating?" Bolton asked. "If our research were to get into foreign hands, it'd be disastrous."

"How so?" Baylee asked.

"We've reached a stage that it can be transposed to humans," Bolton said. "Here in the U.S., the FDA won't allow that. To be honest, they might never allow it. It's one thing to carry out clinical trials on mice, quite another thing to do that on babies. But if the Russians were to get their hands on this? Do you think Putin would have any qualms about testing on human subjects?"

"Super soldiers," Clay said. "I'm sure the Chinese are already working on it."

"Sure, but more than that. Wars aren't fought on the ground anymore, not the real ones, anyway. They're fought with technology. If the Russians can transpose our research onto humans, well then, in a generation they'll have a huge advantage. Our testing is producing mice that are ten times smarter than their peers. Just imagine that."

"Speaking of Russia," Clay said. "Can you tell me what you were doing there back in '94 and '95?"

"Hiking."

"The whole time?"

Bolton shifted in his seat. "What is it you're asking?"

"You just brought up that it would be disastrous if Russia got their hands on the technology you currently possess, yet you failed to tell us that you spent almost a full year there."

"That was a quarter of a century ago," Bolton said.

"Sounds like you stayed on after your buddy returned home," Clay said. "In Perm, was it? Why?"

"I met a girl," Bolton said.

"Young and in love," Clay said. "You keep up with her?"

"No. Absolutely not. Can we get this discussion back on track?" Bolton said.

"Perhaps it would help if we understood how JOHNS has leaped ahead of the world in genetic engineering." Baylee asked.

Bolton stared at her for almost a minute before answering. "I must remind you that you are bound by our NDA," he said. She nodded, and he looked at Clay, who also nodded. "The problem with genome engineering—and it is genome by the way, and not genetic—is the lack of test subjects."

Clay held up a hand. "Back up a bit, cowboy."

Bolton sighed. "So, twenty years ago, genetic engineering was more random because we didn't have the knowledge or technology to manipulate genes at the micro, site-specific level, which is what we do today with genome engineering. And, yes, you guessed it, those 'sites' are where mutations related to various superior abilities occur. The problem is that you need lots and lots of subjects to find the original mutations. To find people who are immune to certain diseases, we have to locate mutations within their genomes that might explain the reason for their being prone to getting—or not getting—a disease. The same can be said for strength and intelligence."

"A mutation?" Baylee asked.

"A gene mutation is a permanent alteration in the DNA sequence that makes up a gene, such that the sequence differs from what is found in most people."

"And you need a few thousand subjects or something to determine the mutations to the DNA that might make somebody immune to cancer or super smart or overly strong?" Clay asked.

Bolton laughed. "Millions, Mr. Wolfe. There are countless possible mutations, and there is no way of knowing which ones are responsible, not with our technology, so far anyway, so we need millions of sample subjects to make headway in our research. By comparing the traits of the successful, we can narrow down which mutation might be responsible for that success."

"That begs the question," Baylee said. "Where'd you get millions of subjects?"

"The work is done for us by the ancestry companies."

"On the people who want to trace their ancestry to find out where they came from?" Clay asked.

"All the rage these days. People spit in a cup and send it off to have their DNA tested so they can discover that their great-grandfather was actually of Native American descent, or some such thing," Bolton said. "It also provides us with all the sample subjects that we need to determine mutations that make them smarter and stronger."

"How so?" Baylee asked.

"For intelligence, we cross-reference the mutations of their DNA against their IQ tests, SAT scores, and a host of other markers. For strength, we look for college and professional athletes."

"Isn't that information private?"

"We're trying to create a better world," Bolton said.

"Just to be clear, you are stealing the information?" Clay asked.

"It is anonymized so no individual could be identified."

"You hacked into their information without their knowledge? Sounds like stealing to me," Clay said.

"A matter of semantics."

"How about ethically wrong?" Baylee asked.

"Ethically wrong? To rid people of disease? To make them stronger? Smarter? Hell, we can give them blue eyes if their parents want. Blond hair. Make them taller. What's wrong with any of that?"

"And this done during the embryo stage?" Clay asked. "Through microscopic injection or something like that?"

"Very good, Mr. Wolfe. Yes. This process is called germline engineering and will ensure that not only the... mouse... but their offspring will carry on the altered mutations that make them healthy, strong, and intelligent."

Clay leaned back. He had several cards that he'd not yet played. "Aren't you concerned about playing God, Mr. Bolton?"

Bolton slapped the table. "God? God gave us disease and weakness and ignorance. God made us fragile. We are trying to create just the opposite of what God has provided us with."

"Who are you to decide?"

"The question is moot, Mr. Wolfe," Bolton said. "We're only testing this out on mice, after all, and the decision is not mine to make. Somebody further down the line, and not so many years from now, will make that call. Believe me, genome engineering will take place in our lifetime."

Clay took this to mean that Rex Bolton would have no qualms about playing God if given the opportunity. "What do you know about Area 38?" he asked.

"Area 38? What about it?"

"Tell me about it. First of all, what is it?" Clay said.

"I know nothing about Area 38."

Clay let the silence build before replying. "You have thirty-seven research labs, Rex. But I want to know about the thirty-eighth one."

"I've no idea what you're talking about."

"Aren't you the chief operating officer?"

"Yes."

"Yet, you don't know about Area 38?"

"You're talking rubbish, Mr. Wolfe. Perhaps we made a mistake in hiring a private investigator with mush for brains." Bolton's face was red, and his voice was rising in anger. "As a matter of fact, we've been paying you for the past ten days to find out exactly nothing. And now, you want to fabricate something to appear that you have found out something."

"What happened to Chad Gagnon?" Clay asked.

"Chad Gagnon? What the hell are you talking about?"

"When you initially hired us, you mentioned that one of your security team had disappeared. Chad Gagnon. What happened to him?"

"He quit. Wasn't up to it."

"And nobody knows where he is. Not even the police," Clay said.

"I'm not sure what you are insinuating." Bolton stood up and walked to the door, opening it. "I have a Zoom conference I'm late for."

"He seemed to be on the defensive," Baylee said.

They were driving back to Port Essex in Clay's Jeep. The day was overcast, and there was a cool breeze coming in off the water.

"You think? Was it just me, or was he hiding something?" Clay asked.

"You certainly struck a nerve."

"Did you notice how he got all puffed up when I asked him about playing God?"

"*God? God gave us disease and weakness and ignorance,*" Baylee said in her deepest voice.

"Is that your impression of Rex Bolton? I think you need more haughtiness."

"Yeah? Let's hear it."

Clay raised his chin and turned to look down his nose at Baylee while he drove. "*We are trying to create just the opposite of what God has provided us with.*" He then changed to a poorly attempted French accent. "I fart in your general direction. Your mother was a hamster, and your father smelt of elderberries!"

"Ha," Baylee said to the Monty Python reference. "Do you think those are really mice or are they newts?"

"He turned me into a newt," Clay said, continuing the Monty Python banter.

"A newt?"

"I got bettah."

"But seriously, that Area 38 thing really seemed to set him off. You definitely touched a nerve there, and notice, he didn't really deny it," Baylee said, once she had finished laughing. "What do you suppose that's all about?"

Clay's phone rang and he looked at the screen. He didn't recognize the number, but it was originating from East Essex. "Hello," he said, putting it on speaker and laying it on his lap.

"Mr. Wolfe?" The voice was brusque.

"Yes."

"This is Jane Withee at Johnson Laboratories. Mr. Bolton has requested that I let you know your services are no longer needed. You can submit your final bill through the usual channels. Thank you."

The phone went dead.

"That sucks," Baylee said. "The place was starting to grow on me."

"Odd, don't you think? We question Bolton about Russian connections, Area 38, and Chad Gagnon…"

"And next thing you know, we're fired," Baylee finished.

"You want to get dinner tonight?" Clay asked. "Hash it out over a meal? I can come by and pick you up after you feed Ollie and Flash. Or we can just go straight over and do it together?"

"Do it together?" she asked.

Clay blushed. "Feed the pets. Maybe take Flash for a walk."

"Gotta take a rain check. I'm on Kalinda duty. Aisha is going down to Portland tonight."

"Yep, forgot about that," Clay said, wondering what his Friday night held now.

After dropping Baylee back at the office, Clay decided to visit Victoria. He texted her and got an immediate reply to come on over. He put the phone back under the parking brake where he kept it while driving and contemplated what he was doing. He considered texting her back and telling her he couldn't make it after all, that something had come up, but knew that would be hollow.

What were his real intentions, he wondered? He knew that sooner or later he would have to at least have a conversation with the woman. It wasn't in his nature to be rude to women he'd just slept with, but the whole fatherhood thing had so many complications that it left his head spinning. Sure, he enjoyed the sex. She had seemed to be open to engaging in fornication without strings attached—well, she did want one particular string, namely, a child. No, he didn't want to father a child with Victoria, but now that seemed part of the equation. And then another part of his brain asked, what was the big deal in creating a child who would grow up wealthy and with the best of everything, after all? But fatherless...

With these thoughts swirling through his brain, he arrived and rang the bell. The manservant opened the door and ushered him in. Clay still don't know his name. He thought he should try.

"Clay Wolfe. I don't believe I've gotten your name yet?"

"I am Mekhi." The man shook his hand with a firm grip.

"Do you live here on the premises, Mekhi?"

"Ms. Haas is in the solarium. Right this way."

The solarium proved to be a glassed-in sunroom. Mekhi poured Clay a scotch without asking. Victoria was sitting on a loveseat, aqua in color. She almost appeared to be a bronze sculpture as she sat immobile looking out the window. Every feature was perfectly put together, her hair pulled tight to her head with hairspray and pins.

"Sit," she said, patting the spot next to her.

"You are a vision of loveliness," he said, settling next to her.

"Hello, Clay. I thought I'd be seeing you before now," she said.

"I'm sorry. Been busy with a case."

"I thought you might be avoiding me."

"Not at all." Inside, Clay thought that he may have been doing just that.

"Was the sex so bad?"

Clay blushed. What was it about women making him blush, he wondered? "It was fantastic," he said.

"Are you afraid of the finer things in life, Clay?"

"The finer things in life?"

"You seem to have a flourishing business, yet you live in an apartment above your grandfather's garage."

"Don't suppose I see any need for anything more than that." Clay looked around the opulence of the solarium that was larger than his entire living space.

"How old is that automobile you drive?"

"The Jeep? Seven or eight years, I guess."

Victoria nodded. "And I offer you $20,000, and you turn me down."

"I suppose I don't feel the need to be paid to have sex with you." How did this conversation get so far off-kilter, he wondered? He figured he'd come over and set down some new ground rules, and now here he was back on his haunches taking a beating.

"Yet, it's been ten days since you last came over. You say it was fantastic. You even turn down the money. Where've you been?"

"I told you that I had misgivings about fathering a child that I wouldn't be involved with."

"And I told you that I'd consider letting him or her know who you were."

"Do we split custody?"

"Do you want to split custody?"

Clay took a large swig of scotch. The burn felt good. "No. Guess I'm not ready to be a dad."

"So, what's the problem?"

"I don't believe that children should grow up without a father."

"I, for one, would have fared much better without one."

Clay stared down at his glass. "Not all fathers are bad."

"You know what he did to me."

"It was terrible. I'm just saying that I'm not that man."

"It would mean so much to me, Clay," Victoria said, a tear rolling down her cheek. "To have a child of my own to love would be like mending a terrible wound in my soul. I need this."

Back to that summer after graduation, Clay had been determined to let Victoria down gently. Before he could, she'd relayed to him that he was the only good thing in her life—the only reason she didn't end her own life—her one shining beacon of light.

"A child needs a father for certain things, at least," Clay said. "To play catch with, take fishing, things like that."

Victoria was staring intently at him. The loveseat was small, and their legs pressed together. She grasped his upper thigh in her hand. "That's only a problem for poor people, Clay. Our child will have the best tutors and role models that money can buy."

"Not sure that that is true," Clay said, his mouth dry.

"What part?"

"That only poor people need a father."

"What is a father? A man who donates his sperm—that's all a father is. I'll make sure that our child is given every opportunity at success in life. As a matter of fact, there are *things* that only the truly wealthy have access to that will increase our child's quality of life. Possibilities that the ordinary peasant doesn't even know about."

Clay thought about his childhood with no father or mother. Grandpops had been great. They had never hurt for money. It still sucked. "I'd like to continue seeing you," Clay said. "But I don't want to get you pregnant."

"Seeing me? You mean fucking me?" Her eyes were hard now, and the mask of civility had been peeled away.

"No, well, yes but… no. We can go out. Have dinner. Go to a show."

"I'm looking for a man to father my child. Are you willing to be that man?"

"No, I guess I'm not."

"You judge me for what happened to me and who I am, but maybe you should take a look in the mirror, bucko. What are you, anyway? Headed towards forty without anything real in your life, strutting around town thinking you're hot as shit because you are a private dick and willing to pull it out for any of the local girls who don't know better. Live in an apartment above your grandfather's garage? Good God, man, you are pathetic."

"I don't judge you," Clay said. Truth be told, he hadn't really grasped what she'd said past that. He had never once judged her. "I just don't want to have a baby with you."

"I am going to have to ask you to leave. If you reconsider, you know how to reach me." She turned away from him and picked up the magazine she'd been looking at when he came in.

Chapter 13

SATURDAY, AUGUST 1ST

The past two weeks had been uneventful. Baylee was kept fairly busy with Kalinda while Clay had picked up a job investigating a personal injury fraud case at BIW. In his free time, he tried looking for the man who'd hit Westy in the head with a hammer, but to no avail. Victoria wasn't answering her phone, and when Clay stopped by, Mekhi told him that she wasn't receiving visitors.

The state police had deemed the death of Daryl Allen an accident. The official statement was that he'd run the stolen boat, Westy's, into the rocks at the Pumpkin Ledges, struck his head, and then drowned. Mary Jordan and Chad Gagnon had both been listed as missing persons. The staties were doubtful that the duffel bag Westy witnessed was actually the cut-up body of the local journalist. Gagnon had recently split from his girlfriend, and the police thought, had quite possibly just decided to take off.

As far as the case at JOHNS, the reality was that there had been no theft, and therefore nothing really to investigate. Still, the details gnawed at the back of Clay's consciousness, popping up at random times to tease him—often at bedtime, sometimes in the middle of the night, but also during the day, like now. He and Baylee knew something was going on. They just couldn't seem to find a way in, something or someone to help them understand what had motivated all of these seemingly random occurrences.

Westy managed to get his boat hauled into the dock, where he was determined to fix it instead of scuttling the vessel that had been handed down to him by his father. This had come at a bad time of the fishing season for him, but luckily Kalinda had just chartered him to take her out on his sailboat, offering a thousand bucks for a four-hour sail. Not only would the income be nice, but his wife, Faith, was ecstatic to meet the pop singer. She was currently stocking the schooner, the *Freya*—named after the Norse goddess of love, fertility, sorcery, gold, war, and death.

Faith had returned from her sister's place about a week earlier, and had been particularly cold, unhappy with having been sent away. When Baylee had texted Westy about this excursion, it'd been a godsend. Even more than the money, it had thawed the cold shoulder Faith had been giving him since her return. Joe was spending the day with a friend, it was beautiful out, and all was right with the world.

Kalinda had insisted that Clay come along, as she'd not yet met him, but had heard a lot about him from Baylee. Thus, the three of them—Westy, Faith, and Clay—had the windjammer ready to go when the Cadillac Escalade with the tinted windows pulled into the wharf. Baylee got out with two people while the SUV drove off. They all wore masks for safety.

The woman, who must be Kalinda, was dressed casually in capris and a pullover sweatshirt that said *Port Essex*. Her hair was coiled into tight braids, perhaps twelve of them, pulled back from her face, showcasing angular features, her cheekbones pronounced and offsetting a delicate chin. It was the eyes, fierce and accented by thin, yet arresting, eyebrows that drew the most attention.

The man beside her was a few inches over six feet, towering at least a foot over Kalinda's diminutive frame. He was thin with wide shoulders, had a beard that ran along his jawline, and dark eyes that suggested a Middle Eastern ancestry. He wore a baseball cap pulled low over his face and now slipped dark glasses on as he walked down to the wharf.

These details Clay recorded in a split second, his eyes quickly drawn to Baylee, who wore white chinos that hugged her shapely legs, and a three-quarter sleeve shirt of turquoise cotton that left little to the imagination. She also had a baseball cap on that simply had the number 3 on it and dark glasses with white rims shoved up above the bill.

"Clay Wolfe, Weston Beck, this is Kalinda and her husband, John."

John stepped forward with a firm grip. "Good to meet you."

Kalinda nodded. "I have heard much about both of you, especially you, Clay," she said.

"Great to meet you both," Clay said.

Westy nodded.

Faith emerged from the cabin of the schooner and stepped onto the wharf with an awestruck look upon her face. "Oh, my goodness, it's really you. I love your music," she said.

"This is Westy's wife, Faith, and first mate for our excursion today," Baylee said.

"I love your top," Kalinda said.

Faith was wearing a long-sleeve ocean blue T-shirt with a turtleneck for ultimate sun protection.

"Thank you. I just bought it." Faith could not control the wide smile that spilled out of her mouth.

Clay hid his own smile because Westy had just been complaining about the $120 T-shirt his wife had recently bought.

"Is this all of us?" Westy asked, looking up the drive in the direction that the SUV had gone.

"Yes," Kalinda said. "Aisha is going to do some shopping. I figured I'd be safe enough with the entire Wolfe & Baker enterprises represented, don't you think?"

"And rumor has it, according to Baylee, you used to be a SEAL?" John asked.

"Yep."

"Well, thank you for your service."

"We're all good to set sail," Westy said.

Clay led the way, as no one else seemed to move. The rest followed him, Faith taking the wheel while Westy cast off. The day was just 78° with a light wind coming from the west and not a cloud in the sky. They eased out of the harbor, passing between Spruce Island and the Point before putting up the sails.

Westy replaced Faith at the wheel so she could take drink orders. Clay followed her down into the cabin to help deliver the cocktails, also bringing up a platter of cheese and crackers. There were shrimp and lobster rolls for later. Clay grinned again, realizing that Faith had gone all out to impress Kalinda. He knew that if it were up to Westy, his friend would've had a cooler with a few Buds and some PB & Js.

They made small talk as they sailed northeast up the coast of Maine, Westy half-heartedly interjecting the occasional tour guide information about islands, expensive homes, and the seals lying on the rocks before lapsing back into easy silence. Faith had Kalinda cornered, peppering her with questions about fashion, music, travel, and celebrities. That left Baylee, Clay, and John discussing mostly what John and Kalinda had done in Port Essex so far, how their visit was coming to an end, and what they yet wanted to do.

"You been out to the Botanical Gardens?" Clay asked.

"Twice," John said. "Once was enough for me."

"Never been, myself," Clay said.

"Smart man," John said.

"Men," Baylee sighed.

"Pemaquid Lighthouse on the left," Westy said. "Kinda famous."

"Have you ever toured Johnson Laboratories?" John asked.

Clay and Baylee exchanged sidelong glances. "Just recently, actually," Clay said. "Baylee mentioned that Kalinda was doing a jingle for them, or something like that?"

"Yes, they're making revolutionary changes in the treatment of diseases, even eradicating them, apparently, at the prenatal stage," John said.

"You mean, before birth?" Clay asked.

"That's what I've heard," John said.

"You mean, with mice, right?" Baylee asked.

"Uh, yes, with mice. They've been experimenting with some kind of special mice, or something like that."

"SHAIM," Clay said. "SuperHuman Advanced Intelligence Mice."

"Yes, that's it. Kalinda has been doing some free marketing for them to promote the work they're doing," John said.

"I hear they are on the verge of a breakthrough that may allow them to rid the world of cancer," Clay said.

"What are you all talking about?" Kalinda asked, sitting down between John and Clay.

"The work that JOHNS is doing to end cancer," John said.

"Krisper, or something like that, right?" Clay asked.

"CRISPR. It's an acronym for Clustered Regularly Interspaced Short Palindromic Repeats," Kalinda said. "Which basically means a process to remove bad mutations from the baby at an embryonic stage, ensuring that this change is heritable, and will continue generation after generation."

Baylee looked at Kalinda with new admiration. "You must have really gotten into all that material we put together for you. And here I thought a crisper was just another drawer in my refrigerator."

Kalinda laughed lightly. "Johnson Labs is also an impressive corporate neighbor in the area. They donate money to all sorts of local charities, build baseball parks, and make voluntary property tax payments even though they are exempt. They pour money into the local schools through programs like STEM."

"They do a lot of good around here, that's for sure," Clay said. "When will this CRISPR become available for people?"

"I don't know," Kalinda said. "It sure would be nice to prevent your child from ever developing cancer, wouldn't it?"

"That is the Louds Island church," Westy was saying. "It was built in 1913 from the lumber of the Malaga Island school after the inhabitants were forced off the island." He shook his head. "That was not a shining moment in Maine history. Some took their houses apart and moved them to the mainland. Those were the lucky ones. Some of them ended up committed to a state institution for life."

"Forced off?" Kalinda asked. "Why?"

"They were Black, brown, native, and poor Irish, and rich white people wanted the island," Westy said. "My grandad told me that after the Civil War, there were a lot of homeless vets who maybe hadn't integrated well when they came home after the war. Back then, no one owned the islands, and so they were kind of like free real estate. So, with a garden and fish from the sea, they could make a living for themselves."

Kalinda had hung on Westy's words. "How come you know so much about this place?" she asked.

"When you fish a stretch of coast for as long as my family has," he answered, "you tend to know everything about it. All the families, the legends, the stories, good and bad." His voice trailed off.

"Baylee," Faith asked brightly, sensing a change of subject to something more upbeat was in order, "will you help me get the shrimp and lobster rolls?"

"Can I get anybody another drink?" Clay asked.

*   *   *

"You taking the *Freya* out of the water?" Clay asked Westy.

It was hours later, and Aisha had returned to pick up Kalinda, John, and Baylee. Faith had gone with them, squealing in delight at Kalinda's invitation to see the house on the Point, and then Baylee would bring her home.

"Nope. Think I might as well use it for fishing," Westy said. "I've paid for the mooring, after all."

"They seem to be good people," Clay said, "Kalinda and John."

"Not bad for people from away," Westy said.

"Am I right in thinking that you're more grumpy than normal?"

"We going to talk about our feelings now? Have an Oprah moment?"

Clay poured himself another finger of the Bowmore, and then on second thought, doubled it. They were sitting across from each other on the stern deck of the sailboat drinking brown liquor.

"How's things with Faith?" Clay asked.

"Let's just say Kalinda made her day."

"Joe doing well?"

"Fair to middlin."

"You going to tell me what's eating you?"

"I suppose it might be that some dude with a skinny neck hit me in the head with a hammer, and he's still walking around somewhere." Westy stared hard at Clay. "How many times have I had your back?" he asked.

"What? What's that supposed to mean?"

"All through school. On the football field. When that bald-headed freak was trying to kill you, and the first son of God was going to sacrifice you?"

Clay had to admit that having Westy at his back had proven very helpful throughout the years. The man wasn't somebody to mess with. But a protest was necessary. "I've had your back plenty of times. Got you out of that temple, didn't I?"

"Wouldn't've been there in the first place if it weren't for you."

"Okay, okay, well, I beg to differ. In what way don't I have your back now?"

"Remember in high school when I was over to Alice Dean's house and her parents were out? And you called me because some guys from up the road were giving you a bad time out to the quarry?"

Clay did remember. The guys, four in number, from a rival football team, had come to a party in the woods at the request of a group of girls. Clay had stopped by, wearing his letter jacket, and they'd started in on him. "Sure, I remember that," he said.

"What'd I do?"

"You came on over, and we kicked their asses," Clay said. He didn't mention that Westy had taken on three of them while Clay had wrestled with the fourth.

"I walked out on a sure thing with Alice to come save your sorry ass."

"What are you saying?"

"I'm saying some guy hit me in the head with a hammer, and you aren't doing a fucking thing."

Well, put that way, Clay thought, his friend had a point. It was time to find the guy who had hammered Westy, and maybe the Russian who had been present.

"Yeah, you're right. Sorry about that," Clay said.

"What do you suggest we do about it?"

"I guess we could start off canvassing the neighborhood where… the house you saw them at."

"Okay," Westy said grudgingly. "Shouldn't have had to bring it up, is all I'm saying."

"No, you shouldn't have. Not much of an excuse, but I seem to have a lot of moving pieces in my life right now."

"I'm not a moving piece."

"No. You're rock solid. I love you, man. Let's fix this, and I won't let it happen again."

"You're not going to kiss me, are you?"

Chapter 14

SUNDAY, AUGUST 2ND

Clive Miller sat in the back of the white cargo van with the Johnson Laboratory insignia on the front doors. This was critical, as he was in the parking lot of that same establishment, just outside the administrative building. A heavy curtain blocked the view of anyone passing the back of the van where he sat comfortably with headphones on. He was virtually invisible in plain sight. He liked that.

Clive was staring at a photo of Baylee Baker on his phone. He was not much for reading. He did not do Facebook, Twitter, Instagram or any other social media. What else was there to do when waiting than to fantasize? Through the headphones there was the sound of breathing, the rustle of paper, and the clatter of a keyboard. Earlier, there had been a telephone call. Clive knew that there was to be a meeting in about five minutes, the reason for his being here in the parking lot, sitting in the back of the van, waiting, and fantasizing about Baylee Baker.

He'd been furious when that fellow had escaped, the man he now knew was Weston Beck, former SEAL, and friend to Clay Wolfe. If Clive had but known the man was a former SEAL, he might've taken more precautions. Perhaps he would've given him several more blows with the hammer before carting him to the boat and taking him off to be deposited in Davy Jones Locker. Clive knew that he'd been greedy. That it was his own fault. He'd wanted to watch the man's eyes as they battered a hole in the bottom of his boat. Clive had wanted to soak up the stench of the man's fear as he realized he was about to die, drowned in his own boat.

Of course, this way was better. Weston Beck would die slowly, of that Clive could be sure, just not right off. It wasn't that he was scared of the man, even if there was a hardness to his eyes, a flat stare that gave away nothing. He had been a SEAL after all, built like a barrel with muscles and he probably knew how to fight hand-to-hand, with a knife, and naturally knew his way around firearms with the best of them. But, no, Clive Miller was not afraid of him.

Clive just needed to bide his time, work up to the finale with this particular adversary. The National Hockey League's Stanley Cup Playoffs did not start out with the two best teams pitted against each other. Rather, it followed a system that whittled away the lesser opponents one by one until there were only two left standing—or skating, in that instance—and then they commenced the final battle. Weston Beck would get his comeuppance soon enough, but there were several early rounds leading up to that final one.

Clive could feel his skin crawling. He needed release. He needed to kill. At the same time, he wasn't dumb. He knew that Bolts kept him on a tight leash, and that killing Weston Beck was not, at the time, necessary or even desirable, as it would draw more attention. Clive thought that he might be given the green light to make Clay Wolfe disappear, since the fancy boy PI was stirring up a pot that didn't need to be stirred, merely simmered. But then Wolfe had been taken off the Johnson Labs job, and that reward was pulled from Clive's grasp.

The sound of a knock came through the headphones followed by a voice commanding somebody to come in.

"Hey, boss. Sorry I'm late."

"Not to worry, HL," the boss said. "Sit down."

"We back on tap?" HL asked.

"Yes. Area 38 has a customer coming in on Tuesday."

"The singer?"

"No. She had to postpone. Got a cold. Something about being out on a boat," the boss said.

"So, who?"

"Lady that was on the wait list. Local."

There was a pause. "Is she ready?" HL asked.

"She has the green light from the team. Not my call. I just bring them in and collect the money."

"Can't believe somebody would pay $20 million."

"For them it's like twenty bucks," the boss said. "You'd pay more than that I'd wager to make your kid super-smart and able to kick ass on the playground, wouldn't you?"

"Sure would, boss. That's a no-brainer."

"You'll make sure that Area 38 is prepared?"

"Yep. We picking her up at 2:00 a.m.?"

"Yes. Here's her name and address."

"Husband?"

"No. Single woman."

"Bring her home Friday morning at 2:00 a.m.?" HL asked.

"Yes."

"When am I getting the bonus you promised?"

"Soon."

"She as good looking as that singer?"

"No more mistakes, HL," the boss said. "I do not know what you were thinking... if you *were* thinking. Gagnon could've sent us both to jail."

"I got it, boss. It won't happen again."

There was the sound of a door banging shut and then nothing but breathing, rustling, and clacking. Clive took off the headphones. Bolts would be happy. He liked it when Bolts was happy.

Clive's eyes flickered back to the image of Baylee Baker on his phone. He needed to wait fifteen minutes or so to make sure that HL was gone before he climbed back into the front of the van and went home for the night. He studied her face, the brown eyes, the delicate but strong features, and the shiny white teeth. Baylee's breasts were ample but not too large, and her waist rose to solid shoulders in the shape of a V. The photo didn't show her ass, but he'd viewed it enough times to picture it in his mind.

He could feel the excitement tingling in his body, making his skin vibrate, shallowing his breathing, and a tightening in his belly in anticipation. Clive felt his erection grow until it was a caged and wild monster throbbing to be let out. The time was coming, but not yet. He couldn't make Bolts mad at him; he didn't like it when Bolts was mad at him.

In the meantime, he'd have to settle for the fantasy, putting off the ultimate satisfaction of his carnal and savage desire with half measures. Clive unbuttoned his pants and pulled the zipper down, his hand crawling into his briefs and grasping his member. He gasped. It was good. Not the real thing, but it would suffice, at least until he had Baylee Baker laid bare and twitching before him. The image rocked him to the very core, and if HL had passed by the van then, he'd certainly have wondered at the feral caterwaul from within. Lucky for Clive, the man was long gone.

Chapter 15

MONDAY, AUGUST 3RD

"What do we know so far?" Clay asked.

Westy was sitting across from him in the office. The swelling on his brow had gone down, but the ugly scar and discoloring remained. It was just past 8:00 in the morning, and neither Baylee nor Crystal was in yet.

"I know what the guy looks like," Westy said. "If he ever ventures out from the rock he's hiding under."

"You think he's still around somewhere?" Clay asked.

"Yep. If leaving was an option, he wouldn't have taken the chance of hammering me. He would've just disappeared, and that would be the end of it. No, he's hiding out in the area somewhere working on something that's not over yet, and he's got a big secret, one big enough to kill for."

"And he's got a partner," Clay said. "Vlad, the Russian."

"Not so much partner in crime as somebody he's doing business with. And Vlad is scared stiff of our guy, that I can tell you for sure. He didn't like one bit of what was going on, but he wasn't going to open his mouth and end up like Daryl."

"Daryl would be a good place to start our search."

"Except for the fact that he's dead," Westy said.

"Does make it a bit harder, but he's the most tangible thing we've got, except the house they took you to, and that appears to be a dead end, although I think we should follow up on it anyway. People don't always tell the police everything."

"The owner moved into a retirement community?"

"Yeah," Clay said, looking at a piece of paper on his desk. "Gerald Paine. Born and raised in that cottage, now ninety-three. His son and daughter came up from down south. Jed Paine from Georgia and Susan Salisbury from The Villages in Orlando. Moved him in about two months back, got him settled, and went back home."

"The daughter's retired?"

"Yeah. Her husband made a bunch of money in tech, and they moved there from New York City about four years ago."

"What about the son?"

"Lawyer in Savannah."

"Not really the sort of people you'd connect to some cold-blooded murderer. How about grandkids?"

"Don't know. I'll get Crystal on it when she comes in," Clay said.

"You said they were thinking of selling the cottage?"

"Undecided."

"Who else has keys?"

"Other than the old man and the elderly kids?"

"Maybe a grandkid? Maybe a realtor they had do a walk-through? Or the neighbor, to come over and check that no critters get into the house?"

"Good thought. I'll call both," Clay looked at his notes, "Jed and Susan." He underlined their names on the paper.

"You should have Baylee call them," Westy said.

"Why's that?"

"People like her."

"Are you suggesting they don't like me?"

Westy shrugged. "Just an idea."

"I suppose you think we should have her knock on the neighbor's doors as well?"

"Nah, we probably have as good a chance of prying information out of Mainers as she does, which is somewhere between slim and none."

"What else we got?"

"The journalist in the duffel bag," Westy said.

"Mary Jordan. The police discounted what you said. Yet, missing, she still is."

"They just didn't want to deal with a murder investigation. A simple missing person case, and the staties can wash their hands of it and go home to their wives and kids and not have to bumble around Port Essex."

"So we're thinking there's a definite connection, from what Cloutier said and those cryptic notes, that she is missing… killed… because of the story she was working on."

"Which we have no idea what it was about," Westy said.

"Except the notebook that Cloutier found that said," Clay looked at the paper on his desk, "Chad Gagnon, Area 38, Jane Doe, and playing God."

"Gagnon is the missing security officer from JOHNS?"

"Yes. Things seem to keep circling back to JOHNS."

"What about the rest of it?"

"JOHNS has thirty-seven laboratories."

Westy nodded. "Seems to be too much to be coincidence."

"Jane Doe is an alias for an anonymous person."

"Like a source that doesn't want her name in print, or someone who is unidentified." Westy leaned forward onto the desk, the tattoos on his massive forearms rippling like living things. "How about playing God?"

"Some people think that's what they're doing out there. Messing around with genomes and genetics and DNA and all that shit to change God's creation—us—into something different than He intended."

The outer door opened and a second later, Baylee came into the office. "Morning, you two. Didn't know you were here, or I would've gotten you a breakfast sandwich."

Clay had eaten breakfast at the diner as he did almost every single morning. That is not to say he wasn't slightly disappointed to miss a bacon, egg, and cheese biscuit from Wake and Bake. He wondered idly if the place was applying for a marijuana license. It seemed the perfect complement to their delicious baked items and the bakery name was perfect. Perhaps he should suggest it.

But far more delicious looking was Baylee, Clay thought. He figured it was probably politically incorrect to think of a woman like that, so, wisely kept his mouth shut, but it was harder to police one's own thoughts. She wore a single piece, white outfit that rose from mid-calf to thin shoulder straps, the white bringing out the bronze of her skin. This, Clay barely noticed, as it was the sparkle in her eyes and twist to her mouth that made his stomach do flips.

Baylee settled into her desk, opening what was indeed a bacon, egg, and cheese on a biscuit, before looking up. "Oh, sorry, is this some sort of private meeting?"

"Not at all," Clay said.

"Just no women allowed," Westy said.

"Probably why you joined the SEAL program," Baylee said. "Feeling threatened by women like you are."

Westy laughed. "How was the rest of your weekend?"

"You mean after our boating excursion, Captain Weston?"

"Yes. And Captain Weston does have a nice ring to it."

"Quiet. Went out to dinner Saturday night with Tammy. Spent Sunday at home reading and working in the yard. Thanks for the sailboat ride, by the way. That was fun."

"Your client paid for it," Westy said.

"Money is not a problem for her," Baylee said. "What are you boys up to this morning?"

"We thought we might go out and find the guy who hammered Westy," Clay said.

"The guy who blindsided me," Westy said.

"The wound in your head seems to be in the front," Baylee said.

"You free to help out?" Clay asked.

"As much as I would like to find the man who so cowardly attacked my friend, Captain Weston Beck, all I got is today. I'm with Kalinda the rest of the week."

"I thought she was gone all week?" Clay asked.

"Yeah, me too. But she caught a cold and had to cancel her plans. Her husband, John, is going to fly down to Boston on business, taking Aisha with him, leaving me on 24/7 duty tomorrow morning through Saturday afternoon."

"You're staying at her house?" Clay asked.

"Yep. Bringing Flash with me. Kalinda said that Rodriguez, her Chihuahua, would love the company," Baylee said.

The outside door opened. "Holy fuck, it's raining buckets out there." Crystal stomped into the outer office, cursing as she came in. A few seconds later she appeared in the doorway. "Don't look like any of you got rained on," she said.

"Morning, Crystal," Clay said. He turned and looked out the window where the rain was, indeed, coming down in buckets.

"Glad you left the 'good' off of that statement," Crystal replied.

"We been needing the rain," Westy said.

"Left my fucking umbrella at home," Crystal said.

"That sucks," Baylee said.

"Is this a secret meeting with no administrative assistants allowed, or do you want me to come in?" Crystal asked.

"Pull up a chair," Clay said. The woman didn't really need an umbrella, he thought, not with that much hairspray. The rain just rolled off her head as if she were wearing a helmet.

Crystal sat down next to Westy. "You got another one of those?" she asked Baylee, eying her sandwich.

"Sure," Baylee said, pulling one out of the bag and tossing it to her.

"Whoa, what's up with that?" Westy asked.

"Didn't know you were here, and Clay always goes to the diner," Baylee said. "I bring Crystal a sandwich every Monday. Next time, call to let me know you'll be here."

"What's up?" Crystal asked.

"We're going to find the guy who… blindsided Westy with a hammer," Clay said.

Crystal guffawed, a hoarseness from too many cigarettes and too much bad coffee over the years, like the coarse rasp of #24-grit sandpaper over rough wood. "We need another case like we need a hole in the head." She laughed again at her own joke.

Clay suppressed his own laugh. "My schedule is free for the week," he said. "Baylee's open today. And as far as I can tell, you mostly spend your time on Facebook."

"Nah, not since I got turned onto TikTok. That is some funny shit," Crystal said.

"Well, if you can fit it in, will you see what you can find out on these two?" Clay wrote the names Jed Paine and Susan Salisbury down on a piece of paper. "These are the adult children of the guy who owns the cottage where Westy was attacked. Find out everything you can on them, extended family, but especially their children, and possibly even grandkids."

"What for?"

"We want to know who might have had access to the cottage."

"Gotcha, boss." Crystal saluted. "Anything else?"

"Get Baylee Jed and Susan's phone numbers so she can call and talk to them."

"Righto, boss." Crystal stood and moved toward the door.

Clay looked at Baylee. "Same thing. Who might have access to the cottage?"

"Okay, I can do that. How about Chad Gagnon, the security guard? You want me to see what I can find out about him?"

"That'd be great. Westy and I are going to go and knock on doors in the neighborhood where he got attacked, buy Cloutier lunch and pick her brain, and see if we can't dig up something on what Daryl Allen was involved in."

"Well, you know how to find me," Baylee said, swiveling in her chair around to face her computer. "You boys go out and play now."

Clay and Westy split up to canvass the neighborhood. There was still police tape fluttering in the wind at the cottage where Westy had come to be tied to a chair with a divot in his head. It was not that the investigation was active, but rather that the police hadn't bothered taking the yellow ribbon down. With nobody hustling to get back into the house, it didn't really matter.

There was one road lined with houses that ran along the inlet, and Clay went one way and Westy the other, down one side of the street and back on the far side. Everybody knew Gerald. It sounded like he was gregarious in a sarcastic redneck sort of way that had increased with age. Nobody had seen anything out of the ordinary at the house since Jed and Susan had come and gone. No cars. No visitors. No lights on. Nobody had a key or knew if Gerald hid one somewhere.

With nothing gleaned, but with impeccable timing, they met back at the house directly across the street from the Paine Cottage, as the neighbors all called it, many with a smirk, as if the term Paine might have more than one meaning.

"Find anything more than nothing?" Clay asked.

"Nope. He didn't like kids riding their bikes on his lawn."

"Liked to fish, almost every morning at the crack of dawn," Clay said.

"Last one is the charm," Westy said. He raised his hand and knocked on the door.

"What do you want?" A thin, old man yanked the door open before Westy's knuckles could descend a second time.

"Hello, Mr...." Westy said.

"Beaulieu. Nathan Beaulieu. Who the hell are you?"

"My name is Weston Beck, and I was wondering if I might ask you some questions?"

"I'm already right with the Lord, and I don't vote." Beaulieu started to shut the door.

"It's about Gerald Paine," Clay said over Westy's broad but short shoulder.

"If Gerry owes you money, it don't got nothin' to do with me."

Westy stuck his foot in the door to prevent it from closing. "We were wondering if you might know of anybody staying at his cottage, say, about two weeks back?"

Beaulieu looked like he wanted to stomp on Westy's foot, but then suddenly paused and looked up at his face. "You're the fellow that got struck in the forehead with a hammer and was almost dumped out to sea," he said. "Come on inside where I can get a better look at your head."

"How'd you know all that?" Clay asked, following Westy into the house that was perhaps half the size of a trailer. Shades were drawn on the few windows and the interior was dark even in the middle of the day.

"One look at his head is how I knew," Beaulieu said. "And some fellow sure enough got whacked over at Gerry's a few weeks back. Police were around asking folks about it."

"What'd they ask you?" Clay said.

"Nothing."

"I thought you said the police were asking questions?"

"Not to me."

"Why not?"

"Wasn't here."

Clay could feel just the faint flame of hope burning. "Did you see anything the night of July 7th?" he asked.

"Nope. I'm usually in bed pretty early."

"How about earlier?"

"A car parked down past my house about five o'clock. There's a little path down to the water and folks do that once in a while. Don't care for it much, I don't, and I was thinking about giving them a piece of my mind, but then this fellow gets out and walks up the street. He stops right in front of my place and looks all around. Knew he couldn't see me, but gave me the creeps, it did, all the same."

"What'd he look like?" Westy asked.

"Pretty average except for his neck made him look like a heron, kinda jutting forward and long as the damn winter," Beaulieu said.

"That's the one who did this," Westy said, touching his wound.

"What'd he do then?" Clay asked Beaulieu.

"He hustled across the street and went into Gerry's place."

"Did he have a key?"

"I think so. He fiddled with something at the door before opening it."

"Then what?"

"What do you mean?"

"What happened next?" Westy asked.

"I made some dinner and ate it in front of a ball game. Sure am glad baseball came back on. Course, it goes too late, so I went to bed. Watched the rest the next day on take two."

"You didn't see anything else?" Westy asked.

"Nope. Didn't think much of it. Figured it was a renter, or a realtor, or something like that." The man shuffled to the window and peeked out through the curtains.

"How about the car? What kind of car was it?" Clay asked.

"Truck. Dark colored."

"What kind of truck? Ford? Chevy?" Westy asked.

"No idea. Don't know trucks that much."

Clay's hopes drizzled back down. "Well, thank you, Mr. Beaulieu."

"I did write down the license plate," Beaulieu said, "you know, him looking suspicious and all. I figured that's what Magnum would do."

"Who's Magnum, anyway?" Westy asked as Clay finished recounting the story to Cloutier. They were at Kurt's Deli waiting for their subs with beers in hand, sitting outside at a picnic table.

"Tom Selleck. He played a PI in a TV series back in the '80s set in Hawaii," Cloutier said. "All beaches and babes and fast cars."

"Ah, before our time," Westy said, looking at Cloutier sideways.

"Right. I forgot you were both babies for a second." Cloutier took a sip and mumbled something that may have been a curse attached to an insult on Westy's damaged forehead.

"Guy with a mustache, right?" Clay asked.

"That's the one," Cloutier said.

"Yeah, private investigator, smarter than me, though. I've watched a few reruns in the winter and wonder why I'm in Maine and he's running around Oahu," Clay said. "I think they did a remake a couple of years back."

"You should check it out," Cloutier said to Westy. "He's a former SEAL."

"Lots of women in bikinis," Clay added.

"Best part," Cloutier said.

The three of them clicked glasses. Tony, the owner, who had bought the deli from Kurt, brought their subs over to them, said hello, exchanged pleasantries, and got back to work.

"So, what's up?" Cloutier asked.

"We decided that if the police weren't going to do anything that we'd take it upon ourselves to hunt down the guy who hammered Westy and most likely killed your journalist," Clay said.

"Mary."

Clay nodded. "I'm thinking the police contacted everybody related, neighbors, and the like. If you could duplicate that list for us to follow up on, and maybe come up with an angle they did *not* look into?"

"The story she was working on," Cloutier said. "Mary was always hiding in the shadows. Afraid of her own."

"Sounds like with good reason this time," Clay said.

"I'd say she certainly got into something over her head," Cloutier said.

Clay nodded again. "That seems to be the elephant in the room."

"I shared the notebook with the police, but they didn't seem to give it much credence," Cloutier said. "Chad Gagnon. Area 38. Jane Doe. Playing God."

"Not much to go on there," Westy said. "A missing man, an unknown place, an alias, and a reference to spiritual work."

"It'd help if we could find the man, locate the place, name the alias, and get religion," Clay said. "Other than that, you have any idea what she was working on?"

Cloutier shook her head. "We were going to sit down to discuss it the day after she went missing. She told me that it was likely to go big—*New York Times*, *Washington Post* big."

"We're going to dig into the missing man, Chad Gagnon. I think he might be related to Area 38," Clay said. "Out to JOHNS, where he worked, they have thirty-seven laboratories. And it has been suggested by critics that they are 'playing God' out there."

"Or thirty-eight laboratories," Westy said.

"Any and all ideas to find out who Jane Doe is are appreciated, 'cause we're stumped," Clay said. "Ask around the newsroom. Double-check her files. Go through her computer for something the police may have missed. Anything would be of help. If Mary was truly working on a huge story, Jane Doe might be the whistle blower."

"I've done it once, except going over the computer, which we just got back, but I can take a second look," Cloutier said.

Chapter 16

When they got back to the office, Westy climbed into his truck and headed home for a bit. They had plans to meet at Lucky Linda's around 3:00, early for serious drinking, but prime time to find Daryl Allen's fishermen friends plowing through beers.

Clay made a mental note to check in with Murphy, and then laughed to himself. Of course, Murphy would be there. His regular favorite spot, every day from late morning until about 5:00, was at the Seal Bar. Once the Fourth of July came, though, Port Essex filled up with summer people, residents and tourists, and the harbor edge bar/restaurant overflowed, which pushed the local regulars across the street and up the hill to the slightly rougher Lucky Linda's.

Murphy would know who Daryl Allen's friends had been. Maybe, more importantly, he'd know who his enemies had been. Either way, the Irishman would be able to point them in a direction.

Clay pecked out a quick text to Murphy: Me and Westy coming by Lucky Linda's around 3. Would love to be introduced to Daryl Allen's friends.

Clay didn't hold out much hope that Murphy would view the text. Even though he carried his cell phone with him, it was still habit for him to only look at messages at home.

Clay envied Murphy his total disdain for social media—no, really his complete dismissal of the overwhelming social media crush that the world seemed to be going through. As of late, Clay had found himself incessantly responding to those pinging notifications from Twitter, Instagram, Snapchat, and even Facebook on the rare occasion. He couldn't quite fathom why he needed to know what his college friend, Desmond, had for breakfast, or view pictures of his second cousin's cats, for that matter. It had been seven years since he'd seen his second cousin, but he daily saw her cat doing any variety of feline things.

It was hard to imagine that he was now thirty-six years old. True, some days he felt older than that, but usually, Clay wondered where the years had gone. His parents had been married for twelve years at his age. It was also the age at which they'd died in the car crash. If he were to die now, today, what legacy would he leave behind?

He was single, had never been in a relationship longer than six months, had no children and few friends, although those few were solid and not superficial. It seemed that some people collected acquaintances like baseball cards, to be taken out once a year and looked at before putting them back in the box. This was not Clay's way. His criteria were high, and if a person didn't meet them, well then, they deserved politeness but not some casual friendship based upon flimsy notions of social niceties that never went any deeper than the passing smile or how-di-do.

Of course, he'd never remained close with a woman he'd had sex with, perhaps underlining the fact that he avoided relationships with women he could actually be friends with—in the bedroom, that is. Victoria was of that mold. Pretty, intelligent, and nice enough, if you could get past that recent tirade and personal attack after he had refused to father her child. But she would never enter into his circle of trust, a very small circle, indeed, reserved for only a few, with entrance granted grudgingly, and generally only after having survived dire events together.

He didn't understand exactly how he already knew Victoria would never make it into that inner circle. Maybe it was in how the two of them were wired, in their DNA, at which thought Clay chuckled out loud. That would explain a lot. Perhaps he could get JOHNS to help him out, the image of asking Rex Bolton for his input making him laugh again. No, he couldn't explain it, but Victoria would never achieve the same status as Westy, Baylee, Cloutier, or even Crystal and Murphy.

Westy had been his friend since elementary school, so Clay was willing to lay his life on the line for the ex-SEAL. Sure, the man was, in so many ways, different than him, but at the core, they shared the same values. Clay had only known Baylee for a few years now, but, even with his high criteria for friendship, there had been a connection between them from the day she walked into his office shortly after killing her husband, a spark that had only grown stronger with each passing day and shared adventure. Then there was Cloutier who had interviewed him after his state championship football victory all those years ago. He hadn't gotten to know her well until he returned to Port Essex as an ex-Boston homicide detective. Joe Murphy was seventy years old, a former IRA fighter, and a clam digger, who had managed to enter Clay's sphere of trust and friendship. And of course, there was Crystal, who'd hired him to investigate a heroin ring, was a former drug user herself, but had somehow morphed into a friend who now also happened to be his administrative assistant.

What a motley group, Clay thought with a sardonic grin as he climbed the stairs to his office. A former SEAL, a woman who'd killed her husband, a gay newspaper editor in a fishing village, a rebel clam digger, and a former heroin addict. This was his group. These were his people. His tribe.

"Hey doll, you find out anything while I was out?" he said to Crystal in his best Sam Spade growl as he pushed open the door.

"Jed and Susan each have two brats, who I guess are grown brats in their thirties, sort of like you," Crystal said. "One of them lives in Maine, down in Portland, the rest live elsewhere. Three grandkids, but all under the age of ten."

"We should focus in on the one in Portland. I bet they would be the one to be entrusted with a key or to have knowledge of who might be staying at the Paine Cottage."

"My thoughts exactly," Crystal said. "Great fucking minds think alike."

"You find out anything about them?"

"Just the names and contact information. Baylee added that to her list when calling Jed and Susan. I can dig deeper if you want."

"What's the name of the brat in Portland?"

"Chris Salisbury."

"See what you can turn up on him. Maybe he owes people money or associates with criminals or has a drug problem or whatever."

"Sure thing, boss."

Clay headed for the inner door, which was closed, suggesting Baylee was making phone calls and didn't want to be interrupted by Crystal cursing in the background.

"That other thing you texted me about, boss? The license plate number. You want the owner's name?"

Clay stopped dead and turned on his heel. He'd quite forgotten that he'd texted Crystal the number supplied by the neighbor across the street. "You got it?"

"Fellow by the name of Clive Miller. Address is a post office box in Brunswick."

"No other address?"

"Yeah, sure, just around the corner from here," Crystal said. "No, there's no other fucking address or I'd've said something. What do you think I am, some kinda junkie?"

Clay had no choice but to resort to his Sam Spade growl. "You're a good man, sister," he said and slid into the interior office, closing the door behind him.

"Did Crystal just ask you if you thought she was a junkie?" Baylee said with a smirk.

"She sure did."

"What'd you say?"

"Plenty—in my head."

"You're not afraid of that tiny spitfire, are you?"

"Downright terrified," Clay said. "How're you making out here?" He went over and sat behind his desk, which was kitty-corner to Baylee's. She swiveled her chair to face him, her knee brushing his.

"Spoke to the son, Jed. He wasn't much help. He did allow that his sister Susan's son lived in Portland and that he might have a key. Susan won't be off the golf course until close to five. I'll give her another jingle before I go home." Baylee leaned back in her chair and stretched her arms high overhead. "What was the license plate you had Crystal run?" she asked.

"Guy across the street, old codger by the name of Nathan something or other, said he saw a guy park down the street and then go into the Paine Cottage. His description fit that of the guy who hammered Westy."

"When?"

"Same day."

"Crystal get a name for you?"

"Yep. That's all, though. Nothing else, so far. She's going to dig deeper. See what else she can come up with. Clive Miller's the name."

"I'll see what I can find on him."

"I'm meeting Westy at Lucky Linda's in a few," Clay said. "Maybe after I leave, you can ask Crystal to run Clive through the LocateNOW software."

"You really are afraid of that fiery little Acadian, aren't you?"

"I prefer to call it 'prudent'," Clay said.

"Probably quite a few Clive Millers in the world."

"Focus on any with a criminal record or military background, or a connection to Maine."

"Military background?" Baylee asked.

"If the guy got the upper hand on Westy, it suggests some sort of training."

"How about any connection to Johnson Laboratories?"

"JOHNS?"

"Everything seems to keep circling back to them," Baylee said.

"Yes, it does." Clay shifted in his chair, so his leg came in contact with Baylee's. "You find out anything on Chad Gagnon?"

Baylee grabbed a piece of paper from her desk without moving her leg. "He's twenty-seven, goes to the gym almost every day, is a local boy who got out of the Marines about a year ago after serving eight, did some lobstering, and worked the last six months at JOHNS."

"Police turned up nothing?"

"Nope. Not as far as I can tell. I'm going to have coffee with Officer Tracy in a bit to see what the PD knows."

"The new chief won't much like that."

"Yeah, she's gonna come over to my house. It's her day off and we *are* friends, after all, so hopefully it doesn't come back to bite her in the ass."

"You want to come over to Lucky Linda's with me and Westy after you get done?

"What'd you say you were going there for?"

"That was Daryl Allen's hangout. I'm thinking that a bunch of his buddies will be there around three. Thought we'd see if anybody knows what he might've been into."

"I'd love to go hang out with you and your redneck pals and be ogled by drunk fishermen, but I got a bunch of things I need to take care of before heading over to Kalinda's for the week. I'll have to take a rain check." Baylee placed her hand on his knee. "But you boys have fun."

"You have any free time this week?"

"Nope. Aisha is gone, so I'm on 24/7."

"You're done Saturday?"

"Yep."

"How about we get dinner together Saturday night and catch up on what's going on?" Clay asked. He was very aware of her hand still on his knee.

"What is going on?" Baylee asked playfully, squeezing his knee.

Clay steadied himself before replying. "Hopefully, by then, we should know a lot more about Clive Miller. Maybe we'll even have tracked him down and put him behind bars."

"Ha," Baylee said. "You're going to have to stop Westy from tearing him to pieces when you find him, if you want to put him behind bars, that is."

Her eyes were so large and round, Clay thought, so entrancing and deep, he had a hard time tearing his gaze away. He finally turned to look out the window, clearing his throat. "I'll keep in touch," he said thickly.

*   *   *

Baylee climbed into her Subaru feeling like she might cry. When she was with Clay it was like the clouds cleared and the sun lit up the world and things began to grow and thrive around her. They had a chemistry that was undeniable. It tore a hole in her heart just to know that she wouldn't see him all week as she played guard to Kalinda. She knew that they were destined to be together, that they would, at some point, deepen this relationship that consumed them. But then he'd go off and start fucking some other woman.

It seemed that the current flavor of the month was Victoria Haas, accomplished fashion designer, CEO, and heiress to the Haas family fortune. She was rich, glamorous, and had done things in her life that Baylee Baker could never imagine. Graduating high school had been Baylee's major achievement to date, and how did that match up with Victoria fucking Haas, who'd been awarded the CFDA fashion award for emerging American designer when she was twenty-eight years old? Twenty-eight. (Sometimes, she reflected, there was a place in the world for a little Facebook stalking.)

All that said, Baylee knew that Clay pined for her, but for some reason, he wouldn't take that final step to bridge the gap that separated them. She understood that it was a fear of commitment—hell, she had similar issues herself, so she didn't push the envelope too hard or too fast. Her own issues aside—and yes, she knew, her abusive marriage and its violent end would always be issues—she sometimes felt in psychic pain at Clay's inability to move forward, taking even a small step out of the mire he seemed to create for himself.

It was so hard to wait, and in the meantime, there Clay was fucking Victoria. And they *were* sleeping together, that Baylee knew, because that was where he had been coming from the night Westy got hammered. They weren't playing Parcheesi at that time of night, that was for sure. Baylee's emotions ran from tears to anger as she thought of the two of them being intimate together. She told herself she could wait until the time was right. But it was hard, so hard, and that anger would have to find a place to go, and soon, lest she explode.

* * *

Westy was at the bar with Murphy when Clay walked in. Lucky Linda's was a late-night place for bikers, the blue-collar twenty-something crowd, and those meeting for trysts away from their usual, more savory, haunts. When hired to find evidence on a cheating spouse, this was one of the first places Clay would come. For ten months of the year, it was fairly quiet until 8:00 or 9:00 at night, at which time it began to pick up. The food was greasy and fit only for those with a drunk palate, the ambiance tending to darkness and inebriation.

Nonetheless, this was where the daytime regulars from the Seal Bar retreated for the months of July and August when the summer crowd arrived in full force. The only other choice not overrun by these sun birds was the Side Bar, and that, hard as it was to believe, was a major step down from Lucky Linda's.

The bar was a large horseshoe shape, a rustic wood countertop gouged with graffiti. About twenty stools circled the rough planks, and a broad array of liquor bottles filled the shelves in front of the cracked mirror. There was, for some reason, no IPA on tap. Clay knew that he'd have to hope that the Jameson he ordered would kill any germs in the glass it came in.

There were a few tables scattered around on the off chance that some tourists got lost and came up the hill by mistake, looking for a meal and some local character. These tables would be safely removed before the crowds arrived later for the serious drinking.

Even though it was Monday night, there was a band playing later, a cross between '80s rock and contemporary punk. A sign proclaimed that "Nightmare on Commercial Way" would be kicking off at 10:00. Clay had made the mistake of attending one of their gigs the year before. He hoped that he was long gone by 10:00.

"Murph," Clay said, settling onto a barstool next to the man. Westy sat on the far side.

"Clay, me lad. Good to see you."

Murphy secretly always made Clay think of Dobby, from Harry Potter, but he kept that to himself, mostly so as to not admit that he'd been a fan of that particular fantasy wizarding series. When Clay had first met Murphy, the man had been about five-foot-six, but had appeared to shrink over the past couple of years. His once wiry body now appeared frail. He was in his seventies, his face lined to prove it, and his hair tousled white. Even though he now spent his days in bars rather than out on the clam flats, his hand was still steady, and his blue eyes sparkled. He wore a white T-shirt with a torn sleeve and a brown wool vest over it.

"How've you been?" Clay asked.

"Not bad for a *dosser*," Murphy said.

"Dosser?" Clay knew that when the man fell into his Irish brogue it usually meant he was working a pretty good buzz.

"You know, me lad, somebody who doesn't work, just messes about."

Murphy had arrived in Port Essex long before Clay was born, running from something in Ireland—that, from the rumors over the years, Clay had pieced together as mostly likely some sort of involvement in the IRA. He had spent the last fifty years as a clammer, and seemingly had socked away a stash of money, as now, in retirement, he was able to spend his days in bars drinking Jameson whiskey, which was far from the cheap stuff.

"You want I should buy you something to eat?" Clay asked, eying the man's diminutive figure.

"Ha. Here? I might be drunk but I'm not stupid. I got a wee bit of soup left over at home. That'll do me fine." He finished the brown liquor in his glass and set it back down with a click. "You can buy me a Jameson, though, that you can do."

Clay made eye contact with the bartender, pointed at Murphy's glass, and then held up two fingers. The woman poured a double into Murphy's glass. "I'll take one as well," Clay said. "Give me a couple of rocks."

"Haven't seen much of you, Clay. Where you been hiding out?"

"You know, the Covid-19, and the fact that I'm trying to cut down on my day-drinking."

"So, you don't need anything of me? This is purely social?"

"Wouldn't've bought you a drink if it was purely social," Clay said. "I'd make you buy me one."

"An old man living off a government check? That's what's wrong with today's world. No respect for the elderly."

"You said something about Daryl Allen hanging out here, around this time of day?" Clay asked. "Any of his buddies here now?"

"Sure, me laddie, those fellows over there—see the two sitting with the two standing behind them? They all run in the same circle. Been kicked out of here more times than the Red Sox have won games this year, but a week later, back they are."

Clay ordered a pitcher of beer for the men. The bartender filled it with Natural Light without asking. Clay leaned forward to look at Westy. "You know any of them?"

"Yep. Not to play checkers with, though."

"What say we go talk to them?"

The pitcher was delivered across the way, the bartender said something and nodded at Clay, and the men raised their glasses in thanks—all but one, that is, who glared at him in a surly manner.

"As long as I can go home and take a shower later," Westy said.

"Another one for my friend when he's ready," Clay said to the bartender nodding at Murphy's glass.

They worked their way around the toe of the horseshoe to the other side.

"Hello, gentlemen. I'm Clay Wolfe, and this is Weston Beck."

"Hey, Westy," one of the men said. "Heard you got your boat sunk?"

"You the one from the newspaper, ain't ya?" A medium-size man with solid cheekbones said. "The private detective dude."

"That's what we wanted to ask you about, Andy," Westy said. "Seeing as Daryl Allen was on it at the time, and you all were friends with him."

"You're not one of those fancy boys, are you?" the man who had been glaring asked, directing the question at Clay.

"Chill out, Dale," the shortest of the men said. "They bought us a pitcher."

"Sorry to hear about Daryl," Clay said. "Sounded like he was a good man."

"He was a good fucking patriot, that he was," Andy said. He raised his glass. "To Daryl."

"Any idea of who might've wanted to harm him?" Westy asked as he set his bottle of Budweiser back on the bar. "And why he was in my boat?"

"Figured you let him borrow it," Dale of the glare said craftily. "Been wondering if you sabotaged the thing."

"I didn't lend him my boat. You know better than that."

"What was he doing on it, then?"

Clay nodded at the bartender for another pitcher of beer. This brought smiles to three of the men's faces. "We think Daryl was killed," he said. "Murdered, actually."

"And planted on my boat to make it look like he stole it and then got sunk in the Pumpkin Ledges."

"Daryl wasn't killed," Dale said. He'd managed to pour a fresh beer from the pitcher.

"You think he steered into the Pumpkin Ledges on purpose?" Westy asked.

The four men all looked at their feet, the two standing, shuffling, the two sitting, squirming.

"Sounds like if he was murdered, you'd be the prime suspect, Westy," Solid Cheekbones said. "Him being on your boat and all."

"Yeah, but I didn't kill him." Westy met his stare. "So, who did?"

"Was he having a good fishing season?" Clay asked.

"Hell, yeah," Andy said. "He been buying... was buying rounds for a few weeks before he was found dead. Fucking guy never bought a round in a night, and all of a sudden he's throwing money—"

"Shut up, Andy," Dale said.

"Some loose change to spend, huh?" Clay asked. "You guys all having a good season?"

"Scallops ain't bad," Shorty said.

"Not enough to be throwing money around, though, huh?" Clay said. He set his empty glass down and the bartender handed him another Jameson. Across the way, Murphy smiled and tipped his glass.

"Daryl pick up some sort of side job?" Westy asked.

"He said he was running a fucking ferry service, is what he said," Andy said.

"For who?" Clay asked.

Andy shook his head. "Didn't say."

"He say anything about Russians?" Clay asked.

"Daryl was a good fucking patriot," Andy said.

"Come November, this here country is going to have to decide whether it wants communism or freedom," Dale said. "And Daryl, he wanted freedom, that's what I can tell you."

"I saw him picking up a Russian fellow off a Russian fishing boat right before he died," Westy said. "Sounds to me like he was in bed with the commies, if you ask me."

"That's a lie," Solid Cheekbones said.

Westy turned his level look at him, and in that instant, Dale launched forward out of his chair, striking Westy, who barely stumbled backward a half-step before grabbing the man by the throat.

Andy swung a roundhouse blow at Westy, which Clay stepped in front of, blocking it with his forearm and thrusting a short right jab into the man's face. Westy stepped forward and slammed Dale's head into the bar, knocking drinks all around the horseshoe onto the floor and into the laps of pissed-off patrons.

Solid Cheekbones punched Clay in the ear, sending him stumbling back. He righted himself and sent a punch to the man's solar plexus, a whoosh of stale-beer air coming out of his gasping mouth. Then it was on like Donkey Kong. The entire place erupted in a swirling melee of violence.

A stool crashed into Clay's back from a random patron, possibly one who'd had their drink spilled. He fell to his knees, and a woman with big hair and long nails came at him, flashing those daggers at his face. He knocked her to the floor as Andy kicked him in the side, and Clay gritted his teeth against the pain of the steel-toed boot. He swiveled on his knees and grabbed the man's leg and twisted, sending him crashing to the floor.

Clay fought his way to his feet, seeing Westy grab a man and lift him overhead and throw him into the wall, shaking the entire building. The bar had descended into a flying, churning ruckus of human beings being pummeled and pummeling in equal volume. In the midst of the brouhaha, Clay glanced over to see Murphy, still sitting at the bar, drink in hand.

Then the cops arrived.

Chapter 17

WEDNESDAY, AUGUST 5TH

Grandpops had come and bailed Clay and Westy out of jail two nights earlier. Just this past winter, they would've been let out with a mild scolding, but that was before Grandpops' good friend, Chief Knight, had retired. The new chief had no such allegiances, was a by-the-book stickler, and seemed ticked off that Clay had the nerve to operate as a private investigator in his town. It was 2:00 a.m. before they were let out with a summons for court.

Clay stopped down from his over-the-garage apartment to check in with Grandpops before going off to the diner for breakfast and then work. He'd a few scrapes and bruises but nothing all that serious. One of the fishermen had been hospitalized and was pressing charges against Westy for assault. Clay didn't recognize the name, so it must have been either Solid Cheekbones or Shorty. There was a dim recollection of Westy throwing a man into a wall, and it was this incident that Clay figured was the reason for the assault charge.

"Coffee?" Grandpops asked. He was sitting on the front porch with the *Portland Press Herald* spread out in front of him.

"Sure, I'll grab a cup and join you," Clay said.

He went through the house to the kitchen and grabbed a cup and put some of the gourmet creamer in and then filled it from the pot. He'd grown up in this house, raised by his grandfather since the age of eight. The man had helped him with his homework. Counseled him on bullies and girls. Attended every one of his sporting events. Picked him up at the quarry when he was too drunk to drive.

Gene Wolfe had steered him clear of trouble, and gave him the opportunity to go off to college in Boston, and then supported him in joining the Boston PD, where Clay eventually became a homicide detective. When he decided to move back home four years ago, Grandpops had paid for the space above the garage to be remodeled into an apartment.

Clay sat down in one of the Adirondack chairs on the porch overlooking downtown Port Essex and the harbor. Commercial Way was mostly obstructed from view, but boats could be seen trundling their way through the harbor, most of them heading out for fishing, lobstering, or tourists with their own boats getting an early start. Sightseeing tours wouldn't start for another hour. It wasn't yet 8:00 in the morning.

Gene Wolfe, Clay thought, could best be described as a silver fox. He was perhaps an inch over six feet, had gray hair feathered back from his face, and a beard of the same color coming to a point on his chin. He'd always had an athletic build, but as of late, that'd turned to thin, if not quite frail. He still kept busy at the gym, going to music venues, and dancing, as well as watching sports on television.

"You recovered from your barroom brawl?" Grandpops asked.

"Mostly," Clay replied.

"You still haven't told me what that was all about."

"Me and Westy have been looking for the guy who whacked him in the forehead. Our best lead, Daryl Allen, who was mixed up in the attack, is dead. We thought we might poke around some of his friends and see what they knew."

"Yes? And did you find out anything?"

"Sure," Clay said. "They take offense at the mere thought that their deceased friend was fraternizing with Russians."

"And, I take it, Daryl was indeed seen with a Russian."

Clay told him about Westy seeing Daryl picking up a man from a ship with a Russian name, and then later following Daryl, leading to the hammering, kidnapping, and subsequent attempted murder.

"Why is some fisherman in Port Essex ferrying a Russian around, and why does the Russian need a boat?" Grandpops asked.

"We think it might have to do with Johnson Laboratories and the work they're doing there on genome editing," Clay said. "As for Daryl and his boat, if the Russian was smuggled in and out, well, no TSA records so he was never here. So, maybe espionage?"

"Okay, Johnson Labs, that's the fellows who had you sign the NDA, correct?" Grandpops asked.

"Yep."

"And you think the Russians might be stealing or buying scientific discoveries involving those superior mice?"

"The thought had crossed my mind."

"Hmm. Is this just mice, or do you think this… science has been applied to human beings?"

"No idea, but I doubt that creating superior mice is the reason for all the ruckus," Clay said.

Grandpops took a slow, contemplative sip of his coffee. "JOHNS has been around for almost a hundred years now. The founder, B.B. Knutson, was renowned for his cancer research using mice. After leaving as the head of a large university, he came to East Essex and started up Johnson Laboratories. But, if cancer research was his life's work, his passion was eugenics."

"Eugenics?" Clay asked.

"The concept of improving the human race by suppressing the propagation of inferior beings."

"Propagation? You mean reproduction? How do you do that? I mean, is that even legal?"

"B.B. Knutson advocated deterring certain gene pools from reproducing and went so far as to push for sterilization of inferior human beings."

"Who was deemed inferior?"

"Remember a few weeks back you came home from that sail when Westy was telling all of you about the inhabitants of Malaga Island being driven from their homes? I could venture a guess that those—how did you describe them—poor, Black, Indian, and Irish? Well," Grandpops said. "I could be wrong, but they tick all the boxes. Perhaps you could have that little whip-saw of a receptionist research it further."

* * *

"What the fuck does he mean calling me a *whip-saw*?" Crystal asked. "I mean, what does that even mean?"

Clay grinned. His Grandpops' old-fashioned image might put up the hackles of most women, but he thought that Crystal wouldn't be offended, and rather, would feel complimented. "I believe he was saying that you attack a problem from two sides and see your way through until you've reached the tipping point."

"That doesn't help a whole lot, but if you're suggesting it's a good thing, that works for me. You don't think your Grandpops is looking for a younger woman in his life, do you?" Crystal arched her eyebrows in what she obviously thought was a sexy manner.

"You should ask him yourself," Clay said. "But first, do you mind looking up this B.B. Knutson? Seems he was obsessed with creating a superior race through eugenics."

"Why do you suppose they made people sterile back in the 1920s?" Crystal asked.

"Add that to the list," Clay said. "Anything more on that Clive Miller?"

"Baylee said you're scared of me. Is that true?"

"You *are* a whip-saw."

Crystal moved and clicked the mouse. "I came up with eighty possible hits. Three live in New England, but don't fit the type. Seven with military backgrounds. Four with criminal records."

"How about criminal records first."

"Two were OUIs. One was burglary. The last one was assault."

"Where did the assault occur?"

"Brunswick, Maine. Charges were dropped. Looks like he joined the military right afterwards. Spent seven years in before being court-martialed for killing a captive kid that he claimed was Taliban."

"Ding-ding, we have a winner, chicken dinner," Clay said. "Brunswick is where Clive has the P.O. box, right?"

"Whatever that chicken dinner thing means, but yes," Crystal said. "He was nineteen at the time. Beat the shit out of his boss. Something about too many smoke breaks."

"Sounds like our guy. See what you can dig up on him."

"Gotcha, boss."

Crystal went back out to her desk.

Clay texted Baylee. Any word on Chris Salisbury? The grandson of the cottage owner who lived in Portland.

Said he had a key and gave it to local guy to do some maintenance. Never got it back.

Guy have a name?

Daryl Allen.

Clay looked at his phone. Not that this really helped, now that Daryl was dead. He pecked out his reply. That doesn't help much.

Heard you tore up the town Monday night.

Clay had been evasive of her questioning texts the day before. Hanging with Westy. What would you expect?

Boys.

Men. Clay texted. With adolescent minds. Yes. Officer Tracey said there were zero leads on Gagnon. He just disappeared off the face of the earth.

Did they search JOHNS?

Top to bottom. Nothing.

Clay closed his eyes. How did a person just disappear, he wondered, then tapped out a reply. Could've ended up in a duffel bag in the Atlantic Ocean.

Or flew town because his girlfriend dumped him. Official police viewpoint, anyway.

Easy version, you mean.

Yep. Banquet Friday night at JOHNS. Fundraiser. Kalinda singing. Invited you along if you want to come.

I'll check my schedule.

I already did. You're drinking alone at the Pelican Perch. Maybe you can break that engagement?

In.

Clay set the phone down on his desk and leaned back in his chair. The office was a gloomier place without Baylee's presence. Her comment about him drinking alone at the Pelican Perch Friday night struck a little too close to home.

Maybe he should try and make things work with Victoria, he thought, even though he was having a difficult time banishing Baylee from his mind. What would be so bad about fathering a child with the woman? Maybe over the course of creating a new life, something more might blossom between them. He enjoyed her company. She was smart, witty, with a caustic side that he liked. She was beautiful in her own way. Wealthy. The sex had been fantastic. What could possibly go wrong?

Without realizing he was doing it, Clay texted Victoria. Can I see you?

He stared at the phone for a minute, and then googled 'eugenics'. He knew that Wikipedia was not the most reliable source, but he clicked on it anyway. It was the quickest way to basic information, and he could always fact-check things later.

The eugenics movement, he read, began in the U.K. in the late 19th century and spread around the world, including the U.S. The concept was to create a superior race by encouraging those believed to have better genes to reproduce and discouraging those with deficient genes from procreating. This proved difficult to accomplish. Yet, in the early

20ᵗʰ century, the U.S. led the world in forced sterilization of certain people. The mentally ill, the physically handicapped, the deaf, blind, and dumb, and those who had a low IQ were forcibly sterilized. In some countries, popular belief, fueled by firebrand politicians, came to view entire races as inferior, stretching to include women who were promiscuous, too, under the guise that they were feeble-minded.

In all, at least 65,000 people in the U.S. were forcibly sterilized until the practice fell out of favor before WWII. One big factor was what was going on in Nazi Germany under Adolph Hitler, who pointed out that their extermination of what they considered inferior races to create a *master* race was not so far different than what was being practiced in the U.S. This, then, had been what the founder of JOHNS had believed in, the sterilization of inferior humans to create a superior gene pool unpolluted by the presence of the weak, sick, or dull-witted. Now, 100 years later, the institution seemed to be chasing the same goal from a different direction.

Clay looked at his phone, but there was no reply from Victoria. She was most definitely ghosting him. He stood up, sliding his phone into his pocket, and walked out past Crystal with a wave of his hand, saying that he was going out for a bit and would be back. It was time to take the bull by the horns, Clay figured, and pay Victoria a visit. He was, as yet, undecided on what he wanted the nature of their relationship to be, but talking it out certainly couldn't hurt, could it?

As Clay pulled into the drive of Victoria's estate, his mind was churning with a jumble of thoughts. Why had he walked away from this woman? Again, he pointed out to himself, she was smart, beautiful, wealthy, witty, and great in bed. What was there not to like? What was his hang-up about fathering a child?

At the same time, Clay felt like an outsider as he approached the door. He furtively looked to see if the house had a side entrance that was a little less conspicuous. Mentally squaring his shoulders, he lifted the brass fox door knocker, banging it firmly twice.

The door opened immediately, as if Mekhi had been awaiting his arrival. "Hello, Mr. Wolfe."

"Hi to you as well, Mekhi. Is Victoria home?" Clay felt as if he was in high school picking up a girl for a date and having to dance his way past the over-protective father.

"Ms. Haas is not home at present."

"Just a minute of her time is all I ask."

"Ms. Haas is out of town until Friday, Mr. Wolfe."

"Where did she go?"

"I will let her know that you stopped by." The door closed.

Chapter 18

"I had to claim you as part of my bodyguard service," Kalinda said to Clay. "They were very tight with invitations. You know, with the Covid restrictions. No more than fifty people can be together for an outdoor event."

Clay looked around the four large tents that were set up on the lawn, which was more of a small field, across from the JOHNS administrative building. "There are way more than fifty people here," he said.

"The guidelines, just updated for the latest phase, allow for four areas of people, if it's outdoors, and if they are separated by barriers to prevent intermingling," Baylee said.

There was a rope fence running between the tents and about fifteen feet of space separating them. Clay seriously doubted that this flimsy barrier would keep people from hopping from tent to tent. "I did bring my gun," Clay said, patting his left chest where his Glock rested in its holster.

"Got your nine, huh?" Kalinda said smiling. "I don't actually expect you to be on duty. It was either that or claim that you're planning on making a large donation. Only the wealthiest of the wealthy have been invited."

Clay wondered if Victoria would be here. He still hadn't heard back from her and was thinking that it might be time to pay her another visit. Or he had been thinking... The thought of rekindling things with Victoria had somehow dimmed on seeing Baylee again after a four-day absence.

"I guess that means I can have a few drinks," Clay said. "Did I hear that you're singing for us?"

Kalinda laughed, the mirth tumbling forth like a kaleidoscope. "I've agreed to do three songs."

"If you don't mind me asking, remind me how you and Johnson Labs are connected?"

"They heard that I was going to be spending some time in Port Essex, and they reached out to my people to see if I'd help them with some promotions." Kalinda shrugged. "I asked for a brief on what they do and who they are. My lawyer did some research as well and came back with a very favorable report on the fantastic things they are doing to eradicate disease around the world, so I decided to do some *pro bono* work for them while I'm here. Baylee's local knowledge sealed the deal for me, as they seem to be very good corporate citizens."

"Speaking of your stay, you must be leaving soon. Seems to me you've been here about a month now." Clay was thinking that he'd like to see Baylee back in the office more, and then realized that what he said might be taken as rude. "Not that I'm rushing you off or anything."

Again, the kaleidoscope laugh. "We have indeed overstayed our welcome, or will soon, anyway. We were slated to return home Sunday but have extended our stay for another week."

"Having a hard time leaving our beautiful village?" Clay asked.

"Yes, we are. And then John was called away on business this week. There are some things we were hoping to do before we left that we hadn't gotten to."

"Will you be going out with Westy again on his sailboat?"

"That was a wonderful experience, but, no, sadly, no time for another sail."

Clay noticed three men sidling towards them, almost like they were intending to accidentally bump into Kalinda as a way of introducing themselves. "Can I get you a drink from the bar?" he asked, figuring that he'd monopolized enough of her time.

"No, thank you. I believe that I'll wait for refreshments until after I do my crooning."

The youngest and best-looking of the three men stepped into their space and held out his hand. "Hello, Kalinda, I'm a big fan. My name is Jack Keeton."

Clay had to step back to avoid getting trampled. He took his leave and moved over next to Baylee who was eyeballing the men closely. "No danger there unless you count too much cologne," he said.

"Me thinks I've caught a whiff of scent emanating from your face before," Baylee said.

"Aftershave. Big difference. To heal the shaven skin of the face."

Baylee leaned in close and sniffed. "Mm. Subtle but sexy as hell at the same time. And you *are* looking fine today, Mr. Wolfe."

Clay had on a Madras jacket over khakis, with a pink shirt and matching bow tie. His Hubbard shoes were shined to a gleam, and he'd gotten his hair cut earlier in the day. "And you, Miss Baker, are a vision of loveliness."

Baylee was in a pants suit, the jacket allowing her to conceal her pistol, which she carried in a holster down in her waistband, just the butt sticking out for her to grasp. He'd given her a Smith & Wesson MP Shield for Christmas to replace her outdated old gun. The slimness of this pistol made it more comfortable to carry.

"Any progress on the guy who hammered Westy?" she asked.

"Not so much. Crystal has figured out which Clive Miller we are most likely looking for." He related everything Crystal had discovered, from assault to Afghanistan and his tours in the military. "After he killed a kid that he claimed was Taliban, he got court-martialed and sent stateside only to disappear into oblivion."

"Disappear?"

"No known address. No job. No credit cards. No car payments. The man literally doesn't exist."

"Try telling Westy that."

"The question is, what's he doing in Port Essex? Or what was he doing in East Essex?" Clay resisted the urge to pat her down to see how noticeable the pistol was in her waistband. He couldn't tell by looking. He thought it best not to frisk her. Not without consent, anyway.

"You should ask Chief Roberts," Baylee said. "He's right over there." She nodded her head toward the front of the tent.

Clay looked at the man, out of uniform and in a tailored suit that looked very expensive. "I doubt that he's one of the wealthiest of the wealthy," he said. "Wonder how he got his invite."

"Always a wise idea to stay on the good side of the police department," Baylee said.

"Especially if you happen to be a lawbreaker," Clay said. "You all finished up with Kalinda tomorrow?"

"John and Aisha should be back in the morning, and I'm headed back home. Not that I minded getting paid to spend time on the Point in a mansion."

"You still up for dinner? We can go to Bianchi's."

"Mmm. Cheesy garlic bread."

"Is that a yes?"

"Sure. What time?"

"I'll pick you up at six?"

"Pick me up?" Baylee asked. "My, this is sounding like a real date. Maybe I should buy new underwear?"

Clay was still blushing as he excused himself to go get a drink and left Baylee to her bodyguard duties. She always knew how to needle him, poking and prodding and being just brazen enough to embarrass him. She certainly kept him on his toes. Perhaps it was her way of punishing him for his own adventures.

The directions had been for people to all sit at their assigned table to prevent mingling, but there couldn't have been more than a dozen people actually sitting down. Clay counted eight tables of eight under their tent alone, which suggested that if they were all filled, the fifty-person limit would be exceeded. Waiters wearing masks emblazoned with the Johnson Labs logo sifted through the crowd, presumably to bring cocktails to patrons, most of whom had impatiently approached the bar on their own.

A light and cool breeze drifted down from the northeast, chasing the few puffy white clouds from the sky against the setting sun. Clay worked his way to the front of the bar where he got a double Glenlivet with just a couple cubes of ice. He was working his way to the corner of the tent from whence to people-watch when he ran smack dab into Harley Lange.

"Mr. Wolfe, I'm surprised to find you here," Harley said. "My understanding is that you had been... let go."

"I'm here in another capacity," Clay said.

"Does this new client know that you were fired from your previous employment?" Harley cast a taunting grin at Clay.

"I trust that you understand that we were only doing our job," Clay said. "It was nothing personal."

"Not personal to muck up my life? Maybe not to you, but to me, it was very personal. Where do you get off accusing me of trying to rip off my employer just because I had an affair on my ex-wife?" Harley stepped in close as he spoke, his tone angry, his demeanor menacing. "Have you ever been married, Mr. Wolfe?"

"No, I haven't."

"It's not all it's cracked up to be. As a matter of fact, it can downright suck. My wife was a nag, and cold. And she criticized every single thing I did."

"Plus, you being gay probably didn't help things," Clay said.

"I'm not gay, Mr. Wolfe, I am bisexual."

"My bad," Clay said. "I had reason to believe that the affair, the subsequent divorce, and the desire to keep your sexual orientation to yourself, that all that perhaps made you open to blackmail or bribes. I'm sure that you would've done the same thing in my position."

Harley stepped back. "Maybe I would've, Mr. Wolfe, maybe I would've. It's not always clear what the right thing to do is."

Rex Bolton slapped Clay's shoulder with a friendly clap. "Clay, glad to see you. Harley told me that you were on the guest list. Bodyguard to Kalinda? Should you be drinking?" he asked eyeing the brown liquor in Clay's hand. "Harley, would you mind asking Miss Engel whether she wants Kalinda to sing first or have the silent auction first, and make sure your team is on top of things?"

"Rex, good to see you," Clay said as Harley sauntered off. "Kalinda thought it best if I blended in, sort of like a secret bodyguard."

"Is that right?" Rex's hair was unkempt, his face looking weary despite the bonhomie, as if it'd been a tough day already. "I'll have to consider urging Harley and the security detail to have the occasional drink."

"Might cut down on internal theft," Clay said.

"Attempted theft, my boy, attempted theft. You know what they say, no harm, no foul."

"What brings you to East Essex, Rex? You don't really strike me as a Mainer. You seem more like a city fellow."

"Ah, that's where you're wrong. I love the outdoors. Ever since a hiking trip I took back when I was twenty years old." Rex had a faraway look in his eyes.

"Is that right? Where'd you go?" Clay might even classify Rex's eyes as dreamy.

"A friend and I spent a few months in Europe."

"Was that Europe or Russia? Perm, right? You were telling us about some Russian girl when we interviewed you a month or so ago, now I remember."

Bolton glared at him. "We were hiking in the Ural Mountains."

"So, you came to Maine for the great outdoors?"

"I could do without the eight months of winter."

Clay finished off the brown liquor in his glass. "Why'd you fire me, Rex?"

"I didn't fire you, Clay, so much as let you go. You were no longer needed."

That was not quite how Clay remembered the conversation. If his memory was accurate, it had followed directly on a distinctly uncomfortable conversation, questions about an Area 38 and Chad Gagnon. "What can you tell me about the founder of JOHNS?" he asked instead.

"The founder? You mean way back when?"

"Yes. B.B. Knutson."

"I don't know. I believe he went through the UMaine system before getting a job out west somewhere, some university. Then he came back to Maine in the 1920s and founded JOHNS. What is it you're asking?"

"What do you know about eugenics, Rex?" Clay watched the man's face carefully. There was no tell-tale sign of alarm at the turn the conversation had taken.

"What's this have to do with anything?" He asked, then shrugged and answered. "Eugenics is the study of how to arrange reproduction within a human population to increase the occurrence of heritable characteristics regarded as desirable." Rex scanned the crowd, a bored look crossing his face.

"My understanding is that this was Knutson's original purpose in founding JOHNS, research that justified discouraging certain segments of the population from reproducing, even going so far as government-sanctioned sterilization, with the end goal being a more perfect human race. A master race, if you will. Same thing Hitler wanted, if my memory of history serves me correctly."

Rex's face flamed red, and he swung his eyes back toward Clay. "What are you suggesting?"

"Isn't the work that you're doing here a more advanced form of eugenics, aimed at discouraging certain gene pools from continuing on, to exist at all, actually?"

"Are you accusing JOHNS of something, Mr. Wolfe?"

"What is Area 38, Rex?"

"I should have you thrown out of here."

"It'd certainly cause a dilemma. Kalinda might decide that if her bodyguard was evicted that she'd be unable to sing later. Is that what you want?"

"You're treading on thin ice, Mr. Wolfe."

"What happened to Chad Gagnon?"

Rex stepped close to Clay. The man's breath stank of stale coffee and cigarettes. "Leave it alone, Mr. Wolfe. You've been warned." He turned on his heel and walked off.

Clay shrugged. He needed another drink, anyway. He'd certainly hit a sore spot and not for the first time. The idea of eugenics, Area 38, and Chad Gagnon seemed to be the perfect trifecta to get Rex's goat. What was JOHNS doing that was so secret? At their last meeting, Rex had admitted to the impropriety of accessing ancestry data to do their research to find enough subjects with mutations associated with high IQs and superior strength. They, then in theory, would apply the mutations within these people's DNA to mice, and this was how they were creating the SHAIM, or the SuperHuman Advanced Intelligence Mice.

Even though they were most likely illegally hacking this information from ancestry sites, or simply bribing some lowly IT drone, that was nothing that their team of lawyers couldn't bury in the dusty cobwebs of court proceedings long after anyone still cared. There was more to it. Clay could feel it in his bones. And it had to do with the mysterious Area 38. And the disappearance of Chad Gagnon. And more and more, it seemed, eugenics, even if it were taking the almost innocuous-sounding name of genomic editing.

Were these things even connected to the attempted theft of a mouse, Clay wondered? It seemed likely that an employee had taken a stab at sneaking one of the SHAIM out of the lab, presumably to sell. But to whom? A foreign country, looking to develop the technology to apply to humans to make a master race seemed to be the most likely explanation. If that was the case, Daryl Allen transporting a man from a Russian ship to a cottage where a fellow by the name of Clive Miller tried to kill Westy—well, that was all making more sense.

What Clay couldn't quite place his finger on was what Area 38 had to do with the attempt to steal and sell a mouse to the Russians. Had Chad Gagnon been killed because he'd caught the employee attempting to smuggle the mouse from JOHNS? Clay seriously doubted that a scientist trying to earn a bit of extra cash or cover up some impropriety in their lives could make a man disappear overnight. That suggested somebody else—most likely this Clive Miller person.

Clay found that, while deep in his thoughts, he'd gotten another drink that tasted much like it must be Glenlivet. Waiters appeared carrying covered plates of food, and he realized that dinner was being served.

Clay was surprised to learn that he wasn't sharing a table with Baylee and Kalinda. He was further thrown off when Bridget Engel came and sat down next to him. He was, indeed, at the power table. He noted the governor on Engel's other side. The other five at the table had the arrogance of money, power, and higher class spilling from their pores. He guessed that they were board members. Or potential donors, the richest of the rich, being given star treatment to open their pocketbooks and donate to the research facility. So, Clay thought, why the fuck was he here, as Crystal would put it?

Clay had chosen the filet mignon and smashed potatoes as his entrée over the lobster, not even considering the vegetarian option. The food was exceptional, as was the wine that the waiter kept insisting on pouring into his glass. In between the meal and the dessert, Kalinda belted out an a cappella version of her song about love. Clay thought that it might be called "Can't Live without You." He'd listened to many of her songs over the past few weeks, and while not a fan, had been captivated by the simplicity of the lyrics. He found that he liked this simple, single-voice version better than the overproduced number with instruments. Kalinda truly had a beautiful voice.

His enjoyment was interrupted by Engel leaning over and whispering in his ear. "Would you be interested in further pursuing your investigation at JOHNS?"

Clay continued to listen to the lyrics wafting through the air. He was turned away from Engel, but her nearness, just short of pressed against him, was palpable even before she spoke. After a bit, he shifted slightly, bringing his face, while not quite looking at her, just inches from her lips. "Bolton made it quite clear that my services were no longer needed. I believe his exact words were, 'no harm, no foul.'"

"But you don't believe that, do you?"

"Does it matter what I believe?"

"I understand that you're still making inquiries into the disappearance of Chad Gagnon."

"The interest is linked to something else that I'm investigating."

"I'm concerned about the security of JOHNS, Clay. I'm fearful that our advances in genome editing are going to be stolen, if the research hasn't already been compromised, and that it will be used by others for odious purposes."

Clay turned the last few inches so that he was staring into her eyes. They were a grayish blue, with thin eyebrows penciled in above. "I've been led to understand that Harley Lange can handle any further issues." Behind him, Kalinda continued singing. *Can't say for sure how I feel, Just know for sure, That I can't live without you, And I want you to stay.*

"That's what worries me. I'm concerned that Rex and Harley might be involved in the thievery," Engel whispered. Kalinda finished up the song, and the crowd broke into applause. "I'd like you to continue your investigation and report directly to me. Nobody else."

"I'm told that there has been no theft. What is it you want me to investigate?"

"You'll be my company secret police, Mr. Wolfe. I'm not around all that much and have concerns about Rex Bolton. You'd be my eyes and ears."

"Why do you have concerns about Rex?"

"I first became suspicious a few years back. Remember that ice storm we had in 2016? Everybody lost power for over a week. We had generators but still scaled back to a skeleton staff until everything was up and running fully. I was away in Europe at the time. When I came back, I was looking at the books, and there was a discrepancy. When I brought it to Rex's attention, he was flustered, but passed it off as an accounting error. At the time, I let it go. But lately, I've had this nagging suspicion that something else is going on. I can't put my finger on it, but I believe that money may have been used for something else."

"What do you know of Area 38?" Clay noticed a tattoo of two jagged lines rising above the back of her black dress on her right shoulder.

Engel was silent for a moment. "There is no Area 38. We have only thirty-seven labs here at JOHNS. What are you suggesting?"

"Is it possible that Rex Bolton has created a new, secret lab, here on the grounds, without your knowledge?"

Engel laughed. "I was more thinking along the lines of embezzling money or selling secrets, Mr. Wolfe."

"Perhaps we can talk more in private," Clay said.

Engel slid her hand into his jacket pocket. "This is my personal cell phone number," she said. "Call me in the morning." She stood up and walked off.

Chapter 19

As dessert was being served, Rex Bolton stepped onto a small platform about two feet high, erected in the epicenter of the four tents. All eyes went to him as he started into a spiel about the work JOHNS was doing and how it was dependent on the generous support of so many, especially those present. He then began reading off the winners of the silent auction, asking that the victors arrange payment and pickup of their prizes before the night was concluded. Clay had taken a quick gander at the items earlier, stopping when he noted that dinner at Bianchi's for two had a bid of $5,000. He was planning to spend a $100 at most the next night out with Baylee, and that was if she allowed him to pay, which she probably wouldn't.

He texted Baylee. I think I had the high bid for Bianchi's.

Yeah, right, came back her response almost immediately.

Didn't go back to check but I put a fifty spot down on it.

Yeah, well Kalinda got it for six-grand. Told her about the cheesy bread and she was sold.

Great. Now I feel like a cheapskate.

You can pay for me if it makes you feel better about yourself.

You're on. B. Engel just hired us to investigate JOHNS. Thinks Bolton and Lange might be involved.

Wow. Wouldn't doubt it. Can we talk later? I'm supposed to be keeping a wary eye out for bad guys who want to pop a pop singer.

Call me later. I'll be up.

K.

Clay took a small bite of the crème brûlée. It was crazy-good. Engel had gone off to attend to some business, so he ate hers as well. By then the silent auction was done, and people were standing up to mingle after attacking the bar. He saw no reason to be a loner and followed the masses to the watering hole. He found himself crowded into the second row waiting his turn. He looked around at the massed, unmasked crowd and shook his head, wondering if this was going to be his first super-spreader event.

"Clay Wolfe, I thought I saw you earlier. What brings you here?"

It was Chief Roberts. He was a tall, angular man, slightly stooped forward at the shoulders, with a curved nose like a hawk.

"Good evening, Chief. I'm here in a professional capacity."

"I've heard some rumors that you're sticking your nose in where it doesn't belong."

"Now, where would that be, Chief?"

"Don't joke around with me, young man." The chief stepped forward and ordered himself a gin and tonic.

"Get me a Glenlivet, light on the rocks," Clay said to his back.

The chief had made clear, since taking the job a few months back that he didn't much care for private detectives in his town. He'd been the assistant chief of police in Stamford, Connecticut, before being hired for the job. Clay wasn't sure if Port Essex was a promotion or a demotion for the man. He certainly didn't exude a love for the small coastal town, but then again, Clay doubted the man manifested much joy in any aspect of his life.

"We should talk," Chief Roberts said, turning and handing a glass of brown liquor to Clay. He strode off through the crowd. Clay considered not following, just to make a point, but was far too intrigued for that sort of juvenile response, so he followed.

Chief Roberts entered the no-man's land between two of the tents, putting his back to the flimsy rope barrier in the middle of the space.

"Thanks for the drink," Clay said.

"It was free."

"Did I do something to upset you, Chief?"

"My sources tell me that you've been poking around asking questions about the man who worked here. Chad Gagnon. The one who left town."

Left town, Clay thought? "I was hired by JOHNS to investigate an incident that occurred here. The missing man did come up in the investigation."

"My understanding is that you are no longer being retained by Johnson Laboratories. That your employment has been terminated."

Ah, so you think, Clay thought, but what you don't know is that I have been rehired by the top dog herself. Of course, the first requirement was that he wouldn't tell anybody that he was again on the case. It was very similar to the first rule of fight club, Clay thought, that rule being that there is no fight club.

"Aren't you concerned about recent events in town, Chief?" he asked instead.

"Recent events?" One rather large and bushy eyebrow rose up the man's forehead.

"Gagnon missing. Mary Jordan missing. Did you know she might've been doing a story on JOHNS?"

"I do not know that. Please enlighten me."

Clay kicked himself mentally. What proof did he really have that Jordan had been writing a story about JOHNS? Cloutier had found a notebook in the break room that had Gagnon's name and a few other clues, but was it really Jordan's notebook at all? The police had already dismissed the idea that Westy had seen a bloody duffel bag that may or may not have contained the dismembered body of the journalist.

"How do you explain Daryl Allen being found submerged and quite dead on Weston Beck's boat?" he asked instead.

"I understand that you and Weston Beck are quite friendly," the chief said. "Again, perhaps you can enlighten me. Did Mr. Beck kill the man and sink the boat to hide the evidence?"

"You know that Westy was kidnapped by Allen and two other men. That they were taking him out to sea to dispose of him when he jumped overboard and escaped."

"Do I?" The slow crawl of the caterpillar-like eyebrow up the forehead. "That is Mr. Beck's story, but it is in no way corroborated by anybody or anything else. An equally likely interpretation of events might be that your friend got into an altercation with Allen. During the scuffle, Mr. Beck was struck in the forehead with a blunt object but managed to get the best of the situation and killed Daryl Allen, then tried to hide the evidence by sinking his own boat with the body aboard."

Clay started to reply and stopped. The logic was actually quite rational, he thought. And the chief had slipped up, letting on that Westy was a prime suspect in Daryl Allen's death. This made it all the more imperative to find the goon, Clive Miller, and the mysterious Russian. They were the evidence needed to clear Westy's name. Of course, it was probably important that Westy did *not* kill them when they were found.

"I think you should finish your drink, Mr. Wolfe, and go on home," the chief said. "Rex Bolton has requested that you stay away from JOHNS."

* * *

Baylee took a deep breath. Things were winding down at the charity fundraiser event. Clay had left, with a promise of dinner the following night. For the first time all evening, Kalinda was not being surrounded by eager fans and admirers.

"How often do you perform at something like this?" Baylee asked Kalinda, the two of them sitting at a table in a corner of the tent.

"Too often," Kalinda said. "Way too often."

"I guess it comes with the job."

"Yes, it does. I really don't mind giving back, paying it forward, whatever you want to call it. I just wish people knew how tiring it was, how stressful." She covered her mouth, stifling a yawn.

Baylee wasn't jealous of the pop singer's glitzy lifestyle. Perhaps it wasn't so bad being just little ol' Baylee Baker from Port Essex, Maine, she thought. "You ever think about leaving it behind?"

"I'd like to have a baby," Kalinda said softly. "Take a break for a few years and raise him or her."

"Are you and John trying? If you don't mind my asking," Baylee said.

"Yes. I was actually pregnant last year."

Baylee didn't say anything. She figured the woman would continue the story if she cared to and sensed that she needed to tell somebody. Sometimes the best confidante is the person you've known just a week and from whom you'll most likely never hear again.

Kalinda took a deep breath, a small burbling sound that may have been a sob escaping her mouth. "The baby had Trisomy 21. Down Syndrome. We made the decision to have an abortion."

"That's terrible. I'm so sorry," Baylee said.

"It was the hardest decision of my life. Every single day, the first thought in my head is that I am a murderess."

Baylee lay her hand on Kalinda's shoulder and squeezed.

Kalinda sat quiet, small sobs escaping her. "I was fourteen weeks along."

"Have you thought about trying again?"

"Not if I might ever be faced with that decision again," Kalinda said. "I'd have to know that my baby was going to be healthy. Is that too much to ask?"

Rex Bolton approached the table, and Kalinda dabbed a napkin on her face and stood up with a dazzling smile lighting up her countenance. "That went wonderfully, Rex, don't you think?"

"You were splendid, my dear," he said. He turned to Baylee. "Do you mind if I have a moment alone with her?"

Baylee stood and stepped past him. His glare was not lost upon her as she passed. She stood about fifteen feet away, close enough to provide security, far enough to give privacy.

A figure weaved its way through the tables and chairs toward her. It was Victoria Haas. "So, if it isn't Baylee Baker of Wolfe & Baker Enterprises."

Baylee had never formally met the woman but had stalked her on social media enough to know who she was. "And you are Victoria Haas."

"It appears that we have something in common," Victoria said. A slight slurring of her words indicated that she might've been overserved. "Namely, we are both partners with one Clay Wolfe."

Baylee said nothing, glancing over at Kalinda to make sure she was okay and not paying any attention to this exchange.

"Tell me, are you sleeping with him as well, or are you just business partners?" Victoria's voice had the sharp edge of drunken belligerence.

"Clay and I are business associates," Baylee said. "Nothing more."

"But you want some of that, don't you? Trying to raise yourself up the social ladder and out of the gutter."

"I think it would be best if you got a cab home this evening, Miss Haas."

"You know why Clay will never be with you? Why he won't father your fucking child?"

"No, please, do tell me."

"It's not because you're a husband-killing sociopath—though that might have something to do with it as well." Victoria gave a half-unhinged chuckle and tipped back a glass of brown liquor, swallowing a huge belt.

Baylee looked around for somebody who might distract Victoria, but she could feel her anger growing at the same time, tempered by the fact that she was on the job, and punching this bitch in the face was sadly not part of this night's assignment.

"Do you know what Clay's bloodline is? His blood is absolutely pure, and he'd never mix it with the product of miscegenation. Would never chance producing a mongrel. No, he belongs with somebody of equally pure blood. And you know who that is? Me. So, get your goddamn talons off of my man. He's going to father my child, so you best stay away."

"What does bloodline have to do with anything?" Baylee asked.

"Bloodline is everything. Purity breeds purity."

"In your mind, what constitutes purity?"

Victoria glared at her. "I had him tested you know. Took a sperm sample from the condom after he made love to me and had it analyzed."

"You're one twisted bitch," Baylee said.

"Maybe so, but I'm going to have a child with your boss."

"I think you are afraid." Baylee said, stepping in close, Victoria's stale cigarette and liquor breath making her want to gag. "I think that you are realizing your money and your mommy and daddy don't mean anything. It, and they, can't keep you from being a shallow and vain bitch who will never end up with Clay Wolfe. And, by the way, I'm pretty sure sucking that stuff back is not what the doctor ordered if you are trying to get pregnant."

"He loves me," Victoria said a little too loudly.

Kalinda stepped up behind Baylee. "Is everything okay here?"

"We were just done talking," Baylee said.

"You never breed mutts with pure breeds," Victoria said.

"Victoria, just the woman I wanted to see." Bolton said, stepping up and taking her arm. "I wonder if I could gather a moment of your time?"

*　*　*

The exchange with Chief Roberts was echoing in Clay's mind as he pulled into his driveway. He'd decided to go to the Pelican Perch for a nightcap, instead of to his empty garage apartment. Baylee was with Kalinda. Westy and Murphy were usually lights out by 9:00. Grandpops was probably downstairs watching a ball game, but that was almost as bad as nothing, at least for the first seven innings. He personally thought that the top of the eighth was the perfect time to turn on the baseball game. Cloutier and Denise usually had date night on Fridays as there was no weekend edition of the *Port Essex Register*, giving her the night off.

At least Clay was smart enough to realize that he should park his Jeep and walk down the hill. Especially when Chief Roberts had just told him that he was keeping tabs on him. The man would probably froth at the mouth at the opportunity to see him in jail on OUI charges. Why was the chief so antagonistic? Of course, Clay knew that it was not uncommon for the police department to butt heads with private investigators who were sometimes viewed as operating on their turf. There had been a few PIs in Boston who he didn't care for back when he was a homicide detective.

He walked down the hill to Commercial Way, enjoying the summer air, noting that most of the houses were dark, their inhabitants gone to bed for the night. As he got closer to the main drag, more pedestrians and cars appeared. The Pelican Perch was just across the street, and Clay climbed the steps looking forward to another drink. He thought it best if he stuck with beer as he bellied up to the bar.

The bartender was a woman named Darcy. He'd slept with her the previous winter, just once was enough—or more than enough to prove awkward. She had a green streak in her blonde hair. Clay tried to remember if it was the same color as last time he'd seen her. After their date and romp in his room back in February, he'd avoided the downstairs bar where she worked. He wasn't sure why. She was nice, smart, pretty, and adventurous in bed. Of course, she was divorced, and living with her parents. This was the first time Clay had seen her up top at the Pelican Perch.

"Hello, Clay. What're you drinking?"

Cool. Definitely cool. "Stowaway," he said.

"How've you been?" she asked, handing him the frothy beer.

"I've been good. You?" he said.

"Okay, I guess," she said.

Darcy moved down the bar to take an order from two men who seemingly had given up the hunt for women on this night and turned to the serious business of drinking, ordering a shot each with a beer chaser. Clay thought about finishing his beer and moving on, but where would he go? The Seal Bar was filled with tourists. He was temporarily banned from Lucky Linda's. Home to an empty apartment?

"Read about you in the paper and that whole cult business," Darcy said, returning.

"Yeah, that was some crazy stuff."

"I suppose that was why you forgot to call or text me?"

"It was a pretty crazy time."

Darcy set another Stowaway in front of him. "You got things straightened out again in your life?"

Clay realized he was being given a pass for avoiding her and was now being offered another chance. "I'm still living above my Grandpops' garage," he said.

"Yeah, I'm still living with my parents," Darcy said. "But I got enough saved, and I'm starting to look for my own place."

"That's great."

"We should catch up."

"I'd like that," Clay said. He figured he owed her at least that much.

"We close in half an hour," she said. "Send the hard cores down to the Seal Bar before they start wanting to pick fights."

Clay's phone buzzed in the pocket of his Madras jacket. He pulled it out. Text from Baylee. You still up?

Yep. Give me five minutes and I'll call you.

K.

Clay dropped his phone back in his pocket but held onto the two items he'd pulled out with it. The first was a business card that simply said, Bridget Engel, CEO, Johnson Laboratories, and a phone number.

The second was folded like a letter, and then in half again. He opened it. **CHECK THE GRAVEYARD**. Typed in bold letters. Nothing else.

Chapter 20

SATURDAY, AUGUST 8TH

There was a banging on the doors that might have been the Gestapo come to take him away, Clay thought, so insistent was the pounding. He looked at his phone. It was 7:00 in the morning. On a Saturday.

The night before, he'd paid his bill and hustled out the door, calling Baylee before he'd reached the bottom of the Pelican Perch stairs. Darcy had cast him a surprised look that as quickly passed over into indifference as he promised to catch up with her sometime.

He'd shared the note in his pocket with Baylee, and they'd come to the conclusion that it had to refer to the legacy cemetery in the middle of Johnson Laboratories. But what was there to check? Clay had a sneaking suspicion, but he was not yet ready to share it. If he was wrong, he'd most surely look like an idiot.

By the time he'd reached home, they had moved on from the graveyard to talk about Kalinda and her involvement with JOHNS. It certainly seemed to be on the up and up, but why did everything keep circling back to this research facility that experimented on mice?

Bang. Bang. Bang.

"Okay, hold your horses," Clay called, pulling on a pair of shorts and a T-shirt.

Bang. Bang. Bang.

He jerked open the door to find Westy standing their crossly. "What?"

"Your door was locked." Westy brushed past him into the

apartment. "Since when do you lock your door?"

"Since I decided to keep out annoying visitors," Clay said. Truth be told, he thought, he'd started locking it the day after Westy had taken a hammer to the head. "What's the ruckus all about?"

"I think I got a hit on our guy, Clive," Westy said.

"Coffee?" Clay asked, turning the Keurig on.

Westy ignored him. "Murphy's been sharing the police sketch around over at Lucky Linda's. Guy yesterday said it looked an awful lot like his neighbor. Said that some odd fellow moved in about a year back who looked exactly like the sketch right down to the elongated neck."

"You know how many false calls the police get on the police sketches every time they post them?" Clay asked. "Let's just say that if I had a nickel for every time, I'd have a pocketful of change."

Westy leveled a stare at him. It said, 'shut the fuck up.' "This guy, Troy is his name, says that his neighbor is a real odd duck. Hardly leaves the house. Doesn't seem like he has a job. Drives a fucking Chevy Silverado. What's wrong with Ford, you know?"

"Sounds like a pathological killer to me," Clay said. "They always drive Chevvies." He took the first sip of coffee. That was better.

"Now, this is out in the country, so the houses aren't real close." Westy sat down at the small kitchen table across from Clay, who was already sitting. "Troy was out walking his dog about a month back, and he hears a woman yell, sounded like she was in pain. Now, Troy ain't a real big guy or anything, so he doesn't do anything, but it eats at him. A little bit later he calls the police, saying there is a disturbance, some sort of domestic dispute or something."

Clay's interest was piqued. "And what did the police find?"

"Nothing. When they came, the house was quiet. Nobody answered the door. They went away."

"Okay. False alarm?"

"Or, our boy Clive had finished the job on Mary Jordan, turned off the lights, and didn't answer the door."

"Seems like a stretch to me."

"I pressed him a bit on when it was, and he finally said he thought it was most likely 'bout a month ago, so, early in July. His wife works late on Tuesdays, and he gets a pizza for dinner on his way home, is how he narrowed it down."

"July 7th is the day Mary Jordan went missing."

"Bingo. Now, I know, it might be nothing." He held up his hands in supplication, and Clay knew the ask was coming. "But I was thinking Saturday morning might be a good time to stop by and check if it is the same pencil-neck fuck that hit me with a hammer."

"Sounds pretty thin, still."

"Oh, and the guy said that he thinks his name is Clive. They only talked the once, back when he moved in, but that name kind of stuck with him. Clive."

"Okay. Let me change." Clay finished his cup of coffee, slid a to-go mug under the Keurig spout, flipped a new pod in, hit the button, and went back into his bedroom.

The sky was overcast but there was no rain in the forecast. They took the Jeep. The fresh air and second cup of coffee helped wash away the last vestiges of sleep and hangover. The address Westy gave was back inland in the official town of Essex, which was not much more than a town hall, fire station, and a store with gas pumps out front.

They took a right at the store and followed the road out a few miles before banging a left, followed by a right. The houses got farther and farther apart.

"That's where Troy lives," Westy said, pointing. "Our guy lives in the next house on the right."

Clay drove slowly past the driveway. He pulled a U-turn in the road, going down in the ditch on both sides to accomplish the task. The Jeep was not real sharp on turning. He parked on the side, short of the house. "What's the play?"

"Figured we'd go knock on the door and if I recognize the fellow,

I beat the fuck out of him and then we haul him off to the police."

"I imagine that if you recognize him, he'll also recognize you, making it unlikely that he'll open the door."

"Okay, you knock on the door, I hide in the bushes, and then I push you out of the way and beat the fuck out of him."

Clay looked over at Westy and realized his friend was grinning at him.

"How about I watch the back in case he runs while you go to the front door. If he answers, I'll come around, we'll subdue him, and take him back to the PD."

"You packing?" Clay asked.

Westy nodded.

"Let's do it, then." Clay had put on pants and a sports jacket, mostly to cover his shoulder holster. Not only had he started locking his door, but he'd started carrying his Glock everywhere. He figured that Westy had his Sig Sauer and Ka-Bar blade on him. Then he remembered that Westy had lost both of those the night he'd gotten hit with a hammer.

Westy got out and crossed the road into the woods. Clay gave him five minutes to get into position and then drove up to the house, parking in front of the garage. He peeked in the small, square window. There was a Chevy Silverado parked in it. The license plate matched. He fought the urge to check his pistol. If the man was watching, that would be a terrible tell. Clay walked to the door and knocked.

The house was quiet. It was tucked back about forty yards from the road. No houses could be seen in either direction through the trees. Looked to be about a three-bedroom modular, Clay guessed. Lawn was slightly overgrown.

Clay knocked again. He called out. No answer. No sign or sound of life. He walked around back. Westy emerged from the trees.

"Nobody home?" Westy asked.

"Truck in the garage," Clay replied.

"What do you think?"

Clay pulled two sets of rubber gloves from his jacket pocket. He

kept a box in his Jeep for times such as these. Old habit. "Put these on."
He took a look at the sliding door, noting with satisfaction that it was
an outside slider, went around to his Jeep and got a screwdriver from
the back. It took him just seconds to pry the door upward, freeing the
latch, and pushing the door open.

"They teach you that at the police academy?" Westy asked.

They stepped into the kitchen/dining room, pulling their pistols
out as they did. "Hello," Clay called out.

There was no answer. Westy went to the right and Clay entered
what could best be described as a family room. It was empty. Not a
picture on the wall. Nothing. He went through the entrance to the
right, into the foyer with stairs leading up. Westy was emerging from
the other side. He shook his head once to signify nothing and then
started up the stairs. Clay stood at the bottom with his Glock pointed
upward until Westy reached the top and then followed him up.

There were four doors. All open. Bathroom. Empty. Clay went into
what was most likely the master bedroom, which showed a hint of life.
The walls were still bare, and the bed made without a crease. There
was a closet with clothes hanging and two pairs of shoes on the floor.
The dresser held more clothes. No documents. No hidden weapons.
Nothing at all incriminating. He stepped back into the hallway. The
next bedroom was an office. There was a laptop on a desk. Clay did
not have the talent to pry that particular item open. Before he could
look through the papers in the drawer, he was interrupted by an
exclamation from Westy.

Clay stepped quickly into the hallway and over to the third
bedroom. Across the way, Westy was standing in front of, but not
blocking, a locker holding a substantial stash of weapons of all kinds.

"This guy has more guns than I do," Westy said.

"Guess we should call the police," Clay said.

"Tell them that we broke into a house and found a bunch of guns?"

"There're some papers in an office across the hall. Maybe
something will turn up there."

"Didn't check the basement yet," Westy said. "We should clear that before rifling through papers."

They went back down the stairs, through the foyer, to the cellar door. Clay had put his pistol back in the holster, confident that the house was empty, as had Westy. The door had a keyed deadbolt, uncommon for the typical basement door. The door opened stiffly, and Clay realized it was heavier than a normal interior door.

"Soundproof," Westy said.

Clay pulled his pistol back out as did Westy.

There was a light switch on the left side at the top of the stairs. Clay eased his way down with his Glock held out in front of him. Westy followed a few steps behind. The right side of the basement held nothing at all. The left side was walled off with a door. Clay opened the door, noting that it was also soundproof.

He stepped through quickly, Westy filling the doorway behind him. The room was a normal basement room, cement floor, roughly finished walls, and a single light dangling from the ceiling. In the middle of the room, underneath the light, was a cast iron bed with no mattress. There were restraints in the four corners of the bed. Next to it was a table whose top was littered with tools—pliers, saws, and knives. Everything was clean and shiny, the air redolent of antiseptic.

Clay stepped to the bed and crouched down. There was a hair entwined in the ironwork. He left it alone. "Can we call the police now?" he asked.

"And say that we broke into a house and found a hidden room with a bed, wrist and ankle restraints, and a hair?"

"Something like that."

They went back upstairs. "Odd that his truck is in the garage," Westy said.

"Must have another vehicle. Can't imagine he's out for a walk."

"We gonna fake a B & E?"

"Seems to make sense."

On the way out, Westy kicked in the front door of the house. The ride back to town was quiet, both men contemplating that what they had surely stumbled across was a murder scene, and, given the evidence of extensive clean-up, what must have been a particularly grisly one. They went to Clay's office. He had several burner phones in the bottom drawer of his desk. He called the police to say that he'd just witnessed a house being broken into and gave the address. Clay added that the house was owned by Clive Miller and that he was the man who'd abducted Mary Jordan and hit a local man, Weston Beck, in the head with a hammer.

"Chief Roberts is going to know that it was one of the two of us who called," Westy said.

"Yeah, probably, but not a hundred percent. Plus, he can't prove a thing."

"Bet he hauls us both in."

"Blood don't rat," Clay said.

"Blood don't rat," Westy said.

In fifth grade one late spring day, they'd skipped school to go fishing. When it was time to go home, they became increasingly worried that one or the other would confess—Westy to his parents, or Clay to Grandpops—about what they'd done. They decided to cut their thumbs and press them together to become blood brothers and came up with an oath of allegiance. They'd repeated this mantra many times over the years, but not recently.

"I'm going to head home if we're done breaking the law," Westy said.

"You want a ride back to your truck?"

"Nah, it'll take me two minutes to walk it." Westy lumbered through the door and out the front.

Clay texted Cloutier. Can I buy you breakfast at the diner?

Had oatmeal but could eat again. When?

Ten minutes?

Sure.

Clay checked his emails, and then went out the door, locking it behind him. He dropped the burner phone into the dumpster next to his building and walked up the hill to the diner. Cloutier was pulling into the parking lot as he arrived.

"You working today?" Clay asked. She couldn't have gotten here this quickly from her home on the Point.

"Just catching up on a few things." Her eyes were red and her face puffy, perhaps from a lack of sleep.

They went in and grabbed a booth for some privacy. "How's Denise?" he asked.

"Fine." Cloutier waved at a waitress walking by and asked for coffee. "Is this truly just a social get-together?"

"Nope," Clay said. "I think we figured out the name of the man who most likely killed your reporter."

"Mary," Cloutier said. "Her name is... was Mary."

"Yes. We found a guy who got the license plate number of a man he saw going into the cottage where Westy almost bought it."

The owner, Alice herself, came and took their order. She'd been forced into waitressing because the diner couldn't find anybody willing to work in the time of Covid. Cloutier got French toast with fruit, and Clay ordered a potato and egg skillet with bacon.

"Yeah, what would Magnum do," Cloutier said, once Alice had walked off.

"What's that?" Clay asked distractedly.

"You already told me that. The guy wrote down the plate because that's what Magnum would do."

"Ah, yes, that's right. Well, Crystal got the name. Clive Miller. We were pretty much able to zero in on a Clive Miller who has a P.O. box in Brunswick. That's where we were stuck. Man doesn't seem to do credit or own anything, as far as we can tell. But Murphy found a guy who was neighbors with this odd duck of a man whose name happens to be Clive. Turns out, back on July 7th—the day Mary went missing—this guy, Troy, hears screams from the house and calls the police."

"Let me guess. The police didn't find anything out of the ordinary."

"House was quiet with nobody home and locked up tight as a drum."

"You update the police with the new information?" Cloutier asked.

"Me and Westy went out there this morning. Nobody home, but the sliding door popped right open on the back of the house like somebody was expecting us, so we went on in. There's a soundproof room down in the basement with a bed with restraints and tools for cutting. Stunk like Lysol."

"Motherfucker," Cloutier said.

"Looked like a long strand of black hair caught in the iron frame. Not likely to be Clive's. Westy said his hair was fairly short."

"She did have long, black hair, so thick, I used to envy her." She shook her head. "What'd you do?"

"Anonymous tip to the police."

"You didn't want to park down the street and wait for him to come home?"

Clay stared without seeing. Of course, that's what they should have done, he thought. The guy was probably just off to the store or the gym or something like that, and they'd ruined the opportunity. On top of that, they'd sent the police in to make sure that Clive didn't ever return to the house. "Didn't seem like he'd been staying there lately. House had an empty feel," is what he said.

"No matter now," Cloutier said. "I found another clue that Mary left behind. On her desk calendar, up in the right-hand corner in tiny letters she wrote two names, Harley Lange/Jane Doe. With a question mark."

"You think her source was pointing a finger at Harley?"

"I don't know. Maybe."

"It seems to make sense. Who better to cover up wrongdoing on the JOHNS campus than the head of security?"

"Not that we even know what crime is being committed," Cloutier said.

"I was at some fundraiser out there last night, and somebody slipped a note in my pocket. It said to check the graveyard."

"Check the graveyard?"

"Yep."

"Know what it means?"

"You ever been out to JOHNS?" Clay asked.

"No."

"The place is built around an old graveyard. Some wealthy family donated the land years back with the stipulation that the cemetery in the middle of the land be left alone. I'd imagine that'd be the graveyard that somebody is suggesting that I check."

"You think that this Clive Miller and JOHNS are related?"

"You said that Mary was doing a story on JOHNS, not that you knew what about, but nonetheless, it was something big. Then she comes up missing. Later, three men plan on killing Westy and dumping him and a duffel bag that supposedly held a dead body out to sea. The man who said this was Clive Miller. It seems there's definitely a connection between JOHNS and Clive. I'm just not sure what it is."

The food arrived along with a coffee refill.

"I guess you should check the graveyard," Cloutier said. "Will they let you now that they've removed you from the case?"

"Funny enough, last night, Bridget Engel asked me to continue my investigation. She wants me reporting only to her and doesn't want anybody to know that I'm on the case. She suspects Bolton and Lange of embezzling money and possibly selling secrets to the highest bidder."

"Lange again, huh?" Cloutier asked around a mouthful of French toast.

"His name does keep coming up."

"If you're supposed to keep your sleuthing secret, then you can't very well go waltzing in and demanding a tour of the graveyard, now, can you?"

"Yeah, well, just to make matters worse, I also ran into Chief Roberts at the same gig. We had a nice chat during which he vouchsafed that if he caught me nosing around out to JOHNS, he'd run me out of town on a rail."

"Vouchsafed, did he? And on a rail?" Cloutier asked. "Promise me you'll never become a writer."

"What's wrong with 'on a rail'? It was a thing back in olden times where a bunch of people would make you straddle a fence post and then carry you out of town. Sometimes they'd tar and feather you, just for good measure."

"Can't say that sounds very pleasant. Did he really say he was going to run you out of town on a rail?"

"No, I might be exaggerating slightly. But he didn't seem too happy with me nosing around."

"Making it difficult to go investigate a graveyard in broad daylight."

"It does sound like it might be a night journey," Clay said. "A wonderful time to be digging around in a cemetery."

Chapter 21

Clive Miller was furious. It was almost as if he could feel his blood boiling. He'd seen Clay Wolfe walk up to his door and knock. He almost shot him then and there. It was probably a good thing that he didn't. When he'd seen the private detective step around the side of the house headed for the back door, Clive had stepped into the basement stairwell with his pistol drawn.

How had the man found him, Clive wondered? He'd been about to peek out the door when he'd heard a solid thunk. He'd realized it was his sliding door being popped open, a trick he'd used once or twice himself. It was not nearly as satisfying to have your own home invaded in this fashion. It would've been so easy to step out and shoot Wolfe in the face, pop-pop, or maybe just disable him and take him down into the playroom in the basement for some prolonged fun, Clive thought, but he was glad that he hadn't acted on that impulse.

The reason he'd not stepped out and braced Wolfe was because Bolts had ordered him to leave that particular man alone. Something about his disappearance raising too many red flags and bringing too much attention to the project at hand. The same hands-off order went for Weston Beck, who Clive assumed was the second pair of footsteps he heard in the house. In retrospect, he realized that Bolts' order probably saved his life, as stepping out against two trained men was exponentially dicier than one.

It was when the two men eased up the stairs, right over his head, that Clive made his move, chancing it that there were no others with the two men. He stepped quietly out into the kitchen. The sliding door had been jacked off the slider, and he didn't waste any time stepping through the opening and disappearing into the cover of the woods behind the house, then making his way silently around the side where he could observe them leaving. Sure enough, he saw Weston's stocky form emerge from the front door, followed by Clay.

After Weston had kicked out his front door and they'd driven off, he'd gone back into the house and got his guns and cutting tools. Knowing he didn't have much time, he'd tossed these things into the back of the truck, turned on a gas burner, lit a rag doused in gasoline, and tossed it into the foyer. As Clive had been pulling onto the road, there was a hollow boom behind him, and then flames had leapt from the windows of the house.

He had to dump the truck as well. Clive knew that. It was the one thing in his name that could be traced to him. He was no dummy. The reason that the lug of a former SEAL had kicked out the door was to send the police over. The coppers would sure find it interesting to discover the house burning to the ground. Suspicions would be raised. The house had been rented under the name Clive Jones.

Did that fucking Clay Wolfe get the license plate to his truck? Or maybe that was how he found him. Either way, the truck had to go. He'd meant to change the tags out to the Clive Jones name a dozen times. He'd bought the damn thing right after they kicked his ass out of the military and before Bolts found him. Should have sold it, especially as he now had the money to get something nicer. Maybe it was because the Chevy was some sort of connection to his former self that he couldn't quite let go.

It didn't matter if the police found the truck. It belonged to Clive Miller, a man who no longer existed. The truck and an unused P.O. box in Brunswick were the last bits of who he'd once been. He also didn't want to make it easy for them. He stopped in at the Port Essex Total Value hardware store, located on Route 29 heading back into town. He bought an angle grinder. Then he went and rented a room at the Town Motel for a week. He stashed the guns and cutting tools, cleaned out the truck, wiped it down, and called Bolts.

After arranging for a pickup, he drove the truck out northeast of JOHNS along the coast to a place where he knew he could pull off out of sight just short of a drop to ocean rocks below. He took the plates off, smashed the windshield to get at the VIN number on the dashboard with the angle grinder. He then opened the hood and found the second VIN near the strut tower and ground that off. The final one was just inside the driver's side door. A four-door truck pulled up just as he was finishing. In it were two men who Bolts used for light muscle on occasion.

They helped him push the car to the edge. He had them pause while he lit a rolled-up T-shirt soaked in gasoline and stuffed it into the gas tank. Ignoring their nervous looks, Clive opened the door, threw the angle grinder into the backseat, peeled off his rubber gloves, tossed them in as well, and kicked the door shut with his foot. He nodded for them to go ahead and push the truck over the edge. It bounced and crashed the thirty feet to the rocks below, flames shooting out its windows. There was no explosion, as that only happened in movies, but the truck was flaming pretty good as they drove off.

The man whose truck they were riding in, Jeff or something, was not too happy when Clive told him he'd be keeping the vehicle, at least for the day. He started to argue, saw the look in Clive's eyes, and shut up, handing over the keys. Clive drove around, trying to think things through. Bolts had told him to not touch Wolfe or Beck, but nothing had been said about Baylee Baker. He would wait for it to get dark, and then he'd go pay her a visit. He knew where she lived.

At 5:00 he went back to his motel room and prepared for his date. He thought he'd most likely snatch her and take her to a cottage he owned in North Whitefield, which was about thirty miles away. Then, he'd be able to take his time with her. His mood would be much improved when he showed up Monday morning for work. He cackled, a sound that was in no way merry. The phone rang. It was Bolts. Clive got soundly reamed out. It didn't improve his mood in the slightest bit.

When it was dark, just about 8:00 p.m., he brought the cutting tools back out to the truck. He had his Heckler & Koch VP9 pistol in a shoulder holster and went back inside for the Barrett M82 anti-materiel rifle—so-called because it was designed to take out war materiel like armored cars rather than combatants. The thing literally blew shit up and could shoot a man through a brick wall. It was his favorite.

Clive looked in the rearview mirror as he pulled onto the road and saw bloodshot eyes staring back, eyes that were red with anger and tequila. As he drove, he worked on a breathing exercise. If he were overly angry, he'd kill the girl too quickly, stealing his pleasure. He had to calm himself so that he could draw out the foreplay. Twenty-four hours, he promised himself, one full day after reaching the cottage, he would allow himself to finish. Not one minute sooner.

He drove past the girl's house. Her car, an aging Subaru, was parked out front of the garage. Good. She was home. He'd planned this out weeks ago, so he knew right where to go to pull off the road into a small meadow, behind some trees, all but invisible in the dark. Clive left the cutting tools in the truck along with the rifle, but took a roll of duct tape along. He'd incapacitate her, bind her securely, return with the truck, and off to the cottage for a blissful weekend he'd go.

Clive crept around the house looking in the windows. There was a light on in the kitchen and in the living room, but nobody seemed to be home. Her basset hound was lying on the couch next to an orange cat with one eye. She'd have to come home to care for her pets, he reasoned, and broke a pane of glass on the back door. The dog came lumbering over and Clive considered killing the canine, but then had the delicious thought of slaughtering the floppy-eared beast in front of Baylee prior to heading off to the weekend in the cottage. The dog was woofing at him and followed him to a bedroom where he locked the stupid mutt in.

Then Clive sat down to wait for Baylee Baker to come home.

* * *

Clay knew that Baylee didn't like him dressed too much like a dandy. Actually, she called him a pretty boy when he went overboard on the duds. But it was a date. And he did want to impress her. So, he had arrived at her house around 7:00 to pick her up dressed modestly, he thought, wearing the brick-colored chinos and a blue short-sleeve shirt with a floral design and his brown Hubbard shoes. With his dark glasses and the top down on his Jeep, he hoped that he was presenting the perfect combination of well-dressed and rugged.

Baylee came to the door in a blue, off-the-shoulder, floral mini-dress that pretty much made his insides melt. He was glad of his own choice, even if his shirt was perhaps too close to matching her dress. She looked at Clay, nodded approvingly, looked at the Jeep, and went back inside the house. Clay stepped in and patted Flash until Baylee came back with a baseball cap on that said *chill* on it. It didn't match her dress. She still looked fantastic in it.

Bianchi's didn't take reservations, and there was about a forty-minute wait. Claudia, the hostess, winked at Clay, and suggested he go to the bar for a drink. She followed them back and pointed them to a two-person table in the corner. It helped to be a regular during tourist time.

Baylee ordered a blueberry lemonade and Clay got a scotch. And, of course, they immediately ordered the cheesy garlic bread.

"What are you doing later?" Clay asked.

Baylee looked coyly at him. "Why, Mr. Wolfe, are you propositioning me?"

"And what if I was?"

"I'm on my way to my grandmother's house, Mr. Wolfe."

Luckily, the drinks arrived, sparing him the pain of replying. He'd been about to say, 'but what big eyes you have', forgetting that this was Little Red Riding Hood's line and not his. He was glad he'd been spared from making a fool of himself. Baylee ordered a pesto cream linguine, and Clay chose Alfonso's Attitude, a combination of sausages and hot peppers over penne.

"I was wondering if I might bring you to a graveyard later this evening, is why I was asking," Clay said.

"Aren't you the romantic one?" Baylee said, taking a sip of her blueberry lemonade.

"You know the note I told you about on the phone last night, the mysterious message in my pocket to check the graveyard?"

"I meant to ask you who you might've gotten close enough for them to slip that in."

"It could have been anybody. It was pretty crowded."

"Not quite a super-spreader but I'd have to give it a C- on the social distancing and masking," Baylee agreed. "Who all did you converse with last night?"

"Bunch of people."

"You sat at dinner with Engel. I saw her leaning into you and whispering in your ear."

Clay looked at her to see if there was a hint of jealousy on her face, but if there was, she hid it well. "She did put her business card in my pocket."

"You think she put the note in at the same time?"

"I wondered about that, but don't you think she would've just said something? I mean, she was engaging my services to continue the investigation on the down-low. One would think that if she wanted to point me at the cemetery she would've just said so."

"Or Engel might want to build plausible deniability," Baylee said.

"That could be," Clay said. "She certainly could've easily slipped the note into my pocket."

"But, to answer your question, Mr. Wolfe, I would love to go to a graveyard tonight with you. Were you thinking after dinner?"

"Long after dinner. Westy and I were thinking after midnight would be best."

"Oh, we're going to bring that third wheel along?" Baylee smirked. "Just like you to need a chaperone to keep you out of trouble."

"I was counting on his SEAL training to keep us both of out of trouble."

The garlic bread arrived, and conversation died as they dipped into the cheesy deliciousness, scooping small portions of marinara sauce onto the bread with soft, buttery garlic cloves.

"I didn't tell you on the phone last night, but I had an interesting conversation at the fundraiser myself," Baylee said.

"Oh?" Clay caught something in her tone and paused with a piece of bread halfway to his mouth.

"Your girlfriend told me to back off, that you were hers."

"My girlfriend?"

"Victoria Haas. She said that you were sleeping together."

"Why did she tell you to back off?"

"Are you sleeping with her?"

Clay sighed. "I did have sex with her. Twice. But it's over."

"Does *she* know that?"

"Yes."

"And now she's angry, thinking that I stole you from her."

"What did she say?" Clay asked.

"She called me a mongrel. A mutt. Said that we could never *breed*—her words, not mine—because you're a pure blood and I'm mixed. How does she even know that I'm part Native American?" Baylee's face was flushed and her eyes flashing, the memory of the previous evening hot within her.

"Right? How does she know I'm a pure blood?" Clay asked. "I feel like I'm in a vampire movie."

Baylee flushed.

"What?" Clay asked.

"She had you tested."

"Tested?"

Baylee looked up from the table and met his gaze. "She took your sperm from a condom. Said you came through with flying colors, whatever that means."

Small house salads arrived, saving Clay an immediate reply. Now he felt like he was in a soap opera. Bleu cheese dressing for Clay and creamy ranch for Baylee, he noted inanely.

"I'm sorry," Clay said. "I haven't spoken with Victoria in weeks."

"She was obviously drunk," Baylee said.

"Why did she attack you?"

"She seemed to think that there's something between us. That you turned her down because of me."

"Is there something between us?" Clay asked.

"We work together."

"I don't think I know how to be in a real relationship with a woman."

Baylee laughed. "I think that's the most honest thing you've said to me since we met." She paused, took a breath. "But, hey, like I have so many positive male relationships in my history."

"What if it didn't work out?"

"I don't know."

"I don't want to lose you as a partner."

"And I don't want to lose my job."

They finished the salads in silent contemplation.

The owner and chef, Enzo Bianchi, came out from the kitchen with a bottle of wine and two glasses. "A glass of red on the house?" he asked.

Clay was not one to look a gift horse in the mouth, but this would be his only glass to go with the scotch he'd already had. It was looking to be a very promising night, and he didn't want alcohol impinging upon his time with Baylee, nor safety later at JOHNS. Enzo chatted with them for a few minutes about this and that, paying tribute to the fact that they were regulars.

When the waitress brought out their entrées, he took his leave to let them eat. "He knows you well enough to not push a white wine on you," Clay said.

"I take all my dates here," Baylee replied.

"Where does this leave us?" Clay asked.

"Do you mean, what will we do between dinner and midnight?" Baylee asked around a mouthful of pesto cream linguine.

"That seems to be the time we might get into trouble," Clay said.

"That's a long time for dessert," Baylee said. "We might have to just take small bites."

"What are you suggesting?"

"Let's take it one step at a time. Perhaps we're both ready for this."

"And if it doesn't work out?"

"We go back to being business partners and friends. I will not be another one of your bimbo exes, that's for sure."

Clay's mind was swirling with a strange mix of desire for Baylee and fear that it might not work out—the chemistry might not be there, or he would somehow fuck it up, and where would that leave them in the big picture? It was difficult to be business partners and friends with a person you'd had bad sex with, or so he surmised, never really having experienced that combination before. Back when he was with Boston PD there had been a disastrous night with a fellow officer, based mostly on her insistence on talking in what she may have thought was a sexy voice while they copulated. She was in another department, though, and he had been able to avoid seeing her after.

A strand of spaghetti with pesto cream sauce suddenly hit Clay in the forehead and stuck there, one side hanging down over his eye.

"You're not going to get lucky if you attack your food like a starving man and ignore me," Baylee said.

Clay grinned and pulled the pasta from his face and put it in his mouth. "Mm. Good," he said. "Sorry, I was lost in thought."

"Care to share?"

"Thoughts of you, of course."

"I bet. Did any of them have me dressing up as a Swedish goatherd?"

"Maybe."

"That sounds better than what I was babbling on about. Do you want to share details?"

They finished eating, talking and flirting and enjoying each other's company immensely. Once they were done, they quite hurriedly got the check, Baylee allowing Clay to pay. Baylee hooked her arm through Clay's and pressed against him as they went to leave, sending excruciatingly delicious tingles throughout his body. The front door opened before they reached it, and Kalinda and John came through the opening.

"Baylee, Clay, hello!" Kalinda was the first one to react.

"Hi," Clay and Baylee said in unison.

"Ah, of course," Baylee said. "You bought the dinner for two at the auction last night."

"Better be good," John said, a wry smile on his face.

"We don't have many chances to use it before we go back to the West Coast," Kalinda said.

"You're here all week, aren't you?" Clay asked.

"We have another engagement, um, Tuesday, and we won't be back until Thursday or Friday, and then we leave first thing Sunday morning."

"Anything you need me to check on while you're gone?" Baylee asked.

"I don't think so. Aisha will care for the dog and be at the house."

"She's not going with you?" Baylee asked.

"No."

The hostess came over to seat Kalinda and John, and they said their goodbyes. Clay was not in the mood for small talk, as he had more pressing things to do. Aisha was sitting in the driver's seat of the SUV out front, and they waved to her as they climbed into the Jeep.

Clay reached over with his right hand and laid it lightly on Baylee's thigh. She quivered slightly under his touch.

"A little strange that they're going somewhere without Aisha, don't you think?" Baylee asked in a husky voice.

"Maybe they want to be alone," Clay said, his fingers lightly stroking the inside of her leg. "Must be hard to always have somebody else at your side. They're probably going to shack up in some beautiful hotel and order room service, and spend a few days just the two of them alone."

"That could be." Baylee reached over and caressed his cheek with her hand. "I can understand that feeling."

It was three miles to Baylee's house, and Clay had no recollection of the drive or how it was possible that they didn't crash.

Somehow, they were in her driveway, and Clay got out and followed Baylee to the front door. She was fumbling with her key when he embraced her from behind. She dropped the keys and twisted around in his arms, their lips coming hungrily together. They were both breathing heavily, their hands exploring, searching, and fondling each other.

"Let me unlock the door so we can go inside." Baylee tried to pull away, although not that insistently.

Clay reached down and grabbed the keys from the ground and unlocked the door, his body still pressed against her body. He kissed her again, his lips trying to be gentle, but struggling with that ability. He turned the door handle and the door flew open under their pressure, the two of them stumbling into the living room like drunks off the street.

A man sat in the dark on the couch with a pistol aimed at them.

"What?" Baylee asked as Clay stiffened up.

"You have a visitor," he said.

"What the…?"

The man sat in the shadows, but a pistol was clearly visible in his hand. He had a narrow face with ears that protruded like hunks of cauliflower from the sides of his head and an unnaturally long neck.

"Clive Miller," Clay said.

Baylee gasped and turned around. "What're you doing in my house?"

"I'm the big bad wolf and I've come for you," Clive hissed. "Close the fucking door before you let all the bugs in."

Clay weighed his options. He could go for his Glock in his shoulder holster. He could grab Baylee and try to pull her through the door behind him. He could rush the man. The fourth option seemed to be the only one that didn't get them both immediately killed. Clay pulled the door shut and turned back toward the weasel-faced killer.

"Smart man. You get a gold star." Clive stood up, stepping to the side, keeping them under his sights. "Now, Baylee, take Clay's gun out real slow and lay it on the floor. No funny business."

Baylee turned back to Clay who gave a slight nod, indicating to go ahead, and a look that said don't pull anything funny. Clive had what looked to be a Heckler & Koch in his hand, complete with a sound suppressor. Nobody would hear a thing if he shot the both of them. The fact that he hadn't done so already meant something. What, Clay was not sure, but something.

Baylee took Clay's Glock and lay it carefully on the floor. "Where's Flash? You didn't hurt my dog, did you, you bastard?"

"The mutt with the elephant ears is fine, for now." As if to back up that statement, a howl came from the bedroom. "Why don't you both step to your right three paces?"

"Does your Russian friend know you're here?" Clay asked.

"Ha. Russian friend? That fucking stooge from the night your buddy almost bought the farm doesn't know nothing no more." Clive stepped forward, crouched down, never taking the ominous pistol off the two of them, and plucked Clay's gun from the floor.

"Have a seat," he said, waving at the couch. He tossed the Glock into the corner of the room.

"Who do you work for, then?" Clay asked, taking Baylee's arm and steering the two of them to the couch.

"Who says I work for anybody?" Clive sat down in the armchair facing them.

"Your kind always works for somebody else," Clay said. "A lackey, if you will."

Clive pressed his lips together but showed no other signs of rising to the bait. He reached into his pocket and tossed something onto Baylee's lap. "Put those on him. In the front is fine." They were a set of black zip-tie handcuffs.

"What do you want with us?" Baylee asked.

Clive raised the pistol and pointed it at Clay's head. "Your choice, Miss Baker. Put the cuffs on him, or I shoot him in the face."

Baylee put the figure eight plastic restraints over Clay's wrists.

"Tighten them."

She did.

"How did you find my house, Mr. Wolfe?" Clive asked.

"Phone book at the booth down on Commercial Way had you listed." Clay shrugged. "Under A for asshole."

Clive stood and stepped forward in one fluid motion and crashed the pistol across the side of Clay's face. "You don't seem to understand the rules," he said.

Clay spit to the side. "Hope you didn't bend your sound suppressor," he said. "Could be bad if you fire it in that state. Could blow up in your hand." Blood spooled from his nose.

Clive hesitated and looked at his gun. Clay tried to hook his foot around the man's ankle and jerk him from his feet, but Clive was too quick, stepping nimbly to the side and throwing a left-handed hook into the side of Clay's head. Baylee lunged forward but sprawled over Clay's feet and fell on the floor in front of Clive. He grabbed her by the hair and slammed her face down into the floor before hoisting her to her feet and flinging her back onto the couch next to Clay.

"We seem to have a failure to communicate," Clive said. His voice had gone from a hiss to shrill, and his eyes seemed to glow in his skull. "Now, I'd like to know how you found me."

"Passing your picture around. Guy down at the bar recognized you," Clay said. There was a slight whistling noise, and he realized it was coming from his own nose.

"Yeah? Who?"

"Don't know." Clay shook his head. "Third hand information by the time it got to me. Said your name was Clive."

"I'm going to ask you this once and once only, so make sure you get the answer correct. How do you know the name Clive Miller?"

Clay licked his lips. They tasted like iron. "Somebody got your license plate from the cottage over in East Essex."

Clive stared at the two of them as if trying to decide. "You know my name. You've seen my face." He walked around behind the couch.

Clay twisted his head around to see the man. Baylee was moaning slightly, apparently dazed from her head being smashed into the floor. Flash was now howling nonstop from the bedroom.

"Don't look at me," Clive said.

Clay looked instead at Baylee, who gave him a small wink, perhaps not as dazed as she appeared. "You can walk away from this," he said.

"I'm sorry, Mr. Wolfe, but the rules have changed. I'm sure that my employer will understand."

"I knew you were a lackey, Clive. I could see it in your eyes."

"I'm going to kill you, Mr. Wolfe. In a perfect world, I'd keep you alive so you could watch what I do with your girlfriend. Her, I'll have my fun with. Let me give you the rundown on my plans."

Clive broke into a chilling description of debauchery that made Clay wince, and he knew that he had to give it one more attempt. His life was already forfeited, but if he could damage the depraved sociopath behind him, or distract him, maybe Baylee could still escape. He could feel the barrel of the gun come to rest at the base of his skull, a firm pressure that might have been reassuring in a different circumstance.

Clay focused again on Baylee and followed her eyes down to her hand. In it, she held a nail file, one of those longer ones, perhaps three inches, with a point. Gripped by her small fingers, it almost looked like a dagger. He looked back up, her split lip trailing a bit of blood down her chin, and she mouthed the word *one*.

"You got any idea how many cuts to the human body can be made, and yet it will live on? Sure, in horrible pain and agony, but live, it will." Clive appeared to be coming to the end of his debased rendition of what he planned to do to Baylee.

Two.

"I am sorry that you'll miss all of the fun, Mr. Wolfe, but I have to say goodbye now."

Three.

Baylee drove her hand holding the nail file upward as Clay jerked his head sideways. The thin point pierced the bottom of Clive's chin, breaking when it hit the jawbone about half an inch in. Clive pulled the trigger twice, the bullets missing Clay's head by inches, instead burrowing into the floor.

Clay stood and dove over the couch with his hands extended in front of him, knocking Clive backwards and the pistol from his hands. It went clattering to the floor. Clive drove the palm of his hand into Clay's chin, who in turn, swung his manacled hands in a roundhouse that caught the man in the side of the head.

Baylee was scrambling across the floor to grab the gun. As she reached the weapon, Clive turned and ran out the back door. There was no clear shot, and Clay had no chance of catching him, his hands still fettered in front of him. Instead, he went to the corner where his Glock lay, picking the weapon up and turning to pursue.

Baylee was at the back door. "He's gone," she said. "We should call the police."

"I'm going to call Westy. Can you cut these things off me?" Clay held out his zip-tied hands. "You call the police."

Chapter 22

Westy lived just a mile or so down the road from Baylee, so the three of them were in the yard in lawn chairs when the patrol car pulled into the driveway. The two officers sat in the vehicle on the road for a few seconds, calling in what they saw so far, Clay figured from experience. They stepped out of the car with guns drawn and assured themselves that the perpetrator was not in the house or present nearby.

Clay knew one of the officers slightly. Thus, he was able to talk them out of calling an ambulance. It probably helped that they'd had a chance to stop Clay's bleeding nose and Baylee's bloodied lip, as well as cleaned up a bit outside. They hadn't touched the room, knowing it was a crime scene, but just exited the house before the police arrived.

Officer Richards, a woman who sometimes played basketball with Clay, took their statements while the other cop went about closing down the crime scene. It was attempted murder, after all, even if no killing had actually occurred. A couple cars stopped to see what was going on, the occupants getting out and approaching to get a better look until being warned to stay off the property.

When Chief Roberts pulled into the driveway, Clay groaned, knowing that they were in for a grilling. The man had made it plain the other night that he didn't like Clay snooping around. It was probable that the chief just didn't like private investigators muddying the waters of any official investigation. And these waters were muddied. It was possible that the chief truly thought that Westy was tied up in the death of Daryl Allen, thus casting a suspicious light upon Clay as well. Or maybe the chief and Bolton were poker buddies.

"Hey, Chief, two days in a row. Go figure, huh?" Clay said.

Chief Roberts ignored him for the moment and went to consult with the cop pulling yellow caution tape around the perimeter. More cars stopped on the road. Clay's phone buzzed in his pocket. It was a text from Victoria Haas. We NEED to talk. Not a good time, Clay thought.

He started to put the phone back and the phone buzzed in his hand again. This one from Cloutier. Everybody okay?

Couple bumps but fine.

When can I get the scoop?

Chief Roberts himself is here. Doubt I will see the light of day for quite some time. Tomorrow morning?

Don't talk to any other media. This, with a smiley face. Glad you're OK.

Chief Roberts came over. "You sure you don't want medical attention?"

"No, we're fine," Clay said.

"And you, Miss Baker? Are you fine, as well?" Chief Roberts asked.

"Fit as a fiddle," she said.

"Were you here for the incident?" Chief Roberts directed this question at Westy.

"No, sir. I was home," he said.

"Why don't you go there now?" the chief said.

"This was the same guy who hammered Westy in the head," Clay said.

"Is that right?" the chief asked. "How do you know that?"

"He's the same pencil-neck fucker that Westy described. Can't be two guys that odd-looking in Port Essex." Clay almost added that it was in retaliation for hunting him down at his house today and setting the police on him. Then he remembered that they'd made the call anonymously, and their presence there would just hurt them in the eyes of the chief. "Any leads on the missing journalist?" he asked instead. "Mary Jordan."

"Okay, then, let's bring all three of you down to the station for your statements," Chief Roberts said.

Westy shot Clay a look that promised a beating at some later time.

"What about my dog and cat?" Baylee asked. Flash was leashed and sitting next to her while Ollie was in a cat carrier and not looking very happy about it.

Chief Roberts pursed his lips. "Do you have something you can do with them? Your house will be off limits until at least tomorrow."

"We can drop them off with Grandpops," Clay said. And perhaps get some legal advice while we are there, he thought, but didn't say.

"I want you at the station in fifteen minutes," Chief Roberts snapped. "All three of you."

They made it to the station in twenty minutes. They brought Grandpops—Gene—with them as counsel. Luckily, he wasn't one of those older people that went to bed before dark in the summer but was, in fact, still up watching a game on television. Even with him there, it was a full three hours before they got out of the station. They were treated hostilely, as if they had perpetrated the attack, and not the other way around, with the chief sitting in on part of the statement and setting a tone that was more suspicious interrogation than sympathetic investigation.

"You staying with us, honey?" Gene asked Baylee in the parking lot.

Clay cringed at the term, but knew Baylee was okay with it. The man was in his eighties, after all. "Yes, she is," he said.

"You're going home, I take it, Weston?" Gene asked.

"Yep. A bit later." Westy's Ford F-150 was parked next to Clay's Jeep.

"Grandpops, do you mind driving the Jeep home?" Clay asked.

"What? Why? I thought the two of you were coming to my, to our, house?"

"We are," Clay said. "But we have something to do first."

"What?" Gene asked.

"Tell you tomorrow," Clay said, giving the older man a meaningful look. "Plausible deniability."

Westy parked the Ford F-150 in a small marina just down the road from Johnson Laboratories. It was 2:00 a.m. Clay and Baylee sat next to him in the front seat. In the back was a bag they'd picked up from Westy's house. In the canvas bag were three pairs of night vision goggles—leaving Clay to wonder why his friend had one pair, much less three—and an M4 assault rifle. Westy, the former SEAL, had an entire weapons locker at home, but these few items, along with the Sig Sauer P226 on his belt and a Ka-Bar blade sheathed on his ankle, seemed sufficient for a recon mission. Clay had commented in passing that Westy had replaced the pistol and knife so fast after losing them in the original altercation with Clive. Westy had just looked at him and remarked plainly that it was like walking around naked without them.

"Let me get this straight," Westy said. "We're trespassing on a classified research facility on the basis that you found a note in your pocket after a party that said, 'check the graveyard.' Is that the long and short of it?"

"Pretty much," Clay said.

"That, and the fact that Mary Jordan was doing a story about JOHNS, and her notes indicated there was an informer who she called Jane Doe, and something about an Area 38," Baylee added.

"That makes perfect sense. Everybody knows that graveyard is another name for Area 38." Westy sighed and opened his door. "What is it we're looking for?"

"A secret lab where they are doing genome testing and manipulation on human beings," Clay said.

"Genome testing and manipulation? You mean they're altering human DNA like in actual living humans? Not just mice?"

"Just a theory, but it's the logical next step. The mice are just the minor leagues."

Westy nodded. "Like they were doing with the mice. Weren't they injecting these mutations into the fetus of the pregnant momma mouse?"

"Technically, the embryo," Baylee said.

"Meaning they need pregnant women to practice, or test, on?" Westy asked. "That's effed up." He got out, as did Clay and Baylee, stepping to the back of the truck across from each other. It was quite peaceful, if a tiny bit cool, as Maine summer nights tend to be. Moonlight glinted on the calm water, the occasional clank of the moored boats' rigging and the soft slap of water against their sides the only noises.

"Just a theory," Clay said again.

"What woman is going to allow her unborn baby to be tested?" Westy asked.

"You got it backwards, pal. We think maybe these people are actually paying for the privilege. For the right amount of money, most people would do just about anything to make their babies smarter and stronger," Clay said.

"How is it, again, that these scientists are able to make mice smarter and stronger, and how could that be transposed to humans?" Westy asked.

Clay took a deep breath. "As best I understand it, they have compiled the data on millions of mice by taking blood samples, thus getting their DNA. They run this through their computer program and locate a mutation in the DNA strand of those mice determined to be stronger, and a different mutation in the ones deemed to be smarter. Then they use this thing called CRISPR—"

"That an acronym?" Westy asked.

"Yeah, but don't ask me what it stands for. I could tell you and then there would be two of us who had no idea what I just said," Clay replied.

"Three," Baylee said.

"Anyway, this process called CRISPR allows the scientists to implant this mutant DNA into the embryo of momma mouse, and *voilà*, the baby mice come out smarter and stronger," Clay said.

"Isn't mutation a bad thing?" Westy asked. "I mean, mutants are freaks, aren't they?"

Baylee pulled out her phone. "Kalinda was going on earlier about how JOHNS is trying to cure certain childhood genetic killers like sickle cell anemia and brittle bone disease by introducing mutations that 'fix' the errant genes. So, I looked it up afterward. A mutation can also be a break, or a sudden departure from, the parent type in one or more heritable characteristics, caused by a change in a gene or a chromosome."

"Meaning, in this case, a change for the better," Westy said.

"I think Wolverine is a mutant, and he isn't all bad," Clay said.

"Bad?" Baylee said. "That man is mighty fine."

"I mean that he is a mutant who possesses animal-keen senses, enhanced physical capabilities, a healing factor, and three retractable claws in each hand," Clay said. "I was *not* saying how good-looking he is or isn't."

"Well, he is," Baylee said.

Westy looked back and forth between them. "I guess it was lucky that Clay went back to your house earlier or things might have turned out different," he said.

"Yep. If I hadn't gone in with her to get my…" Clay started to say.

"Book that I borrowed," Baylee finished.

"Huh, how about that? What was the book?" Westy asked.

"We should get going, or we're going to still be there when dawn breaks," Clay said.

Westy retrieved the night vision goggles from the depths of a black duffel, handing each of them a pair, pulling his own onto his head. "You don't want to look at light with these things on. If you do, you're going to wish you hadn't."

"This thing is heavy," Baylee said, pulling the goggles onto her own head.

"Pretty soon you can opt for an eye injection instead of this outdated tech," Westy said glibly.

"An eye injection?" Clay asked, grimacing. "You're shitting me."

"Nope," Westy said. "Funny enough, the experiment has already proved successful on mice. Maybe right here, for all I know. It works for up to ten weeks, or so I read." He pulled the M4 from the bag and led the way towards the woods at the edge of the parking lot.

"I think I'm okay with the weight," Baylee said. "Better that than a needle in my eye."

"Just so you know, these things drastically narrow your field of vision," Westy said. "So it's important to turn your head left and right to see the big picture."

"Good to know," Clay said. "Wouldn't want to wander by Harley Lange or one of his security team. Especially seeing as if we get caught, we're all going to jail."

"We *have* been retained by the CEO, Bridget Engel, to investigate the facility," Baylee said. "How do you turn this thing on?" Baylee pulled the goggles down over her eyes.

Westy showed her. "Single file, follow me. My hand goes up, we all stop and shut up," he said.

"Wow, everything's green," Baylee said.

Clay's phone buzzed. It was a text from Victoria. Where are you? Why aren't you home? Your Jeep is here. I need to talk to you. He turned the phone off and put it back in his pocket. In the night silence, the buzzing had sounded like the Indianapolis 500. He certainly had a knack for attracting whack jobs, he thought, and then reversed this thought as kissing Baylee earlier filled his mind.

"Who's texting you at two in the morning?" Baylee asked.

"Nobody."

"You think Bolton is behind the whole thing?" Westy asked as they walked slowly through the woods.

"Don't know. If there is a secret lab on the premises, it would be hard to keep the chief operating officer from knowing about it," Clay said.

"That means Engel is in on it, too," Westy said.

"Not necessarily," Clay replied. "As CEO, she has little to do with the actual operation of the facility. It was Bolton who told us that she's rarely ever around, as her duties often take her around the world."

"While the cat is away, the mice will play," Westy said.

"Ha," Baylee said.

Westy stopped and held up his hand. He stood stock still for a minute and then lowered it. "Fence," he said, stepping forward. He pulled the Ka-Bar blade from his ankle sheath. The weapon doubled as a utility tool, and within a minute, he'd cut a hole large enough for them to slip through.

"Don't forget where the hole is. Right in front of this cluster of birch trees," Clay said. "In case we're in a hurry on our way back and don't have time to cut our way through."

"Or we get split up," Westy said.

"Great," Baylee said. "Now I feel like I'm in a mouse trap." When neither man reacted, she said, "C'mon, that was a good one. Stuck in a mouse trap? That's some funny, right there."

"As long as it doesn't hold true," Clay said grimly.

After another hundred yards or so, there were dim lights up to the right on the hill, and soon after, lights down on the left. Clay had mapped out the JOHNS setup earlier to share with Westy how the facility was a series of buildings clustered around a U-shaped road that curved around the sprawling cemetery at its center. They were approaching from the open end of the U, so as to not cross any roads or pass by any buildings.

They continued in silence. Harley Lange had shared with Clay and Baylee that the security details checked the buildings every couple of hours, walking the road. It was highly unlikely the interlopers would cross paths with any of them given the direction they were coming from.

Westy raised his hand again, and they came to a stop. He stepped aside and gestured for them to come even with him. A small clearing was in front of them, and upon closer inspection, Clay saw that among the grass were seemingly randomly placed grave markers of all shapes and sizes. It appeared to be meticulously taken care of, as far as could be seen wearing night vision goggles. As if on cue, the moon, about three-quarters full, broke through the clouds of the night sky.

Clay pushed his goggles up on his forehead. It was a relief to escape the blinding green, and he realized how narrow his view had been. Westy and Baylee followed suit.

"What now?" Baylee asked.

"Looks like a graveyard to me," Westy said.

"How about the shed?" Clay asked. He pointed at the structure on the far side of the small plot of graves.

"I'll cover you if you want to walk through the middle of the cemetery," Westy said. "Maybe you'll spot something amiss."

Clay went to the right and Baylee went to the left while Westy covered them with the M4. They crossed over the fifty or so yards without incident. Baylee went to the front of the shack. It was not really a shack, Clay thought, surveying the structure, which was actually a small building made of concrete block. He walked carefully around it, figuring it to be about fifteen feet long by ten feet wide. There were no windows. There was a wide door that could be raised straight up just like a garage door, probably to get the large grounds-keeping mowers in and out.

"That thing is reinforced steel," Westy said, having skirted the edge of the clearing in the protection of the trees before coming to join them. "No way we're getting it open."

"Not like they can hide much in there," Clay said. "Which kind of begs the question—why the reinforced steel?"

"Those big mowers cost a fortune!" Baylee said. "Maybe you can get Engel to let you in Monday morning to have a look-see. She does seem to like you."

Up on the hill they heard a motor kick to life. Clay figured it was a four-wheeler. Probably security going on their rounds, he guessed. It started down the hill toward them.

"Time to scram," Westy said.

They skirted back around the cemetery. There seemed to be nothing out of order. From the far end they watched as a four-wheeler pull up to the concrete shed, the driver alighting and tugging on the door. He seemed satisfied that it was locked tight, climbed back aboard, and drove on down the hill.

They traversed their way back to the truck without incident and headed home. The first light of the new day was just tinging the edge of the sky. It'd been a long night, but there was an underlying sexual tension racing in Clay's blood. Should he invite Baylee up to his place above the garage to finish what had been started some seven hours ago, he wondered? Or was the moment gone? Baylee sagged against his body in the front of the truck, her fatigue obvious, but there was a comfort there that was undeniable.

"Am I dropping you both off at your place?" Westy asked.

"Yes," Clay said. "Baylee's house is a crime scene until at least tomorrow—I mean, sometime today."

To himself, Clay wondered if she would be in the big house with Gene, or in the apartment above the garage with him.

Baylee leaned her head on his shoulder. "Thanks," she murmured into his ear, nestling in comfortably.

Clay pulled his phone out to check the time. He had to turn it back on. There were five text messages from Victoria. He stole a glance at Baylee. Her eyes were closed. Carefully, Clay clicked on Victoria's name and the string of messages popped up in bubbles next to VH.

I really need to talk with you.

Why are you avoiding me?

Where are you? I stopped by.

You're being an ass.

I am pregnant.

Chapter 23

SUNDAY, AUGUST 9TH

Clay showed Baylee to the guest room in Grandpop's house.

"Are you joining me?" she asked.

"I don't think it's the right time," he said.

"Sort of a bad sign, wasn't it?"

"Maybe a warning that we're rushing things."

Baylee nodded, turned her back, and pulled the door closed.

Clay stood there for a long moment and then went to his childhood room where he texted Victoria back. I will come by your house at ten.

Clay woke up with a start. Light was streaming in his eyes. Where was he? And then the events of the day and night before came thundering back into his mind. Paying a visit to Clive Miller's house and torture chamber. Dinner with Baylee. The kiss. The current. Clive Miller waiting for them. Seconds from death. Baylee saving him. Going to JOHNS and searching the graveyard. Nothing. Victoria pregnant.

Clay figured that she was telling him this because he was the father. That thought had been enough for his battered body and exhausted mind to direct Baylee upstairs into the guest room. He thought about sitting guard down on the couch, but his brain pleaded for a mattress, and he sacked out in his childhood room. Right next door to Baylee. He looked at his phone. It was just past 9:00 in the morning. Sunday.

What had woken him? Was it just the sun? He reached under the pillow and his hand found the Glock. Clay swung his legs to the floor and stood up. His face ached but his fatigued body seemed to have recuperated somewhat after four hours of sleep. The door to Baylee's room was cracked, and he eased it open far enough to peek inside. She was fast asleep on her side, facing him, her hair spread across her dark features, a tiny snore sliding from her mouth, the whole scene as peaceful as a Christmas card.

He thought about what it would be like to crawl in behind her and drape his arm over, his hand cupping her stomach, and holding her tight. He took a moment to cherish this fantasy of fiction over reality, before stepping back and making his way quietly down the stairs. Grandpops was sitting on the front porch reading the *Maine Sunday Telegram* and drinking a cup of coffee. Clay went to the kitchen and got a cup and joined him outside.

"Morning, Grandpops," he said, settling into a rocking chair.

"Your face is bruised up a bit," Gene said. "Is that why Baylee chose to sleep in a separate room?"

"Anything of interest in the paper?" Clay asked, changing the subject.

"House burned down yesterday morning over in Essex. Five towns had to come in to contain the blaze."

"Out on Woodside Road?" Clay asked. "117 Woodside?"

"Said Woodside, sure enough. Don't think it said what number." Gene looked expectantly at Clay.

"Westy had a lead yesterday morning on the guy who beaned me. We went out, nobody was home, went inside and found a bunch of guns upstairs and what looked to be a torture chamber down in the basement. We called in an anonymous tip and left."

"House burns down and erases any possible evidence. He pays a visit to Baylee to get you to back off, but then you show up with her, and his plans change," Gene said.

"I don't think he was sending a message. Remember his sick ass descriptions of what he planned to do to Baylee? His anger got the better of him, and she was going to pay for what I did."

"What's going on between you and Baylee?" Gene asked. "Not that it's any of my business."

Clay thought of Victoria. "Nothing," he said. "Nothing at all."

Gene nodded. It wasn't a very convincing nod. "Sure," he said.

Clay stood up. "You got that pea shooter of yours around? Might be a good idea to throw it in your pocket. I need to shower and run out and take care of something. Should be back by noon."

Mekhi answered the door and ushered Clay through the house to the pool. There was no offer of bathing trunks nor fine, aged brown liquor. This is what kids do to you, Clay thought wryly. Victoria was sitting at the table where they'd last shared drinks before her belittling attack. Today she had a Poland Spring water and a glass. She was not her normal oh-so-put-together self, her hair unbrushed, and hands clutching a red silk robe with flowers. Her eyes matched the robe.

"Hi," Clay said, sitting down.

Victoria nodded. "You haven't been returning my messages."

"I've been busy."

"Where were you last night? I stopped by your place about 2:00 a.m. No Clay Wolfe."

Clay pondered this further step into her irrationality after the increasingly sharp and paranoid texts and her behavior towards Baylee. So what should he tell her? The truth was complicated. An easy lie seemed wrong. He chose flippant. "I had a rodent problem."

"You are a fucking rat is what you are."

"Why are you angry?" Clay snapped back. "This is what you wanted, isn't it? To have a baby and have me walk away."

"I love you."

Clay stared at her. This was crazy, he thought, wondering if he was in the movie *Fatal Attraction* and Victoria was playing Glenn Close. "You told me you wanted nothing to do with me after you got pregnant."

"You can fuck me but not marry me?"

"Victoria, what the hell is going on with you? One moment you're lovey-dovey, then you're stalking me, and the next you're batshit crazy," he said, standing up. "I think it best if we talk about this another time."

"I'm sorry," Victoria said. "I'm sorry, sorry, sorry. I don't know what's come over me. Probably these hormone pills I've been taking. Please, sit down. Our baby is going to be so perfect. You'll see. Our genes will make a perfect match. You won't be able to stay away."

Stay away from the child or from her, Clay wondered? "How do you know the… quality of my genes?" he asked.

"Who said anything about that?"

"Baylee said you two had a run-in the other night at the fundraiser."

"I wasn't myself, I'm sorry."

He sat back down. "She said you were drunk. And now I find out you're pregnant?"

"These pills are messing me all up, Clay. That's why I need you."

"Are you certain?"

Victoria cackled. "Certain of what? That I need you? Or that I'm pregnant and you're the father?"

"All of the above, I guess."

"I *am* most definitely pregnant. I visited the doctor. You're the only man I've slept with… recently. That makes two yesses."

"We had sex only a month ago. Isn't that quick?"

"You think it takes that long for the sperm to swim upstream?"

"I mean, to know you're pregnant?" Clay found his face flushing.

"Thirty-two days. I had an annual check-up last Friday. Said I was feeling a bit queasy. Bingo. Looks like you have strong swimmers." Victoria laughed without mirth.

Clay thought back to the day. Swimming in the pool. Drinks. Following her to the bedroom. *Like Russian roulette*, Victoria said. *What are the chances? Let's just try it out.* He'd given in, prey to his baser desires, his rational thought swept by the wayside.

"How do you know our baby is going to be perfect?"

Victoria's bottom lip quivered. "Promise you won't be mad?"

Clay held her gaze without replying.

"I had your DNA tested."

"What? How?"

"I, uh, took the condom from our first night together and had the... semen analyzed."

He suddenly felt ill, like he was in the presence of something grotesque and ugly. He took a deep breath. "That is just fucking sick. It's so... invasive, not to mention paranoid, inappropriate, and just plain gross. What is wrong with you?"

"Look around you, Clay." Victoria's eyes blazed again. "Children being born with disease, physical handicaps, mental retardation... do you want our kid to be messed up from day one, or worse yet, just average? I had to be sure. I *have* to be sure. I will do whatever it takes to make sure that my child is superior in every way."

All of a sudden, another thought came screaming through his head. If JOHNS was doing human testing to create super babies, wouldn't Victoria Haas be at the front of that line? Her whole concept of having a child seemed a bit like an experiment.

Clay shook his head. It was too much information. Too hard. Too fast. "You're certain that you're pregnant?"

"Yes. One-hundred percent."

"And I'm the father?"

"Yes."

How does one ask, Clay wondered, if the mother of their child was planning on having a micro-injection into her newly-formed embryo in order to make this egg, once matured and out of the womb, into a stronger and smarter human being?

"Are you taking vitamins?" he asked.

"Our baby will be fine," she said. "Better than fine."

Victoria's phone buzzed, and she looked at it, typed something, and set it down.

"I could sure use a drink," Clay said.

"Me, too," Victoria said. She measured him with her eyes. "I'll get you a double. You can drink for both of us." She got up and walked toward the house.

Clay picked up her phone, which had not timed out yet, and hit the email icon. He wasn't sure what he was looking for. Perhaps something from JOHNS or Bolton or Lange. There didn't seem to be anything out of the ordinary. He exited and clicked on the text messages. How much time did he have? It didn't take long to put two cubes in a glass and pour liquor into it. Maybe she would have to use the bathroom, he thought, especially being pregnant and all, or did that not come until later?

Clay's name was second on the list of recent text messages. There were others, none that rang any bells, though.

And then there it was. RB. Somehow, he knew that RB was Rex Bolton. Clay clicked on the text trail. There was only one message to which Victoria had replied okay. Harley will pick you up Tuesday at 2 a.m.

The door opened, and Victoria came back out with his drink. Clay slid the phone casually onto the table face down, blocking his actions from view with his body.

"Thank you," he said, taking the glass. He didn't actually want a drink but thought it less suspicious if he drank it after having asked for it. "You would never—"

"I've reconsidered our being together," she interrupted him. "I think we should continue to see each other. Who knows? Maybe we'll find it in ourselves to commit to a relationship."

"Seeing each other?"

Victoria ran her fingers up his inner thigh. "Starting with right now," she said. "There are poorer reasons for people to be together than great sex."

Clay put his hand over hers. "I believe I need some time to process," he said.

She pushed her hand further. "I understand. How about we test the waters and see if last time was just a fluke. That might help you process."

Clay stood up, setting down the mostly-full glass. His head was spinning, and not from the scotch. Jesus, first woebegone pregnant mother, then accusatory harpy, and now sultry seductress, all in the span of fifteen minutes. What could be next, he wondered? "I need a few days to sort some things out and roll this all through my mind."

"It's that bitch, Baylee Baker, isn't it?" Victoria settled back in her seat with the look of a woman who was not used to being refused. "Thursday. Noon. I expect your answer. In person."

*   *   *

Clay wasn't sure how he got back to Grandpops' house, other than he must've driven himself, because the next thing he knew, he was pulling into the driveway. He was going to be a father. The thought filled his mind to the point that he was unable to explore it further, what that might entail or mean for the rest of his life and everyone in it, or even what it was that he wanted. Westy's truck and Crystal's car were parked in front of him. He got out of the Jeep, and another thought came bustling into his head, tamping down the fact that he was going to be a father. How was he going to tell Baylee?

The living room had been turned into a war room. Crystal and Cloutier were both clacking intently away on laptops as they sat side-by-side on one sofa. Baylee was filling Murphy in on the gist of what had happened the day before on the second sofa, indicating that he'd just arrived. Westy was in one of the Wydmire armchairs talking on his phone while Grandpops was in the other looking at a map.

"What's going on?" Clay asked.

"Where you been?" Baylee asked, pausing in her recounting of their graveyard visit.

Where indeed, Clay thought? "Gathering information."

"I made a few calls," Baylee said. "Thought we could use some help."

Westy put his phone down. "And what do you bring us, oh, fearless leader?"

"What do we think is happening out to JOHNS?" Clay asked.

"Somebody's stealing fucking mice," Crystal said.

"But no mice have actually been stolen," Cloutier said.

"I had a thought on that," Baylee said. "Let's start with the basics. We get hired because somebody tried to steal a SHAIM, or a SuperHuman Above Intelligence Mouse." Baylee stood up and began to pace as she talked. "But they failed. That links together with Daryl Allen transporting a Russian dude from what may be a Russian spy ship. One would think that the two are related. That Clive Miller, who is later spotted with this Russian, is orchestrating a sale to the Russians. But Clive is not the conductor of this orchestra. He is a lackey who works for somebody else."

"Rex Bolton?" Cloutier said. "I'm not buying it. Bolton must have access to steal a mouse. Couldn't he waltz in after hours, put a mouse in his pocket, and then walk back out?"

"I'm sure there must be cameras," Gene said.

"Everywhere but the bathroom," Clay said.

"Did you look at the cameras?" Gene asked.

"No. Harley Lange said that there was nothing incriminating on them," Clay said slowly.

"If Bolton and Harley were working together, one would think they could smuggle a... what do you call it? Super mouse out," Westy said.

"SHAIM," Baylee said. "And who is to say they didn't?"

"What are you suggestimh?" Cloutier asked.

"That Bolton and Harley have conspired together to steal a SHAIM and sell it to the Russians." Baylee stopped by the hallway to the kitchen and faced the group as a whole. "It wouldn't be hard for them to do. As we just said, either of them could walk in there anytime they wanted and back out with a mouse. All Harley has to do is turn off the camera or erase the footage or something like that. What's the problem with that?" she asked.

"A mouse is missing," Clay had an idea where Baylee might be going with this.

"Exactly," Baylee said. "The dead mouse in the bathroom wasn't being snuck out, it was being smuggled in. It was to replace the SHAIM they'd already stolen."

"They couldn't just put a regular ol' mouse in with a bunch of super mice," Westy said. "The scientists were bound to catch on. So, they brought a dead mouse in. Hard to tell if the little guy is smart or strong when he's already dead."

"Why'd they leave it in the bathroom and make it look like it was an attempt to steal it?" Murphy asked. He had a drink glass in his hand.

"I'm betting there's a whole bunch of protocols if a healthy SHAIM is suddenly found dead in its home in the lab. Tests and whatnot," Baylee said.

"An autopsy," Westy said.

"Which would show that this particular mouse wasn't genetically superior," Cloutier said.

"But, if it's found suffocated in a box in the bathroom, there'd be no need to do an autopsy, if that is the right term when talking about a mouse," Baylee said. "Cause of death would be obvious."

"Son of a bitch," Crystal said.

"Under your theory, they already stole a SHAIM," Clay said. "We were hired to putz around like they were concerned. Once the spotlight dimmed, Bolton dismissed us from the case."

"Not much can be done about it now," Cloutier said.

"We can't even prove somebody stole a mouse now, much less that it was Bolton and Harley," Westy said. "Because there is no record of one missing."

"Unless you get them to exhume the body and do tests to prove it wasn't a super mouse," Cloutier said.

"Ha," Westy said. "That's pretty funny. We're talking about a mouse, here. I doubt they buried it. Probably cremated its remains, it being a clean research lab and all."

"Unless they plan to do it again, once the heat subsides," Baylee said. "Then we could catch them in the act."

"What would they need another mouse for?" Westy asked.

"Or something else," Clay said.

"Something else?" Gene asked.

"Why would a SHAIM be all that valuable to the Russians?" Clay asked. "I mean, one would think that the technology for mouse experimentation is readily accessible at some level."

"Unless it can be proven that micro-injections of DNA mutations, or genome editing, can be transferable to human beings," Baylee said.

"What the fuck are you talking about?" Crystal asked.

"We've been thinking that they might be creating super babies in a hidden lab called Area 38," Baylee said. "That's what we were looking for last night in the cemetery. Clay got a cryptic message about checking the graveyard, and we thought it might be referring to the one out to JOHNS."

"Find anything?"

"Nope."

"You're suggesting they're doing human experimentation on unborn babies?" Cloutier asked. "Who in the hell would sign up for that?"

"I might have an idea," Clay said.

"You going to share?" Westy asked. "Or is this like the cryptic note you found in your pocket?"

"Maybe the whole operation is past the experimentation stage," Clay said slowly. "What if they already have the ability to create babies that are smarter and stronger than normal?"

"Is that even legal?" Cloutier asked.

"The legality of human genome editing is a gray area, or perhaps even murkier than that," Gene said. "But it's highly unethical at this time, and banned by the FDA here in the U.S."

"Thus, a secret lab, called Area 38," Baylee said.

"How the fuck do they find customers for that sort of thing?" Crystal asked.

"They market to a niche of very wealthy people," Clay said. "People who can afford the high cost of having superior children."

"Sort of like that college scandal where kids were having their SATs taken for them and getting in based on sports they never even played," Crystal said. "What the fuck's that actress's name? Lori Loughlin? She paid $500,000 in bribes so her spoiled kids could go to USC. That is seriously fucked up."

"You got enough money, half a million isn't a whole lot of dough to give your kid a leg up on the competition," Clay said. "Imagine what it'd be worth to implant superior genes into them? Stronger and smarter than everybody else? How much would that be worth?"

"We should turn this over to the FDA," Gene said. "Let them figure it out."

"Turn *what* over?" Clay asked.

"You got a better idea?" Westy asked.

"We find this Area 38, and catch Bolton and Harley red-handed, and *then* we turn it over to the FDA," Clay said.

"Oh, easy as fucking pie," Crystal said.

"You have a thought, don't you?" Baylee asked.

"I do." Clay went and stood at one of the two windows looking out over downtown Port Essex and the harbor beyond. "A little over a month ago I was approached by Victoria Haas with a proposition to father her child."

"To father her child?" Gene asked.

"She offered me money to impregnate her. I turned down the money." Clay clasped his hands firmly behind his back.

"But not the impregnating?" Baylee asked. "Tell me you are fucking kidding me?"

"I had no intention of… I told her I was not interested in having a child under those circumstances," Clay said, turning back to face the group.

"What circumstances?" Gene asked.

"A business arrangement with a woman I barely knew," Clay said.

"So, you used a condom the first time. But there was a second time, wasn't there?" Baylee said. "And I bet your knight left his shining armor at home."

Clay bit his lip on a reply that he knew would sound pathetic and empty. He most certainly did not have the moral high ground here. "I may have used poor judgment. I *did* use poor judgment."

"The night Westy got hammered," Baylee said, her eyes widening. "That's the second time you fucked her."

Clay nodded. Baylee took two steps forward and punched him in the face, knocking him backward into the window. "You suck," she said, and stormed out of the room.

Clay went to follow her, but Cloutier held up her hand, following Baylee out of the room herself.

Chapter 24

MONDAY, AUGUST 10TH

Baylee was sitting on her rope-swing bench overlooking Essex Harbor with a cup of coffee in hand and her foot rubbing Flash's belly. There was a path from the back of her house to this spot, an oasis of beauty that was her happy place. She'd been there since sunrise, unable to sleep, thoughts of Clive Miller's attack and Clay Wolfe's deceit filling her mind in a chaotic jumble of fear, anger, and betrayal. The anger was obvious at what had been done to her by these two men, as was the fear of what Clive was yet capable of, but what particular fear was associated with Clay, she wondered?

Her ruminations through the sleepless night and early morning had determined that what she feared most in life was losing him. Just two days earlier things had been going so well, and she'd opened up to taking their relationship to a new level, a further dangerous intimacy, already so much more than just the physical act of sex, which hadn't happened anyway, thank God. And yet she had opened herself up to allowing him into her inner being, a vault long locked. And she'd cracked the door only to find he'd already betrayed her and had his back turned, ready to leave.

At least, she thought, he'd been honest. And to be fair, she'd already come to the conclusion that Victoria and Clay had shared more than drinks that evening when Westy had gone missing. It was everything since that somehow made it different, like Victoria confronting her at the party, the bizarre insinuations about her.

"So what are we going to do, Flash?" she asked the basset hound.

Just keep rubbing my belly, Flash answered with his eyes.

Baylee heard footsteps behind her. She imagined it could be Clive Miller come to kill her, but was certain it was Clay Wolfe come to apologize. She didn't know what her response would be to either scenario.

"Morning," Clay said, stepping into her view. "I brought you a breakfast sandwich from the diner."

She stared at him but allowed her hand to take the offering.

"I'm sorry, Baylee," he said. "I don't know what I was thinking. I'm an ass."

She opened up the egg, sausage, and biscuit, taking a tiny bite to see if it would be sandpaper going down. It was surprisingly good. She wasn't sure of when she'd eaten last. Perhaps her dinner at Bianchi's with Clay?

"Can I sit?" he asked.

She nodded at the spot next to her on the swing.

He sat, and they stared across the water at Port Essex for several minutes.

"We had sex twice," Clay said. "The first time, after I left, she took a sample of my semen and had it analyzed."

"The second time?"

"I was stupid."

"And me?"

"I have no interest in a relationship with Victoria Haas. I've made that clear to her."

"She is going to be the mother of your child."

Clay nodded. "Yes."

"I've been thinking," Baylee said, "about what we said at Bianchi's. When we decided to test the waters of intimacy. We said if it didn't work, we'd scale it back, no questions asked, no regrets."

Clay nodded. His eyes glistened.

"Well, it didn't work. No regrets. We will continue to work together, be partners in a business sense, and hopefully friends."

"Okay."

"What's the plan for tonight?"

*　*　*

"Got an interesting hit for you, boss," Crystal said. It was noon, and the gang had reassembled at Gene's house to talk strategy for that night.

Clay had been trying desperately to let his mind accept the fact that he was going to be a father, and to begin to deal with the practical implications. He'd be the father of a child whose mother he didn't love. While across the room was the woman he *did* love. Plus, that sad, sick Victoria was planning on making this tiny embryo superior, no matter the risk.

"Yeah," he said. "What's that?"

"I friended Rex Bolton on Facebook. This gave me access to his friends."

"Bolton accepted your friend request?" Clay was still only half paying attention.

"Fuck no, he accepted a friend request from Mila Pappan, a young PhD candidate in Biomedical Sciences who happens to have perfect skin and huge knockers," Crystal said.

The room laughed as Clay asked, "Who are you?"

"I'm not just a pretty face," Crystal said. "Anyway, one of his friends is named Lada Kotova."

"A Russian," Westy said.

"Turns out Miss Lada Kotova was born in Perm, Russia, which also happens to be where Rex Bolton spent a large chunk of time the year he was kicked out of MIT." Crystal looked around the circle of faces, all now paying rapt attention. "Kotova now lives in Moscow and works for Misha Communications."

"Interesting," Clay said. "But it's not crazy to think that Bolton would keep up with an old friend, even if she happens to be in Russia."

"That's true," Crystal said. "But would you find it more useful if you knew that Misha Communications is widely believed to be a front for the FSB?"

"Who is the FSB?" Cloutier asked.

"The new KGB," Westy said. "Modernized, efficient, and ruthless. The right hand of Putin."

"It might be time to include the authorities," Gene said.

"Who?" Clay asked. "I don't even know who to go to. The FDA monitors genome editing. Do they even have 'people'?"

"I'll look into it," Cloutier said. "If not the FDA, I'm sure the CIA would be interested in this potential threat to national security."

"A bit of a stretch to think that we have a national security issue just because Bolton knew a woman years ago who *might* be involved with the FSB," Clay said. "But worth looking into I guess."

"Okay, boss. I'll keep digging," Crystal said.

"Whatever happened to that brother and sister who owned the cottage Clive Miller stayed at?" Westy asked.

"Big fat zero," Crystal said.

"Remember," Baylee said, "the grandson, who lives down in Portland, did give a key to Daryl Allen, sadly now very dead, to check on the house. So, dead end there."

"What's the plan tonight?" Gene asked.

"I was thinking we'd stake out Victoria's house, and when Harley came to get her, we'd follow them to Area 38," Clay said.

"That seems simple enough," Cloutier said.

"What do you think about putting a tracking device on her?" Westy asked.

"I suppose you have one?" Clay asked.

"Yep. Just got to figure out how to get it on her."

"How big is it?" Cloutier asked.

"Size of a pencil eraser," Westy said.

Cloutier pulled the gold bracelet from her wrist. It was hollowed out, the two ends going into one another to attach to her wrist. "Would it fit in here?" she asked.

Westy looked. "Sure."

"How do we get her to wear it?" Clay asked.

An hour later, Clay found himself knocking on the door of Victoria's house. He'd gone with Westy to his house, inserted the tracking device into the hollow bracelet, and now stood on the doorstep of the mother of his future child feeling as nervous as if he was about to propose.

* * *

Westy had just packed his wife and son into the car to go visit her sister for their safety. She was pretty pissed off about it. Again. But he had a good sixth sense when it came down to the shit hitting the fan, and his Spidey sense was tingling all over. He was perusing his weapons locker for the evening's festivities when the knock came at the door.

He stuffed the Sig Sauer into the back of his waistband and stepped to the living room window, looking out at an angle to see the doorstep, but not be seen. It was the police. His first thought was that something had happened to Faith and Joe, but they'd just left, so it had to be something else. There was no way the police would show up that quickly.

Had something happened to Clay or Baylee, Westy wondered? Perhaps Clive Miller had come back to finish the job. If that were the case, there wasn't a crevice in the entire world that that man could slither into to escape the vengeance of Westy. As it was, Westy was guessing that the man had messed up Clay and Baylee finally hooking up the other night. That was reason enough to beat Clive Miller to a pulp.

Clay going into Baylee's house after a dinner date could have been totally innocuous, something as simple as he'd left a book there, but Westy would bet good money he'd planned on grabbing more than that. The way they had both carefully danced around the fortuitous—and deeply suspicious—circumstances of Clay entering the house with Baylee, which most certainly saved her from pain and possible death. And Baylee's reaction in punching Clay when she realized he'd fathered a child with Victoria Haas was further proof.

Westy had few real friends, and he didn't really fit into the fishing community. He liked to read books and watch classic movies. Clay Wolfe was his friend. And Baylee Baker was good for Clay. Westy had never had a friend who was a woman until the past few years when he'd gotten to know Baylee, and Cloutier as well. When he opened his front door, the last thing he expected to hear was that the policemen were there for him.

"Weston Beck?" the officer at the door asked. His partner stood about ten steps back with his hand hovering over the pistol at his hip.

"Yes. What seems to be the problem?"

"We have a warrant for your arrest," the officer said.

"What?"

"For the murder of Daryl Allen."

"That's crazy."

"You have the right to remain silent. You have…"

As the officer droned away through the Miranda Rights, Westy's mind buzzed. The killing of Daryl Allen? Clay had mentioned that the chief had suggested he was a suspect. Wouldn't they bring him in for questioning first if they really believed he'd done it? What evidence had they obtained that convinced a judge to issue a warrant for his arrest?"

"…one will be provided for you."

"I have a pistol in my back waistband," Westy said firm and clear.

*   *   *

Murphy thought it best to curtail his normal consumption of alcohol to the barest minimum, not too much to impair his judgment, but just enough to stay alive and keep the shakes at bay. He also thought it wise to take a nap if he planned on being up all night. His normal day consisted of fishing at dawn, the bar by 9:00 in the morning, and home before 6:00 for dinner, usually something simple he heated up. He rarely drank at home, so that by the time he went to bed at 9:00 p.m., he'd largely sobered up.

So it was that Joe Murphy found himself lying in bed staring at the ceiling just after noontime trying to sleep. He couldn't remember the last time he'd taken a nap. Maybe never. It was not in his DNA. Especially not without the normal level of consumed alcohol in his system, that was for sure. It was almost a relief when the front door was smashed open. At least it beat trying to take a nap.

"ICE." A voice rang out. "Get on the floor."

Murphy alit from bed with an agility not bad for an old drunk, or so he told himself. What could ICE want with him, he wondered? But deep down he knew. Some fifty years ago, he'd fled his native Ireland. He'd been caught up in the whole IRA movement, fighting the good fight, trying to end British rule, but his revolutionary fervor ended because of one mission that concluded with the wrong people dead. Innocent people. Not by his own hand, but it may as well have been.

Three days after an explosion that killed innocent people, Joe Murphy had found himself on a steamer headed to Iceland, and from there he found passage to Halifax, and then finally, Portland, Maine. He had no official papers, but he was white and spoke English, even if with a lingering brogue. He thought it best to leave the city behind and ease into a small town that reminded him somewhat of the village he grew up in. Port Essex had become his home.

Murphy became a clammer, at first dealing in cash only, and then over time establishing a bank account, an address, identification, and had for all intents and purposes, became a U.S. resident. But his entire existence was built on that first lie, for he was not technically a citizen. Why would immigration officials suddenly care, he thought, as a man in a fluorescent yellow vest over body armor burst into his room and threw him to the floor on his face.

*   *   *

The gathering was smaller that evening. Clay, Baylee, Crystal, Cloutier, and Gene made small talk while waiting for Westy and Murphy to arrive.

"How'd your proposal go?" Baylee asked drily.

"I simply pledged to be a father to the child and gave her the bracelet as my commitment to that end," Clay said. "Don't know if she'll wear it or not."

"Shouldn't need it. I don't think we'll lose her, after all."

"It wasn't a proposal," Clay said.

That seemed to silence conversation.

"Where's Weston and Joe Murphy?" Gene asked after a bit.

"Don't know," Clay said. "Neither one is answering their phone."

"Anything you want me to look into in the meantime?" Cloutier asked.

"Did you ever take a look-see at those companies that Engel sits on the board of?" Clay directed the question at Crystal.

"Not at the top of my fucking list," Crystal said.

"You wanna give me the names?" Cloutier asked.

"Another thing," Clay said, grabbing a piece of paper and a pen. "Engel has a tattoo on her shoulder. Two jagged lines." He drew the parallel lines on the paper. "Check and see if this means anything."

After an hour, Clay and Baylee took a ride out to Westy's house, and Crystal and Cloutier drove over to Murphy's, while Gene stayed home in case either of the men showed up.

They returned within the half-hour with similar stories. Murphy's neighbor, a crusty old fellow by the name of Edgar, said that ICE agents had taken the Irishman away. At Westy's house, the police were still there, combing the house for proof that he was a murderer.

Gene Wolfe put on his lawyer cap and went to the police station to represent Westy, and to see where ICE may have taken Murphy. This left just the four of them to plan and carry out the early morning mission to follow Victoria Haas to her mysterious rendezvous with Bolton at 2:00 a.m.

Chapter 25

TUESDAY, AUGUST 11TH

White van leaving JOHNS. The text from Cloutier flashed up on Clay's phone.

K., Clay replied.

He and Baylee were in his Jeep on the town-side of Victoria's house. It was highly unlikely that she would leave in the other direction, as it only looped out further around the point before returning to town. With the arrest of Westy and detention of Murphy, the revised plan had Cloutier and Crystal parked outside the entrance of JOHNS with Clay and Baylee down the street from Victoria's driveway. Originally, Westy and Murphy would've been on the other side of the house keeping an eye out, but with the tracking device, it most likely didn't matter. Gene was down at the police station with Westy. Nobody knew where Murphy was.

Clay and Baylee sat in the Jeep in a wharf parking lot that, surprisingly for this midnight hour, had several vehicles in it, mostly trucks. He wondered whether they no longer worked, or perhaps they'd been left behind by lobstermen who'd had one too many drinks. The reality was more likely that neighbors were using the lot for their own purposes.

The conversation had been strained, the elephant in the Jeep being Clay's impending fatherhood. That, coupled with the fact that they were currently staking out the house of the woman who was going to birth his child, and then follow her to a scientific lab to undergo some as yet unknown procedure involving the baby.

"So, we wait for the van to come get... her... and we follow it to this secret lab," Baylee said breaking the silence. "Then what?"

"We determine its location, and Cloutier calls the FDA who call the local police."

Cloutier had finally gotten hold of a person at the FDA who could make decisions at this level, and, while he was skeptical, her clout as a journalist had led to a begrudging agreement to give her his cell phone number. Whether or not he'd answer the phone at 2:00 in the morning, Clay had his doubts. That meant that the decision would be his as to whether or not to bust into this Area 38 to stop the procedure from going forward.

It was quite a conundrum, he thought with a sardonic grin. Did he really want to prevent his unborn child from being superior?

"What if the dude doesn't answer the phone?" Baylee asked.

What, indeed, Clay thought? "Lab isn't going anywhere," he said. "Guess we just call in the cavalry in the morning when people wake up."

"You afraid that might be too late?"

"Too late?"

"For your kid."

"We should've seen the van by now," Clay said. About an hour earlier there'd been a smattering of cars with the closing of the bars. Since then, nothing.

Baylee drew a deep breath, breaking the silence. "I'm only going to ask you this once, then we'll never speak of it again. How exactly did you come to get that woman pregnant? I don't mean the details but how did you end up there, in that situation with someone it seems you hardly knew?"

"I dated her after I graduated high school," Clay said. "I wasn't actually all that into her, but she shared a secret with me, a pretty shitty secret about... let's just say her father was pretty twisted.

Somehow that bonded us together, and I couldn't seem to break things off."

"What secret?"

Clay hesitated, never having broken this confidence before. "She discovered that her father had been filming her naked. When she was in the shower, mostly."

"Fuck. That's messed up. What was he doing with the film?"

"She came home from school early one day and found him in front of the television, masturbating as he watched her shower."

"Double fuck," Baylee said. "But how does that translate into you making her pregnant almost twenty years later?"

"She invited me over. Said she wanted to discuss something. I felt obligated to hear her out, thought it might have something to do with her father and that incident."

"Did it?"

"No. She asked me to sire her child."

"Sire? What are you? Some champion stallion?"

"Apparently. She offered me $20,000. No strings attached."

"Wow. Pretty good money. And she's a good-looking woman."

"I told her no, but we ended up in the sack anyway. I used a condom."

"You telling me it broke?"

"Couple days later I went back over. I had a few drinks. She was particularly persuasive. I was a little drunk and a lot stupid."

"Fucking rich people," Baylee said. "They get their way one way or another, don't they?"

Clay's phone buzzed in his hand. It was a call from Cloutier. "Hello," he said.

"The van is back, what do we do?" Cloutier sounded stressed.

"Back? We haven't seen it." Clay looked at the time: 2:20 a.m.

"No movement on the tracker," Baylee said.

"It just pulled into the road up to JOHNS."

"Was Harley Lange driving?"

"We couldn't tell. It's dark out."

Fair enough, Clay thought. How had they missed it? Had Victoria snuck out of the house? It would appear that she didn't think enough of his commitment bracelet to be wearing it. "Try and see where it goes," he said.

"Maybe she was being picked up somewhere else," Baylee said. "Didn't you say her parents live next door?"

That they did, Clay thought, and they couldn't see the parents' driveway from here, as it was around the corner. "Follow them, but don't let them see you," he said into the phone. "We're on our way."

It was a fifteen-minute drive to JOHNS. Clay did it in ten. Cloutier and Crystal were in a dark corner of the parking lot just past the administration building.

"Where'd they go?" Clay asked through the window.

"Down there." Cloutier pointed to the faint dirt road leading down the hill. Toward the graveyard.

Baylee got out of the Jeep. Clay followed. "What are you doing?" he asked.

"Going down to the graveyard, I guess." Baylee reached through the neck of her T-shirt and pulled her Smith & Wesson Shield from the holster sewn into the tank top underneath.

"If we're not back in twenty minutes call your boy at the FDA," Clay said pulling out his Glock. "Might as well call the police. If you don't hear from us in twenty, things have definitely gone south."

Clay followed Baylee across and down the side of the road, a nearly-full moon illuminating their way. The road was rutted with grass growing up in the middle between the tire tracks. It looked to be rarely used.

At first, they were out in an open space, but within fifty yards, entered the woods. The trees seemed to be a combination of red maple, white pine, and northern red oak. They were old growth trees, untouched for over a hundred years, in Clay's estimation, with lush foliage blocking the light.

Streams of moonlight managed to pierce through gaps in the branches, falling like spotlights at a Broadway production, creating dancing shadows all around them with the shifting wind. There was a sinister vibe in the air, far different than a few nights before when they had been there and found nothing. As they rounded a corner and emerged on the edge of the graveyard, the stones reflecting the light, there was nothing, still.

No white van. There were no makeshift tents with scientists in frocks dancing around the plots like macabre minions of Satan as they interfered with God's plan for the human race. Nothing. They circled the tree line surrounding the diminutive cemetery. There was no other road out. No path through the forest for which a van to go, not even enough of a crease in the façade for Clay's Jeep to attempt passage.

Clay pulled out his phone and texted Cloutier. You sure van came down this way and has not left?

Yes.

Start the clock over. Give us 20 more before calling in the troops.

K.

"The shed?" Clay asked Baylee.

"Got to be."

"How about you get behind one of those gravestones over there, and I'll go check the door."

Baylee wrinkled her nose. The markers were about two-feet high, rounded at the top, and covered in moss and mold. "Think I'd rather be in the line of fire than lying on top of a dead person in a cemetery," she said.

"Better than *being* the dead person," Clay said. "You get into place. I'm going to go around to the back and sidle up to the front." He walked off, following the circle of the woods around.

Baylee decided that all-fours would be the wisest approach across the moonlit cemetery, crawling her way forward, until she reached a headstone with an excellent vantage of the front of the caretaker's shed. She'd no sooner gotten into position than Clay emerged from the rear of the building and slid his way along the wall.

Clay looked across the graveyard but was unable to see Baylee, which was a good thing, for if he couldn't see her, then the bad guys couldn't either. If Clive Miller was out there, this was most certainly a deadly game they were playing.

He reached down and grasped the handle of the garage-like door and pulled. It slid up—the reinforced steel heavy but gliding easily on rollers as it was raised. Clay stepped to the side, holding his Glock in front of him, standing kitty-corner to the opening. It was dark inside, but even through the gloom, he could tell that the space was empty.

What the hell, Clay thought. How had this van disappeared? He pulled his phone out and turned the flashlight on to see better. If Clive Miller was out there, Clay was a sitting target, but no gunshot split the night air. He stepped into the box-like space. It was ten feet wide by fifteen feet long and absolutely empty. Not quite empty, he realized, as he spotted a black box on the back wall. He pulled black gloves on his hands.

Baylee stepped into the opening as he approached the black box. She faced out, guarding against enemies that were not there. The front of the box slid up like a breaker panel. There were two black buttons inside. Clay looked over at Baylee, mentally shrugged, and pushed the top button. The floor vibrated under their feet, but that was it, nothing more.

"What was that?" Baylee asked.

"I'm not sure," Clay said. But he had an idea. "Come inside another couple of steps."

Baylee took two steps backward into the shed. Clay pushed the bottom button. The floor under them vibrated again, and then started descending. "It's an elevator," he said. "Be ready for anything."

The walls didn't go down along with them, just the floor, lumbering its way downward slowly for what Clay guessed must be two stories before they reached a brightly illuminated room obviously part of a much larger structure excavated from under the shed. There was a white van parked off to the right. Several desks, empty, sat off to the left. There was a door behind them. Clay and Baylee made eye contact and approached the door from either side. Baylee pulled open the door as Clay pointed his pistol. There were stairs going up.

Clay pulled out his phone to text Cloutier, but there was no service. Baylee touched his shoulder and pointed at the far wall where another door beckoned. They approached the door carefully, each stepping to one side. Clay held up one finger, then two, and then three, pulling the door wide and stepping through the opening. Baylee followed a step behind, their pistols raised in front of them.

To their right was a glassed-in room with a single bed in the middle and various pieces of medical equipment surrounding it. There were four people inside fiddling with various things. They wore the scrubs, powder blue, of medical personnel.

Across the way, at a desk, sat Rex Bolton, facing them. Across from him, with their backs to Clay and Baylee, were a man and a woman.

To their left were two men holding assault rifles pointed at them. Behind them were several more desks and television monitors filling the walls. The middle screen showed the shed, or elevator, on the side of the graveyard.

"Welcome, Mr. Wolfe and Miss Baker," Bolton said, standing up.

The woman and man spun around. It was Kalinda and her husband, John. "What are they doing here?" Kalinda asked.

Chapter 26

"Your weapons, please," a voice from behind said. "Lay them gently on the floor."

Clay risked a look over his shoulder. It was Harley Lange standing behind them like some western gunfighter, a pistol in either hand, pointed at their heads.

"What's going on?" Kalinda demanded loudly.

"Your guns," Harley said. "On the floor."

The two goons off to the side fanned out slightly, creating a crossfire zone.

Baylee had her Smith & Wesson pointed at Bolton's head.

"Baylee, what's going on?" Kalinda asked.

"I might ask you the same," Baylee said.

Bolton stood up and positioned himself behind Kalinda. "Everybody relax, there is an easy solution to this."

"Drop your weapons," Harley said. "Now."

They had little choice, Clay thought. The best option was to delay until the cavalry showed up. The shed was open, and the lift was down. It wouldn't take the police long to figure out where they were. How long had it been? Clay looked sideways at Baylee and nodded slightly. The two of them knelt and lay their pistols carefully on the ground and stood back up.

"What the hell?" Kalinda asked.

Bolton stepped out from behind the desk and passed by Kalinda and John, motioning for Clay and Baylee to step away from their guns. He picked the weapons up and walked them back over to his desk.

"You're well aware that this procedure is ethically questionable in the eyes of the FDA, my dear," Bolton said. "We made that abundantly clear."

"What does that have to do with Clay and Baylee?" Kalinda asked.

"Ah, that's right, they're on your security detail," Bolton said. "That might explain why they're here."

"Boss, I should bring the lift back up and secure the shed door," Harley said. "As a matter of fact, I should probably sweep the area. I doubt these two came alone. They probably have a spotter out there watching their backs. Probably that SEAL fisherman, Beck."

"Weston Beck is in jail on murder charges," Bolton said. "And the Irishman, Joe Murphy, has been mopped up by ICE. Seems his immigration status is a bit spotty. But, yes, it would be a good idea to secure the vehicle entrance and check the grounds. That damn journalist, Marie Cloutier, might be out there. You should be able to handle her on your own."

"Somebody tell me what the fuck is going on," Kalinda snarled.

"You're here to get a microinjection that will make your unborn baby like Clark Kent, minus the aversion to kryptonite," Bolton said. "I believe it's time to turn you over to the doctors while the rest of us step into the other room to take care of some unfinished business. Please step into the other room, Mr. and Mrs. Kaya."

Is that Kalinda's last name, Clay thought? He wasn't even aware she had a last name. Kalinda Kaya had a pretty nice ring to it. Clay looked around. They'd been moved ten feet from the doorway. Would it be possible for him and Baylee to dash through the door and pull it shut behind them, he wondered? Then run across the room to the stairs and escape up and out? Not likely.

One of the men stepped out of the glassed-in medical room. "We're ready."

Bolton waved at Kalinda and John. "Go ahead."

"I still don't understand what Clay and Baylee are doing here?" Kalinda said again.

"Please proceed into the other room. I'll handle them," Bolton said.

"Are you going to hurt them?"

Bolton laughed. "No, we won't hurt them. We're scientists and doctors, not thugs and killers. Now, go ahead."

"I'm not sure that this is a good idea," John said.

"You've already paid $20 million for tonight's procedure," Bolton said. "We allowed you to postpone last week because of your cold, but it's now or never. No refunds. Your choice."

"They're going to kill us," Baylee said.

Bolton laughed. "We're going to remove you and call the police. You've broken in here and threatened us with weapons."

"You're operating an illegal genome editing program," Clay said. "You can't afford to let us live."

"There is nothing illegal about what we're doing here," Bolton.

"Then why are you performing the procedure in a secret facility underneath a graveyard in the middle of the night?" Baylee asked.

"What we're doing here may be frowned upon by certain organizations, sort of like PETA complained about our treatment of mice. *Mice*. Go figure. We're trying to improve the lives of millions, and they're worried about the treatment of mice." Bolton waved his hand at the open door. "We can discuss this in the other room." He turned back to Kalinda and John. "It's now or never." He pointed at the glassed-in medical room.

"You're just going to turn them over to the police?" Kalinda asked.

"I promise. What else can I do?"

Kalinda looked at her husband. "What do you think?"

"We paid a lot of money."

Kalinda stole a glance at Baylee. "I'm sorry. This might be my only chance to have a healthy baby." She walked toward the operating theater with John in tow.

"He's a liar," Baylee said. "They're going to kill us."

"I don't believe that. I can't believe that." Kalinda said, looking at the floor. Then she and John went through the door, the doctor following and closing it behind them.

"That room is soundproof," Bolton said. "And has one-way mirrors. We can kill you here and now and nobody would be the wiser. Or you can step into the next room." He gestured to the doorway.

Clay shrugged and walked to the door. Pull Baylee through behind him, slam the door, and run for it, or just delay, he wondered? Would Harley find Cloutier and Crystal? What would he do to them? With the shed locked and the lift back up to level, it was unlikely that the police would realize that the shed was actually an elevator, especially if the box with the up and down buttons was hidden.

If Harley was comfortable the police would turn up nothing, then there would be no reason to harm Cloutier and Crystal, or so Clay figured. But there would also be no help coming. He walked through the door, turning toward the stairs. That seemed to be the only viable option out of here.

"Have a seat," Bolton said.

Clay looked at him and then back toward the desk most immediately in front of the door to the stairs. There was a chair behind it and also one to the side. He motioned for Baylee to sit at the one behind the desk and took the other for himself. The two goons stood about ten feet away, their eyes unblinking and their hands steady on their weapons. Professionals, Clay guessed, and not just off-the-street hired muscle. They had the look of soldiers of fortune. Buzz cuts and hard eyes that looked twenty feet past you and, at the same time, missed nothing at all.

"What now?" Clay asked.

"We wait for the all-clear sign from Harley, and then we take you out of here." Bolton pulled a chair from the other desk around to face them, careful not to get too close to the two interlopers or in the way of the goons that Clay had now decided were mercs.

"And do what with us? Turn us over to your boy, Clive?" Baylee asked.

"Clive?" Bolton wrinkled his brow. "Not sure what you mean by that."

"Are you going to kill us?" Clay asked.

"No, of course not."

"You're lying," Clay said. "Yeah, what you are doing here is a gray area when it comes to the law, but at the same time, you know that the FDA and the entire scientific community frown heavily upon it. If you don't go to jail, you'll at least be blackballed from ever working in any health care facility again."

"Your friend in there, the pop singer, is the last one. After she's done, we're wrapping up operations. I'd hoped to do a few more, but your snooping has ruined that. I still have enough money to go away and never have to work again."

"Perhaps to Russia to visit Lada Kotova," Clay said.

Bolton's face tightened. "What do you know of Lada?"

"You mean the lost love of your life who now works in Russian intelligence?"

"How do you know that?" Bolton composed his facial features. "No matter. That ship has sailed."

"What do you mean?" Baylee asked.

"I don't see why I shouldn't tell you," Bolton said with a sigh. "I'll be long gone before you're released. Oh, don't worry, it won't be more than three or four days, but that'll be long enough, and I promise that you won't be harmed."

"What ship has sailed?" Clay asked.

"For the record, I was never a traitor to my country," Bolton said. He looked at the two mercs. "I considered it. And you're right about Lada being the love of my life. How you know, I have no idea. She contacted me five years ago. She even came to visit me a few times, and the sex was every bit as wonderful as it was all those years ago when I was young. It was as if I were in my early twenties again." He lapsed into silence, staring into the space over Clay's head.

"You weren't selling secrets about SHAIM to a Russian guy named

Vlad who was sneaking into Port Essex from the spy ship, *Ivan Sereda?*" Clay asked.

"You certainly know more than I would've guessed," Bolton said, coming back to the present. "Vlad was my go-between. Lada set the whole thing up. She introduced me to Vlad, and we made arrangements for me to… transfer information." Bolton rubbed his lined face.

"The SHAIM that you stole from the Black Lab?" Baylee asked.

"You know there was no theft," Bolton said.

"Oh, you stole a SHAIM, alright, and then you covered it up with a regular mouse. Not a superhuman mouse, just a regular mouse in a trap."

"The two of you are full of surprises. The truth is, I did steal a SHAIM, but then I changed my mind. I disposed of it." Bolton rubbed his forehead with his hand. "I was going to tell Vlad to go to hell, that I wasn't a traitor to my country, the next time I saw him. But he never came back."

"When'd you last see him?" Clay asked.

"It was the Fourth of July," Bolton said without hesitation.

Three days before the man was seen with Clive Miller and Daryl Allen when Westy got hammered, Clay thought. Then another thought popped into his head. "That was also the day that Chad Gagnon disappeared," he said. "Did you have something to do with that?"

"Yes, yes I did." Bolton drummed his fingers on the desk. "He wandered in on us down here, just like you did. I believe he's in California enjoying the hundred grand I offered him to keep his big mouth shut and go away."

"Chad Gagnon is alive and well?"

"Enjoying being young in the sun with money in his pocket, would be my guess," Bolton said. "I'd offer you the same deal to keep your mouths shut. Hell, I'd offer the two of you a million to keep this between us, but somehow, I don't think you'd take it. Or would you?"

"You'd give us a million to go away and shut up?" Clay asked.

"Money could be in your bank account tomorrow."

"I suppose it'd be well worth it. You could go back to microinjecting mutated DNA into embryos for—what'd you say Kalinda paid you? Twenty million? How many have you done?"

"No, I'm all done. I know when to hold 'em and when to fold 'em. Now is the time to fold, take my winnings, and go away."

"Back to Russia," Baylee said. "You sure you didn't sell classified information about creating superhumans to the FSB? To Putin?"

"I absolutely did not," Bolton said. "I was tempted by Lada's... charms, let us say, but thought better of it. Vlad missed our meeting, and Lada has been trying to contact me ever since. I've ignored her. Another reason to disappear from the grid, I guess, as it appears that I've now pissed off the FSB."

"You *did* know that she was FSB?" Clay asked.

"I had her looked into," Bolton said. "She told me she'd been hired by the WHO and that the work we were doing with the mice was something the whole world should benefit from. I bought that story at first, but then became suspicious. When my guy found out the truth and told me, that's when I decided to pull the plug on the whole operation."

"You didn't pull the plug, though, did you? Vlad just never came back," Clay said. He was beginning to piece together what was going on.

"I was going to pull the plug," Bolton said. "Where the hell is Harley?" He stood up, stalked over to the door and pulled it open, looking up the stairs. There was nothing, not a sound, just the dark void of the elevator shaft. He closed the door and walked back around in front of Clay and Baylee.

"And I don't suppose you had Mary Jordan killed, either, did you?" Clay asked.

"Who the fuck is Mary Jordan?" Bolton asked.

"And you really don't know a man by the name of Clive Miller? Narrow face, thin neck, mean eyes?" Clay asked.

Bolton shook his head. "Just to be clear—what is your answer to a cool million to keep your mouths shut?"

"And go away?" Clay asked.

"Not necessarily. *I* am going away. Somewhere where the authorities will never be able to find me and possibly drag me through years of trials, but it would be a relief to know that they weren't actually looking for me."

The walls of the room rumbled. "What the hell is he doing coming down in the lift?" Bolton asked.

There were eight people on the lift. Seven of them were police officers. The last was Harley Lange.

The two mercenaries looked at Bolton, then laid their rifles on the ground and put their hands up. Clay got the distinct impression that they'd done the murderous math and quickly realized the aggravation of a minor gun possession charge wasn't worth the risk.

Chapter 27

The seven police officers were only the first wave of the law enforcement tide that descended on Johnson Laboratories that night. Blue lights and sirens split the night, bringing local and state police, while helicopters flew in with a variety of FDA and FBI personnel, all trying to claim jurisdiction in a situation in which nobody understood who really was responsible for what.

Clay, Baylee, Bolton, Harley, the two goons, Kalinda, John, and the four scientist-doctors were carted back to the Port Essex jail during this wild melee. Two drunk and disorderly occupants, a shoplifter, and a vandal were released to help make room, but even then, it was quite a crowd.

Clay and Baylee were put into a small conference room, not quite on the horizon of being accused of any wrongdoing, but asked not to leave at the same time. Then they were left alone, the station abuzz outside their closed door.

"What do you think will happen to Kalinda and her husband?" Baylee asked.

"Seems to be a gray area," Clay said. "Don't see how they can be charged with anything. But public opinion might be harsh on them."

"Not sure who will be upset by them wanting to have a healthier, smarter, and stronger baby."

"What did Mary Jordan's notes say? Playing God? I think plenty of people will be enraged over their decision to interfere with God's plan, whatever the hell that might be."

"And what do you think?" Baylee asked.

Clay stared at his beautiful partner, this very smart woman he was in love with, and then thought about the other woman he wasn't in love with, the one who was going to have his child. He felt little but confusion and pain. "I guess I'm glad it wasn't Victoria who was there to get the operation."

"It does seem a slippery slope, I'm with you on that."

"I don't know. My gut tells me it's wrong, but my mind asks why."

Baylee nodded. "I guess I kind of feel the same way. Glad that it wasn't your baby momma in there, not that Kalinda had a chance to go through with the procedure. But as you said, I'm sure there's going to be some flack over this one."

"When I saw the message from RB about a 2:00 a.m. pickup, I was certain that she was going to JOHNS. Guess I was wrong about her. She just seems the type to want to give her child every advantage, whether it was legal or not."

"Quite some coincidence," Baylee said, raising her eyebrows meaningfully.

"Yeah, for sure." Clay's throat was dry, and a nagging voice was pushing him to see the forest and not the thicket of tangled trees that was the situation in front of him. "Did you get the impression Harley brought the police down the lift without any coercion?"

"They handcuffed him, same as the others, and took him away," Baylee said. "He must be sitting in a cell around here somewhere."

The door opened, and Westy walked in, followed by Gene Wolfe. Westy looked pretty normal for a man who'd recently been arrested for murder and then plucked from his cell at 4:00 in the morning. Gene was not showing any of his eighty-four years of age, his eyes twinkling with energy. This had been a great adventure so far for him. He'd been missing the thrill of the legal system.

"What the hell happened out there?" Westy asked.

"Are you free?" Clay asked.

"Some lieutenant woke me and told me they needed my cell,"

Westy said. "Gene was in the chief's office when we walked by and he waved me in. It appears they haven't dropped the murder charges against me yet, but they seem to be trusting me not to amscray out of this low-security conference room."

"I'm not sure what it is, but I believe new evidence has been introduced in Daryl Allen's death," Gene said. "What happened with Victoria tonight?"

"It wasn't Victoria at all," Clay said. "But Cloutier and Crystal saw a white van leave and return to JOHNS, so we hustled over there." Clay went on—with Baylee's interjections and corrections—to share the evening's events at JOHNS during the wee hours of an August morning in East Essex, Maine.

"You're telling me that Bolton was going to hold you for a few days and then let you go once he'd safely left the country?" Gene asked.

"That's what he said. He said he had enough money to disappear. I can believe him. We overheard that they were charging Kalinda twenty million for the procedure. If they've done this five times, that is one heck of a chunk of money." Clay had been sitting, but now he stood and walked to the door, opening and peeking out the crack before shutting it again.

"He doesn't sound like the psychopath who killed a journalist and Daryl Allen," Gene said.

"That was the fucking guy who hit me with a hammer and planned on scattering my corpse in pieces at sea," Westy said.

"Bolton didn't seem to recognize the name Clive Miller," Clay said. "Could be that he's a good liar, but I don't think so. If I had to guess, I don't think he had anything to do with that sick bastard."

"So who does Clive work for?" Baylee asked. "Or is he just some sadistic killer who happened to come up in our investigation into JOHNS?"

"Daryl Allen picked up a man named Vlad off a Russian fishing ship that may actually be a spy ship." Clay came back over to the table and sat down. "Bolton admitted that he'd made arrangements to sell a mouse to the Russians but then changed his mind. Westy sees Clive Miller with Daryl Allen and the Russian, and then Daryl turns up dead."

"And the Russian is missing," Baylee said.

"You think maybe Clive killed them?" Westy asked.

The door opened, and Chief Roberts came in. Even though he'd been roused from his bed at 3:00 in the morning, his uniform was pressed smooth, and his eyes were alert. "I'd like to speak to you in my office," he said to Clay.

"I'm his lawyer," Gene said. "I go where he goes."

"There is no need of a lawyer. He's not being held. He has not been read his Miranda rights. I just want to speak with him in private," Chief Roberts spoke in a clipped tone. "Actually, Miss Baker, you're invited as well."

Clay and Baylee followed the chief back to his office. A police officer sat in a chair next to Harley Lange. The chief nodded, and the officer rose and exited the room. Clay and Baylee sat in chairs next to Harley and the chief went back around behind his desk.

"What were the two of you doing out to Johnson Laboratories in the middle of the night?" Chief Roberts asked.

"We had reason to suspect that there was a secret lab performing genome editing on embryos," Clay said.

"What business was it of yours?"

Clay fidgeted. Certainly, it couldn't hurt to unveil that they'd been hired to investigate what was going on at JOHNS. "We were hired to investigate mysterious circumstances going on at JOHNS."

"Mr. Lange says that you were let go by Rex Bolton."

"We were. But then Bridget Engel rehired us."

The chief stared at him. "And Bolton had no knowledge of this?"

"Engel suspected him of wrongdoing," Clay said, "or at least that's what she told me."

"Wrongdoing?"

"She didn't know *what* was going on, only that *something* was going on."

"And you have something in writing?"

"We hadn't yet... formalized the agreement."

"Isn't that handy?"

"I'm sure that Engel will back up my claim," Clay said. "Is it too early to call the CEO of a company that was just discovered experimenting on pregnant women?"

"She has not been answering her phone."

"Not to tell you your job, but I'm sure you could send somebody to knock on her door."

"Not that it is any of your business, but I did. No answer. Harley suggests that she might be out of town. She is out of town quite a bit, he said."

"Last I knew, Harley was one of the bad guys," Clay said. "Has something changed to make the two of you so chummy?"

"What exactly led you to this supposed secret laboratory in the middle of the night?" the chief asked.

"There's nothing 'supposed' about it." Clay snorted. "I had reason to believe that there was criminal activity and followed up on that information," he added, sounding a bit formal and shirty even to his own ears.

"Did this information come from Kalinda or John Kaya?"

That would be the easy lie, Clay thought. "No."

"Okay, for now," Chief Roberts said. "What did JOHNS originally hire you to do for them, if that's not breaking confidentiality."

"We were hired to investigate an attempt to steal a mouse," Clay said.

"A mouse?"

"Bolton called it a SHAIM. A Superhuman Advanced Intelligence Mouse."

"Who would want to steal a mouse? No matter how special it is?" The chief's evident skepticism, which seemed to be growing with each passing minute, went up a notch.

Clay sighed. If he didn't give the chief something, he and Baylee were going to end up in a cell alongside Bolton, but apparently not Harley. He didn't want to be locked up. There was a suspicion nagging at him that he wanted to follow up on. "We've reason to believe that the SHAIM had already been stolen. A normal mouse was then snuck in, already dead, to replace the stolen SHAIM."

"Why would somebody do that?" Harley blurted out.

"I thought you might be able to tell us that," Clay said.

"I got no idea what you're talking about."

"I believe that Bolton and Harley stole the SHAIM, sold it to the Russians, and then replaced it with a normal mouse." In reality, this was no longer what Clay believed, but it would do for now. "Alive, this mouse would have been obvious. Dead, it looked just like a SHAIM. Maybe a little smaller."

"That's not true," Harley said. "Maybe Bolton, but not me. I never even considered that possibility."

The chief nodded. "I'm sure the CIA will need to speak with you in a few days after they hear about this. Both of you. What other evidence did you have of this?" He looked back at Clay, who shrugged noncommittally.

Clay had no evidence. "How about some give and take," he said. "Why is Harley part of this?"

"Your friend, the *Register* lady, Marie Cloutier, called into the station with a report of something amok out to Johnson Laboratories," Chief Roberts said. "Dispatch didn't give it much credence but was going to send a patrol car to do a drive by. And then, Mr. Lange called in with the whole secret lab thing and thugs with assault rifles. That's why seven officers originally showed up. He has been most helpful with information."

Clay looked at Harley. "You're Jane Doe, aren't you?"

Harley looked confused. "Jane Doe?"

"Were you feeding Mary Jordan information about Area 38?"

Harley licked his lips. "Yes. The whole thing was—*is*—wrong. Who are we to be playing God?"

Now, the chief looked confused. "Jane Doe? Mary Jordan? The missing woman?"

"Harley was leaking the story about JOHNS doing genome editing on human babies to Mary Jordan, a reporter at the *Register*," Clay said. "Guess he was the anonymous source, and thus, she gave him the name Jane Doe."

"Why didn't you just come out with it?" Baylee asked.

"You were right, you know, when you interviewed me," Harley looked like he might cry. "I was being blackmailed about my sexual orientation. Just not by the Russians. It was Bolton. He said at first that I just needed to look the other way, you know, about Area 38, steer my security team clear of there on certain nights. Next thing I knew, he had me picking up the patients and bringing them in."

"And so you tried to leak the story anonymously," Clay said. "But then when Mary Jordan came up missing, you got scared and clammed up."

Harley nodded. "I was scared. Bolton had those two mercenaries on the payroll. I'm sure they're probably the ones who killed her, and I was next if I blabbed."

But it wasn't Bolton and the mercenaries who had murdered Mary Jordan, Clay thought. It was Clive Miller, a sadistic killer who worked for somebody else, Clay had concluded. But he didn't want to tip his hand, not until he was certain. "Tell me something, Harley. Kalinda was supposed to have the procedure done last week, but she caught a cold, and had to postpone. Was last week left blank?"

Harley shook his head. "No. Bolton switched Kalinda out with the woman who was next on the list."

Clay tried to leave it that way, but he knew he couldn't. "Who was?"

"Haas. Victoria Haas. Local woman, so it was easy enough. The switch, I mean."

Chapter 28

It was noon before Gene was able to get Clay and Baylee out of police custody. Once the police were done with them, various state and federal agencies took turns going over every minute detail associated with JOHNS and everything that had happened there. They were only allowed to go home for a break with the promise that they'd return by six o'clock for follow-up interviews, interrogations, and questions.

Clay was given his phone back as they left. There were twenty-seven text messages and four voice mails. He decided to leave them until he got home. Gene drove them back to the house, and Clay was pleasantly surprised to see his Jeep parked in the driveway.

"Cloutier drove it home from JOHNS," Gene said. "Crystal spent the night here and fed the dog and the cat."

Crystal's car was not there, so it appeared she'd vacated the premises.

Flash met them at the door, bouncing around excitedly, not the normal greeting of a basset hound.

"I could use a shower, and then I might close my eyes for a few minutes," Baylee said, yawning.

Gene went and got fresh towels for her. Flash followed the two of them up the stairs.

Clay sat down in the living room, thinking he might go up to his apartment and shower, but first he needed to check his messages. First one was from Cloutier, that she'd brought the Jeep home and wanted to talk about the case, obviously having her journalist cap on. Clay had a few errant and still disordered thoughts about the case tumbling around in his mind, but he wasn't quite ready for that conversation. There were a few things to check first.

Crystal couldn't refrain from swearing even when texting. Went to open the office. Check in when you get the fuck out.

Clay let her know that he and Baylee were at Gene's house and that he'd stop by in a few hours.

Westy had sent a simple text: Let me know when you get out and then let's go kick some ass.

Victoria had left several messages, wanting to speak with him. Clay wondered if she'd been trying to tell him how their destined-to-be-superior child would have amazing abilities. That's what the conversation the other day had been about, he now knew, what she had been hinting at. Not only was he going to be a father, but he was also going to have a kid who was the product of a potentially illegal and certainly unethical procedure. Was this a stigma that would follow the child around through school? *Look, there goes Bobby Haas. He was genetically engineered.*

One thing was clear after last night's debacle at the graveyard. It was time to rethink the entire Clive Miller angle. Clay no longer believed that Bolton was the puppet master pulling Clive's strings. His complete ignorance of the name had seemed genuine, even though the killer might not have been using the name Clive. Also, Bolton was in it for the money, but he was no murderer—otherwise he and Baylee would be long dead. Clay even believed that the man had truly planned to release him and Baylee after he'd safely made his escape to whatever island nation as his retirement destination.

"Sounds like you're going to have a superbaby, Superdaddy." Baylee said, sitting down next to him on the couch. She wore the same pants as the day before but was now wearing his high school football jersey. The front read *Seahawks*, and the back *Wolfe*, both above the number 17. "You don't mind that I dug this out of the drawer up there, do you?"

"No problem," Clay said. He'd left it behind when he went to college and hadn't given it a thought since. It was highly unlikely that it still fit him. Besides, it looked spectacular on Baylee. "Shower feel good?"

"Fabulous," she said. "But tell me, Mr. Wolfe, what are your thoughts about fathering a superbaby?"

"I guess having a son or daughter is pretty cool," he said.

"But?"

"I'm worried about the stigma attached to the birth because of the genome editing. I suppose if we left well enough alone, Bolton would be in a hula skirt somewhere in the southern hemisphere with a coconut shell drink in his hand, and nobody would know that Victoria had had a procedure to make the baby superior."

"Your little wolf cub," Baylee said. She grinned mischievously, signaling that she was going to have a lot of fun at his expense with this particular situation. "Who's going to know?"

"What do you mean?"

"If I know one thing about rich people, it's that they're very good at covering up their dirty laundry. You sprinkle a few million dollars around, and everything smells like roses."

"My child is not going to want for money," Clay said.

"How about a father?"

"What?"

"Is your child going to want for a father?"

"No."

"You gonna tie the knot with the mother?"

"Absolutely not."

Baylee lay her head on Clay's shoulder. "Life sure is complicated, isn't it, Mr. Wolfe?"

A knocking on the door roused Clay from slumber. Baylee jerked awake next to him. They were still on the couch in the living room. Clay looked at his phone to check the time. They'd been asleep about twenty-five minutes. Gene passed through the living room on the way to open the front door. After about a minute of murmured conversation, he came back inside with a man behind him. It was Mekhi.

"He took her, Mr. Wolfe," he said.

"What?" Clay disentangled himself from Baylee and stood up.

"He rang the bell and, when I answered, he was standing there with a gun in his hand. He hit me with it, and when I woke, Miss Haas was gone."

"What are you talking about? Who took Victoria? Took her where?"

"I don't know, Mr. Wolfe. I don't know."

"Who was it?"

"I've never seen him before. It was a man with a narrow face, mean eyes, and a very long neck." Mekhi was agitated, his words spilling out on top of each other. There was a long gash along his temple from his ear to the receding hairline of his forehead.

"Have you ever heard the name Clive Miller before?" Clay asked.

"No. I am sorry."

"How about Bridget Engel?"

"No. Should I have?"

"When did this happen?" The last of the cobwebs were flushed from Clay's mind as the adrenalin kicked in.

"It was about an hour ago. When I came to, I searched the house. Then I went to your office, and the woman there told me you were here."

On cue, Crystal came through the front door, which was still open. "What the fuck's going on?" she asked.

"Did you report this to the police?" Clay asked Mekhi, ignoring Crystal.

"No. I did not."

"Why not?"

"Miss Haas has shared with me certain delicate things that she has been involved with. Things that might not be appropriate for the police to know."

Clay contemplated telling the man that the secret was out of the bag. Harley Lange had already spilled the beans. Bolton was in jail, even if not yet charged with specific crimes, so far only being held as a person of suspicion in an ongoing case.

Clay's phone buzzed. He glanced at it. Text from Baylee. He looked sideways at her and then back at his phone. If she is wearing the bracelet, we can track her.

The receiver was in the Jeep. Last night, he thought that Victoria might've taken the bracelet off, which she most likely did to sleep, but as it turned out, she'd not gone anywhere. Would she be wearing it today, Clay wondered? He'd given it to her as his commitment to be a father to their child, or so he hoped she believed, and the further consideration of whether the two of them would be more than parents to the child they had created.

He nodded to Baylee. "Will you get the... note from Victoria out of the Jeep?"

She muttered a 'no problem' and went out the door.

"How would Victoria contact you, Mekhi?" Clay asked.

"She'd text or call me on my cell phone." He showed the phone in his hand.

"Did you know she was pregnant?"

"She told me that you were the father," Mekhi said.

"So I've been told."

Baylee came rushing back inside. "We have to go," she said.

"You go home in case Victoria shows up. What's your phone number?" Clay asked Mekhi, and then pecked the number into his own phone.

"What the fuck?" Crystal said.

"We'll call you from the road," Clay said as he went out the door.

"The tracker shows her in Waterville," Baylee said as they climbed into the Jeep.

"Waterville?"

"That's what it said."

"Where's Clive taking her?" Clay asked, pulling into the street and flooring the accelerator.

"Beats me."

"Can you call Westy and tell him where we're headed? Be nice if he followed along and brought some guns," Clay said.

"Why don't we pick him up?"

"Sooner or later, Clive is going to take that bracelet off, for one reason or another, and then we'll likely never see Victoria again."

Baylee put the receiver for the tracker into the cupholder and picked up her phone, touching Westy's name in her contacts, and putting it on speaker. It went to voicemail. "Call me back," Baylee said. "Your boy, Clive, kidnapped Victoria Haas, and we're tracking her. She's headed for Waterville and so are we."

"Call and tell Crystal to go over to his house," Clay said. "I'm betting he's asleep."

Baylee did so, finally looking up as the Jeep swung in a particularly aggressive passing maneuver.

Route 29 was not the best road to go fast on, especially in the summer when it was packed with cars, but Clay was managing, zipping in and out like a NASCAR driver.

"What's Clive want with Victoria?" Baylee asked. She was sitting on her hands to keep them from flailing around with every brush with death as they swerved this way and that.

"What's better than stealing a mouse?" Clay asked.

"You think he took her because she…" Baylee trailed off.

"If you want to steal the technology that produces superhuman babies, what better way than to take the pregnant mother hosting that unborn child?"

"Who's Clive working for?"

"Maybe he's working directly for the Russians." Clay figured the traffic would ease up once they got through Wiscasset. He hoped that it wasn't stop-and-go through town, but the middle of a weekday shouldn't be too bad.

"You think so?"

"No."

Baylee's phone rang, a military bugle call to action that she'd put in for Westy. She put it on speaker and clicked to accept the call, holding it out between her and Clay.

"Hello," Clay said.

"What's going on?" Westy asked.

"I need you to get in your truck and head for Waterville," Clay said.

"I'm in my truck going through Port Essex now. Crystal came and banged on my door."

"Did you pack your guns?"

"Yep. A good variety in a bag behind my seat."

"Mekhi showed up at the house and said that some narrow-faced fellow with a long neck knocked him out and took Victoria."

"Clive fucking Miller," Westy said.

"Luckily, she must have the bracelet on with your chip device in it." Clay picked up the tracker. "Looks like they got off an exit in Waterville, and they're now on Route 104 heading towards Skowhegan."

"You know why?"

"Harley Lange told me last… this morning that Victoria had the microinjection, the genetic procedure to make her child a superbaby, had it last week." Clay was happy there was no backup going past Red's Eats in Wiscasset, but still, there was no opportunity to pass, and traffic was going much too slow for him.

The phone was silent for about twenty seconds. "Your kid?"

"So I'm told."

"Where're they going?"

"You got me." Clay banged a right, and the road was wide open in front of him. "Private airfield, maybe?"

"You think he's working for the Russians?"

"No. I think he's working for Bridget Engel."

Chapter 29

They were silent for a minute or so after Clay got off the phone with Westy. This was partially because they were careening down the road at close to eighty miles an hour in a fifty zone, and the Jeep wasn't the most stable of vehicles at high speeds on twisting roads.

"You think Engel is behind all this?" Baylee finally broke the silence.

"Somebody other than Clive is calling the shots."

"What shots are we talking about?"

Clay corrected a skid that almost put them in the ditch. "It seems that Bolton was running the program to alter the DNA of unborn babies and making a pretty penny off this endeavor. He was running the operation underground to avoid oversight, as it is highly illegal. Seems that people with sack loads of money are willing to part with it for the opportunity to have bragging rights on the playground."

"Was Engel involved? And how much—that's really the question, right?"

"I think she rehired us exactly because she wasn't involved in any more than a tacit way but then she thought things might be getting out of control. Bolton thought he was doing it right under her nose, the smug dumbass, just because she was traveling abroad on company business so often."

"But you think she did know about what was going on?"

"Yes. Maybe not at the beginning, maybe not everything. But I'm guessing she has bigger plans. Instead of getting her hands dirty selling superbabies to the wealthy, why not steal the technology wholesale, on the hoof, so to speak. I think Engel plans to deliver an unborn baby whose body contains all the information necessary for somebody to replicate the process. And all wrapped up in the pretty package that's carrying it. Victoria Haas." His tone was grim, his knuckles white as he gripped the wheel in anger.

"You're not going to help anybody out if you kill us on the drive," Baylee said softly.

"Clive Miller is not a nice man," Clay said. "I'm sure that he has strict instructions not to kill her." He blew through a red light just the other side of Augusta and gunned it up the on-ramp to the Interstate, where he opened the Jeep up to ninety miles an hour. "But he might do certain things to her."

"I doubt that Clive will harm her in any way. She's worth too much to him. If he were to kill her, or in any way harm the embryo growing inside of her, she'd be useless to him."

Clay slowed down slightly. "I think Engel is behind it. And she's been pulling his strings from the get-go, always in the far background, which is why we kinda got lost with the Russian angle. I'm still trying to figure out what's driving her. Something's bothering me about her, like those tats. I know I've seen something like that but I couldn't' see the whole thing, only two vertical jagged lines, like half a lightning bolt. Pretty sure I asked Cloutier to look into that. Give her a call and jog her memory. Maybe she had an idea that got lost in all the confusion of recent events."

It was all a moot point if the bracelet was discarded, Clay thought, while Baylee was on the phone. She had it on speaker, but he let her do the talking while he concentrated on driving. He supposed it didn't really matter if it was Engel, Bolton, Clive, or the Russians who'd kidnapped the mother of his unborn child. Well, he knew Clive was involved somehow, as Mekhi had described the man exactly as Clay knew him.

What if Clive had figured out there was a tracker in the bracelet and attached it to a random car, Clay thought with horror? They could be following some traveling salesman or tourist heading home. The GPS said that it was now on Route 201, just the other side of Skowhegan. There wasn't much north and west of Skowhegan. Maybe some rural cabin where Clive intended to have his way with Victoria?

They'd made up some ground and were only about twenty miles behind. Clay came down the hill into the town of Skowhegan and blew through the red light, having seen a small break in the traffic. Baylee yipped next to him, said a hurried goodbye to Cloutier, and hung up the phone.

* * *

Bolts had woken Clive up at 6:00 a.m. that morning with the news that police had arrested Rex Bolton, Harley Lange, the four scientists, and the hired muscle. She had it on good authority that it was Clay Wolfe and Baylee Baker who had busted the whole operation wide open. This was not as disastrous as it could've been, as they'd been just about to tip off Wolfe in that direction, sending out a red herring that was too juicy to pass up while they skedaddled with the real prize.

What it did mean was they had to reset their clocks and proceed with the plan a full twelve hours before schedule. The intention had originally been for Wolfe to lead the authorities to Bolton's secret Area 38 later that night, after Kalinda had had the operation, and they would have kidnapped Victoria Haas in the meantime. No worries, Bolts had said, we just have to do it now. Clive went to gather the prize while Bolts called to make arrangements in Canada.

The manservant, that fellow Mekhi, had answered the door, and Clive had put a gun to his head, knocked him out, and then tied him up. He wasn't supposed to be there, not until 8:00 in the morning when he showed up to make the royal queen her breakfast, but every strategy had kinks, and Clive went with the flow. Bolts had been explicit that there was to be no more killing, only because they were so close to their goal, and it would draw too much attention.

Of course, when he mentioned the part about Mekhi answering the door, and the fact that he hadn't killed the man, Bolts had loosed some pretty choice language in his direction. Clive was getting a little tired of Bolt's changing notions of how things should work, and overall abusive language and attitude. He considered putting a bullet right between those pretty little eyes, but there was something about them that also chilled him, and Clive wasn't somebody who often felt fear. It'd been soon after that day in the café where Engel had killed the mark as well as the witnesses that Clive had first seen the tattoo of two lightning bolts on her shoulder, thus earning her the nickname he'd never said aloud.

They were only about an hour from the Canadian border. Clive knew an off-road trail that would avoid border security. They were basically home free, so what the hell was Bolts bitching about? One hour and they would leave U.S. jurisdiction behind, and then one more to get to the facility. At that point, he'd collect the huge bonus that had been promised, and travel to some rural South American country where he could lie on the beach, drink umbrella drinks, and relax. Clive smiled at the pleasant thought, the idea of the perfect vacation, with money burning a hole in his pocket.

The package was secure, wrists and ankles duct-taped, and on the floor in the back of the crew cab of the new Chevy Silverado he'd recently bought. Clive had opted for the blackout tinted windows as well as the off-road package, so no one could see inside the truck and spot the multi-millionaire fashion heiress. All would be well as long as they didn't get pulled over, and Clive was very careful not to break the speed limit.

They'd just passed through Bingham when he looked in the rearview mirror and saw the black Jeep. It couldn't be. But he knew that license plate. As a matter of fact, it was drilled into his brain so deeply that it itched and burned and caused a seething pain. Clay Wolfe. There appeared to be two people in the vehicle. Probably the delicious Baylee Baker. It was impossible, but there they were. They'd come around a curve no more than forty yards from his bumper but had now fallen back. Had they been following the whole way, he wondered? But no, that was ridiculous, he would've spotted them.

Then it came to Clive that the bastard must've put a tracking device on his truck, but how had he found it? Son-of-a-bitch, Clive thought, but must've said aloud, because Bolts asked him what was wrong.

*   *   *

"Call Westy and let him know that our quarry has continued on Route 201 through Skowhegan," Clay said.

Baylee hit the number and then speaker, holding the phone between them. "Our quarry?" she asked as the phone rang.

"Hello," Westy barked into the phone.

"We're passing through Skowhegan right now. How far back are you?" Clay asked.

"We're almost to the Waterville exit," Westy said. "Christ, man, we started out twenty minutes behind you and now we're a half-hour and I'm flying. How fast you going?"

"Too fast," Baylee said.

"What do you mean we?" Clay asked. "Who's with you?"

"Crystal came with."

"Hi, boss. Baylee," Crystal said.

"Looks like we're going right on through town," Clay said. "We'll let you know if they turn off."

"Who's they?"

"Clive and Victoria, at least. Don't know if there's more."

"Any idea where they're going?" Westy asked.

"Not much between here and Canada," Baylee said.

"You think they're fleeing the country?" Westy asked. "Didn't think Canada was allowing U.S. citizens in during these Covid times."

"Especially not with a kidnap victim in tow."

"GPS says Moscow is just the other side of Bingham," Crystal said.

"Wouldn't that be a hoot if there was a bunch of Russians hiding out in Moscow, Maine."

"Got another call coming in," Baylee said. "We'll let you know if we turn off 201. Try to keep up." She hit a button and then another. "Cloutier, what's up?"

"You asked if I'd come across anything else on Engel. Turns out she's a legacy at JOHNS. Her grandfather was hired as a scientist there in 1946. Then her father. She's the golden child who became CEO."

"Hmmm. Interesting," Clay said. "Was he an immigrant?"

"An immigrant?"

"Can you see if he was new to the U.S. in 1946?" Clay asked.

"Because Engel is a German name, he was a scientist, and it was right after the conclusion of WWII?" Cloutier said slowly as she appeared to piece it all together. "That tattoo on her shoulder you asked about? The jagged lines? It could be the sig rune, ancient symbol for victory. The whole thing looks like a double lightning bolt."

"And?"

"It was the emblem of the SS in Nazi Germany, giving it the double meaning of standing for either SS, or victory, victory."

"Son of a gun. Keep digging."

"Got it. Any luck catching up to your baby mama?"

Baylee laughed. Clay grimaced, and said, "Not yet. Closing the gap as we speak. Keep in touch."

Baylee hung up the phone. She looked at the tracker. "We're only seven miles back now. Let's try not to kill us."

"Crystal is right," Clay said. "We should catch up to them right about in Moscow."

"Then what?"

"We force them off the road, beat the shit out of Clive, and rescue Victoria," Clay said.

"Well, the police took our pistols, and I'm sure that son of a bitch is armed to the teeth," Baylee said.

"Do you have a better suggestion?"

"We tail behind at a safe distance, wait for Westy to catch up, follow them to wherever they're going, and then jump them. Armed."

Clay contemplated this. He wasn't in a very patient mood, but it made a certain amount of sense. "Suppose it wouldn't be a great idea to crash into his vehicle with Victoria aboard."

"Not with her pregnant and all," Baylee said dryly. "What was all that about Engel?"

"Something Grandpops told me about the founder of JOHNS. Guy by the name of B.B. Knutson. Back in the twenties. B.B. opened up the research facility looking to eradicate disease, but his hobby—perhaps 'passion' is a better word—was the eugenics movement."

"Eugenics?" Baylee asked.

Clay slowed as they came into a town, the sign announcing Bingham. "Trying to improve the quality of human life by discouraging reproduction of those with genetic defects or undesirable traits," he said.

"Discouraging reproduction?"

"The movement was pretty big in the 1920s. Its basic tenet was the forced sterilization of those thought to be inferior. But they were broad-minded racists and bigots, so they also believed in restricted immigration, segregation, and even, in the extreme, extermination of certain groups these demented people considered to be worthless—gays, gypsies, cripples."

"What the fuck? In the U.S.?"

"Studies suggest there have been anywhere from sixty to 150,000 sterilizations performed in the U.S. on undesirable elements. Segregation lasted into the 1960s. We still struggle with our immigration policies, even today. Bans on immigration from Muslim countries sound familiar? Just part of the eugenics movement."

"And the connection between the U.S. and Germany?"

Clay had resumed speed on the backside of Bingham, but greatly reduced, since the road now was filled with curves as it followed the Kennebec River, flowing some sixty feet below to their left. "Nazi

Germany adopted our sterilization and eugenics movement. It might be said that this was the basis for their grand plan of a master race."

"And you think that Engel's grandfather might have been a Nazi?"

They came around a corner, and there was a Chevy Silverado no more than a half a football field ahead. Clay hit the brakes and backed off. "That's him. New truck but same make and model."

"Did he see us?"

"Doubt it," Clay said. "Let's see if his speed changes and follow at a safe distance. Makes sense to let Westy and Crystal catch up."

"My bad. I should've been watching the tracker. I got caught up in the whole eugenics, Nazis, and Engel tie-together," Baylee said.

"Seems to make sense to me that if you were a scientist in Germany at the conclusion of the war and needed to relocate fast and discreetly, an institution that was founded upon the principles you believe in would be a great place to disappear into," Clay said.

"I thought the Nazis all fled to South America," Baylee said.

"Not so. It seems the big profile ones did, often to Argentina, Chile, and Brazil," Clay said. "But the smaller fish scattered all over the world. They just caught a former concentration camp guard down to Tennessee and deported him in March. He was ninety-four."

"And why are you just sharing your suspicions now?" Baylee asked.

"It seemed too far-fetched. Easier to believe that Bolton and Lange were the real villains when all the evidence pointed to them," Clay said.

"But then last night, Bolton didn't seem to have any clue who Clive Miller was."

"And his Russian contact just disappeared," Clay said. "That seemed pretty odd. So, I started going back over it in my mind, and there was something nagging about Engel."

"Like what?"

"For one thing, when she hired us in secret, Engel called us her company secret police. That just seemed a bit odd. And why all the secrecy?" Clay pointed to the right at the sign that said *Entering Moscow.*

"You kind of ruined the funny there," Baylee said. "Better if it was Berlin, I suppose."

"Ha," Clay said.

They rode in silence for a few minutes, lost in their thoughts.

"Is that the Kennebec River down there?" Baylee asked, pointing to the left.

"Yep."

And then, a truck came barreling out of an old logging road off to the right. It was gray, had tinted windows, a Chevy Silverado. Clay slammed on the brakes hoping it would go barreling across the front of them and into the gorge that lay below, a piece of his mind screaming that this wouldn't be the best result if Victoria were inside. Instead, the truck swerved into them, the front bumper crunching into the passenger side door and driving them across the road where they came to rest on the edge of the drop off leading to the river below.

Clay's head had been slammed back into the seat on impact. He managed to look to the side where Baylee sat, pinned by the airbag and the dented in door in a deadly grip. And then a motor revved, and the Silverado pushed the Jeep over the edge of the ravine. Clay felt them rolling, once, twice, the Jeep bouncing down the rocks, and he wondered idly if this was how his parents and grandmother had felt at the end. And then... nothing.

Chapter 30

"I should go finish them," Clive said. He and Bolts were standing at the top of the ravine looking down at the Jeep, upside down, wheels still spinning.

"No. Let's get out of here before another car comes along," Bridget Engel said. "The last thing we want is some passerby calling the police and telling them some guy just killed two people, and he's in a Chevy Silverado driving up Route 201. Not many roads to turn off on, probably not until the Forks."

Bolts walked back to the passenger side of the truck. "They're dead. Let's go."

"Can't be sure of that," Clive said. "And there probably aren't any police departments to worry about up here in the williwhacks. Just a sheriff's department stretched too thin."

The sound of a vehicle could be heard and an old truck, covered in rust, operating with a suspect muffler, came trundling up to them and stopped. A man with a gray beard sprouting from his round face stuck his head out the window. "Everything okay here?" he asked.

Engel stepped over to the truck. She had her hand on her H & K compact, which was nestled in a waist holster covered up by her pants suit. At the window, she looked back over her shoulder. There was no way he could see the Jeep below. She hoped that he couldn't see the dented front of the Silverado. "We just stopped to look at the view," she said.

"Awful close to the edge," the man said. "Plus, you best get your back end out of the road or somebody's going to sideswipe you right into the Kennebec."

"Thanks for the advice. We were just moving on."

The man drove off, and Clive and Engel climbed back into the Chevy.

"I think he put a tracking device on my truck," Clive said. "Only thing that makes sense."

"How'd he find your truck? I'm not paying you to be stupid." Engel's eyes had turned the chilling blue that scared the bejesus out of Clive. "Let's drive."

Clive carefully pulled back onto the road and resumed his northwesterly direction. "I gave it a once over just yesterday. I don't have a bug detector. Shit, GPS tracking devices aren't usually hard to find."

"I bet that former SEAL has military-grade tracking devices in his toolbox. Told you it was stupid to go buy the same kind of truck you had before. You probably parked it right out front of the motel, didn't you?"

Clive started to speak, thought better of what he was going to say, and tried a new tack. "So, what do we do about the tracking device?"

"Another hour to the border and then twenty minutes to where we cross. I'll have people meet us just on the other side to pick us up."

"What about the Chevy?"

"They'll dispose of it. One way or another."

"Still would've liked to kill that little pretty boy." Clive thought it best not to mention what he'd hoped to do with Baylee. He didn't think that Engel would care for that. Her being a woman and all. *If* she was a woman, he thought, because she sure didn't act like any woman he'd ever known.

"As I said, good chance he's dead. If he's not, so what? You won't ever see him again. No chance he's getting out of there in the next hour and getting back on our tail."

They were nervous going through Jackman, the only place a sheriff might be posted on the lookout for a Chevy Silverado who'd just slammed a Jeep Wrangler into the rocks along the Kennebec River. But there were no cops, few open businesses, and only a handful of pedestrians. About four miles short of the border and customs, Clive took a right onto the old Route 201, and then another right onto the Campbell Pond Road, before turning left onto a snowmobile/ATV trail. He had to engage the four-wheel drive to get through, branches scratching at the truck sides, its massive tires pulling them over the small boulders that littered the trail.

A few miles later they emerged into a clearing. There was a Suburban and a truck on the far side, both with Canadian plates. Clive drove over to them, and four men got out. They took Victoria Haas from the back and moved her to the Suburban. Clive climbed into the back with one of the men while Engel rode shotgun next to the driver, a thin man of about twenty years of age with blond hair and a ragged goatee of similar color.

Clive gave a small goodbye wave to his Chevy as it drove off, back the way that Clive and Engel had just come, followed by the other truck the Canadians had arrived in. He didn't know who these men were that had met them, but they had the cold efficiency that screamed ex-military.

*　　*　　*

Clay opened his eyes to a blinding light. Where was he and why did his head hurt so bad? It wouldn't be the first time he'd drunk too much and woke up in a strange place with a blinding headache, but that hadn't happened for some years now. Then he realized that he was in his Jeep, hanging upside down, and that the blinding light was the sun reflecting off water just feet from where he was.

"I'm going to undo your seatbelt now," a voice said.

There was a click and Clay felt himself enveloped in arms that felt like slabs of concrete, and he was carefully wrested from behind the air bag and pulled out his driver's side window. It was Westy, Clay realized, as his friend carried him like a baby a few steps from the Jeep.

"Can you sit?" Westy asked.

"Yeah, think so," Clay croaked.

Westy set him down on a rock next to Baylee, who was rubbing her arm. Then Clay remembered the Chevy coming out of the logging trail and blasting them over the side, the impact into Baylee's door and why she was rubbing her right arm and grimacing.

"You okay, boss?"

Clay turned his head to the voice, the movement sending a jolt of pain from his neck right up into his skull, to see Crystal standing there with an uncharacteristically concerned look that might have verged upon maternal.

"Yeah," he said, wondering if he was lying. The earth was swaying underneath him, and the sky seemed to be pulsating like a giant heart, constricting his breathing. "Think so. You okay, Baylee?"

"Sure," she said, flexing her arm. "Arm hurts like hell, but I don't think anything is broken."

"Told you to slow down," Westy said. "These curves are death."

Clay shook his head. "No, it was Clive. He must've seen us following him and pulled into an old road up there. Then he rammed into us, pushing us over the edge." Clay looked up to the road above, some fifty or sixty feet up.

"Closest hospital is back in Skowhegan," Westy said.

"That's not the direction they were headed," Clay said.

"Baylee?" Westy asked.

"It was Engel," she said. "Saw her face plain as day right before they slammed into us. She was sitting shotgun next to the narrow-faced, long-necked dude."

"You passing up medical attention?" Westy asked.

"I'm fine. Let's go catch those Nazi motherfuckers," Baylee said.

"Nazis?" Westy asked.

"I'll tell you in the truck," Clay said. "See if the tracker is still in the Jeep. It was in the middle cupholder when we got hit."

Crystal found the tracker down by the water's edge, luckily, dry and intact. There were six cars stopped when they climbed back onto the road, emerging from the river ravine like zombies. Luckily, there were, as yet, no police.

"Water is freezing," Clay said to the onlookers. "And rocky. If I was y'all I'd pick another swimming hole."

"You take the front, boss," Crystal said. "Us ladies will ride in the back and choose our weapons."

"Thirty-five miles ahead, still on Route 201," Clay said, having to squint at the tracker to read the numbers and direction. "Almost to Jackman."

"Got to be heading to Canada. Think they bribed a customs official to let them through?" Westy asked. He had the truck going forty-five miles an hour on the winding road running alongside the river. And that was too fast.

"That or they're going to sneak over the border," Clay said. "It's all snowmobile and ATV trails up here. No one cares much where the border is."

"What's this about Nazis?" Crystal asked.

"Just a theory," Clay said. "You still got your phone?" he asked Baylee, turning his head slightly and sending more fireworks exploding through his head.

"Yeah, want I should check in with Cloutier?" Without waiting for an answer, Baylee called, putting it on speaker.

It rang twice, and Cloutier answered. "Hey, Baylee."

"You find anything on Engel?"

"Clay with you?"

"Yeah. Westy and Crystal, too. They just picked us up."

"Picked you up?"

"Long story short, Clive Miller just forced us off the road into a ravine by the river. Bridget Engel was riding shotgun."

"No trace of where Franz Engel came from, as far as I can tell," Cloutier said. "But there was a Franz Engel whose name comes up in connection with Treblinka. He was a scientist who had made his name in the German eugenics movement, you know, creating the Aryan master race by excluding bad blood, rah rah."

"Franz is Bridget Engel's grandfather?" Clay asked.

"That's his name. I can't be sure that the two Franzs are the same one," Cloutier said.

"Let's go on the premise that they are," Clay said. "Get Gene to help you research. See if you can find out any association that Bridget might have with the Nazi party or any other group looking for so-called superior blood, preferably white."

"Got it. Where are you four going?"

"Looks like Canada," Clay said.

"Might want to check your phone rates up there," Cloutier said. "Could cost an arm and a leg."

"She hung up," Baylee said, looking at the phone.

Clay thought it interesting that not one of them seemed to think it wise to call the police. Not Westy, the ex-SEAL, Crystal, the ex-heroin addict, Baylee, the ex-domestic abuse victim, nor Clay, the ex-homicide detective. That was just not their way. And if they did phone the Somerset County sheriff's department, what would they say? 'We're chasing a sadistic killer traveling with a Nazi who has kidnapped a woman with mutant DNA strains in her embryo that will make her baby superior.' Right, that'd go over like a lead balloon.

"Got any pistols in that bag back there?" he asked instead of calling law enforcement.

"Got a Walther Q5 Match in there for you," Westy said. "The big one," he said to Baylee who was digging through the canvas bag full of weapons. "I also brought a Colt King Cobra and a Springfield Armory Hellcat for you ladies."

"I got the one with the six-shot chamber already," Crystal said. "That's the Colt, right? Old school. Fuck yeah."

Baylee handed up the Walther to Clay. "Then, this must be the Hellcat. I like that. Good choice, Weston," she said.

They were just about to Jackman when Clay noticed a change in direction. "Looks like they turned to the right just this side of the border," he said. "We're about twenty-five miles back."

"About five miles short of the border is a turn to the right," Baylee said looking at her own phone. "Looks like old Route 201. Takes you down to the Campbell Pond Road."

"That's it," Clay agreed, looking at the tracker. "They're headed northeast. Wait, hold on, they're turning back to the northwest. Doesn't look like a road at all."

"That's where the fuckers are crossing," Crystal said. "Probably a logging road or a snowmobile trail like you said, Clay. Used to snowmobile with a boyfriend back in the day. Awesome trails out of Jackman. We didn't know half the time if we were in the U.S. or Canada."

Clay turned, braving the shooting pain, to give Crystal a wondering look. She used to snowmobile back in the day with a boyfriend in Jackman, he thought. Will wonders never cease? What else didn't he know about this former client, now his administrative assistant?

*   *   *

Clive stepped from the back of the suburban, taking in his surroundings. After only ten minutes they'd gotten to a real road, and after another hour, had arrived at the facility, as Bolts called it. It looked to have been a resort at one time, a two-story hotel plopped down in the woods in the middle of nowhere. A metal fence ran around the grounds, only about six-feet high, more of a reminder to stay out than a real barrier to entry.

The two men—Clive hadn't gotten their names yet—pulled Victoria from the back of the suburban and carried her toward the front door.

"What now?" Clive asked Engel.

"Yes?" she asked.

"What's going to happen to her, for starters?"

"Studies will be done on her and the child growing inside of her."

"Studies?"

"Experiments."

This didn't upset Clive. It merely interested him. Like when he was a kid and killed the neighborhood cat and opened it up to find out what was inside it. "Will you kill her?"

"Not until the baby is born. Then we will no longer have need of her."

"And the child?"

"We will continue to study it as it grows," Engel said. "Hopefully reproduce it. We have the means."

Clive nodded. Made sense. He wanted to ask what they'd be studying it for, but figured he'd be told it was none of his business. "And me?"

"Tonight, you'll choose a destination, and we'll buy you an open-ended ticket. Tobias will take you to the airport in Quebec City tomorrow. Take as long as you want."

"Do you still need me?"

"We always need people with your particular talents," Engel said. "But you deserve a vacation."

"How do you know I'll come back?"

"Because you know that I'll provide you the opportunities that you desire."

"I'd like to take care of some unfinished business in Port Essex before I leave."

"If Wolfe and Baker survived their accident, I'll notify you. I ask that you don't return for them for six months. Then you may do as you please."

Clive wrestled with the order, for an order it was. He'd been waiting so long already. Sure, the natives in whatever far-flung third world paradise he found himself in would slake his appetite for a time. He wasn't sure what he looked forward to more: killing Wolfe slowly or ravishing Baker while he killed her. Both were certainly appealing. Too appealing. Six months might not be possible.

Chapter 31

Westy was driving along the Campbell Pond Road at about ten miles an hour as they all looked to the left. The tracker showed Victoria moving back on a main road on the Canadian side. What they had to find was the track Victoria's vehicle had used so they could cross the border to reach that road. They all saw the Chevy Silverado pull out of the forest at the same time, just about a hundred yards ahead of them, turning in the same direction that they were going.

"That's definitely Clive's truck," Clay said. "The front even has dents and black paint on it."

Another truck pulled out behind it. "What do you think?" Westy asked.

"Gotta follow them," Clay said. He looked at the tracker moving steadily further away off to the left. "They could've found the bug and attached it to a deer for all we know."

"Or they switched vehicles," Baylee said.

"Something with Canadian plates," Crystal said.

Westy drove on past where the two trucks had emerged from, staying a good hundred yards back. They went about a mile and then turned down a dirt road to the left, Westy cruising on past and then turning around, approaching the road from the other direction. The two trucks were out of sight, and he turned down the road to follow.

"We're gonna have to brace them," Clay said. "If Victoria's not in there, we're losing her."

"That tracker is good anywhere in the world," Westy said.

"You said the battery was only good for three days," Clay replied.

"You activated it yesterday? Around noon?" When Clay nodded yes, Westy continued, "That gives us forty-four hours to get to her. Plenty of time."

"Look." Clay pointed to the right where tire tracks led into the trees. "That looks fresh."

"That's not even a snowmobile trail," Westy said. He continued on past, around a corner, and stopped.

"I saw a glint of something back in there," Baylee said. "Not moving."

"Looks like a pond or something on the GPS," Crystal said. "No name, but a blue circle."

Westy opened his door. "I'll go check it out."

"I'm going with you," Clay said. "Baylee, you and Crystal find a place to turn this thing around and go back and block them from leaving, just in case."

"Follow me," Westy said and disappeared into the trees.

Clay was barely able to keep up with him, shambling along, whereas Westy made not a sound. About a hundred yards in, Westy held up his hand. Clay came up alongside of him and stopped where the trees opened onto a clearing. Two men were pushing the Silverado towards an overhang that dropped into a pool of water no more than fifty yards around.

Suddenly all Clay could think of was that they'd killed Victoria and were disposing of the body, dumping her, vehicle and all into some gorge that was probably hundreds of yards deep. "Stop," he yelled, stepping forward with gun pointed.

The two men released the Silverado and turned to face Clay and Westy, the vehicle continuing on and over the precipice. As Clay's eyes swung to the disappearing truck, the two men went for their holstered weapons, and Westy shot them both. Bang. Bang. Two shots. Both in the chest.

Clay approached the two men who were still gasping and choking on the ground. A widening circle of red slowly filled the front of their identical white shirts. "We need to call an ambulance," he said.

Westy crouched down next to him. "They'll be gone in five minutes."

There was a crashing in the trees, and then Baylee and Crystal burst out with pistols in hand. "What happened?" Baylee asked.

Clay started. "I have to check the truck."

He rushed to where the truck had gone over and clambered down the twenty feet or so of bank. The Silverado was half-submerged in the water. Clay walked into the water, but quickly found himself swimming as the bottom fell away under his feet. He had to swim over to the truck. He couldn't get the door to open and had to smash the window, cutting his hand in the process. There was nothing and nobody inside.

"They're not going to go to all the trouble of kidnapping your baby momma just to kill her and dump her in a quarry," Westy said as Clay climbed out of the water and made his way up the bank. "She's safe and sound. We just have to find her."

"Why do you think they were getting rid of Clive's truck?" Clay asked.

"They must've thought that we'd put a tracking device on it, and that's how you found them." Westy grinned. "I'd say it was a waste of a good truck, but it *is* a Chevy."

"Be nice if one of those fellows up there had some information to share," Clay said.

Baylee was on her knees next to one of the men, and Crystal was standing over the second. "Hey, boss," Crystal said. "These fellows are both dead as doornails."

Baylee had a solitary tear leaking down her cheek. "What happened?"

"They were pushing the truck into the water, and I told them to stop." Clay wasn't sure if he was supposed to give Baylee a hug or leave her alone. He settled for squeezing her hand. "They went for their guns."

"And you shot them?"

"Westy did. Both of them. Before I could even squeeze the trigger, they were down on their backs."

"Who the fuck are they?" Crystal asked.

"You got me," Clay said. "They got any identification on them?"

"You can check. I'm not touching them," Crystal said.

"I'll look through the truck," Westy said.

The two men's names were André Berger and Dietrich Fuchs, and both had the same address. Other than that, there was no other indication of who they might be. If the four were going to track down and save Victoria, it was generally agreed, this was not the right time to call the police. That would have to wait until after Victoria was safe and sound.

Westy suggested they take the license plates from the truck, the better to blend in as they were apparently heading to Canada.

They were back in the truck and about to get back on the road when Cloutier called Baylee's phone.

"I was looking into those companies, remember? Where Engel sits on the board of directors," she said. "One of them sort of jumped out at me."

"Yeah? Which one?" Clay replied as Westy turned onto the road the two trucks had originally been traveling—not much more than a track, really.

"Company called Freikorps Iron."

"Yeah." Trees slapped at the windows as Westy wended his way along the narrow path.

"Just on a whim I looked up what the meaning of Freikorps was. They were paramilitary groups in Germany in the late '20s and early '30s that fought against communism and pushed for fascism. Hitler adopted their ideology almost full-scale and used them as his shock troops on his ascendancy to power. One group was known as the Iron Division. Freikorps Iron."

Cloutier now had their full attention. "You are good as gold, girl!" Baylee observed.

"Yeah, keep on going. See if there are any Canadian connections, as that seems to be where we're headed." Clay added. "Keep us in the loop."

"You catch up to them yet?"

"We got slightly sidetracked but are back on the trail now," Clay said, thinking, yeah, we shot two guys. That's getting sidetracked alright.

"Okay, then." Cloutier hung up.

"So that crazy bitch Engel is a fucking Nazi," Crystal said. "Don't you have to shave your head to be a Nazi in modern times, or some such thing?"

"You don't suppose they're taking Victoria to an airport, do you?" Westy asked. "I mean, I don't think there is much of a Nazi presence in Canada."

"Why sneak into Canada just to fly somewhere else?" Clay said. "Heck, they could've flown in and out of Brunswick Executive Airport if they'd wanted."

"Not international, though. Perhaps the Jetport. Maybe the security is laxer in Canadian airports," Westy said. "I mean, nobody wants to blow up their planes and bomb their people."

"Canadians are too cool to blow up," Crystal said.

"They stopped moving," Clay said looking at the tracker.

"Which way?" Westy asked.

Clay looked up. They'd emerged from the woods onto a dirt road that, while not all that wide, looked like a major highway compared to the snowmobile trail they'd just traversed. "Right."

"We're in Canada," Baylee announced.

"No movement at all. Forty-eight miles from here," Clay said.

"Makes me feel better," Westy said. "Killing those two. I figure they were probably Nazis, too. Don't feel hardly bad at all anymore."

Clay didn't think he'd seen Westy's face change at any point. His stoic expression had been the same before, during, and after shooting the two men dead.

"That address the two men had on their driver's licenses?" Baylee said, looking at her phone. "It's forty-six miles from here. In this direction."

*

About an hour later, the four of them were hunkered down in a copse of trees sharing the binoculars to view the mansion. A man lounged by the front door smoking a cigarette. They'd been watching for an hour or so, and he hadn't left, so they figured he was on guard duty, and not just taking a smoke break. They'd seen no other sign of life. The curtains were drawn tight at every window, as if there might indeed be something to hide. There were six vehicles in the driveway, suggesting that there were at least that many people staying there.

The place reminded Clay of the Mount Washington hotel in New Hampshire. The façade was a faded white and the roof of red tiles faded to the color of dried blood, and only the two doors, front and back. It had a regal bearing, even if somewhat tired with age. There was a shed on the side closest to them, and another structure on the far side that might be a garage, hinting that there could be more vehicles.

The only cover for fifty yards around the estate was the copse of trees that hid them. There appeared to be no close neighbors, and this open space was surrounded by thick forest, with only the one road for access.

"We'll go in at dusk," Westy said. This was his specialty, the thing he'd trained for, before deploying to Afghanistan and other places of the world on various missions he never talked about. Back then, no doubt, he'd had a stronger support team. "I'd say about an hour."

"We climbing the fence?" Baylee asked.

"You and I are," Westy said. "We'll drop in on the back and work our way to the side. Me behind that rock there, and you'll take cover by that shed."

"How about us?" Crystal asked.

Westy told them the plan, handing over the remote gate opener he'd taken from the truck back at the quarry. They went over it in detail, smoothed out a few wrinkles, and before they knew it, dusk was descending.

Chapter 32

Crystal drove the truck with Clay lying down on the back seat. The shadows were lengthening around them, the sun low on the horizon at their back, and anticipation of the unknown heightening all their senses. Baylee and Westy had already slipped over the fence and scuttled their way into position within the estate grounds.

Clay worried about putting his friends in danger, but Westy was a former SEAL who seemed to slip naturally back into action when called on, occasions that took him out of his monotonous daily grind as a fisherman. Baylee was his partner in the private investigation business, and Crystal was an employee. This was the job. Well, not usually, Clay thought, a grin creasing his face as he lay prone in the back seat. It was not an everyday occurrence for a case to require them to drive into a Nazi compound in Canada to save the mother of his unborn baby who might or might not turn out to be Superman or Superwoman one day.

Did it matter whether the baby was a boy or a girl, Clay wondered? No. Of course not. Whether Victoria wanted it or not, he was going to be a father to the child, not that that meant being in a relationship with Victoria, other than that of the shared work of parenting, that is. He hoped that Westy was right, and that these whackos weren't going to harm Victoria in any way, for how could that benefit them? A small part of him feared that she'd been kidnapped so they could surgically remove the embryo and do scientific experiments on it—they seemed to be Nazis, after all. That thought he tried to banish.

The truck stopped, and the window went down. There was a

moment of fiddling, and then they moved forward again. Once safely past the gate, Crystal said, "We're in."

Clay held the Walther flat against his chest, bracing himself for what was to come. He wished he had his Glock with him, but the Walther had a nice feel to it, and, if Westy owned it, it must be an excellent weapon. The plan was that the guard out front would approach the truck to see what Crystal wanted and how she'd gotten into the estate. When he did so, Clay would sit up and point the pistol at him, and then they'd restrain him with the zip ties and duct tape Westy had brought along in his gun bag. Simple.

"He's standing up," Crystal said. "Shit, he's pulling his gun out."

"Steady," Clay said. "We can still get the drop on him."

Crystal pulled the truck to a stop. "Here he comes."

"Steady."

"He's got a pistol pointed directly at my face," Crystal said. "Don't tell me to be fucking steady."

"What do you want?" the guard asked from about ten feet away. It sounded like he'd stopped there and was no longer moving forward.

"I'm looking for the Engel house," Crystal said. "Is this it?"

"How'd you get through the gate?"

"It was open."

"Why do you have Dietrich's license plates on your truck?"

Damn, Clay thought, the man was paying attention. Should he sit up and try and shoot the man? If the guy had a gun pointed at Crystal's face, that would likely be the kiss of death for her. Clay always laughed at the movies where everybody stood pointing guns at each other, and nobody pulled the trigger. If you pointed a gun, it was because you meant to use it.

"I don't know what you're talking about," Crystal said.

"Get out of the truck."

Clay heard the front door open, and the diminutive Crystal stepped down from the large truck. "Why are you pointing a gun at me?" she asked innocently.

There was a faint sound, pop-pop, like the clucking sound one might make with their tongue.

"Fuck," Crystal said.

Clay risked a glance out the window. The guard lay face down in the driveway, most of the back of his head missing. Westy. He thought of pulling the body out of sight, but there was no time. Westy had screwed a suppressor onto the end of a sniper rifle he'd brought along. As Clay got out of the truck, Westy came striding across, leaving the rifle behind and carrying his new Sig Sauer in his right hand.

The front door was unlocked. That was a lucky break. Clay surmised that they'd grown overconfident in this rural hideaway. He went through the entrance and into a large hallway with a thirty-foot ceiling. There was no one in sight. A wide staircase climbed its way up to the second floor. Clay motioned for Westy to go to the right, and then as Baylee came through the door, for her to go to the left. Crystal had been directed to stay at the front door. Clay chose the staircase and the second floor.

*   *   *

Westy didn't much care for shooting people, but he did what he had to do. That was three people in one day. He sure hoped they deserved it. The guard had his pistol pointed right at Crystal's head, and there was no guarantee that, even if Westy got the drop on him, he'd have seen the error of his ways and lowered the weapon. Westy had learned the hard way that, if you hesitate when killing-time came, it was likely to be you or a friend who ended up dead, and not the enemy.

It was during his first tour, fresh off the boat, that he learned this lesson. It seemed like one day he was starting BUDS, and the next he was in Iraq in an advance unit leading up to the Battle of Nasiriyah on the Euphrates River in Dhi Qar Province south of Baghdad. That day, he'd been slow to shoot when an old lady pulled a rickety pistol from her burqa and pointed it at Hal Bugbee, and the next thing Westy knew was that his friend's brains were dripping down the side of his face. Never again.

There was a hallway that led to the right, and Westy eased his way in that direction. The first room was a bathroom, empty. The next room had no door and appeared to be some type of sitting room, also empty. He heard voices across the hall, coming from behind a closed door, but he cleared the last room on the right side, a bedroom with two twin beds. The room was orderly, but there were clothes in the closet and bureau, suggesting it was currently in use.

The voices came from the only doorway on the far side of the hallway. They were muffled, and he couldn't hear through the closed door. Westy moved back toward the central hallway and crouched down, his Sig Sauer casually pointed at the room with the voices. He could see Crystal over by the front door, but as of yet, no sign of Baylee or Clay.

If either one of them found Victoria, it was possible that the whole team could escape without any more bloodshed. If they found her and the alarm was sounded, however, Westy would be able to bottle up whoever was in the room down the hall from him without too much trouble. He didn't even want to entertain the idea that her captors may have removed the bracelet and stashed her elsewhere.

Either way, the correct course of action for now was restraint, and he was a very patient man. He hunkered down in a squat, back against the wall, and waited to see what would happen next.

* * *

Baylee watched the truck with Clay and Crystal drive up to the mansion, and then the guard approaching from the entranceway, pistol extended in front of him. It hadn't sounded like much of a plan to her in the first place, but she couldn't come up with anything better. Sure, they could try to convince the authorities, but this was Canada.

Who the hell *were* the authorities? The Mounties? And did they even carry guns?

No, it was better that they took matters into their own hands, but that didn't make her hands shake any less, nor stop the sweat gathering on her brow, as she watched the guard approach the truck with weapon extended. Baylee stole a glance at Westy behind his rock, and she saw him rising at the same time she heard what sounded like two snaps of the fingers. Was he going to just amble right up to the guard, Baylee wondered? She looked back to find the guard face down, and Crystal and Clay climbing out of the truck.

What the hell? Baylee eased out from behind the shed and followed Westy over to the house. The guard was not moving. Where the back of his head should have been now looked like chili in a pot. Baylee had the urge to vomit, but looked away and breathed deeply, getting control of herself. Clay was telling Crystal to keep watch at the door, which was part of the plan. The next step was to go inside, and Baylee found her feet moving before her mind reacted. Once inside, Clay motioned for her to go to the left.

The great hallway was devoid of life. Baylee walked gently, worried that her footsteps would echo throughout the entire house. Clay had reached the first step of the staircase as she moved out of sight down the hallway. There was a bathroom, empty, on the left. The next doorway led to an office, or perhaps a library, as the walls were floor-to-ceiling bookcases filled with hardcovers. Weren't the Nazis into book burning, Baylee thought? She stepped over to look at the titles, expecting to see *Mein Kampf*. The first title was *A People without Space* by Hans Grimm. There was a noise from the hallway, and she spun around, pistol extended in front of her.

Quiet. Baylee stepped back to the door, peering around the edge. Then again, she heard a muffled clattering from across the way—dishes being stacked, she wondered? There was an arched opening a bit further down and across the hallway. She eased her way down, setting each foot lightly down, one after the other, fully aware of her breathing but not able to silence it. There was the sound of voices. Baylee peeked around the corner of the opening.

It was a massive dining room with a table that could sit at least twenty, maybe more. Voices were coming from a door across the way. Baylee figured it led to the kitchen. It was a swinging door, and Baylee pushed it open a crack with one hand, her other grasping the pistol ready for anything. A man and a woman stood in front of a sink, washing and drying dishes, their backs to her. No immediate threat.

Baylee let the door ease shut and turned around. Clive Miller was standing there with a leer on his face.

"Baylee Baker," he breathed, hunger in his voice. Then he punched her in the jaw, lights exploding and darkness cascading as she felt her legs give out, and she fell.

Chapter 33

Clay went up the staircase gingerly at first, but the steps were solid and didn't creak, so he was able to increase his pace. The house felt like a cavernous library in its silence, and he was beginning to have his doubts that anybody was here, much less Victoria. It was quite possible that they'd brought her here, and either discovered the bug in her bracelet, or just took the piece of jewelry from her and then transported her elsewhere.

Then Clay saw the light seeping out from underneath a door, seemingly the only light on upstairs, even though the shadows were lengthening into darkness outside. He held the Walther in two hands like they taught him at the academy as he approached the door. Clay took a deep breath, exhaling, before reaching over with his left hand to test the old-fashioned brass doorknob. It turned.

Another shallow breath and he flung the door open, stepping into the opening with both hands on the pistol. The room was lit up by fluorescent lights. Machines hummed and whizzed throughout the space. A blond-haired man in a white lab coat stood next to a hospital bed holding a clipboard. He wore thick black glasses and was intent on his work. Clay didn't believe that he was armed.

On the hospital bed, stark naked, was Victoria Haas. Heavy leather restraints fastened her legs and arms. There was a gag in her mouth that not only silenced her, but kept her head pinned down on the bed. Her hair had been shaven from her head, as well as from her pubic region, making Clay blush as he tried to remember if that was new. Leads trailing wires were taped to various parts of her body, one even disappearing inside her nether regions.

"Who are you?" the man said.

Clay thought of witty things to say, like, *your worst fucking nightmare,* or perhaps, *the father,* but he chose the simpler path. "Remove the wires and unfasten the restraints." He gestured with the gun, but the man didn't move.

The man looked pointedly over his shoulder at the open door. "Do you have any idea what you're getting into?" he asked.

Clay took two steps and hit him in the cheek with the pistol, not so hard as to disable him, but more a not-so-gentle hint of who was in charge. "Do it."

The man straightened his glasses, touched his cheek, and began to undo the restraints. Clay, the pistol trained on the man, stepped forward to release the gag from Victoria's mouth.

"Clay, what's going on?" she asked.

He stared at her bewildered face and realized that, of course, they hadn't told her why she'd been kidnapped, that they'd taken her because of the superbaby in her belly, so that they could experiment on her and their unborn child.

"Let's get you out of here." Clay grabbed her arm and pulled her to a sitting position. "Can you stand?"

Victoria slid off the bed and toppled to the floor. "You," Clay said, waving his pistol at the man, "Lie down."

"What?"

"Lie the fuck down on the bed." Clay gave him another tap across the cheek, this time splitting the skin in a jagged pattern.

The man, already folded over the bed, rolled the rest of the way on, and over onto his back. Victoria had struggled her way back to her feet and began to fasten his arms. As soon as they were secured, Clay restrained his legs.

"Can we strip him naked and stick things in him?" Victoria asked.

Clay thought that she might be serious. "Later. Put the gag in his mouth."

There were no clothes in the room but there was a sheet folded on a table in the corner and Clay grabbed that and wrapped it around Victoria.

"What is going on?" she asked again.

"We have to get out of here," Clay said. "I'll tell you everything once we're safe."

Clay pulled her arm around his shoulders and did likewise with her, moving her towards the door. Her legs were shaky and moved awkwardly after having been restrained all day, but she was at least able to stand.

"Is Mekhi okay?" Victoria asked.

He put the gun in his waistband to pull the door shut behind them. Two gunshots rang out downstairs. Clay dragged Victoria to the stairs, staggering down the first four steps. As they rounded the curve, Clay saw Westy on the left, looking down the hallway. His friend heard them, risking a quick glance up, holding his finger to his lips and pointing back the way he'd been looking, and then following his own direction.

It was most likely Westy who'd fired, Clay realized, and had the bad guys pinned down. He just had to get Victoria out of the house and into the truck, and they had a chance. There was no sight of Baylee, nor Crystal.

"Who are these people?" Victoria asked.

Clay stumbled and almost let go of her, and when he looked up, he saw with horror that Clive Miller stood on the opposite side of the hall from Westy with a pistol pointed, and a gunshot rang out. Westy's head banged against the wall he was standing next to, and then he fell in a heap, not moving. Clay snapped a shot at Clive, and the man looked up the staircase and fired back as Clay pushed Victoria down.

A man came around the corner by Westy's motionless body, firing rapidly, the bullets fanning Clay's face like a disturbed beehive. Clay turned to face the danger, the pistol coming into his clasped hands with a will of its own. He pulled the trigger, the single bullet drilling the man in the neck.

Clay turned back to see Clive picking Baylee up by the hair and draping her over his shoulder. In the movies, the hero would take the shot and kill the villain and save the girl. Clay knew there was about a fifty/fifty chance that he would hit Baylee. Clive ran out of sight with her over his shoulder toward the back of the house. Clay figured he was going for the back door.

In a tiny fraction of a second, Clay assessed the situation. The house was most likely filled with bad guys. His friend since third grade lay in a heap on the floor, not moving, blood pooling around his head. The mother of his unborn child was naked next to him halfway down a flight of stairs and incapable of walking on her own. And his true love and desire had just been carried out the back door by a sadistic killer.

"Take this," Clay said to Victoria, thrusting the pistol into her hand. "Check on Westy. I'll be right back."

He took three strides clearing nine steps and then vaulted over the side into the hallway leading to the back door. Clive and Baylee were gone, but the door flapped open. Clay ran to the door and saw Clive at the building they surmised to be the garage, going in a side door, Baylee slung over his back. It was about forty yards across, and Clay figured he did it in under five seconds, faster than he'd ever managed the forty-yard dash in high school at football practice. As he came through the door, an engine sprang to life, and the sliding door began to open.

Clive was in the driver's seat of a Range Rover, Baylee spilled into the seat next to him. Clay took two steps to the driver's side window as the vehicle lurched forward, crashing into the door that was not yet open all the way. Clay wrapped his right arm around Clive's neck and was jerked forward with the Land Rover as it crashed through the garage door. He threw a punch with his left, a looping hook that landed but had no real power. Clive snarled and stabbed his thumb into Clay's neck just before they crashed into a parked truck.

Clay was thrown to the ground with the impact, rolling and coming to his feet as Clive came out of the Land Rover with a pistol in hand. Clay stepped at him, feeling the bullet whoosh by his face as he tackled the man to the ground, the gun jarred from his hand and clattering across the gravel driveway. Clive twisted free, rose to his feet, and kicked Clay in the stomach as he tried to rise, sending him toppling back to the ground.

A gunshot rang out by the entrance to the house, but Clay didn't have a chance to see what was going on as Clive stepped in and tried to kick him again. Clay drove his body at Clive's anchor leg as he drew back to kick, sending the man crashing to the ground. He scrambled on top of Clive, his hands grasping the man's neck and squeezing, but Clive managed to jerk a knee into his groin, breaking his hold, and the two men rolled away from each other and came to their feet.

Clay saw Crystal and Engel entangled by the door, both on the ground, while standing in the doorway was a very naked Victoria. He knew he had to end this soon—not just for the sake of his own life, but the fates of the most important people in his life depended on it. He went at Clive as if to tackle him, but then sidestepped at the last second, and Clive teetered off balance. Clay drove a jab with his left into the man's belly, and then came over the top with a hard right that smashed his nose, which split under his fist like a ripe tomato.

Clive tried to grapple with Clay, reaching with his arms, but Clay stepped back out of reach, and then forward again with a quick step, driving another one-two combination into Clive's face, the blows resounding in the air like gunshots, bang-bang, and Clive went down, out cold.

Baylee stepped from the Land Rover with a dazed expression. "Where are we going?"

Clay stood gasping, looking first to Clive to make sure he was truly out, and then over to where Crystal and Engel rolled on the ground in ferocious combat. Victoria no longer stood in the doorway, apparently having disappeared back into the house.

Clay took two steps toward the tussle when a bullet whistled past his ear. Two further gunshots rang out, bang-bang, right on top of each other. He dropped to the ground and looked back at Clive Miller who had gotten to his feet and was standing wide-eyed in shock, a gun held loosely in one hand. He dropped the pistol and then began screaming, his hands clutching at his groin. Baylee, gripping her own weapon, stepped forward and kicked the gun away from him. Clay turned back to help Crystal as Victoria reappeared with a pistol in her hand. Engel rose to her feet, warily looking at the woman she'd kidnapped, who now stood facing her, naked, her body shimmering white in the darkening sky, the pistol in her hand looking like a small cannon.

Crystal punched Engel in the side of her jaw. "Fucking bitch," she said as the CEO of Johnson Laboratories buckled to the ground.

Epilogue

TWO WEEKS LATER

All in all, it could've turned out a lot worse, Clay reflected, as he pulled into Victoria's drive on the Point.

When Clay had gone out the back door to save Baylee, Victoria had crawled down the stairs to Westy's side, losing the covering sheet in the process, finding a pulse, just as two men came down the hall at her. She had pointed and pulled the trigger of the pistol, hitting the front man in the leg, but the second guy kicked the gun from her hand. Once the hallway was clear, Bridget Engel had emerged and told the man to take Victoria to the truck outside.

As they had stepped out the door, Crystal, standing off to the side, shot the man square in the ear. Engel tackled Crystal. This was the glimpse of them rolling around on the ground that Clay had seen as he fought Clive. Victoria went back to retrieve the pistol that had been kicked from her hand. When she pointed it at Engel, Crystal saw her opening, and packed all of the strength in her diminutive body into a punch that knocked Engel to the ground, dazed.

Baylee had found some rope to tie Engel up with. Clive needed no restraints as Baylee's bullet was a direct hit on his penis, one ball exploding so that only particles were found by the medics a bit later. Clay had rushed inside to Westy's side. Westy had a pool of blood around his head, but also had a pulse and good breath sounds. Clay had ripped his own shirt, already tattered and torn, from his body and bound Westy's head as best he could.

The Mounties arrived, two cars with four officers at first, and then an influx of authorities that must've drained the entire country of any policing. Paramedics arrived in profusion, then a medevac helicopter run by Airmedic touched down outside. Clay had insisted they take Westy alone, not wanting him on board with Nazi thugs.

Clay parked his new Jeep Wrangler and went and knocked on the door. Mekhi answered it and told him that Victoria was around back. He walked back warily, not sure what to expect. She was sitting at a table by the pool overlooking the ocean. Clay sat down next to her.

"I'm sorry," Victoria said. "I'm sorry about everything. I think I went a little bit crazy there, maybe the prenatal stuff I was taking, and maybe my own... issues from growing up?"

"I'm sorry that you... we... lost the baby."

"It's my fault. All my fault. Thank you for coming to save me."

"I have to ask." Clay studied her face. "Why did you do it?"

She turned away and thought for a time, so long that Clay wondered if she knew the answer herself. "Who doesn't want their child to be gifted?" she asked finally, her face bleak and weary as she looked him in the eyes.

"But, to alter the genome? To inject mutations into the embryo?"

Victoria shrugged. "Women take prenatal vitamins. Eat better. Give up alcohol and smoking. People are taking their kids to music classes before they can walk, sending them off to camps to get better at this or that, getting private tutors, and on and on and on. How is this any different?"

Clay had no real answer for that. He stood up. "Goodbye, Victoria."

The next stop was at Baylee's house. He hadn't seen her in two weeks, having shut down the office so they could all lick their wounds and assess the damage. Not a phone call. Not a text message. He found her down by the water, sitting in the swing, Flash laying in the sunshine. This time Ollie the one-eyed cat was also there, sitting contentedly next to Baylee.

It looked to be idyllic. Clay wished that he was part of it. Knew he was not.

"Hey, Baylee."

"Hi, Clay."

"How are you?"

She shrugged. "Any update on Westy?" She did not offer for him to sit.

"Clive made a mistake when he shot Westy in the head. Nothing but concrete up there. He got out of the hospital earlier today."

"What's up with Victoria Haas?"

"She had a miscarriage. Lost the baby."

"I'm sorry," Baylee said.

"As am I."

"They going to charge her or Kalinda with anything?"

"Doubt it. They're rich."

"How about Bolton?"

"They managed to find and freeze Bolton's bank account. And they're trying to stick him and the others with a crime, but his father hired him some damn good lawyers. Seems that there is a difference between a ban and a crime. A few years back Congress passed a provision that any human clinical trials must be approved by the FDA. At best, that'll be a slap on the wrist. Of course, they'll all be banished from the scientific community."

"Harley?"

"Harley Lange is cooperating fully," Clay said. "Although this won't look good on his resume, I don't think he'll be in any trouble. Maybe time for a new career, though."

"I read that Clive Miller has been brought back to the States and will be tried for kidnapping and the murder of Mary Jordan, amongst other things," Baylee said. "There was no mention of his mutilated dick or missing ball, though, funny enough."

Clay gave a dry laugh, fighting the urged to squish his legs together. "Couldn't have happened to a better guy," he said.

"What happened to Engel? There's nothing about her in the paper or on the news."

"I think Homeland Security got her. Right about now, she's probably in a cell block that even the President doesn't know about being interrogated with methods best practiced in the shadows."

"Good. She is a hateful woman."

"Cloutier uncovered that she was on a board of a company called Freikorps Iron, which appears to be little more than a front for a Nazi conspiracy ring. Hard to tell yet how many people are involved, but I'm sure they're working Engel over pretty hard to see what she knows."

"She deserves everything she gets."

"I was going to open the office back up tomorrow," Clay said.

"I'll be in," Baylee said, and went back to looking out over the harbor towards the town of Port Essex.

About the Author:

Matt Cost aka Matthew Langdon Cost

Matt Cost is the highly acclaimed, award-winning author of the Mainely Mystery series. The first book, *Mainely Power*, was selected as the Maine Humanities Council Read ME Fiction Book of 2020. This was followed by *Mainely Fear*, *Mainely Money*, and *Mainely Angst*.

I Am Cuba: Fidel Castro and the Cuban Revolution was his first traditionally published novel. He had another historical released in August of 2021, *Love in a Time of Hate*.

Wolfe Trap and *Mind Trap* were the first two Clay Wolfe / Port Essex Mysteries. *Mouse Trap* is the third in this series.

Cost was a history major at Trinity College. He owned a mystery bookstore, a video store, and a gym, before serving a ten-year sentence as a junior high school teacher. In 2014, he was released and began writing. And that's what he does. He writes histories and mysteries.

Cost now lives in Brunswick, Maine, with his wife, Harper. There are four grown children: Brittany, Pearson, Miranda, and Ryan. A chocolate Lab and a basset hound round out the mix. He now spends his days at the computer, writing.

If you enjoyed reading this book,
please consider writing your honest review
and sharing it with other readers.

Many of our Authors are happy to participate in
Book Club and Reader Group discussions.
For more information, contact us at info@encirclepub.com.

Thank you,
Encircle Publications

For news about more exciting new fiction, join us at:

Facebook: www.facebook.com/encirclepub

Instagram: www.instagram.com/encirclepublications

Twitter: twitter.com/encirclepub

Sign up for Encircle Publications newsletter and specials:
eepurl.com/cs8taP